"*Bring Me to Life* is compelling, gripping, and impossible to put down."

—Hon. Michael D Bradbury, District Attorney (Ret.), County of Ventura, California

"The character development of "Ray Scapio" is a delight which brings the reader to view the prosecutor as not only a highly skilled trial litigator, but as a colorful human."

—Brian Tiffany, Retired Deputy Sheriff

"True courthouse drama at its best. The ending was a true surprise!"

—Arturo Gutierrez, Retired Superior Court Judge

"An insightful behind the scenes look at the prosecution of major crimes in a Southern California community. A high-quality level of detail puts you into the prosecutor's shoes in evaluating trial strategy.

—Tony Trembley, Attorney and Camarillo City Council

"This book springs from the creative mind of a man who has spent 40 years investigating and prosecuting some of the most heinous crimes produced by the human condition. This gripping novel interweaves clever story telling with a real-world knowledge of criminology, police procedure, and courtroom strategy. *Bring Me to Life* is a compelling page-turner that culminates with a creative ending that won't be forgotten."

—Bill Haney, Former Homicide Prosecutor

"The Courtroom action was brilliantly written. The twist ending was equally brilliant and stunning yet it fit with the narrative provided."

—Jeff Held, Retired Attorney

"Simon's crime novel is engaging; realistic with vivid characters based on actual people in the system from his thirty-years of experience. I won't spoil it for you but there are great plot twists and surprises. It's a fantastic novel and I can't wait for the next one."

—John Dobroth, Retired Superior Court Judge ,
Actor, and Film Producer

BRING ME TO LIFE

Also by Richard Simon

JAKE'S RUN

BRING ME TO LIFE

A NOVEL

Richard Simon

LIVING LASER PRESS

Bring Me to Life—A Novel

Published by Living Laser Press, Ventura, California

978-0-578-30748-0 (paperback)
Also available in eBook format

Publishing services provided by AuthorImprints

ONE

It was October of 2017 when Jack Macklin was released from prison for sexual assault after receiving an eight-year sentence. Macklin was known as Jack Mack, or just Mack to some he was friendly with. Those who were not were simply scared of him. Jack stood six foot three and weighed around 240 pounds. He was burly and mean looking, a white guy with a full beard and tattoos on his neck, including a skull and crossbones.

In prison, he had joined the Aryan Brotherhood prison gang; he was one of the few sex offenders to be accepted into a prison gang. He claimed it was a false charge by a disgruntled ex-girlfriend, and the leaders of the neo-Nazi prison gang agreed to accept him, figuring he would be a valuable asset, even if they doubted his version of why he was incarcerated. He also had a swastika tattooed on his chest and lightning bolts below his ears, and the fingers of his right hand spelled out *PC 187*. In California, Penal Code section 187 is the section for murder. In prison, the unwritten rules are very clear; you don't put 187 on your body unless you had actually murdered someone. Whether the police knew about it or not doesn't matter. What does matter is that if 187 is tattooed anywhere on an inmate's body, he better have killed someone. Prison-gang culture does not look favorably upon posers. If they think you're a poser, your next pose might be lying dead on the floor with a shank in your neck.

On October 8, Mack moved into an apartment in Ventura, California, on the Avenue—Ventura Avenue. If you said it's on or off the Avenue, everyone knew it was Ventura Avenue you were talking about.

Ventura is a county in Southern California between Los Angeles and Santa Barbara. Cities in Ventura County include those close to Los Angeles County like Simi Valley, made famous by the Rodney King trial and subsequent acquittals, leading to the LA riots; Moorpark; Thousand Oaks; Newbury Park, frequently misspelled Newberry; and Westlake. This is the area referred to as the East County. Ventura County extends through the comparatively quiet and affluent city of Camarillo as you head north on Highway 101 toward Santa Barbara. After Camarillo, you pass a navy beach town called Port Hueneme, then Oxnard and then the city of Ventura. The city of Ventura is gorgeous near the beach, but as you go farther away and into the downtown area and beyond, you get into the poorer section, where gangs and criminals are all too common.

The Avenue goes from the beach through the poor part of town all the way to the industrial area. That industrial area is one of the few parts of Ventura city where there are no homes but many auto body repair shops, manufacturing plants, warehouses, and other buildings that look empty from the outside except for some scattered vehicles driven by the employees.

Mack's apartment was in a relatively low-income section of the Avenue near where the old card club used to be. The club was primarily a Texas hold-em poker club but was also approved for Omaha poker, blackjack, and a few other table games where customers were frequently separated from their money. After the club was robbed at gunpoint by six masked criminals ten years earlier, they relocated to the Ventura auto mall.

Above Ventura and off the 101 from Highway 33 is the quaint little town of Ojai, California. Ojai is Laguna light. Lots of art galleries like Laguna Beach has, but no ocean. Ojai has no gangs, but they do have scorpions. It gets very hot there in the summer and many of the homes are in the hills. Ojai is a nice town for foodies, as there are several upscale farm-to-table restaurants, lots of health food, and some exotic cuisines. Ojai is home to many artists, such as painters and musicians. Definitely an artsy town, a nice place to live if you can handle the summer heat and avoid scorpions.

Also in Ventura County are the middle-class largely Hispanic towns of Fillmore and Santa Paula. From the city of Ventura, the 126 freeway will get you to those hidden gems. For those who like Mexican food, Santa Paula, Fillmore, and Oxnard are heaven on earth. Ventura is not bad, either.

Although Mack's home was seedy and the place was kind of a dump, it was livable, and the rent was cheap. Jack Mack's cousin Paul was the landlord and gave Mack a break, despite what he had been incarcerated for; he was family. Mack's mother had been in and out of jail most of his life and was now living in a residential drug-rehab facility in LA. He did not have much of a relationship with her. His father left his mother when he was four and has had no contact since.

Mack wasn't concerned about the local gangs; he was way too scary to mess with. At thirty-eight years old, he looked back and laughed about how much fun he'd had showing little gang punks they were not nearly as tough as they thought they were. He was the ultimate bully who got off on instilling fear in others. One look at him and the gangbangers knew that wasn't the guy to mess with. That wasn't the guy you came up to in a dark alley and pulled a little robbery on. Gang members like to find easy targets. Jack Mack was a lot of things. An easy target wasn't one of them.

Mack's life had taken a turn in 2008 when he abducted an exotic dancer from Snooky's, a gentlemen's club in a seedy section of Oxnard, forcibly took her to the fields in Oxnard, raped her, and left her naked, battered, and terrified. Mack figured she was a stripper with a probable methamphetamine addiction and that she'd therefore never report the crime—and if she did, nobody would believe her.

In 2008, Mack didn't have any tattoos yet, and at the age of thirty, he was a rather presentable young man. In fact, most fathers would have been OK with him dating their daughters. But if any father's daughter had chosen to do that, it would have been the biggest and possibly last mistake of both father's and daughter's lives. Jack Macklin didn't really *date* women; he abused them, physically, sexually, and emotionally. That is how he liked it. Always had, always would. He was one man who was never going to change.

In the summer of 2008, he had entered Snooky's in Oxnard and paid for a lap dance with Treasure, whose real name was Tina Forsythe, a twenty-six-year-old blond white woman who was quite attractive, with several tattoos, large breasts, and long, polished pink fingernails. "Very pretty but sorta trashy" was how Mack would later describe her during the police interrogation.

What first caught Mack's attention was the MC's introduction of her. Mack had been a little intoxicated already as he heard the voice on the mike say, "All right, ladies and gentlemen, welcome to Snooky's, where we have the most beautiful ladies in town. Let's give it up for our next lovely lady! She is new to our club but has danced at Club Rouge in LA and she's ours now, so show your appreciation with the green paper in your wallets and let's welcome . . . One man's trash is another man's . . . Treasure! It's Treasure up on Stage One." The MC drew out the name "Treasure" like a public address announcer at a Major League ballpark introducing the team's best hitter.

Well, Mack thought that was kinda funny, and he also thought to himself how much pussy he would get if he had that MC's job. He paid for a lap dance with Treasure and he paid extra for the VIP Room. They engaged in small talk before the music started and continued a little after it had begun. He did not reveal much about himself, but she did mention that she was a single mom with an eight-year-old daughter.

She told him the rules about no touching by him. As she gyrated on his lap and as he got hard, he began to forcibly push her face toward his crotch, and she slapped him and said, "We're done." She gave him his money back and said he better leave or the bouncers would throw him out.

Needless to say, he was not a happy man that night. He left the club but waited patiently in the parking lot. Two bouncers escorted her to her car at 2:00 a.m. when her shift ended. He decided not to follow her then but knew he would be coming back. As he drove home that night he cursed under his breath,

"Nobody slaps Jack Mack and gets away with it. Especially not some cunt-ass stripper bitch."

He waited two weeks, then parked in the club's parking lot. He was so mad that first night that he forgot to notice what car she drove. The first night back, he didn't see her, so he figured she didn't work that night. Same thing happened the second night, and he became concerned that maybe she had left that establishment. He called Club Rouge in LA but they would not reveal the stage names of any of the dancers or any other information. Mack decided to try one more time, and he waited in the lot on a Thursday night, the same night of the week that he had been rebuffed by her.

It was around 2:00 a.m., and there she was. She walked out wearing blue jeans and a bikini top with an open Levi's jacket. He recognized her right away, but she was walking and talking with another dancer, a short, small-breasted brunette who seemed very animated as the two talked by their cars. He wasn't going to grab her in front of a witness, so he decided to follow her to see if he could find where she lived. He hoped it wouldn't be some gated community but doubted her stripper wages would allow her to afford to live in that type of residence.

When they had engaged in small talk before he attacked her in the VIP Room, she had revealed that she was a single mom of a daughter but seemed wisely careful not to reveal her city of residence. Mack followed her discreetly and discovered she lived on a residential street in Camarillo, a sleepy town about twenty miles south of Ventura toward Los Angeles. Although a Ventura resident at the time, Mack had frequented a strip-mall bar called Outlaws that wasn't far from her home off of Pickwick Drive. He was proud of how he had tailed her without her seeing him.

The other thing he noticed was that there were no cars in the driveway. He thought about knocking on the door and trying some sort of ruse, but it might be better to plan this out a little more. No, he knew where she lived and that was all he needed for now. Her residence was near Berry Street where the gang hung out, but he figured that would not be a problem. He had seen some of the gangbangers when he went to Outlaws. He wasn't afraid.

He waited a week, then he parked outside her home on a Friday morning at 2:00 a.m. Sure enough, she pulled into her driveway a half hour later. Once she pulled her keys out of the ignition, he ran up to the driver's door and pulled her out. She screamed but he had already covered her mouth and suppressed the sound. He snarled, "You fucking cunt, you think you can slap me and get me booted out. Now you're mine, bitch."

He dragged her, kicking and trying to scream, to his parked car. Mack duct-taped her mouth as she tried to scream. He then tied her wrists. As he drove to the strawberry fields in Oxnard, she was whimpering, believing he would kill her.

Never particularly religious, she prayed more than she ever had in her entire life. She believed she would never see her daughter, her friends, or even her family that she was somewhat estranged from. She wished she had made amends and not told her mother to "fuck off" the last time they talked. She wanted so badly to apologize and tell her mother that she loved her. She believed she would never get that chance. She didn't know if there was a God, but if there was, she sure hoped he was listening.

Mack dragged her into the field and ripped her clothes and forcibly penetrated her. After he finished, he told her that if she mentioned this to anyone, he would kill her. He knew where she lived, and she would never be safe again. He also told her that her eight-year-old girl would be without her mommy. She was relieved to be alive but frightened beyond her wildest imagination.

After he drove away in his gray Camaro, she decided to not report what happened. She was lucky to be alive. She called her mother the next day and apologized profusely for their last conversation and told her how much she loved her. She did not tell her mother about being abducted and raped. She would later. She did tell a couple of the other dancers at Snooky's, though, for their protection.

She told Cinnamon, a beautiful black woman whose real name was Tracy Watters, what had occurred, and that it was the customer she had slapped. Tracy urged Tina to report it. Tracy was studying psychology at Oxnard College and had an interest in working with domestic-violence victims, as she had been a victim herself. For Tracy, dancing was easy money and fit her class schedule. She knew she wasn't going to do it much longer, and she also knew she had to convince Tina to report what happened so it didn't happen to someone else.

Two weeks after the rape and abduction, Tina reported what happened to the Camarillo Sheriff's Department. She was accompanied by Tracy. She was referred to sex crimes detective Melissa Milton. Milton was about five foot six, slender, and very fit, with blond hair; she was white and appeared to be in her early forties. The detective, pleasant and empathetic, listened patiently to the weeping young woman, and she knew three things. First, this definitely happened. Melissa Milton knew a liar when she saw one, and Tina Forsythe was not lying. Second, although she only had the name "Mack," she knew, even if caught, this was going to be a very difficult case. It would be his word against hers, and she was a stripper. With the late reporting there was no DNA or any other definitive physical evidence, but even that would not be conclusive, as he would simply claim that she consented. Milton knew it would be a challenge to convince the district attorney to file charges, but she relished the opportunity to do so.

Unfortunately, she knew she would never get that chance. The crime happened in the fields in Oxnard, so this crime had to be reported to the Oxnard Police Department. Parts of Oxnard are unincorporated, and thus under the jurisdiction of the Ventura County Sheriff's Department. The incorporated part is under the jurisdiction of the Oxnard Police Department. Although Ms. Forsythe was abducted from her home in Camarillo, the sheriff's department had a longtime understanding that where the abduction happens in one city but the rape and or murder happens in another, the case belongs to the town where the rape and or murder occurred. Where the rape occurred was an incorporated part of Oxnard. The only time you might see a joint investigation is in homicide or missing-person cases. Melissa called ahead to the Oxnard Police Department, and their Sex Crime Unit agreed to take the case.

Tina told her story the next day to Detective Ken Lamb. Lamb had received Milton's report, so he knew what the allegation was. Lamb appeared to be in his mid-fifties, with pale skin, silver hair, and a mustache. He had served in the military and proudly displayed medals earned and photographs of himself in a US Army uniform. Tina was less comfortable speaking with him than she had been with Detective Milton the night before, but she told him everything she could remember from that horrible night.

Detective Lamb was able to identify Mack by getting surveillance video from inside the club. The incident in the VIP Room was not captured on video, but he did get still photos off the video from Stage One that Forsythe was able to identify. Lamb asked several of his fellow officers if they knew who the man was. When nobody did, the still photo was sent to every Ventura County law enforcement agency. A patrol officer from Ventura city named Mark Nelson recognized him as Jack Macklin, a man he'd arrested for domestic violence a couple of years earlier.

Detective Lamb constructed a photographic lineup that included Macklin and five other men who looked similar. Macklin was in position number four, which was the first photograph on the bottom row. The photos were selected from booking photos and cropped to conceal the fact that the men in the photographs were incarcerated. It wasn't too hard to get a photo lineup of similar-looking men, because at that time Macklin had not yet gotten the prison tattoos that would make his appearance more menacing and distinct.

Tina Forsythe was called and asked to come to the station. Detective Lamb, who had always had a reputation as a thorough professional, provided her with what they referred to as the photo lineup admonition form. The form explained that she was about to be shown a photographic lineup, and that the person who did the crime may or may not be in the lineup. The form also instructed the person being shown the lineup to only select someone if they recognized the person, and to not feel obligated to make an identification. She signed the form, confirming that she had read it. Upon being shown the lineup she immediately pointed to number four, began crying, and said she was 100 percent sure that was him.

Detective Lamb tracked down Macklin at his address in Ventura and advised Macklin of his right to remain silent and have a lawyer. Surprisingly, Macklin decided to talk. Lamb was further surprised by Macklin's statement. Lamb expected a complete denial, but instead, Macklin claimed they'd had a consensual relationship and that he'd broken it off after they had sex a couple of times. He said it was a case of "a woman scorned," or as Macklin also called it, "stripper's revenge."

Lamb knew Macklin was lying, but it was now Lamb's job to convince the DA to go on with this he-said/she-said case. One good thing he had was that Macklin would have to take the stand to get to the "he said" part. Otherwise, it's just a "she said." Defense attorneys can question jurors and get them to promise that they won't hold a defendant's decision not to testify against him. That is, after all, the constitutional right of every defendant, and juries are not supposed to hold it against a defendant if they don't take the witness stand in their own defense.

The reality is, though, without another side to the story, if the victim is credible and there is no alternative story, prosecutors almost always get to the level of proof beyond a reasonable doubt, and juries convict. Macklin had two convictions, one for theft and the domestic-violence conviction. If he did testify, his credibility could be attacked based upon his having been convicted of crimes of moral turpitude. Theft and domestic violence fall into that category.

He also had convictions for drunk and disorderly conduct and driving under the influence. Those charges would not be considered crimes of moral turpitude and therefore wouldn't be admissible. He was also the prime suspect in an unsolved murder from 2003 when Macklin was twenty-four. An elderly neighbor had been beaten and strangled in his home and money was stolen. The killer had cleaned up the scene enough that there was no physical evidence linking Mack. There was very little likelihood that the fact that Macklin was a suspect in this murder would be heard by a jury. His convictions for simple battery and resisting arrest and public intoxication would not be usable in court either. But the moral turpitude crimes would be enough to call into question his credibility, so it was unlikely Macklin would be called as a witness. No competent prosecutor would use Macklin's self-serving statement, as there was sufficient evidence of ID to go forward. The defense could not get Macklin's story in without putting Macklin on the stand. His statement to Detective Lamb would be barred by the hearsay rule unless the prosecutor was stupid enough to offer it as evidence.

Mack initially had a public defender, but he was working various construction jobs and his cousin Paul loaned him some cash, so he was able to hire a private defense attorney. Mack figured a woman would be best, as it would show the jury that he wasn't a threat to women. If a woman would represent him, sit next to him, even comfort him, how could he be a rapist, some jurors might ask. He hired Simi Valley attorney Melody Hardwick. Hardwick had only been an attorney for five years, having graduated from Pepperdine Law School in Malibu. Hardwick was not the greatest lawyer but was aggressive and hated to lose.

She was what they called a true believer, someone who disliked police and prosecutors and believed they were out to frame and railroad innocent people, and that almost all of her clients in her view were innocent people. She was also not above dirty tactics to achieve her goals. Her reputation in the DA's office was not good; she was known to withhold discovery—information one side is required to provide to the other—and to misrepresent facts to the judge. Several times she did not show up for hearings and was almost held in contempt. The prosecutors called her "Bad Melody."

One of her moments of notoriety was when she was sent to trial in front of Judge Michael Bailes, Courtroom 44. Bailes ran a strict no-nonsense courtroom. The prosecutor on the case was Kevin Epps, a third-year African American prosecutor just promoted to the Felony Unit. The charge was assault with a deadly weapon and infliction of great bodily injury. Epps found out before trial that the treating physician who could establish that the victim suffered great bodily injury was going to be away at a seminar, but Epps did have medical records showing the victim's injuries. Epps advised Hardwick that he did not have the physician, but if she agreed to not object to the medical records, he would use those instead; otherwise he could not start trial until the following week. Hardwick said, "That's not a problem; our defense is self-defense, so I won't object to the records." The trial began, and Epps offered the medical records into evidence once the victim's testimony was completed.

Judge Bailes asked if there was any objection, at which point Hardwick said, "Yes, we object; these records are hearsay." Epps, who was generally even tempered, came unglued and asked to approach the bench. He told the judge of Hardwick's flat-out lie and how she agreed to the records coming in. Hardwick played innocent and said Epps must have misunderstood her. Bailes was frustrated because he knew someone wasn't being truthful and suspected it was Hardwick but could not force her to accept the stipulation she was now denying.

Epps was able to get the records in as a business record—an exception to the prohibition of the use of out-of-court statements or documents—due to the fact that the records were certified, but Hardwick made numerous efforts to have portions blacked out by making various objections. This was also unsuccessful, and the accused was convicted and sentenced to five years in prison. That event spread like wildfire throughout the DA's office, and soon the consensus was that Melody Hardwick was not to be trusted. If you asked Epps even years later what he thought of Hardwick, you could guarantee that the words "lying" and "bitch" would flow smoothly from his lips and almost always in that order.

Epps should have gotten the agreement in writing, but he was used to dealing with the public defender's office, with whom the prosecutors frequently had "handshake" agreements—relying on mutual good faith. Since they had cases together often, it was in neither's best interest to engage in deception. Hardwick wasn't a public defender, however, so no unwritten obligation existed.

Melody Hardwick was a thirty-seven-year-old white woman and had been employed in marketing before going to law school. She was not particularly pretty but she had sex appeal and she flaunted it. She worked out religiously and was extremely toned, and she dressed to show it. Her face was rather angular and harsh looking but her long brown hair and figure got the attention of many men.

Her investigator was a very portly white ex-cop from Port Hueneme who had fallen out of favor with the department.

Lanny Michaels—or Fat Lanny, as most people in the DA's office called him—had a reputation for being willing to do anything to win. Once a handsome and respected member of the Port Hueneme gang task force, Lanny's career went downhill after he began to cut corners to get search warrants. Several of his warrants were tossed out for leaving out information that might have convinced a judge not to approve the search warrant. Lanny was demoted to patrol and began eating heavily, resulting in a weight gain of over a hundred pounds. He and the police department reached a severance agreement, and soon afterward he began working as a private investigator for defense attorneys.

It wasn't long before investigator Michaels tracked down Tina Forsythe, the victim, and told her that the defense was obligated to vigorously defend the accused, and that included doing everything possible to prove she was a liar. He told her that if the judge believed she was lying, she could lose custody of her child. He added he wasn't telling her not to show for court, only that it was her decision . . . and that these are some of the things she needed to think about when deciding whether it was in her best interest to be available for the prosecution for the preliminary hearing or the trial. At the time he contacted her, the preliminary hearing was just five days away.

In California, a preliminary hearing is a probable-cause hearing where the prosecutor puts on enough evidence before a judge to show that there is probable cause to believe that a crime was committed and that the defendant committed it. Unless the prosecutor decides to indict by way of a grand jury, a preliminary hearing is required. Unlike in grand juries, hearsay testimony is allowed in preliminary hearings. What that means is that the lead detective who interviewed the victim can testify as to what the victim told them, including the identification of the accused. In cases such as kidnap for the purpose of rape, most prosecutors like to avoid using hearsay testimony and prefer to call the actual victim to the stand. Doing that gives them a chance to evaluate the strength of their case. If they then are unable to locate the victim or something happens prior to trial, the preliminary hearing transcript would be admissible at trial, since the victim was subject to cross-examination at the preliminary hearing.

Michaels and Hardwick knew that if Tina Forsythe did not show up for the preliminary hearing, one of two things could happen, and both would be very good for the defendant. One possibility was that the DA, without the victim's testimony, could choose not to file the case and the accused would be released with no charges, even after a judge determined that there was probable cause based upon the hearsay testimony of the detective's interview. In that case, even after a holding order by the court finding that the district attorney presented enough evidence to allow the defendant to be arraigned in superior court, the district attorney could announce that no charges would be filed at arraignment and the defendant would be released. Another possibility is that the DA would offer a plea to a lesser charge. Here, since kidnap for rape was a potential life sentence, just about anything less would be a win for the defense. Hardwick and Michaels knew that if they could get a lenient offer due to lack of victim cooperation, Mack would likely serve less than ten years.

It was possible that the DA could choose to proceed anyway and go with an all-out effort to locate the victim and secure her trial testimony. The difficulty would be proceeding without having the benefit of hearing and assessing the victim's prior testimony. Michaels and Hardwick figured a hearsay preliminary hearing without the victim was a good thing for Mack.

The assigned prosecutor in the case was Kate Keller, one of the DA's office's rising stars. A graduate of Texas Tech undergrad and UCLA Law, Kate was both intelligent and extremely charismatic. Her big victory that catapulted her reputation in the DA's office was People v James Anthony Searcy. Searcy was a financial whiz and local real estate mogul accused of date rape. Keller interviewed the victim personally and chose to take the case even though the chances of victory in a he-said/she-said case were slim, especially against a good-looking, suave professional like the accused. She knew she had to prove Searcy lied, otherwise a hung jury was the best she could realistically hope for. The victim was young and attractive but reluctant to go forward. The victim testified well but it appeared the defendant, who claimed consent, would as well, and a tie goes to the defense. At least it should, under the beyond-a-reasonable-doubt standard.

Searcy testified that he and the victim had been to several bars that evening and she drank at least two shots at every bar. Searcy was a member of the Moorpark Country Club and he knew they did not have surveillance cameras, so he said that he and the victim had spent most of the night there before going to more bars, then going to his home in the Camarillo Hills where they had consensual sex. He said he told her the next morning that it was a one-night stand and he didn't want any more to do with her. She retaliated by falsely accusing him of rape.

On direct examination from lawyer Randy Pandrick, a prominent trial lawyer from Los Angeles, Searcy detailed their evening. On cross-examination, Keller got him to say exactly how much alcohol he had at each place and how much she had. Searcy even gave some details about things she said that made him realize she was becoming a little tipsy.

Keller was shocked to hear him say they had been drinking at the Moorpark Country Club. Keller was not a member of the club but had gone there with some friends for drinks at the bar just a month earlier. Once 8:00 p.m. hit, they stopped serving alcohol. Searcy testified that both he and the victim were drinking specific drinks up to one in the morning. In rebuttal, Keller called the president of the Moorpark Country Club and the head bartender and both said they stopped serving alcohol after 8:00 p.m. for the last two months after one of the golfers got drunk late and caused an accident that seriously injured three people. Searcy hadn't been there at night in a while and did not know that. The last time he was at that bar was about three months prior and he was unaware of the change. Once the jury knew Searcy was lying, they found him guilty.

Keller's well-earned victory caused her to be a rising young star in the Ventura County DA's office. Yes, Keller got a little lucky—had she not stopped by the Moorpark Country Club with friends, she would not have known about the alcohol restriction—but Keller was thorough and was known to check every aspect of a defendant's statement anyway. She had won other trials on the strength of hard work and preparation. After the Searcy trial, she checked every detail, and she would not have to rely on luck again.

Ultimately, a hearsay preliminary hearing was held for the case against Macklin after the prosecution was unable to locate the victim, Tina Forsythe. Extensive efforts were made to locate her, but the defense refused to waive time, insisting on a speedy preliminary hearing, giving the prosecution less time to locate their star witness. Macklin was held to answer on the charges. That meant the judge, or magistrate, as they are called for preliminary hearings, believed that the evidence was sufficient to support the conclusion that a crime was probably committed and it was probably the accused that did it.

After extensive discussion in the Sexual Assault Unit among the assigned prosecutor, other sex-crime prosecutors, and the chief deputy, they decided to allow the defendant to plead guilty to forcible rape without the life charge for kidnapping. If the victim were to be located, the DA could withdraw the offer. Macklin, knowing he could face a life sentence, pleaded guilty to forcible rape and received an eight-year sentence.

He served 85 percent of his eight-year prison sentence and was released. On several occasions, however, he violated parole, and he was caught twice. One of the violations was for possession of a knife; he pleaded guilty and went back to prison for sixteen months. After being released on the knife charge, he was pulled in for possession of methamphetamines. He served an additional year for the methamphetamine charge, and was released in 2017. According to his sentence, Macklin would be on parole supervision until 2020. He moved into his sparsely furnished apartment on the Avenue and began working sporadically, doing construction work for acquaintances of his cousin.

He had an older TV with cable. One day he was watching the Santa Barbara–Ventura local 5:00 p.m. news, which reported on the success of the Ventura High School football team, whose season ended in a 42–0 playoff loss. He shook his head upon hearing a report of a UFO sighting in the Ojai hills, and he watched a report about a brush fire in Goleta, near Santa Barbara. It was nice to be a free man again.

At 5:45 p.m., he looked out the window and saw a beautiful young Latina, who looked to be in her early twenties, getting out of the driver's seat of a Honda Civic. She had long, flowing black hair; she greeted a boy who could be her brother with a big laugh and a hug. She may have been the most beautiful girl he had ever seen.

He began to contemplate the mistakes he had made in his life. He was a free man now. He had a new life to live and he was going to live it to the fullest. He was going to get a full-time job and he was going to enjoy all that life had to offer. He would travel and visit new, exotic places. He wanted it all, but to get that, he knew that there was one mistake he could never make again. He walked over to the mirror, stared it down, clenched his teeth and growled, "This time, I'm not leaving a fucking witness."

Daisy Guzman, the young Latina that Macklin had observed, was twenty-four years old. She had temporarily moved back in with her parents on Ventura Avenue. They used to live in East Ventura near Buena High School, but her father's work in the restaurant supply business had fallen off, and they had to sell their home and move to a less expensive area. She was a part-time student at Ventura College studying journalism. Her ambition was to be either a TV news anchor or an investigative reporter. Daisy was smart but could be a little too carefree and wasn't the most dedicated student. Her mind often wandered, and she drifted in college, taking semesters off, which is why she was twenty-four and still not in a four-year university.

She had thought about getting married and being a stay-at-home mom, but she'd had several relationships that didn't work out and was now single again. She never really liked the idea of following in her mother's footsteps and giving up her career upon getting married. But she knew she had to have a career before she could make that decision. Daisy was beginning to accept that starting school, then dropping classes and then starting again, sometimes at a different community college, was not good for her future, and she really needed to apply herself.

She had drifted in her employment as well. In addition to periodic modeling jobs for commercials and music videos, she liked her current Victoria's Secret job at the Pacific View Mall in Ventura, but she had liked other jobs before she got bored. She had worked as a server at several restaurants, including a popular and busy Mexican restaurant in Oxnard called Yolanda's. She had also worked as a receptionist in a law office in Santa Paula.

Daisy never had trouble getting a job. Daisy being beautiful, smart, charismatic, and fully bilingual virtually guaranteed success in any interview. Her problem was sticking with one thing and staying interested. Her father, Jose, was born in Mexico and came over illegally to the US at the age of seventeen. He met Marta, a US citizen born in Mexico. Jose was a mechanic and then moved into restaurant supply; Marta was a legal secretary. They fell in love and got married. He was thirty and she was twenty. Three years later, she gave birth to their first child, Joshua. Four years later, Daisy was born. They also had a son Juan, now eleven years old who, as Daisy's little brother, worshiped his big sister. Joshua, twenty-eight, had moved out after turning twenty, and he married and moved to New Mexico.

Now divorced and paying child support, he was still living in New Mexico.

Like many girls born in the '90s, one or both of her parents had watched *The Dukes of Hazzard* growing up. Daisy Duke, known for her short shorts and long flowing dark hair, was one of the few sex symbols during that time that wasn't blond. The name Daisy was particularly popular in the Latin culture, partially for that reason. Natural blondes of Mexican descent are not common. Like Catherine Bach, the actress who played Daisy Duke, Daisy Guzman was blessed with a natural beauty that, along with her bubbly personality and gorgeous smile, would light up any room she entered. At five foot three, Daisy was a little short for runway modeling, but her long black hair, dark complexion, and well-developed figure still got her some photo shoots for car advertisements and clothing lines. Daisy resembled a younger and shorter version of the actress Jessica Alba but with a darker complexion and black hair. The other comparison she frequently heard was with the late great Tejano singing star Selena.

Something that made Daisy stand out was not just her outer beauty, but her inner beauty. Daisy was nice to everyone, always smiling and laughing. If her parents had a worry, it was that she was too trusting. She always got a lot of attention from men and boys; she knew she was considered beautiful and felt lucky for that gift. She never considered herself better than others because of it. She treated people with kindness and respect, whether they were one of the "beautiful people" or an awkward-looking teenager. In middle school and high school, the bullied and mistreated kids, often mocked by the "popular crowd," never got that treatment from Daisy.

One thing Daisy and her mother, Marta, disagreed on was tattoos. Daisy wanted some tattoos, but her mother was dead set against it and told Daisy that tattoos on girls made them look like cholas—female gang members. Daisy jokingly said, "I'm not a chola, I'm a hyna"—gangster Spanglish for "hot girl in the neighborhood," sometimes also used as "a gang member's girlfriend"—then laughed loudly. After much consideration and reflection, Daisy defied her mother when she got a purple daisy tattooed on her left shoulder on her twenty-second birthday, April 14, 2015. Marta wasn't happy, but the two eventually agreed that would be her last one, at least for a while. Daisy warned Marta that when she earned enough money to move out, she might get more, but while living under Marta's roof she would respect her mother's preference.

Daisy was also a talented singer. This was a good thing, with her resemblance to a famous singer. She had a naturally good voice and her parents knew it from the time she was young, when she would run around the house singing. She never took a voice lesson, though her parents wanted her to.

One night, Daisy went with three other girls to a karaoke bar in Ventura. Daisy was not the designated driver, so she had been drinking a little and some liquid courage came upon her. Her friends had heard her sing and thought she was good, but they had never heard her perform in public because she had not done that yet. All she had done to that point was play around and sing along to music on the car radio.

The way singers got to perform at that bar was to write their first name and last initial on a piece of paper, along with the song they were choosing to sing. If the machine had the requested song, the name would be called. When the MC called the name

Daisy G, Daisy got up and sang the Evanescence hit "Bring Me to Life." She brought down the house, it was so good. She sang a second song, that time in Spanish that brought her a standing ovation.

She did end up putting her rendition of "Bring Me to Life" on YouTube and it generated a lot of hits. One record producer contacted her after seeing the video. Daisy took her name and number and promised to think about it. She also thought about trying out for *The Voice,* but she never went through with that or the opportunity to record. Daisy was beautiful and talented with a great heart and full of kindness. Her one weakness was that she drifted and often didn't follow through with things.

She left her home one morning in mid-October of 2017 and walked to her car. She saw a large tattooed man approaching. He smiled and said hi, as did she. She thought he was kind of handsome in a bad-boy sort of way. He looked to be a little older than those she usually dated, but her last boyfriend was younger and was in a gang, which Daisy did not like. Plus, he turned out to be a little immature and bad tempered when things didn't go his way. She thought the guy she just passed seemed nice, though with those tattoos, he wasn't the type of guy Jose and Marta would want her to date. She did not know it yet, but she would soon learn that the man she saw and greeted would become Daisy Guzman's worst nightmare. That man was Jack Macklin.

TWO

It was August 2, 2017. Jack Macklin was still in prison, having violated parole by possessing a knife, when young deputy district attorney and self-proclaimed rising star Kyle Irby received a phone call that all young prosecutors can expect to get.

Irby had been working felony trials with a vertical assignment. This meant that he reviewed the cases that would be assigned to him rather than having another prosecutor, who wasn't going to try the case, make the decision on whether to file the case. Irby was twenty-nine and had only been in the office for two years but had gotten twenty convictions out of twenty-one trials while assigned to misdemeanors. He was promoted to the DUI Grant Unit that handled the most serious driving-under-the-influence felony cases, including repeat offenders and accidents resulting in injury and even death. Soon after, he was moved to the Serious and Violent Felony Unit. He was considered a possibility for the Homicide Unit soon.

Irby was very well dressed and had every hair in place. He looked like a young good-looking cop or FBI agent—not a beat cop, but maybe a young white-collar investigator, tanned, with blond hair and blue eyes. He never lacked for confidence. He could play the nice guy to a jury, but most of his colleagues considered him to be a self-absorbed asshole.

His only not-guilty verdict was in a driving-under-the-influence case where the defense was that the accused's cousin was actually the driver when the accident happened, because the defendant had a prior DUI conviction for which he was still on probation. The cousin had a clean driving record, although he did have theft and resisting-arrest convictions. Because his driving record was clean, he would do less jail time than the defendant if convicted of driving while intoxicated. At the trial, all the people in the car said the cousin was driving. Irby was cocky and didn't always prepare his cases.

Had he taken the time to prepare, he would have heard a jail call, which are all recorded by the jail and retained, from the defendant to his cousin during which they discussed exactly how the cousin would come in and take the blame, and that the DA wouldn't file against the cousin because they couldn't charge the cousin when they already charged the defendant. Technically they could, but only if they believed the cousin was driving. In that jail call, the defendant begged the cousin to take the fall, saying, "Even if they charge you, it's a first offense, you won't go to jail, and I'll pay you back for the alcohol school."

Irby never bothered to pull defendants' jail calls. That was the only stain on Irby's record, and he loved to brag about how good he believed he was. He never did find out about the jail call that would have won him the case, or more likely, would have resulted in a guilty plea. Neither did anyone else, so it became the proverbial tree falling in the forest with nobody around. "If a tree falls in the forest and nobody hears it, did it fall?" Yes it did, because the tree is still on the ground and the missed opportunity still existed.

On August 2, Irby received an angry phone call from a man identifying himself as Bob Staton. Staton had a heavy southern accent and began to berate Irby about "my boy's case." Staton said that his son was in a neighbor's backyard looking for a Frisbee that had possibly gone over a fence into his neighbor's yard at night. The neighbor had a rifle with buckshot, and when he heard the noise, he called out. When he heard more noise, he fired the gun in the direction of the young man "looking for the Frisbee." In reality, the man's home had been broken into several times, and Mr. Staton's sixteen-year-old son and his friends had been the perpetrators. Irby had rejected charges of assault with a firearm against the homeowner.

Mr. Staton ranted on the phone to Irby about how "that maniac could have killed my boy," et cetera. Staton threatened to go to the district attorney, William (Bill) Reddis, with his complaint. Irby had filed and rejected a lot of cases and did not remember the details of this one, although it did sound vaguely familiar. Additionally, he did not want a citizen complaint to the DA about him, so he calmly said, "Mr. Staton, I don't recall the details of your son's case, but I would be happy to pull the file and meet with you so we can discuss this matter further." Irby asked Staton if he knew the name of the man who had fired at his son. Staton provided the name for Irby, who promised Staton that he would review the file. Staton sounded like he'd calmed down some, and he agreed to come to Irby's office that Friday morning, August 4, at 10:00 a.m.

Irby had a secretary retrieve the file. After reviewing the file, he did have a recollection of having rejected the case. He believed that a Ventura County jury would be sympathetic to the homeowner, especially since the man had used buckshot rather than real bullets and had been the victim of several burglaries.

That Friday morning at 9:58, forty-one-year-old Senior Deputy District Attorney Ray Scapio from the Homicide Unit went to the lobby and asked receptionist Gina Rodriguez to page Kyle Irby and tell him that Mr. Staton had arrived. Ms. Rodriguez was confused, but Scapio smiled and told her, "Go ahead and do it, it will be great."

Rodriguez paged Irby, who went to the front desk and looked into the lobby of the DA's office and saw only Ray Scapio. In a confused voice, Irby called out Bob Staton's name and turned to Rodriguez and asked where he went. Immediately Scapio, in his best fake southern accent, the same one he had used on the phone, said, "You Mr. Irby? I want to talk about my boy's case."

Irby was relieved that he wasn't going to face the wrath of an angry dad, but he was angry at himself for being duped. Irby said, "Fuck you, Scapio, I am gonna get you back. Payback is a bitch, remember that." Scapio was doubled over with laughter, amazed that Irby fell for the joke, while Rodriguez suppressed her snickers. Scapio had made the initial phone call from one of the few remaining phone booths in Ventura, so Irby could never get an answer if the number did show on Irby's phone and he thought about calling back.

Scapio was not only a legendary practical joker in the office, but was one of the best trial lawyers Ventura County had ever had. He had been teaching classes on cross-examination for the last several years. He had not only taught all the "baby" prosecutors when they received their initial training, but he also was a frequent speaker on the topic for the National District

Attorneys Association (NDAA) and the California District Attorneys Association (CDAA).

Scapio had decided that Irby needed a comeuppance and had pulled a stack of rejected cases, looking for one rejected by Irby where Scapio could play the "angry dad" routine. When he came across the rejected case where homeowner Daniel Summers fired buckshot at suspected juvenile thieves who claimed they were just retrieving a Frisbee, he knew that was the perfect case to play his joke. He came up with "Bob Staton" because one of the boys was named Timmy Staton.

Scapio didn't want Irby to call Staton before the meeting, so he told Irby that he was in the process of moving and getting new phones so he would be incommunicado, but he would definitely be there for the meeting. It was easy for Scapio to find a pay phone, as he was quite familiar with the few left in the area. If Scapio had called from his office phone, the display on Irby's office phone would not only display Scapio's number, but it would display his name. Modern technology has made the art of the practical joke about as easy as taking a shower with no water.

Scapio at forty-one looked about ten years younger. Five foot ten and 190 pounds, he was in decent shape, a good-looking man with black hair slicked back. Being of Italian American descent, he liked to play that up by often wearing a light-gray suit with a black shirt and white tie. He looked more like a mob lawyer than a prosecutor in that getup. Some prosecutors would jokingly call him "Vinny" or "Vito," and he would proudly laugh and impersonate a mobster. Scapio was born in New Jersey and had an uncle who was a bookmaker. Scapio himself made frequent trips to Las Vegas to bet on sports, made some local wagers, and played poker since his divorce from Amanda six years prior. They shared joint custody of their ten-year-old daughter, Amy.

Scapio began his career as a prosecutor for Ventura County at the age of twenty-seven in 2003, straight out of Loyola Law School in Los Angeles. One of the great practical jokes pulled when Scapio began his career is one many still remembered. That joke involved the participation of Bill Reddis, the district attorney himself. One might wonder why the DA would get involved in a practical joke involving a rookie in the DA's office with whom he would normally have almost no contact.

Scapio first drew the attention of the district attorney when he tried a driving-under-the-influence case against local DUI specialist Darren Whitford. Whitford charged a lot to go to trial, and as a result, his clients were usually wealthy or the children of wealthy people. Whitford often teamed up with an expert witness named Byron Loadholt, who had a PhD in biology and chemistry.

Loadholt was a critic of Ventura County's approved blood-alcohol testing devices, which relied on gas chromatography. Loadholt would testify that the only reliable testing devices used infrared laser spectroscopy and that gas chromatography is inaccurate, despite state approval of both types of devices. Loadholt also testified that Dr. Steven Courtier was the leading authority on blood-alcohol testing and had supported the use of laser spectroscopy devices.

In addition, Loadholt was a major proponent of a study that was critical of field sobriety tests used by police, sheriffs, and highway patrol officers to assess sobriety in the field. These tests commonly included finger to nose, walk a straight line, heel to toe, counting backward, and standing on one foot to test balance. The study concluded that bartenders outperformed law enforcement personnel in measuring accuracy of field sobriety tests compared to the actual blood-alcohol levels.

Scapio was the only prosecutor in the Misdemeanor Unit to use the term "field sobriety tests." They had always been called "tests," but the misdemeanor supervisor at the time thought it would be a good idea to refer to them as "field sobriety exercises." Scapio thought that was ridiculous; you're not doing push-ups or burpees or running a 40. They were tests, and if you didn't do them right you got arrested; if you did them well, you probably got to drive home. But most prosecutors did not like the pass-fail concept because even some high-blood-alcohol defendants could perform some of the tests well. Scapio thought it would sound disingenuous to use the term "exercises," so he did not stick to the script.

Scapio prepared for Loadholt's testimony by researching prior testimony of Loadholt but also by researching articles written by Courtier. Scapio came upon a recent article published in a relatively obscure scientific journal in which Courtier engaged in a review and analysis of various experts in the field of forensic alcohol analysis and their credibility as witnesses as well as the quality of their work. When he discussed Byron Loadholt, Courtier stated, "Byron Loadholt is a fraud whose work is not worthy of publication in a supermarket tabloid."

Scapio began his cross-examination of Dr. Loadholt by asking about the study comparing bartenders with police officers on measuring sobriety. He asked how many total cases they studied. He asked how many bartenders were involved in the study, and how many police. He asked if any of the bartenders had previous law enforcement training. Had any of the bartenders, if they had prior law enforcement experience, ever arrested someone for driving under the influence? He asked how many police officers that participated in this research had been working driving-under-the-influence cases. He asked what assignments they had. He asked what training they had in driving-under-the-influence investigations and how many arrests they had made for driving under the influence.

Dr. Loadholt did not know any of the answers to those questions. Scapio concluded with the following question, to which an objection was overruled: "So for all we know, there could have been just two bartenders and two police officers, one of the bartenders had previously been a police officer for ten years working patrol and had made 100 arrests for driving under the influence after having had extensive training. The two police could have been fraud investigators who never made a driving-under-the-influence arrest in their careers and had no training. Right?" Loadholt pushed back and said that was highly unlikely. Scapio asked him if he knew anything about the police agencies that were studied, which agencies they were, and what training the officers had. Loadholt had to admit that he did not know.

After some technical cross-examination about the different devices used for testing and measuring breath alcohol and converting that into a blood-alcohol level—which seemed to do nothing but bore the jury—Scapio began to attack Dr. Loadholt for judging field sobriety tests without ever having been an officer or having himself conducted any tests. Scapio concluded his cross-examination by asking about Dr. Courtier and Loadholt's testimony critical of the machine and lab-technician testimony.

He got Loadholt to praise Courtier as the foremost expert in the field. He then asked if Loadholt was aware of what Courtier thought of him. Loadholt said he did not know. Scapio then showed Loadholt the paragraph Courtier wrote about him and asked him to read it to the jury. Loadholt was destroyed; he left the witness box so flustered that he left all his notes on the witness chair. After thirty minutes of deliberation, the jury found the defendant guilty of driving under the influence and driving with a prohibitive blood-alcohol level.

The judge in that case, Patricia Scheinbloom, had been a colleague of DA Reddis's, and Reddis had recommended her to the governor for appointment as a judge. Judge Scheinbloom raved about Scapio's cross in a phone call to DA Reddis. Reddis made it a point to personally congratulate the young DA. When the two men got to talking, one of the great practical jokes of the Ventura County DA's office was born.

The next day, Scapio came into work wearing an earring in his right ear. Reddis called his chief deputy, Alan Farrell, into his office. Farrell was a graduate of Biola University (Bible Institute of Los Angeles) and Pepperdine Law School. Farrell was a pretty conservative man who was not fond of some recent fashion trends. Reddis informed Farrell that Scapio wore an earring and that it was unacceptable. Reddis instructed Farrell to inform Scapio's supervisor, Katrina Waverly, to inform Scapio that earrings on men were unacceptable. Waverly was a young supervisor at just thirty-three, and she had no problem with the earring. She didn't like the fact that Scapio defied her on not saying "field sobriety exercises," but she knew he got good trial results and relished going to trial.

She called Scapio into her office and told him of the district attorney's order regarding the earring. She emphasized that it did not bother her, but that she was obligated to communicate the DA's request and she hoped he would comply. Scapio was defiant and said that when he is in trial, he would not wear an earring, as jurors might feel the same way as the DA. He said it would not be in his interest to alienate any jurors, but when not in trial, he wanted to exercise his personal expression and wear one. Waverly was distressed; she knew Scapio was good and did not want him to be terminated or to resign but she could not get him to compromise. Scapio felt bad. He liked Waverly and knew he was putting her in some distress, but he did think it was for the purpose of humor, which, in Scapio's mind, was the greater good.

After being told that Scapio wasn't budging on the earrings, Reddis blew up and said, "I want that snot-nosed rookie asshole fired!" Farrell actually tried to talk Reddis off the ledge. Reddis agreed to have a meeting in his office at 1:00 p.m. the next day. Waverly and Farrell were first to arrive and sat uncomfortably staring at the photographs in Reddis's office.

Reddis was a rather proud forty-eight-year-old Irish American and he had photographs of famous Irish pubs throughout the world. His father worked as a deputy in the DA's office in the 1980s when controversial anti-death penalty Supreme Court Justice Rose Bird was voted out of office. Jeremy Reddis retired in 1989 and had been very active statewide in the campaign to oust Bird. He had a photograph of a sign with a circle with a red line through it meaning "No" next to an autographed picture of disgraced baseball star Pete Rose, who had been banned from the Hall of Fame, despite being the all-time hits leader, due to his gambling on the sport. Next to the large poster of Rose was another poster, this one of former Celtics star Larry Bird. Reddis had spelled out "No Rose Bird" via the three posters in his office.

When Jeremy Reddis retired, he essentially willed his prized set of posters to his son, who began his own career in 1992 after having previously been a probation officer and a park ranger in Northern California. Years after the ouster of Bird as a justice and long after her passing, Bill Reddis was still proudly displaying the "No Rose Bird" poster configuration he inherited from his father.

Ten years after Bill started his career as an attorney, the district attorney opted to retire, and he ended up endorsing Reddis to be his successor. Reddis won a hotly contested election against another prosecutor and a local attorney specializing in civil practice.

Reddis congratulated Scapio on his trial victory and told him of Judge Scheinbloom's comments. The older Reddis and younger Scapio bonded over sports and their love of trying cases. As they continued talking, the topic of pulling jokes on people came up, and Reddis proposed they pull one on his misdemeanor supervisor and chief deputy.

On the morning of the big meeting over Scapio's earring insubordination, Scapio entered Reddis's office wearing the same earring in his right ear. Farrell immediately asked him if he really thought this was worth it. Waverly said she really hated to see him leave over this because he had the potential of being a great prosecutor. As Scapio shrugged his shoulders and said, "Oh well," Reddis walked into his office wearing two huge hoop earrings, one on each ear. He then said, "I heard someone has a problem with earrings," and burst out laughing. Waverly was relieved and laughed. Scapio took off his earring and said, "I got a trial I'm starting tomorrow, so no earring; besides, they look better on women." He then turned to Waverly and said, "That wasn't sexist, was it?" and Waverly practically fell out of her chair laughing. Farrell just shook his head, looked at Scapio and Reddis, and said "Well played, you guys got me."

THREE

It was April 24, 2015, when a young woman was found murdered in the garage of her home in Newbury Park. Macklin was incarcerated on one of his parole violations at the time. The woman was twenty-nine-year-old Jessica Braden. Her ex-boyfriend Allen McCarty, thirty-one, was the immediate suspect. McCarty, the son of a very wealthy Camarillo physician, was a local tennis pro who was known to have a bad temper. The police had been called on several instances to abuse allegations involving McCarty and Braden, with Braden having called 911 to report that she was assaulted. A couple of times, she recanted the allegations and ended up getting back together with McCarty. He was convicted on one of the instances when she had visible injuries, and he was placed on probation. A previous case was rejected for prosecution.

Jessica had recently broken up with McCarty after four years of dating, and she told several of her close friends that McCarty had called her and threatened to kill her if she didn't get back together with him. He had also left a threatening voice mail, but unfortunately, she had erased it. She talked with some friends about getting a restraining order and was upset that she had erased the phone threat before realizing that she could use it to get the restraining order.

Jessica Braden was a pretty woman with blond hair and ivory skin who had graduated from Newbury Park High School and attended Moorpark College for two years, studying nursing, before she changed course. She decided that she wanted to cut hair, and she got her cosmetology license. She had met McCarty through one of her clients.

McCarty was a very good-looking man and quite a smooth talker. The first several months of dating, Braden always said, were perfect, but then she saw him becoming more controlling. He did not want her to hang out with her friends. He repeatedly would call her and if he could not reach her, he would accuse her of cheating on him. It wasn't long after he began restricting her activities and becoming more possessive that he began the physical abuse.

As sheriff's homicide detective Miguel Cuevas researched the history of 911 calls and incident reports, he knew he had to get a search warrant for McCarty's residence. Cuevas worked his homicide cases with partner Kenny Rollins. At fifty-six, Rollins was the veteran, and Cuevas at forty was the youngster. Cuevas was Hispanic and was short for a cop at five foot eight; his 220 pounds meant he did look like he could have spent a little bit too much time at the donut shop. Clean shaven, with a round bald head, he was intimidating, but he also had a great way of relating to suspects and was good at getting confessions. Rollins was bald on top but had white hair on the sides and a big white handlebar mustache and a slightly ruddy complexion. Everyone called him "Monopoly" or "Monopoly Man" for his resemblance to the bald, mustachioed character pictured on the Monopoly cards and game board.

Rollins and Cuevas would never be cast in Hollywood to play cops, but as prosecutors say, "We don't get our witnesses from central casting." That line is almost as frequently used to justify less than perfectly likable witnesses to a jury as the quote, "When the crime happens in hell, your witnesses aren't going to be angels." Yeah, Cuevas and Rollins were not picked by central casting, but they were great homicide detectives. Juries liked them too because they were humble, honest, and down to earth. Rollins may have looked like the Monopoly guy, but if he set his sights on you as a suspect, there was no "get out of jail free" card.

The murder was discovered when Braden's mother and father could not reach her. They became concerned when they had called Jessica the previous evening and the call went to voice mail. The following morning she did not call back, and subsequent calls went to voice mail. Jessica's parents feared the worst because Jessica had expressed fear of McCarty.

The sheriff's department was called out to check the well-being of the resident. Braden lived alone in a two-bedroom house about a mile from the high school off North Reino Road. She'd previously had a roommate she split the rent on the house with, but that roommate decided to move in with her boyfriend. Braden got some help from her parents to cover the rent after her roommate's half share was gone.

The ex-roommate, Michelle Harrington, twenty-six, was a server at Cronies in Ventura, a popular local sports bar and restaurant on Johnson Drive near the 101 freeway. She had been working at the Cronies in Newbury Park, but upon moving to Oxnard Shores she asked to be transferred to the Ventura

Cronies because it was closer. Harrington would be one of the witnesses who told of the victim's controlling ex-boyfriend and some of the problems they had.

Deputies first searched the house and did not find anyone inside. There were drawers pulled open in the bedroom and items strewn about as if either someone was looking for something to steal, or someone was trying to make it look that way. There were no obvious signs of a struggle or any visible evidence of blood inside the home. Deputies called out the victim's name, but there was no answer. They searched every room, every closet, and every bathroom, but still no sign of the victim.

There was a one-car garage attached to the house, so the deputies entered the garage through the closed but unlocked interior door. They found signs of a struggle: a desk near the door entering the garage from the house was overturned, and numerous items were on the floor. Farther into the garage, lying on the floor next to the driver's side front tire of her 2014 silver Lexus, was the body of twenty-nine-year-old Jessica Braden.

Patrol deputies called the station, requesting forensics and homicide investigators. The medical examiner's office was also notified. It was 10:10 a.m. when Jessica Braden's body was found.

The forensics team arrived around the same time as Rollins and Cuevas. The head forensic scientist was forty-three-year-old Sean Murphy. Only about five foot seven, with red hair and a light Irish complexion, he looked somewhat like a leprechaun, so it's no surprise that Murphy had been given the moniker "Lucky Charms" after the cereal with the leprechaun on the box.

Murphy had only been in the US for six years, having studied forensic science in his native Dublin. He had a thick Irish accent, and Ventura County juries loved him. The word in the DA's office was if you got Murphy on the stand, you won your case. Before Murphy, people used to think maybe a British accent or a southern accent would create the most ethos or credibility with jurors, but after Murphy, even the public defenders knew that nothing beat the Irish accent. He was kind of like MMA fighter Conor McGregor, without the cussing and the tattoos.

Murphy's specialty was blood-spatter interpretation, and there was a decent amount of spatter to interpret in Braden's garage. After Murphy surveyed the scene for about ten minutes, Cuevas approached him and said, "So what are we looking at, Lucky Charms?"

"Well, the ME will give you the details," Murphy replied, "but I think this poor young lady was stabbed a lot of times by somebody who was really pissed off at her. You can see her tank top is drenched, and I already see at least five punctures to her chest and neck. It also looks like he finished her off by slashing her throat. I say 'finished her off' because it bled a lot, so she was probably still breathing when the son of a bitch did that. I couldn't tell you when this happened—the ME might—but I can tell you that the body is cold, so it's likely she's been dead a while and appears to be in rigor mortis.

"He probably took the knife with him and went back through the door into the house and got out from inside the house. I see two blood drops from a higher-up angle that probably came from the bloody knife being held around waist high, based on the shape of the drops. I'll photograph those for sure and collect them in case he cut himself and it's his blood or a mixture. There are only the two drops though, so he probably put the knife in a pocket or something, then escaped through the door leading to the garage. There is some cast-off spatter which appears low velocity, so as he was stabbing her, some of the blood from the blade of the knife flew off and landed; that is probably going to be victim's blood.

"I'm gonna go inside in a bit to check for blood he might have tracked from his shoes. I expect to find some that the patrol guys might have missed as I track from the garage interior door to the front and back door of the house, but it'll more likely be found toward the front, as that should be the fastest escape route. I expect a neighbor might have heard a scream but didn't call 911. I gotta think with the multiple stab wounds she would have howled like a banshee and somebody probably heard her. Maybe the bastard covered her mouth—I mean I assume the killer is a he, but I guess you never know these days, do you—anyway yeah, she probably screamed at least a few times.

"If you're able to find the clothes he was wearing, there'll be blood spatter unless he thoroughly washed them. Your killer is likely right handed, based on the location of the stab wounds, and it looks like—but I can't be sure till I watch the autopsy and get a clear look at the stab wounds—she was stabbed while standing and also while on the ground. I am basing this on what looks like the angles of entry, but I won't know this for sure until the autopsy."

Cuevas thanked Lucky Charms and then immediately began to focus on finding out about the victim, because this case needed to be at least considered a possible domestic-violence homicide. First, women who are murdered are most often murdered by a romantic partner or ex-partner. Second, the scene appeared staged to look like a home-invasion burglary. Cuevas and Rollins both concluded, after noting no evidence of forced entry and the garage door being closed, that the killer either entered with his or her own key, or the victim let her killer in. A confrontation occurred and the killer chased her into the garage and murdered her. The killer re-entered the home, making a bad attempt to make it look like a home invasion by ransacking some drawers; he was in a hurry to get out of there, so he didn't take any valuables. It would later be determined that there was some valuable jewelry and money not taken, and there would never be evidence that anything was taken.

Murphy examined the inside of the home more carefully than the initial patrol deputies and noticed that some of the clothing strewn on the bed had blood transfer or smear patterns consistent with the killer having blood on his or her hands and transferring it onto the clothing being pulled out. There were also some barely visible stains leading from the garage interior door to the front door of the home and some bloodstains on the driveway. Unfortunately, no shoe-tread patterns could be located that had sufficient detail to be helpful for comparison with a later-collected shoe. He did find a few blood drops elsewhere inside the house.

* * *

Rollins and Cuevas had the unpleasant but necessary task of notifying the next of kin. They needed to find out if she was in a relationship or had a recent breakup. They would need to procure a search warrant with a judge's approval before evidence would be destroyed by her killer, so time was of the essence.

Upon speaking with the victim's family, including her parents, Diane and Phillip, and her siblings, Sheree and David, as well as ex-roommate Michelle Harrington, suspicion focused on the ex-boyfriend.

Cuevas and Rollins visited McCarty at his home, and it seemed to both detectives that he was trying hard to act like he did not know of Jessica's death. Strangely, he asked no questions about the details of the murder. Innocent people frequently inquire about details such as where the victim was killed, how the victim died, and if they had any suspects. Braden's parents asked those questions and more, despite the fact that they were devastated and clearly grief-stricken. Braden's parents asked those questions and more and added their suspicion of ex-boyfriend McCarty.

Cuevas noticed a bandage on McCarty's right index finger and sarcastically asked, "What happened? Cut yourself shaving?"

"I can be clumsy sometimes. I cut it chopping celery," McCarty replied. Not long after, the detectives asked where he had been during the time period that it was believed the murder occurred. McCarty said, "I think I might need a lawyer here."

"That's up to you," Cuevas said, "but we want to eliminate people." He explained that if McCarty was innocent, it would be helpful to clear him as soon as possible to be able to move on to other suspects.

"I didn't do anything, but I want a lawyer before I say anything else," McCarty replied.

Rollins asked McCarty if he was willing to give them a cheek swab for the purpose of eliminating him by DNA. Both detectives explained to him that it would be a really simple procedure where they would just put a Q-tip in his mouth and press it lightly against the inside of his cheek, and they would have their

DNA sample. If he had nothing to do with his ex-girlfriend's death, the DNA would clear him and allow the detectives to move on more quickly and increase the chances of catching the real killer.

McCarty declined and said, "Get a warrant. Now, if you're not going to arrest me, our conversation is over."

Cuevas photographed the bandage on the finger. The two detectives left the house and began to walk back to their unmarked police car. As they walked, Cuevas noticed that the trash was out by the curb awaiting pickup. Cuevas pointed it out to Rollins and said, "Let's check it out. You never know."

Rollins muttered, "Abandoned property. Why not?" Rollins was referring to the law that says once you put your trash out to be collected, you have abandoned your possessory interest in the items in the trash can because you are throwing them out. That means police can search the trash can without first obtaining a warrant. This is important, because at this point in the investigation, they don't have probable cause to obtain a search warrant. McCarty wasn't going to consent, because they had asked him if they could search the house, and his response was "Get a warrant."

They also noticed a new 2015 Porsche registered to McCarty in the driveway that looked like it was freshly detailed both inside and out. They would not end up getting any evidence out of his car.

There were two trash cans by the curb in front of the residence. The blue one contained just newspapers. The green one contained discarded food and clothing items as well as plastic and paper bags. The detectives quietly moved the trash cans, hoping not to be noticed by McCarty. Once they were several houses away and out of a window's view from McCarty's home, they dumped the trash cans onto the grass area of another house.

The two detectives immediately began searching and found two items of obvious significance. Near the bottom of the green trash can was a yellow button-down shirt with visible blood spatter on it. The shirt was not drenched with blood, but there was enough visible spatter to indicate that the wearer of the shirt was physically close to a traumatic occurrence. The shirt would be collected and photographed from multiple angles and would be extensively examined by Lucky Charms. The spatter appeared, based on the detectives' training and experience, to be low-velocity spatter.

Blood spatter is evaluated by the size, shape, and angle of the blood drops. Larger drops are called low velocity and are consistent with stab wounds, as opposed to medium-velocity spatter (medium-sized drops), which is consistent with blunt-force trauma such as a pipe or baseball bat. Smaller drops that look more like spray, which is called high-velocity spatter, is most consistent with someone using a firearm.

There was also a pair of black tennis shoes that appeared to be new, so they would not be likely to be tossed in the trash, but there they were, a pair of size 10 Nikes. There were several blood drops on each of the shoes. Oddly, there had been no pants among the trash. Rollins speculated that McCarty may have liked the pants enough that he was unwilling to toss them out, so McCarty thoroughly washed them instead. Even if they got a warrant, it would be unlikely that there would be incriminating evidence like blood still present and detectable on the pants.

* * *

It took over three months to analyze all the evidence collected and get DNA results back. The real world is not like the CSI shows where they get the results in less than an hour minus commercials. They did get a warrant and never did locate any bloody pants or the murder weapon, but they also got a warrant for McCarty's DNA, which he then provided without resistance.

As the DNA results began to come in, it was clear that sometimes things are exactly as they seem. In fact, that's probably the case 98 percent of the time. It's the old principle known as Occam's razor: the simplest explanation is likely the true explanation.

Several blood drops inside the victim's home were collected. Most belonged to the victim, but two were unquestionably McCarty's blood. The odds of it being some other random person's blood and not McCarty's were astronomical. Basically, the earth's population would have to multiply over 100 billion times before you would find a person other than Allen McCarty who would possess the same genetic markers.

The blood spatter on the shirt and shoes recovered from the trash can at McCarty's front yard all belonged to the victim. The odds of it being someone else's were just as astronomical. The same was true of the victim's blood found inside her home, although that blood did not suggest who her killer was. The blood on the clothing items that appeared to be ransacked from the home was determined to be mostly the victim's blood, but there was one brassiere that contained a mixture of the victim's and McCarty's blood.

The lab was able to determine this thanks to a new field of DNA testing known as Starmix or STRmix, meaning "short tandem repeats mixture." These short tandem repeats are genetic markers that repeat in short repetitive tracts, and the numbers of times they repeat are genetic markers used in DNA analysis. They are used to separate out mixtures of more than one source to identify each individual contributor to a DNA mixture. It used to be very difficult to determine the sources of the DNA when there was a mixture, but with advances in the science by companies like Cybergenetics in Pennsylvania using a system called TrueAllele and county labs using STRmix, these mixtures can now be separated and identified.

Ultimately, what this meant for the case against McCarty was that blood from a cut on McCarty's hand transferred along with the victim's blood onto one of the objects that was pulled out of the victim's drawer after she was stabbed to death. The blood pattern was described as a smear or wipe rather than spatter and therefore consistent with McCarty stabbing the victim to death and cutting his hand in the process, and pulling clothing belonging to the victim out of the drawers while transferring the victim's blood he got on himself as well as the blood from his own cut hand.

All the blood collected from the garage, including the two drops that Murphy thought might be from the killer, turned out to be the victim's blood. The two drops must have dripped off the knife before the killer put the knife in his pants. This might have been the result of the killer standing in the garage while holding the knife and contemplating his next move before putting the knife in his pants.

* * *

It was 10:00 a.m. on a Thursday and there was a slate of daytime baseball games set for August 24. Scapio got in his car, a 2011

CLS 550, and headed for Buena Lanes, a bowling alley in Ventura. Scapio had signed out to four different courtrooms and the credit union but not to his real destination, the local bowling alley near the 101. He headed out to Victoria Avenue and drove a couple of miles before turning onto the street leading to the alley.

Scapio knew that there was a phone booth at the bowling alley. There are very few left, but Scapio knew the closest one was at Buena Lanes, and he did not want the call he was about to make to be traceable. He stood in front of the pay phone, dropped in the coins, and dialed the number. There was no wait to use the phone, as pay phones were rarely used in 2015, and Scapio wondered how long this phone would be available.

A nice young woman answered the phone with the phrase, "Sports Today, who am I speaking with?" and Scapio replied, "This is RS32452." The young woman responded, "How can I help you, RS?"

Scapio replied, "Give me the Cubs listing Arrieta as the starting pitcher in that game over the Reds listing Romano to win $100. Give me the Tigers listing Fulmer over the Yankees for a flat $100. Give me the over in the Phillies-Marlins game to win $100. Give me the Red Sox, Sale pitching versus the Indians Bauer under 7.5 runs to win $100, and finally for just action, no listed pitchers, give me White Sox over the Twins for a flat $100." He didn't need to ask the betting lines or what the total runs were because he just used his iPhone to check VegasInsider.com for the baseball lines, and the offshore service he was using would not vary much from Vegas Insider. Scapio continued, "That's all for today, thanks." And the young woman replied, "Thank you, RS, and best of luck."

Scapio bet on sports. It was a hobby, but it was no longer legal. He used to have an account with PinnacleSports.com, but once the federal government passed an internet betting ban that was attached as a rider to a port security bill during the George W. Bush administration, internet sports betting became illegal except in Nevada. One of Scapio's college buddies from Cal State Northridge got Scapio access to the betting service he'd just called.

He knew baseball. He'd played baseball in college and now did modestly well betting on baseball, though he usually gave away those winnings by betting on the NFL. This time, Scapio won three of the five bets he'd just placed. The White Sox beat the Twins 5-1, and the Tigers beat the Yankees in a big upset as Scapio's $100 bet netted him a $210 profit, so he would get his $100 back plus another $210. He unfortunately lost the Cubs bet when the Reds beat them 5-2. Scapio took the Cubs even at -180—bet $180 to win $100—because their pitcher, Jake Arrieta, had been pitching as well as anyone in baseball. Unfortunately, the Cubs bullpen blew the lead for Arrieta and the Cubs lost the game late.

Scapio lost the under in the Red Sox game badly. Sale and Bauer were two superb pitchers that year, but both had miserable days and the final was 13-7, soaring way past the 7.5 runs that Scapio was hoping the game would not exceed. He did win the over total on the Phillies-Marlins easily, as the final was 9-8, totaling 17 runs and far exceeding the 8 posted total by the bookies. For the day, he won three and lost two and hit a big underdog on the Tigers. He lost a smaller favorite on the Cubs, but overall, he had a nice day.

After placing the bets, Scapio got back in his car and drove back to the government center. When he returned, he had a phone message that he was needed for a sentencing in Courtroom 27. He immediately hustled to Courtroom 27 and apologized to the judge for being late, then proceeded with the sentencing. Scapio rarely made a calendar error because he did not want to get caught being absent from court while making his phone booth trips. This was one of the rare times he messed up, but there were no consequences. Scapio tried to limit his phone booth trips to his lunch break, but when there were early day-games he wanted to bet on during the week, he had to be cagey. Fortunately for him, he only made these trips about once every two weeks, and he really had to like the games a lot to leave for the Buena Lanes phone booth and bet.

When he bet games, he would call his friend from college who lived in Los Angeles, the friend who had set him up with the account. He would tell him that he made bets, which he called SGEs. In Scapio's mind, he was not violating the criminal laws that he was sworn to uphold except for significant games, so SGE stood for "significant-game exception." Every two weeks, Scapio's college buddy would meet with Cory, who was a runner for the bookie service, and settle up. If he and Scapio made money combined, Cory would pay; if they lost, Scapio's buddy would pay Cory and then Scapio and his friend would settle with each other. The friend's name was Eric Goren and they played baseball together at Northridge. Goren was currently a high school baseball coach in West LA.

Scapio was an honest prosecutor who always sought the truth, would never withhold exculpatory evidence, and would never prosecute someone he did not believe was guilty. He was well respected by defense attorneys, but he lived by his own code. In his initial interview, he was asked whether there was any type of case that he would refuse to prosecute, and he said he would not prosecute bookies as long as they paid their winners. He said that he did not believe it should be illegal. They hired him anyway. When he answered that question, he wasn't betting except in Las Vegas, but after a couple of years in the office, he started up again.

* * *

Detectives Cuevas and Rollins had kept DA Reddis informed of the Braden-case DNA results as they trickled in from the crime lab. It was the first week of November when Cuevas called Reddis and informed him that they would like the district attorney to file their case and charge McCarty with the murder of his former girlfriend. Reddis requested that they come in the following afternoon, and he informed them that his chief assistant DA Brad Hollinger (who had taken over a couple of years earlier, after Farrell retired), his Major Crimes supervisor Katrina Waverly, and his chief deputy DA Matt Flynn would be present for the meeting.

The next day, Cuevas and Rollins arrived at 1:30 for the 1:45 scheduled meeting. At 1:45, they were escorted into the office of the district attorney by the receptionist on duty.

As they entered the office, Rollins immediately noticed Flynn, and there was a moment of discomfort for both. Rollins did not like Flynn, and the feeling was mutual. Flynn stood six foot four and had played basketball at the University of Texas Arlington. He was in his late forties, with a lean build, pale complexion, and short gray hair. The source of the animosity between Flynn and Rollins was that Flynn had prosecuted Oxnard officer Michael Lester, a friend and colleague of Rollins, for excessive force six years earlier. Rollins had been Lester's partner when Lester had worked for the sheriff's department four years before the incident where Lester was charged.

* * *

After a high-speed chase and a foot pursuit, Lester had caught gang member Miguel Solis. After Solis was handcuffed, he rolled from his stomach to his back and kicked at Lester, who then struck Solis with his baton approximately fifteen times. Lester maintained that the force was reasonable, as Solis was still resisting and kicking at him. Two civilians witnessed the encounter, with very different recollections. One said that Solis stopped kicking after he was hit with the baton once, and Lester continued to strike him numerous times while calling Solis a "gangbanging piece of shit." The second witness was farther away and said that Solis was trying to kick the deputy the entire time. He also said he did not hear what was said, but that Solis was also yelling and sounded very angry.

Flynn established that the nineteen-year-old witness whose testimony favored the Oxnard officer was planning on becoming a deputy sheriff and that the witness's father was an LAPD detective. Two officers who heard Lester's call for backup arrived toward the end of the confrontation but did back up Lester's testimony by saying that when they arrived, Solis was trying to kick the officer and thought the officer might have even been kicked "in the nuts."

In his closing, Flynn argued to the jury that this officer was part of the "blue wall of silence," meaning cops won't "rat out" bad cops, and that Lester was a bad cop. This argument infuriated all of law enforcement, and for the rest of his career, Flynn would have a hard time with them—particularly the leaders of that community, leadership that included Rollins. The jury ended up deadlocked 7–5 for acquittal. Flynn further infuriated law enforcement by requesting the trial judge reset the case for trial. The judge declined Flynn's request.

Reddis also lost some law enforcement support over that case for a period of time, but he was a great schmoozer and worked very hard to regain their trust, and largely succeeded.

Reddis had a lot of confidence in Flynn, but he had advised Flynn during that trial not to argue the blue wall of silence, and Flynn ignored his advice. Reddis didn't punish Flynn, because he didn't *order* Flynn not to make the argument. Reddis told law enforcement that it was not his decision to issue the charge in the Lester case, but that since it was entirely a credibility call, he left that decision up to his deputy.

Before becoming DA, Reddis had earned great respect from the cops. He was always making himself available to review search warrants at any time of day or night. He knew he was lucky that he was married to an ex-cop, otherwise not many spouses would put up with all the after-hours search warrant duty he did. He also was tight with the narcotics detectives, as he frequently attended busts with them and even wore a bulletproof vest and entered homes. He was a cops' DA, so he had gained their respect.

Reddis believed when it came to excessive-force cases, there was an us-against-them mentality that led to an unwillingness of many police to cooperate and be truthful against a fellow officer. He also believed that the problem was greater in other parts of the country but did exist in Ventura County. He was working behind the scenes to reform training and change mentality among younger members of law enforcement. Unfortunately, Flynn's argument undid all the hard work that Reddis had put in, and it would take an event years later in Minnesota for the training to incorporate elimination of the code of silence.

Flynn did sincerely believe in the case and also believed that most police would turn in a crooked cop or one committing sexual or domestic-violence offenses, but he further believed that when it came to excessive force against criminals, the us-versus-them mentality prevailed. Flynn maintained that regardless of who he offended, the code of silence continued to be a problem in law enforcement. The truth was, Reddis had a great relationship with the police but he felt it vital to have someone in upper management be the skeptic, and Flynn was that man.

Flynn offered to shake Rollins's hand, but Rollins declined and gruffly mumbled, "Hey Flynn," as Cuevas successfully suppressed his own laughter at the awkwardness of the situation. Hollinger and Waverly did shake hands with both detectives.

Rollins laid out the case against McCarty in a kind of closing argument that most prosecutors would be happy to deliver. Waverly asked if Lucky Charms could say that the blood on the clothes was necessarily from the murder or if it could be from some other event. Rollins said his understanding was the best that could be said was it was consistent with the murder.

Flynn, perhaps trying to redeem himself with the detectives, said, "Any other explanation would be ridiculous; McCarty would have to be the unluckiest guy on the planet to have that blood come from some other time he happened to beat or stab her, but some other guy did this murder. That would be the OJ defense all over again."

Waverly then pointed out that OJ got off, at which point Rollins could not restrain himself. Looking right at Flynn, he said, "Yeah, and OJ's scumbag lawyers argued that the police planted evidence. Maybe they even argued the blue wall of silence; wonder where I've heard that phrase before."

Flynn put his arms up in the air and said, "Hey Rollins, I'm on your side here, I want this case filed."

Reddis stepped in and said, "OK, guys, it's time to let that go. We're going to file this case. We're gonna get a far better jury here than what they got in downtown LA, and McCarty being a local athlete isn't gonna do shit for him in Ventura County."

Reddis added that McCarty was likely to hire a top-notch defense attorney, and they were gonna need to put their best on it. Reddis asked Rollins and Cuevas if they had anyone they thought would be good, based on their experience. Cuevas immediately stated, "I like Scapio. I saw him do the cross on the defendant on one murder where the woman had her husband killed in Camarillo a couple of years ago, and it was absolutely beautiful."

Rollins agreed, saying, "Scapio is great and so is Keller, and you have a rising star in Michelle Church. I know she's only thirty-two at most and hasn't been in homicides for even a year yet, but I had a four-defendant robbery case with her, with four defense attorneys, and she took them all apart as they kept objecting and getting overruled. She came back and completely flustered them with objections that the judge ruled her way on. That was a complex case, but her PowerPoint presentation put it all together.

"I don't know Church, haven't worked with her yet, but I do know Scapio is really good, and that guy that came over from Riverside, Keith Harris, is great too. The other homicide guy I have been impressed with is the black dude, Kevin Epps. He is real sharp and always prepared." Flynn was going to make a comment about Scapio but decided to make that comment when the detectives were not around.

Reddis said that he and his chiefs would have a meeting to discuss who to assign the case to, and he got on the phone. "Barbara, reserve the executive conference room for tomorrow at 1:30." He then enthusiastically shook Cuevas's and Rollins's hands and said, "Great job guys, loved the trash-can search. You guys are the best, and guys like you are the reason we are the safest county west of the Mississippi. When we decide who you'll be working with, I'll let you know. Before the meeting tomorrow, if there's anyone you're not comfortable working with for whatever reason, call me. Have great day, guys, and we'll talk tomorrow."

The next day was the day of the big meeting. Cuevas had called Reddis to discuss a potential press conference—who would conduct it and where it would be held—but neither Rollins nor Cuevas had called to disqualify any potential prosecutors. In attendance for the meeting were the same people from the previous day: chief assistant Brad Hollinger, Reddis's number two; chief deputy Matt Flynn; and Katrina Waverly, the supervisor of the Homicide Unit who'd been Scapio's supervisor back when he was in misdemeanors and he and Reddis pulled the earring joke. She was again supervising Scapio, this time in the Homicide Unit.

Also at the meeting was chief deputy Fred Boylan. Boylan was in charge of special operations, which included internal investigations and political corruption. Boylan was a veteran of the DA's office who was graying at sixty-five but still very fit. He was of half-Irish and half-Syrian descent and had intense brown eyes and a unibrow that few would ever tease him about (though Scapio did once sneak a poster of famous unibrow basketball player Anthony Davis with the caption "Long Lost Son" and put it on Boylan's office wall). Boylan was sharp and intense, a graduate of Berkeley's Boalt Hall law school, one of the most respected law schools in the country. Boylan knew all the attorneys in the Homicide Unit, and though he'd never seen them in trial, his wise counsel would still be valued.

Also present at the meeting was chief of the Investigation Bureau, Jim Katz. Katz had been hired away from the Oxnard Police Department and had worked at both offices as an investigator for trials in homicides and serious and violent felonies, which would include robbery, home burglary, assaults with deadly weapons, attempted murders, and other crimes involving great danger or violence. He developed a good rapport with the attorneys he worked with. He was promoted to bureau chief after five years working cases.

Katz was sixty-one. His twenty-seven-year-old daughter had just finished law school and passed the bar and was clerking in the DA's office, hoping to be hired. His son Ricky, thirty, was a California highway patrol officer stationed in Ventura. Katz stood six foot four, which made him the same height as Flynn, although Katz didn't skip many meals and had more girth than Flynn. Katz had a good voice and was a cantor at the only synagogue in Ventura.

Reddis opened the meeting by saying he would ask each for a name or two that they would like to see assigned to this case and why they thought their suggestion was a good choice. He added that this case was going to get national media attention. It wouldn't be quite the circus that OJ was in Los Angeles, but it could be one of the biggest cases their county had ever seen, given that McCarty had played professional tennis at several majors, including the US Open and the Australian Open.

Reddis said, "We are going to need someone who's a highly skilled trial lawyer and who'll be able to handle the media exposure. They'll need to be dedicated and live up to the highest ethical standards. We can't risk losing this case, or winning, then having it tossed on appeal and have to do it all over again. We have to send a message here, and that is, if you kill someone in this county, you are going down. If we lose a burglary case, not too many people know about it. The victim might lose some jewelry and a TV or DVD player. The guy will likely get caught doing it again and we'll have better luck next time.

"If we lose a murder case, it's front-page news, and other criminals see that and think, 'Wow, maybe I can get away with it.' Public safety," Reddis emphasized, "is the biggest reason we need to win this case. Based on the evidence, we have no doubt that McCarty is our guy. Now we need the best person to convince a jury of that." Reddis went on to add that it was also necessary to avoid a manslaughter verdict where the defendant might only serve ten years.

Reddis turned to Waverly. "As Major Crimes supervisor, what are your thoughts about who should get this case?"

"Either Scapio or Keller," she replied. She said Michelle Church would be her third choice, as Church had shown great talent, but she hadn't been in Major Crimes long and had only had three homicide trials. Waverly said Epps was very good too but had only tried two homicides and had not attended the National Homicide Symposium in Monterey yet, though he was next on the list. She assigned the more complex cases to prosecutors who had attended the symposium.

Keller, Waverly said, had been extremely successful in winning first-degree convictions when they thought they'd get a second degree at best, and she was great with juries.

Waverly said that Scapio might seem a little disorganized—"His office, for example, is a complete wreck"—but she thought his cross-examinations were amazing. The Braden murder was a case where the defendant could testify and could come across well if not effectively cross-examined. Scapio was also great with experts.

Reddis turned to Hollinger and asked his thoughts. Hollinger was fifty-two and a runner in excellent shape, tanned from the miles he put in. Rather than fight going bald, he gave in years ago and had a completely shaved head, smooth as a bowling ball. Hollinger grew up in the Midwest but came to California for UCLA law school.

He was a skilled prosecutor who had tried some high-profile cases himself. He liked trying cases and kept a murder-for-hire case after he became a chief deputy. He did get a conviction but vowed never to try a case again as long as he was a chief deputy, making policy decisions and overseeing internal investigations as well as managing two separate divisions in the DA's office. He found working the trial extremely stressful while trying to balance other duties. Besides, he liked the pay raise he got as a chief deputy and did not want to take the pay cut that would go with returning to homicides and giving up his chief deputy position. Hollinger said that he thought the case should go to a homicide prosecutor, but he didn't have any experience watching any of them, so he couldn't give a recommendation.

Reddis turned to Katz and asked if he had any thoughts, to which the bureau chief replied by relating a story about a legendary cross-examination he saw Scapio do. Katz was working violent crimes in his first year as a DA investigator and he got assigned to a stabbing inside a bar. Scapio was the assigned prosecutor.

* * *

The defendant in that case was a Thousand Oaks gang member who stabbed a guy during a fight. The defendant was also a well-off white kid who was good-looking and arrogant. His parents were very upper crust. The judge had already gutted the prosecutor's case by excluding all the defendant's past acts of violence and all evidence of his gang membership. Scapio was furious about the judge's ruling, which had made the prosecutor's case that much tougher. The victim was a young Hispanic who had once been in a gang and had gang tattoos. The judge ruled that the victim's gang past could come in.

This was basically a he said/he said, with no others at the bar willing to say they saw it. Scapio had joked that if all those people inside the bar were where they said they were, the bathroom had to be the largest anywhere in the world. The one thing the prosecution did have was that when the defendant was arrested four days after the stabbing, he had a knife on him. The prosecution had a witness, who was a former friend of the defendant, who said he asked the defendant why he always carried a knife. According to the witness, the defendant said, "So some big-mouth bitch-ass doesn't talk shit. But if he disrespects me, I'll shank that mother fucker."

The defense felt they needed to counter, so they put the defendant's mother on the witness stand. She was an attractive woman and very well dressed. Everything was Chanel except the purse, which was Louis Vuitton. Scapio leaned over to Katz and whispered, "Isn't that purse a Lewis Vitten? I pronounced that right, didn't I?" causing a chuckle from Katz and the bailiff, who overheard him.

The defendant's mother testified for about an hour on direct examination—friendly questions from her son's attorney—about their charming mother-son relationship and how he was still a momma's boy, and she gushed on with praise for her son's peaceful nature. Scapio could tell that at least some jurors were eating it up. Finally, at the end of direct, she said that her son always carried a knife because he knew someone who was kidnapped at knifepoint and sexually assaulted.

Scapio argued the mother's testimony about the son's loving nature opened the door to his violent history and gang membership. The judge, a former public defender, ruled that the testimony about the defendant's gang membership and violent past was too prejudicial and was still excluded. The judge was flat-out wrong, and Katz said he felt the case was lost when the judge made that ruling.

Scapio began cross by asking when this kidnap and sexual assault happened, and the witness answered April 5, 2006. Scapio asked if the incident was in the paper, and she said no. Scapio asked if there was a police report filed and she answered no. Many lecturers on cross-examination say, "Never ask a question that you don't know the answer to." Scapio never believed in that rule. The defendant's mother was a late decision by the defense, and Scapio had no discovery—reports about what the witness will say before they actually testify—so he felt he had to ask the next question. Scapio looked her in the eye and said, "If there was no police report, and it wasn't in the paper, how can you be sure of the exact date?"

After a dramatic pause and some tears, she said, "Because I'll never forget the day that I was kidnapped at knifepoint and sexually assaulted. I was left tied up and beaten outside an abandoned farm." There was an audible gasp from a juror. Katz said his first thought was that if they hadn't lost this case when the judge made his ruling, they'd lost now for sure.

But Scapio stood up—he usually did his cross-examinations seated—looked the witness right in the eye, and asked, "Do you think this is some kind of a game we're playing?"

The witness appeared to be offended and said, "This is no game. I thought my life was over that day, and now my son's life is on the line, so no, I don't think this is a game, and it certainly isn't fun."

Scapio looked at her and said, "Well, the reason I asked that is that you testified on direct examination by your son's lawyer for almost an hour, and you never once said it was you that was sexually assaulted. Were you waiting to spring it on me on cross so I would look dumb in front of this jury, and you could score points for your son?"

The witness stammered and said she was embarrassed to say it was her. Scapio pounced and began firing questions in rapid succession. "You didn't think I would ask about who the victim was? Did you discuss with your son's lawyer withholding the identity of the victim?" She said that she had not discussed that. Scapio followed up with, "Well, if you were embarrassed, why didn't you tell your son's lawyer that you would rather not disclose that it was you?" She then said she did mention that to him. Scapio was quick to point out that she just contradicted herself because she just said she didn't discuss withholding the identity of the victim with her son's lawyer. She then responded that she had forgotten, but yes, they did talk about it.

Scapio then asked if the lawyer said that this question would come up on cross-examination. The witness was completely flustered and said she didn't remember if that was discussed. Scapio then asked, "So if it was discussed, then it was your strategy to hold back until cross so you could spring it on me?"

The answer was a stammering, "I don't remember if we discussed that or not."

"OK, you forgot to tell us on direct that you were the victim, you now don't remember if you discussed not mentioning it on direct with your son's lawyer, and you forgot whether you discussed the possibility that I would ask. So, let me ask you this, 'cause I do hate having stuff just sprung on me. Is there anything else you forgot to say that you might spring on me?"

The witness answered, "Not that I know of."

Scapio then said, "Let's be sure. I have a watch on. I am going to let it go for one full minute to let you think if there is anything else you forgot or were too embarrassed to tell us." After an objection was overruled, Scapio waited a full minute of awkward silence. The witness was finally asked if there was anything, and she said no.

Scapio asked if she saw the assailant's face or the type of car he drove, if she thought about the possibility that reporting it could save someone else or the possibility his DNA could be found at the scene or on the rope. At this point, her answers no longer mattered. Her credibility and her son's, before he even testified, were destroyed as soon as Scapio fired out the "Do you think this is some kind of game we're playing" line of questioning.

* * *

Katz told Reddis that the vast majority of attorneys would have frozen at the answer she gave about never forgetting the day she was kidnapped, tied up, and sexually assaulted, but Scapio won the case because he reacted and figured it out. Nobody thought he would win that case, but he did. Katz concluded, "Scapio is your man, and if you ask the guy who survived that stabbing or any of his family members, they will tell you the same thing."

It was at this point that Matt Flynn spoke, and he made it very clear he was not a fan of Scapio's. Flynn began by saying that Scapio was poorly organized. He mentioned the messiness of Scapio's office and talked about files on the floor and loose CDs and DVDs on his desk.

Flynn described Scapio as insubordinate. He explained that when he was Scapio's supervisor, he repeatedly told him to clean his office, and Scapio would say he would but never did. Flynn said he confronted Scapio about this, and Scapio showed him a perfect formation of large paper clips on top of his credenza. The rest of the office was a mess, but all he did to satisfy Flynn's demand for neatness was to "create some OCD-inspired formation with paper clips."

Flynn asserted that the black shirts and wild ties that Scapio would sometimes wear in trial were a poor representation of the seriousness of his duties. Flynn added that there were rumors that Scapio placed illegal wagers, and everyone knew he traveled frequently to Las Vegas.

Reddis asked Flynn if he thought Scapio was a skilled trial lawyer. Flynn admitted that he was but said that if Reddis picked Scapio, Scapio would embarrass the DA's office and jeopardize Reddis's hold on the county as the elected district attorney.

Flynn then suggested Kyle Irby. Flynn said Irby was very skilled and a guy who played it by the book. His office was as meticulous as his wardrobe. No mob-boss attire. Flynn sang Irby's praises, calling him likable, believable, and totally respectable.

Waverly was not having it, as she pointed out that Irby was currently prosecuting serious and violent felonies but not homicides. He had been in misdemeanors and general felonies and the driving-under-the-influence grant, and had never tried a homicide or gone to a homicide training conference put on by CDAA. Waverly said she had seven superb trial lawyers in homicides and pleaded with Reddis not to go outside the Homicide Unit, as it would send the wrong message. Appointing someone with no homicide experience to the biggest murder trial in Ventura County would essentially say that nobody in her unit was good enough to do the big case, so they had to go outside. She added that the selection of the smooth but unproven Irby would decimate the morale of the Homicide Unit and could cost them the conviction.

Flynn backed off on the Irby selection but renewed his diatribe against Scapio. He raised the incident from a couple of years back when Scapio did not document a deal he made with an informant who he gave leniency to in exchange for testimony against the leader of a robbery ring. Scapio successfully prosecuted the leader and disclosed the deal to the defense but could not document that he cleared the deal with his supervisor. Scapio insisted that he did get permission from the supervisor, but he admitted to failing to document it. The supervisor did not recall giving Scapio permission to grant leniency.

Reddis responded that they did put a memo in Scapio's file urging him to document such deals with a confirmatory email to the supervisor, but Reddis pointed out that the actual deal was fair and that Scapio put away a very dangerous guy and was very effective in getting that conviction. Scapio had also fully disclosed the deal. Flynn persisted, saying, "I still think Scapio is the wrong lawyer for this." Flynn added that they'd had other evidence, and he thought that letting the informant plead to a three-year sentence when the informant could have received fifteen years was unduly lenient. He said that if he had been Scapio's supervisor at that time, with the other evidence they had, he would not have granted approval for that deal. But Flynn saw that point was going nowhere, because Reddis simply shook his head no and said nothing.

With one last card to play, Flynn laid it out. "I was hoping not to bring this up, but remember after his divorce he dated a victim in a felony battery case. The defendant saw them out at dinner together after the trial, and we had to do an entire internal on that. Maybe he dates the victim's best friend or something and the case gets tossed because our prosecutor was screwing someone who testified in the case."

For the first time in the meeting, Reddis was visibly angry. "Matt," he said, "do you remember Alicia Woodard, the first African American woman to make detective at the Oxnard Police Department?" Flynn, very embarrassed, nodded yes.

Reddis then said, "Do you know what her name is now?" Flynn did not even respond. Reddis said, "It's Alicia Reddis, and do you know how I met my *wife*?" Flynn quietly responded no. Reddis leaned forward, his face the color of the first three letters of his last name, jaw clenched tight, and said, "On a case, after she testified for me on a major drug bust. I asked her out when the case was over. And the rest, as they say, is history." Reddis went on to point out that Scapio was cleared in that internal investigation, and that there was no evidence they dated before or during the trial. Reddis added that Scapio had to go through an internal for a girl he only got to first base with, and they only went out three times. "We're lucky he didn't sue our asses. I get that you don't like Scapio, but please promise me that as long as you work here you will never bring up that stupid investigation again." Flynn nodded quickly.

Reddis was intimidating, not only because he was the DA, but because he looked like someone you didn't want mad at you. Even though his college days were long ago, he still had his college-baseball-catcher build: stocky, with virtually no neck. When he glared into you, his head and wide shoulders were right in front of you, but there was almost nothing visible separating them. Scapio once said to him, "You know, the one way you could never be murdered is by strangulation, 'cause you gotta have a neck for that and you don't have one." Reddis was done hearing from Flynn, and Flynn knew it.

Reddis asked if anyone had any additional thoughts or suggestions. Nobody said anything further. Boylan had been going to recommend sex-crime prosecutor Trisha Quantrill. She was a rock star in the Sex Crime Unit and there was no doubt she was good. Quantrill did get assigned a couple of homicides and did very well with them but had twice turned down a chance to be in homicides because she had kids in middle school and thought that a homicide assignment was just going to force her to take too much time away from her kids. Boylan knew how good she was because seven years before, he worked a couple of robbery cases with her. She'd had a great five-year run in the Sex Crime Unit. Boylan decided to back off, however, because of how strong Waverly's pitch was that it had to be someone in homicides.

Reddis looked around the room. "I am going to pick someone who is ethical, fair, and a great trial lawyer who is gonna get justice for the victim and her family. That's the most important thing, not whether he wears goofy ties or made a clerical mistake in not sending a confirmatory email." He picked up the phone and, staring straight at Flynn, said, "Barbara, call Ray Scapio and tell him to meet me in my office tomorrow morning at 9:00 a.m." After hanging up he announced, "Obviously from my call, you know I'm giving Scapio the case."

When Scapio got the word he was to meet Reddis the next morning, his heart raced. He figured he was either getting the McCarty case, or he screwed up something so badly that the head DA wanted to meet with him, or they found out that he was betting on sports. Scapio wasn't particularly religious, but he prayed that it was not the latter.

Scapio arrived at Reddis's office ten minutes early. He was relieved when Reddis motioned him in and joked about this being "the first time you were ten minutes early for anything." Then Reddis said, "I take it you heard about the tennis player's girlfriend being murdered." Scapio said that he had been following the news on it. Reddis then told him that the case was ready for filing, "and I trust you with it."

Scapio thanked him and told him he would work his butt off to get justice and confirm Reddis's faith in him. They shook hands, and as Scapio was leaving, Reddis said, "Hey Scapio, don't fuck this up." Then he smiled and said, "OK, get outta here—and congratulations. I know you'll do a great job."

FOUR

It was the middle of October 2017 when Jared Plant, his wife Rachel, and their son Billy and daughter Anna were going to go bowling at the Ojai Bowl in the early afternoon. The Plants were both thirty-five years old. Jared worked on an oil derrick off the coast of Santa Barbara. His job for a large oil company took him away from his family for weeks at a time. Other times he would go weeks without working, but when he did work the pay was quite good. Rachel was working as a legal secretary for a prominent family law firm in Ventura.

Plant was a muscular, athletic man who had been a high school football star and played in community college in Ventura. Rachel was very attractive and got married right out of high school to her first husband and high school sweetheart, Mike Willis, but they quickly grew apart and ended the marriage. Rachel began to work as a secretary after the divorce, and a mutual friend set her up with Jared; they hit it off, and not too long after, Rachel gave birth to Anna. They got married a year later and had been married for fourteen years. Billy was eleven years old and Anna was fifteen.

The bowling excursion took place on a slightly overcast Saturday, but that day was not going to be remembered for the weather or how any of them bowled. It would be remembered for the odd stranger they met that day.

It was early afternoon when Jared parked the car in the bowling alley parking lot. As they headed in, they saw a line forming behind a man sitting at a table selling muffins. The man looked to be in his thirties. The only thing they would really remember about what he looked like was how he was dressed. He had bright lime-green plaid shorts and a black polo-style shirt. Jared whispered to Rachel, "The next time you criticize what I'm wearing, remember this guy." The man was short but very wiry and strong looking.

They heard the couple in front of them saying that these muffins were the best they had ever tasted. Jared and Rachel smiled at their children and said, "OK, we are each having just one, no matter how good they are." When they got to the front, they asked the man what flavors he had, and he said just the one, it's just regular plain flavor. Each muffin cost $1.25 and they each had one.

Rachel was shocked at the lightness and airiness of the muffin and was even more amazed at how delicious it was. Jared said, "This may be the best muffin I have ever had." Both children begged their parents for one more, but Rachel said, "No, dinner will be in a few hours, after we get home." The man announced that he was sorry, but he had only five muffins left. When the Plants had finished their delicious muffins, they went inside and rented bowling shoes.

After each bowled a few frames, the man selling the muffins took the lane next to them. He put his shoes on and selected his ball from the racks. He then started to fiddle with the computer display and said to Mr. and Mrs. Plant that he had not done this before, and he did not know how to set it to track his score. Jared was familiar with the process and explained it to the man, who seemed to catch on.

Then the man began bowling. His first three rolls were gutter balls. After each throw, he would jump up and make hand signals to the ball, but that didn't keep it out of the gutter. He next tried moving positions and altering his wrist angle upon release, talking to the ball and making wild gestures. Soon he began to improve, and he did little celebration dances after a good roll. Anna gestured toward him and whispered to her parents, "Why is the muffin guy so weird?"

They all took to watching the man's antics. He would dance when he liked his roll, but when he would miss a one-pin spare, which he did a lot, he would tilt his head and make a screechy sound that was just odd. Other bowlers would stop when he was about to roll to see what he might do next. Rachel glanced at his scores and noticed that he started out with a 76 in his first game but was up to the low 100 range in the next two. When Jared rolled a strike, the man congratulated him. When Anna, Rachel, or Billy rolled a strike, he did one of his dances for them.

The Plants began to gather their things to go, and the man told them to have a great day and said that he was going to roll the last game and leave. As they walked out, they laughed when they heard one of his screeching noises. They agreed the man might have mental health issues but seemed like a nice, rather than scary, and unusual person. They had no idea what they had just witnessed, nor would they ever. He was oddly athletic when he jumped—he jumped unusually high and his movements were very fast—yet his rolling of the ball and his entire approach seemed off. He had trouble timing his steps, often stopping before the limit line and going back. For someone so strong and wiry looking, his bowling was pretty much terrible.

For years after that, they would joke about that day. Anna would always refer to the man as "green plaid shorts guy," and Billy would call him the "muffin man." It would be a memory that would stay with them for the rest of their lives.

FIVE

Scapio had a 10:00 a.m. meeting with Cuevas and Rollins before he would file the murder charge. But first, he had to be in Courtroom 12 for arraignment for a gang homicide case. He called that case's defense attorney to tell her he had a key 10:00 a.m. meeting he had to attend—he didn't mention that the meeting was on the McCarty case—so he was hoping she could be at the arraignment at 9:00.

Lydia Crespino was a public defender who was not viewed by prosecutors as a "true believer." She did not think virtually all police and some prosecutors were racist Neanderthals who took great pleasure in violating the civil rights of those they suspected were criminals. Crespino was respected by cops and prosecutors yet was a very talented defense attorney.

Crespino was in her early forties and wanted to become a judge, so she was at the phase of her career where she did not want to offend prosecutors whose recommendations she figured she would need in order to get appointed by the governor. Crespino told Scapio that she had a sentencing hearing in Courtroom 47 at 8:30 a.m. but she would go to Courtroom 12 as soon as her hearing was over. She thought it might not be right at nine, since she expected the prosecutor to present victim-impact statements. She told Scapio that she would go to Courtroom 12 as soon as her sentencing was over and added with a laugh that "we paisanos"—in this case, fellow Italian Americans—"need to have each other's backs." She also said that she was going to ask to put the arraignment over a couple of weeks.

At 9:00 a.m., Scapio went down to court for the arraignment and saw defense attorney Brian Canning. Canning was thin and in his early thirties, with jet black hair, long sideburns, and a goatee. Scapio once told him he looked like every bad guy in every western ever made. Scapio had a big smile on his face as he sauntered up to Canning and said, "What are you doing here? Isn't there some stagecoach you and the James brothers haven't robbed yet?"

Canning, who took pride in his old west villain gunslinger look, shot back with, "Hey, tell me again how the lawyer for the Gambino crime family ever got hired to work in the DA's office?"

Scapio laughed and said, "I think it was that 'keep your friends close and your enemies closer' thing, and then I decided I actually like it here. Who knew?"

Then another defense attorney asked Scapio who he had in the Monday night game. "If I was a betting man," Scapio replied, "I'd take the Jets and the ten points." Scapio then joked, "I guess that's one phrase I can't credibly use."

The attorney asked, "When are you heading to Vegas next?"

Scapio said he "just got a new case that's gonna be high profile, so I might not get there again this year or for March Madness next year. I'd like to, but if not, hopefully June for some baseball action and lounging around the pool."

Crespino, wearing a gray dress, black jacket, and black high heels, arrived at 9:15 and told Scapio that she wanted to just continue the arraignment for a couple of weeks so she could review the discovery. At around 9:30 the case was called, and a new date was set. The parents and sister of victim were in the courtroom, along with the DA's victim advocate, Sandra Goldberg.

After the continued arraignment, Scapio spoke to the victim's family members. He explained why the case was delayed and added that it was common for defense attorneys to delay having their clients enter a plea until they have had a chance to review the discovery—the police reports and other evidence the DA's office is required to turn over to the defense. The victim's sister, who was a seventeen-year-old high school student, asked if they had a good case. Scapio said they did, but there were two witnesses that would need to remain cooperative; that was always the challenge when the charge was murder and there was a gang and a firearm-use enhancement.

Carlos Acevedo, a Northside gang member, was charged with shooting a gang member from rival Southside—South Oxnard—at a party. Acevedo, whose gang moniker was appropriately "Sniper," had fled the scene in a 2014 green Toyota. He was stopped with three other gang members in the car. One of them gave him up—told police in an interview who did it—and the gun in the back seat was determined to be the gun used to shoot the victim, twenty-one-year-old Nelson Castillo.

The victim's sister, Gabriella Castillo, could not hold back her tears. Her mother, Norma, said her son had really been doing better and had been trying to get out of the gang. Scapio assured both the family members that the DA's office would do whatever was needed to secure the witnesses, including relocating them in the DA's witness protection program.

Sandra Goldberg explained the case process in detail, including how the family could file a claim with the state victims-of-crime compensation fund. Goldberg had been a victim's advocate for seven years, after getting her psychology degree at UCLA. She really knew how to relate to victims. At thirty-four, Goldberg was one of the younger advocates, but she worked well even with much older family members of victims. She was tall and slender, with wavy blond hair and a peachy complexion, and was attractive in a librarian sort of way.

Scapio liked her because she would handle many of the questions victims' family members had. That meant Scapio didn't need to have long phone conversations with victims' family members while he lost valuable time that could be spent working with the investigators to improve the case and plug whatever holes might exist. He had experienced hour-long conversations with grieving family members and really felt that was the job of the advocate, and his was to shore up the case.

* * *

Once Scapio concluded his business in court he hurried back to his office, arriving ten minutes early. Cuevas was already there. Cuevas said Rollins was in the bathroom—"Probably had too much coffee and is pissing it out." About a minute later, Rollins walked in. Scapio shook hands with both detectives and said that he was excited about the McCarty case and working with the detectives.

Rollins and Cuevas said they were really happy with Reddis's choice and Cuevas added that there was no unanimity on that.

Scapio said he was sure it was that "asshole Flynn." Cuevas said he was not confirming or denying anything. Rollins laughed and said, "All that shit is supposed to be secret, but Cuevas here doesn't really believe in secrecy."

Scapio said, "It doesn't matter; I knew Flynn would do everything he could to keep me from getting that case. He has been trying to fuck my career for the last five years. If it was up to him, I'd be trying DUIs and shoplifts till I fuckin' quit." One of the other things Flynn didn't like about Scapio was his tendency to swear, though he was always a choir boy in court unless he was quoting someone else directly who had used foul language. Scapio swore a lot. Flynn was religious, but he wasn't totally averse to swearing and he did it occasionally. He just didn't like how often Scapio did it.

Scapio's first order of business was to file the charging document, called a criminal complaint. He knew it would just be one charge: murder under Penal Code section 187, with a special allegation that would add one year. The special allegation was that the murder was committed with the use of a knife.

Scapio didn't want to charge first-degree murder, which requires proof of premeditation and deliberation. He could add it after the preliminary hearing if there was proof of it. One of the reasons Scapio did not want to charge it now was he was not sure yet if McCarty intended to kill her when he arrived at the victim's home, first-degree murder, or only decided to do so after he got angry that she wouldn't take him back, second-degree murder.

The penalty difference would be that first-degree murder carries a sentence of twenty-five years to life in California, and second-degree murder carries fifteen to life. That means upon a conviction for first-degree murder, McCarty would have to serve twenty-five years before a parole board could decide to parole him and a governor could agree to release him. For second-degree murder it would be fifteen years before he could be released on parole. The one year for the knife allegation would make it twenty-six to life or sixteen to life, depending on the degree.

Scapio also could use the threat of elevating the charge to first degree as leverage to induce a guilty plea to second-degree murder, though Scapio understood that defendants rarely pleaded guilty to charges that carried a life sentence where parole was allowed but not guaranteed.

If a first-degree charge could be made, it would be filed as a special allegation, requiring a separate finding by the jury after a guilty verdict. This would prevent a hung jury where the jury deadlocks between first and second degree. As a special allegation, the jury could convict of murder and be unable to agree on the degree, and the defendant would stand convicted of second degree. A separate charge of first-degree murder would result in a hung jury if six jurors thought it was first degree and six thought it was second degree.

Scapio reviewed all the reports and asked some questions about the status of all the lab results to make sure that there wasn't any lab work that had not been completed. He then entered all the subpoena information on his computer and drafted the charging document.

Once the charges were filed, McCarty became subject to arrest. Rollins and Cuevas were planning on picking him up that afternoon and putting the cuffs on him. They figured McCarty thought he had gotten away with it, and they took pleasure in giving killers the bad news. Unfortunately, McCarty was out of the country for several months, so the arrest was delayed. He finally returned to the US in late January of 2016.

* * *

It was February 15, 2016, when McCarty was led away in handcuffs. He may have been scared, but he acted as confident as ever and yelled, "When they drop my case or I get acquitted, I am gonna fuckin' sue your fuckin' asses and take every penny you got. You won't be able to get a job as a fuckin' rent-a-cop at the mall!"

The fifteenth was Monday, and McCarty appeared in court the next day in handcuffs and the jail-issued orange jumpsuit. Appearing in court with Scapio was Senior Deputy District Attorney Woody Holdman, forty-three. Holdman was a bookish little man whose presence was the result of a meeting with Reddis.

On the eleventh, Reddis had called Scapio into his office. When Scapio arrived, it was just Reddis and his second in command, Brad Hollinger. Scapio was relieved that Flynn wasn't there. When Scapio took a seat, Reddis brought up the issue of a second chair. Reddis asked Scapio if he had anyone in mind, and Scapio said, "Holdman."

A second chair sits at the lead prosecutor's side at the table in court. The second chair may have witnesses that they handle on both direct and cross-examination. The second chair rarely makes the opening statement or closing argument.

Holdman, at first, would seem like an odd choice. He'd only had five jury trials in his twelve-year career. Holdman was the research attorney of the district attorney's Writs and Appeals Division. That meant he did legal research and defended some of the DA's office's appeals when defendants were convicted and sought appellate court review to find error to reverse the conviction. Holdman worked on the cases the DA's office handled directly, and he also worked closely with the attorney general's office in California on the larger cases that went up on appeal. Also, if the DA's office believed a judge erred in dismissing a case or excluding evidence in a pretrial ruling, Holdman was the one who wrote the argument, called a writ, asking the local court of appeal to reverse the trial court.

Holdman had worked with Scapio on two writs where Scapio challenged the exclusion of evidence by the trial court. On one, Scapio was prosecuting a serial arsonist who had set fires in every neighborhood where he lived from age eleven on. Scapio sought to offer thirty years of fires starting in neighborhoods where the arsonist lived and then offer evidence of the fires stopping after the arsonist moved out. The trial judge ruled there were no significant similarities between the fires, as they were set to trash cans, trees, cars, and debris piled against fences, and the fires were set with a common open flame such as a match or lighter. The trial court also ruled that the other fires should be excluded as more prejudicial than probative, meaning that the jury would lose their objectivity and just convict once they heard that evidence.

Holdman found very few cases that raised the same issue in California but researched every state and found similar cases allowing the evidence in. Scapio had written a brief advocating for the admissibility. Holdman did the research in two days and significantly expanded on Scapio's ten-page brief with a sixty-eight-page brief, which resulted in the local court of appeal reversing the trial court and holding that the presence of the defendant in each neighborhood was the key similarity, so it did not matter that the fires themselves were different.

The court of appeal also reversed the trial court by finding that the existence of numerous previous fires could be used to support the contention that the fires were intentional in origin as opposed to the product of some unknown accident. After the court of appeal's reversals, a jury heard evidence of the history of fires in the defendant's neighborhood and the defendant was found guilty; that conviction was affirmed by the California Supreme Court.

The other appellate court case Scapio worked on with Holdman involved a search of the trunk of a gang member's car where multiple firearms were located along with narcotics and stolen checks and credit cards. The trial court suppressed the evidence based on a ruling that the police search was illegal. Holdman got the court of appeal to reverse and rule that the search was, in fact, legal.

Scapio was very impressed with Holdman's work. They became good friends and often went to lunch together. Scapio said that Holdman was the best legal writer he had ever known.

Reddis was also fond of Holdman, as Holdman represented the DA in lawsuits. A few years earlier, the district attorney's office had been sued by a disgruntled investigator who had alleged mistreatment by the DA and the investigation bureau of the DA's office for not assigning him high-profile cases despite having some excellent performance reviews. The trial was transferred to Santa Barbara County because it was believed the Ventura judges should be disqualified from hearing and trying a lawsuit against the current district attorney. The DA's office hired an outside law firm for the trial. Holdman worked alongside the outside firm, which was based in Los Angeles. The jury found against Reddis and the DA's office. Santa Barbara juries are generally less favorable to the government than Ventura County juries. The jury awarded the plaintiff $1.9 million.

Holdman appealed and wrote a short but right-to-the-point brief, arguing that not getting high-profile cases was not an actual damage that could be awarded. The plaintiff did not lose pay or benefits and was not demoted to a lower assignment. The court of appeal reversed the findings of the jury and the case settled out of court for $128,500 just to make it go away. This was a fraction of the jury's reversed award, so Reddis was also quite the fan of Holdman.

Scapio wanted Holdman to handle a few witnesses so that Holdman would be seen doing something in front of the jury, but Scapio primarily wanted Holdman for his writing and research skills. Scapio had asked Holdman, before the meeting with Reddis, if Holdman would be interested in being Scapio's second chair, and Holdman did not hesitate. Holdman didn't really want to handle any witnesses, but Scapio insisted he do so, because he didn't want the jury thinking Holdman was some high-priced jury consultant. Reddis also thought picking Holdman to second chair the McCarty case was a good idea, albeit one he had not thought of. Reddis thought Keller would be a great choice too, but Scapio, though praising her, said he really wanted Holdman's expertise in law-and-motion work, the research for and preparation of written motions before the court.

* * *

Scapio and Holdman, who was wearing his signature bow tie, arrived in court early for McCarty's arraignment. Scapio had not gotten any calls from a private attorney, so he assumed McCarty would continue his arraignment to obtain private counsel. Scapio figured that McCarty made too much money to qualify for the services of the public defender's office. The public defender would review what is called a green sheet, which is a green-colored questionnaire, inquiring about the person's income, property ownership, and debts. The public defender had been known to accept a few clients who seemed to make a little too much money, but in a high-profile case like this, it would be unlikely that the public defender's office would accept McCarty as a client.

About five minutes before the scheduled arraignment, Attorney Sam Vandenbalk arrived with his entourage of young lawyers. Vandenbalk was about fifty years old, with silver hair and icy blue eyes. He was somewhat of a local celebrity because he was often a guest on Fox News and Court TV to discuss legal issues involving political figures. Vandenbalk was a former prosecutor who tried several murder cases while he was a deputy district attorney. He was confident to a fault and treated investigators like servants, so few liked working with him. He was good in court though. He left the DA's office after he ran an unsuccessful campaign against Reddis. After the election, he chose to go out and open his own law firm, and he did have some major victories, including getting a gang member off on a murder. Vandenbalk was not above questionable tactics and loved to try his cases in the media. He often hired the infamous Fat Lanny as his investigator.

Scapio and Holdman introduced themselves to the victim's family members, who were all in attendance at the arraignment. Scapio explained the process and the likelihood that Vandenbalk would continue the arraignment since he'd just come in on the case and didn't have any reports yet. As Scapio and Holdman went to the front of the courtroom, Vandenbalk approached Scapio and shook his hand and said, "Ray, I really am sorry you got this case. Losing a high-profile case is a career ender. But if you see Marcia Clark, give her my best," and then laughed.

Scapio replied that maybe McCarty should ask OJ what prison is like, 'cause that's where OJ is and where McCarty is gonna end up. Maybe OJ could tell him if they have a wing for washed-up ex-jocks like Vandenbalk's client. Vandenbalk replied, "Yeah, maybe after the acquittal, he might try and steal some tennis rackets back."

Scapio replied, "I guess that would be racketeering," then added, "It's OK though; we'll get him for murder, so we won't have to do some Al Capone bullshit charge to nail your guy."

Vandenbalk then turned toward Holdman and said, "Aren't you the most useless thing I have seen in a few weeks. Who needs an appellate lawyer when the result will be a complete exoneration? Since you like to write, maybe Scapio here will let you write the apology letter to my client."

"OK, asshole," Scapio said, "when do you want the arraignment to be? I can get you the discovery by the end of the week."

Vandenbalk replied that he better get it sooner than that, "because we're doing the arraignment today and setting a preliminary hearing within ten days, because my client isn't waiving time."

This is exactly what OJ Simpson's lawyers did, led by Johnnie Cochran. Vandenbalk did figure his client was probably guilty, and the longer the prosecutor had to prepare, the better the prosecution would do, and the more likely his client would be convicted. There was also a greater likelihood that with more time, additional damaging evidence might be found.

A preliminary hearing was set for nine days out. Scapio argued for no bail, relying on the defendant's wealth and incentive to flee and his frequent trips to foreign countries. Defense countered with his ties to the community and lack of prior criminal history. The judge set the bail at $1,000,000.

Scapio was not happy that this case was going to be fast tracked. He had several other cases and still needed to work on those, and he had scheduled a five-day Las Vegas trip in a month and knew he might have to cancel those plans. He was really glad that he chose Holdman as his second chair. Holdman could devote his full time to writing and filing motions. Scapio could spend his time with trial prep and working with his technical staff and computer graphics people to create exhibits for the eventual jury.

As soon as the arraignment was over, Scapio asked the court to issue a gag order because "defense counsel likes to try his cases in the media."

The judge in the arraignment court declined to do that but said, "If a need does arise, you can file a motion."

As Vandenbalk and his entourage of staff left the courtroom, the press was right there, and immediately Vandenbalk said that McCarty was innocent and wanted to be exonerated in a timely manner. He said that it's horrible to be falsely accused, and that he feels badly for the family of the victim, but he looks forward to the complete exoneration of his client. The next day, McCarty posted 10 percent of the bail and was released with an electronic monitor attached to his ankle.

The first motion that needed to be filed was the gag order, and Holdman got right on it. As an exhibit attached to the motion, Holdman found every article that covered Vandenbalk's comments proclaiming McCarty's innocence. Every Ventura County newspaper covered it, as did the *Los Angeles Times* and several Santa Barbara newspapers. The local TV station covering Ventura and Santa Barbara also featured Vandenbalk's comments. The story was covered online as well, and those articles were printed out and attached to the motion to keep defense counsel from tainting the eventual jury panel.

The motion was quickly set for a hearing on the Tuesday prior to the next Thursday's preliminary hearing. Holdman also found that McCarty's lawyer proclamation of innocence made the ESPN crawl, the ticker that scrolls across the bottom of the screen, and Holdman photographed the image and attached it as an exhibit to the gag order motion.

The motion was heard before Judge Catherine Carillo, a former public defender with a defense-oriented worldview. Scapio decided not to exercise a challenge against her, because although he felt she was lenient on sentencing, she was reasonably good on the law.

The day before the hearing on the gag order was scheduled to take place, Vandenbalk filed a motion for change of venue to move the case out of Ventura County, based upon the contention that the accused could not get a fair jury due to extensive pretrial publicity. The irony is that part of the publicity came from the defense. Scapio thought it was reminiscent of the minor who kills his parents, then asks for the court's mercy because he is now an orphan. Scapio and Holdman had anticipated that Vandenbalk would file such a motion, as Ventura County juries tend to be good for prosecutors and unlikely to believe a defense that accuses police of planting or fabricating evidence. A more defense-friendly jury might be found in Los Angeles or Santa Barbara.

Judge Carillo ruled on the gag order request but would need more time to hear the change-of-venue motion, and the prosecution would need time to file their response to the request to change venue. This would cause the preliminary hearing to be delayed, since the court would have to decide whether Ventura County was the proper venue or county to hear the case before any preliminary hearing could occur.

The judge agreed with the prosecution on the gag order but issued a slightly narrower ruling than what Scapio and Holdman had sought. Both sides were ordered not to discuss the merits of the case, the evidence, or the investigations. They were limited to discussing scheduling and procedure only. Judge Carillo had to back out of the change-of-venue motion because she had a scheduled vacation when Vandenbalk was requesting it be held.

Judge Kevin Curtis, a former deputy district attorney and private defense attorney after leaving the DA's office twelve years earlier, was assigned the change-of-venue motion. The defense was hoping to move the trial to Santa Barbara County, which is about sixty miles north of Ventura. Santa Barbara is more liberal and less pro-police than Ventura. Santa Barbara public defenders are frequently elected as judges in Santa Barbara County. In Ventura County, public defenders are never elected and can only become judges if a governor appoints them. Carillo was appointed by the governor to her seat as a superior court judge, as was Curtis.

The scheduling of the motion for change of venue worked for Scapio because it allowed him to make his trip to Las Vegas to bet on the college basketball tournament. He might have wished he had stayed home for that one, though, as he had some bad luck in the basketball games, losing some big bets by one point, including a meaningless forty-foot shot at the buzzer, making the underdog an 8-point loser rather than an 11-point loser. Not good for Scapio, who had the favorite at -9 points. Scapio bet them because the favorite hit 76 percent of their free throws as a team, so they would likely be leading when they would be sent to the line with desperate last-minute fouls. Scapio had been nervously congratulating himself while the favorite made their last seven free throws down the stretch to take the 6-point lead to 11, even as the underdog made some shots. With one second left on the clock, a sophomore guard launched a 40-foot three-pointer that swished and killed Scapio's spread.

He tried to win it back at the poker table but was still bothered by the 40-foot shot. He played unusually recklessly and lost another $300 at the table. Scapio had some gambling successes in the past, but March 2016 was not one of them. He was happy to get back to focusing on the McCarty case. He also had six other homicide cases but was told by Waverly that she would try to keep new cases from coming his way, since his plate was very full.

Curtis ruled on April 11 that the defense had so far shown no evidence that they could not select a fair and impartial jury in Ventura County, and he denied the motion to change venue. Curtis did rule that if the defense could provide additional facts or data establishing that an impartial jury could not be found, they could revisit the motion before the case went to trial.

The venue motion was denied, and the preliminary hearing remained set for Tuesday, April 19, 2016.

Vandenbalk looked at Scapio as they were leaving the courtroom and said, "I hope you like research, because I am gonna drown you guys in so much paperwork, you won't have time to prepare for trial."

Scapio replied, "I hope that wasn't an admission that you are gonna file bad-faith frivolous motions, 'cause if you are, I am sure the state bar would love to hear from you in a formal setting." Vandenbalk immediately walked back his comment and said all his motions were going to be good ones because there are so many issues in this case. Scapio replied, "Yeah, just like the one we just did. That was the worst change-of-venue motion I have ever seen." Vandenbalk then said that he wouldn't win every motion, but that will be fine; once he won the trial, the other stuff wouldn't matter.

Reddis was relieved that Scapio got the limited press gag order. Reddis respected Scapio's skills as a trial lawyer but considered him to be somewhat of a loose cannon when it came to dealing with the press. Scapio was always accessible to the press and would often be interviewed on high-profile cases that he was assigned.

As a result of being considered "quotable," the local reporter for the *Ventura County Star* was always happy to cover a Scapio case. Stephanie Ruiz was twenty-nine and very attractive. Scapio had a crush on her but never asked her out on a date, although he had thought about it after his divorce became final. He once asked her what she was doing for Valentine's Day, ostensibly just to be friendly, but really as a slightly more subtle way of asking if she was seeing anyone. Depending on her answer, Scapio thought he might pursue something.

When her answer started with the sentence, "My boyfriend is taking me to," Scapio didn't pay attention to the rest.

Reddis decided it might be time to have a word with Scapio to make sure he didn't violate his own requested gag order. When Scapio entered Reddis's office, the DA asked Scapio to have a seat, then told him now that he got this gag order in place, he better be sure he follows it. Scapio assured him he would follow the order. Reddis told him, "You are a great trial lawyer, but sometimes you make me nervous. Remember the fake acquittal?"

This was a reference to what was not Scapio's finest idea, although it was certainly outside the box. Four years prior, Scapio had prosecuted Jaime Mendoza for attempted murder. Mendoza came from a wealthy family in Mexico but was an outcast. He was a three-striker who had stabbed a man twenty-five times but didn't kill him. It was done because the victim had made a pass at Mendoza's girlfriend. Mendoza was out on bond during the trial. The evidence was going very badly for him, so he left the courthouse and was driven across the border. He skipped out on his bond and the trial continued in absentia, meaning without the defendant. Scapio was allowed to argue that the defendant's voluntary absence was consciousness of guilt that the jurors could consider.

Scapio knew Mendoza would be convicted, so Scapio came up with an idea that he told his supervisor about. "What we should do is, after the jury convicts, we take the verdict without notifying the press. Then we explain to the convicting jury that they would be asked to announce a second verdict with the press there. The guilty verdict would be filed away, but the jury would come back in the courtroom in front of the press and announce that the verdict was not guilty."

The press would run the story. Mendoza, whose family was not in the courtroom, would not know that the acquittal verdict was fake. The press wouldn't know it was a fake acquittal. Mendoza would hear of the fake exoneration and would come back from Mexico and would then be arrested and serve thirty-six to life. As Scapio was enthusiastically telling his supervisor how he would say how disappointed and shocked he was by the acquittal but that he had to respect the decision of the jury, his supervisor, Waverly, looked at him like he had lost his mind.

Waverly liked Scapio but did feel the need to inform Reddis, to make sure she wasn't completely wrong in thinking this idea was nuts. Reddis agreed that it was nuts. Reddis talked to him and simply said, "No, we are not doing that."

The day after Scapio was assigned the McCarty case, Flynn was upset with himself that he had neglected to bring up Scapio's fake acquittal idea as a reason to persuade Reddis to assign a different prosecutor, instead of bringing up his dating a victim. Once Reddis reacted angrily toward Flynn's bringing up that topic, he knew mentioning the fake acquittal idea would never change Reddis's mind about giving the big case to Scapio.

Reddis began to explain to Scapio that they needed to do everything by the book. Reddis added that he didn't want anything approaching "your fake acquittal idea." Scapio explained that he ran it by his supervisor before he did anything, and that he never would have just done it.

The real truth is that Scapio almost proposed it to the judge and defense attorney without ever going to his supervisor. He made a last-minute instinctive decision that he better not just do this without getting approval. A month earlier, Flynn was his supervisor and Scapio would have just proposed it to the judge and the defense without mentioning it to Flynn. He knew Flynn would not approve and probably would have suggested demoting Scapio.

Scapio watched Reddis do "the duck" as he explained that he did run it by his supervisor. Everyone who had been in Reddis's office knew that when you got "the duck" from him, it wasn't good. When Reddis pursed his lips into a duck face and nodded his head up and down while listening, or more likely pretending to listen, that meant he was trying to look empathetic with his facial expression and nodding. He was communicating that he cared about what you were saying, but there was no way you were getting what you wanted.

If you asked for a promotion to a more prestigious or interesting assignment and Reddis gave you the duck, you were not getting that promotion. If you were receiving a demotion or were being moved to an assignment you didn't want and Reddis gave you the duck, you were getting demoted or you were stuck with that assignment. Basically, if there was something you wanted to convince Reddis of and you got the duck, you didn't convince him. He just wanted you to believe that he had thought about what you requested and you got fair consideration. Scapio wasn't sure that Reddis was even aware that he did the duck and why.

Scapio knew all he could do was thank Reddis for having faith in him and promise there would be no acquittals in this case, real or fake. Reddis laughed and said, "You may have slowed down a little on the softball field, maybe you have to stop at third or play it on a hop in the field now. But as far as your mental quickness, you haven't slowed a bit. That's why I picked you. Now go kick some ass."

Reddis was still of the opinion that the "fake acquittal" was one of the dumbest and craziest ideas anyone ever had, and he wasn't buying that it's all OK because it was nixed by a supervisor first. He did have to admit that it was creative. That said, despite his doing the duck, Reddis was placing his faith in Scapio.

* * *

Contrary to his outward display of confidence, Vandenbalk knew he had problems. How was he going to explain away the DNA? For that, he hired Frank Andrews, a physicist who graduated from Cal Tech in 2004. Andrews had once taught physics at Occidental College and then at his alma mater, but for the last five years he had been a jack-of-all-trades as a forensic expert. Andrews made a fortune testifying that the laws of physics supported his version of the facts.

Despite having no training in accident reconstruction, his expertise in physics allowed him to clear the hurdle and testify in vehicle accident cases. Frequently he was flat-out wrong in his analysis, but juries were impressed with his credentials, and opposing attorneys rarely had success cross-examining him beyond establishing his lack of experience in the field. He would parry that line of questioning by repeating that accident reconstruction is simple physics, and that is all you need to know. He often testified in ballistics cases on things like bullet trajectory, and he would frequently testify in use-of-force and police-shooting cases. He even defended police officers in civil suits, if the city paid enough, depending on who hired him first.

He had achieved a bit of fame as one of four experts in an arson case who helped free an innocent man from death row. Bradley Upshaw of Lewiston, Idaho, had been convicted of arson and murder based on junk science from a fire marshal. Upshaw fled from a fire in his home but was unable to save his five-year-old daughter who slept in an adjacent bedroom. Upshaw had been separated from his wife and they were divorcing, partly because Upshaw had a drinking problem and was abusive. He was not, however, an arsonist or a murderer. The fire marshal testified that, due to heavy charring on the floor wood that made the wood resemble the skin of an alligator and spalling of the walls of the home (cracking or chipping of concrete due to rapid temperature change), this was an intentionally set fire with the use of an accelerant such as gasoline. The defense provided no counter expert in this case and the jury found Upshaw guilty and sentenced him to death.

Andrews and the three fire experts who testified at Upshaw's motion for a new trial—after Upshaw had already spent twelve years behind bars—were correct when they said that the heavy charring on the floor wood was just an indication that a fire had burned long enough to create flashover. Flashover is when fire burns long enough that it transforms from a fire in a room to a room completely engulfed in flames. Once a fire burns to the ceiling, it has nowhere to go but down. The heavy charring just means the room was very hot, and that can occur from an accelerated gasoline fire or a slow-burning fire that could be of accidental origin. Spalling is due to rapid temperature change, and that can occur from a rapidly burning accelerated arson fire, but it can also occur when a hot burning fire is sprayed with water by the firefighters. When that happens, you get the same spalling or cracking in concrete or brick that you would get from a gasoline fire.

The fire marshal had not even noticed the electrical short in the daughter's room, but the fire experts who were contacted by the defense reviewed the scene photographs and saw evidence of an electrical short based upon burn patterns near an outlet, indicating the fire started there. The three fire investigators, who were with different agencies in different states but were active in training conducted by the National Association of Arson Investigators, agreed to work for free for Upshaw's release after viewing the evidence.

The defense was aware of Andrews and thought it would be good to have a physicist on board along with three trained and respected fire investigators who were up to date on the latest science related to fire investigations. Andrews was an expert on physics, which is the basis for the principles of fire behavior and burn-pattern analysis. Andrews took more credit than he deserved, as he was not the driving force behind the exoneration but was brought on to add to the strength and credibility of the claim of innocence, but he still did contribute to the release of an innocent man.

He really milked this in his testimony, so jurors would see him as a brilliant scientist who helped free an innocent man. Andrews testified on the defense side in forty-three criminal cases; twenty-two resulted in acquittals and another seven resulted in hung juries. Only fourteen resulted in convictions. Since the typical prosecutor's office obtains convictions in over 80 percent of jury trials, Andrews's record was phenomenal. His success was equally impressive in civil cases; he boasted positive outcomes in over 70 percent of those trials. Andrews was expensive, but his scholarly demeanor and background made him a powerful witness and well worth the money.

Vandenbalk still had a problem. How was Andrews, impressive as he was, going to convince the jury of an innocent explanation for blood spatter on the accused's shirt and shoes? Moreover, how was he going to explain the blood drops his client left at the victim's home? Andrews simply told Vandenbalk that he would have to run some tests, but he had a pretty good idea how he could make it work.

* * *

Scapio and Holdman were preparing for the preliminary hearing as well as motions to file for when they got to trial. Holdman was going to do the direct examination of Detectives Cuevas and Rollins for the finding of the clothes in the trash can, the DNA collection, and the initial conversation with McCarty. Scapio would do the direct examinations of the other witnesses, which would include Lucky Charms and the patrol officers who found the body and some of the scene evidence, and Maria Aguilar, who was the lab analyst for the DNA testing, as well as the county medical examiner, who determined the cause of death and approximate time of death. The prosecutors had subpoenaed McCarty's phone records plus cell-tower data.

One interesting fact was that McCarty was frequently on his phone, and his phone was very active at almost all times except the six-hour time period surrounding the estimated time of death of Jessica Braden. The medical examiner estimated Braden's time of death to be around 1:00 a.m. on the morning of the twenty-third. The next-door neighbor sleeping thought he heard a woman scream at a little after 1:00 a.m. but was uncertain at the time whether he had been dreaming. His wife did not hear anything. The neighbor across the street also thought she heard two loud screams at around 1:15 a.m. and almost called 911 but didn't hear anything after that. There was no cell-phone activity to indicate McCarty's phone was turned on from 10:00 p.m. on the twenty-second until after 4:00 a.m. on the twenty-third. It would certainly appear McCarty deliberately shut his phone off so that it could not be tracked during that time period.

This evidence supported the premeditation allegation that they added to the charge. Shutting off his phone was strong circumstantial evidence that he intended to kill her and didn't want his phone to be tracked.

The phone evidence was also strong evidence that McCarty was the person who murdered Jessica Braden. It would have to be a pretty weird coincidence that the only time he appears to have shut his phone off for any extended period was during the hours surrounding the brutal murder of the woman he had recently threatened for breaking up with him. Scapio knew that DNA evidence was powerful, but it became unassailable if corroborated by other evidence. Coincidences rarely exist in reality, but defense attorneys need juries to believe in coincidences. The more farfetched the coincidence is, the more akin it is to believing in Santa Claus and the tooth fairy.

Scapio already knew he was going to pile up the coincidences, and in his closing he was going to repeat to the jury that very line—that believing in all these coincidences was like believing in Santa Claus and the tooth fairy. In fact, since the legendary tooth fairy was a tiny creature that sprinkled dust, it had to be Santa Claus who had the knife, came through the chimney, and fled into the night with the reindeer getaway car, 'cause it couldn't have been the defendant—the man who threatened to kill her if she broke up with him, abused her in the past, left his DNA outside after mysteriously cutting his hand chopping celery, threw away clothes with her blood on them for some other reason besides having murdered her, and just happened to shut his phone off so he could not be tracked at that time and never did it before.

Scapio was excited about this case. He also relished the idea of beating the arrogant Vandenbalk, but he knew he had to be careful there. Scapio understood that the worst mindset prosecutors can have is to make it about the defense attorney. He always considered the trial like a football game. He was a defensive lineman, the quarterback was the defendant, and the defense attorney was an offensive lineman trying to protect the quarterback. The prosecutor's job was to sack the quarterback, and to do that you just had to get by the offensive lineman trying to get in your way, but you must always maintain your focus on the quarterback.

Scapio believed that top-notch defense lawyers fell into two types. The first was the credible defense attorney. These lawyers were nice, and you could work around each other's schedules. Judges liked them because they were very professional and made things easy. They were often willing to stipulate to facts and events, meaning they'd agree to call some facts undisputed, so the jury was not burdened with deciding them or hearing evidence on basic things both sides agree on. They often limit the issues to things that go to the heart of the charges. They will frequently concede the guilt of the accused but to a lesser charge like theft in robbery cases or manslaughter in murder cases.

Judges like these lawyers and so do juries. Lydia Crespino was an example of this type.

Vandenbalk, however, fell into the second category. This type of lawyer was a warrior. Warriors had boundless energy and they fought everything. The warrior would do everything to anger the prosecutor and throw them off their game. An angry prosecutor was a mistake-prone prosecutor. The warrior could cause the prosecutor to miss evidence, make comments that get an admonition from the judge, lose credibility with the juries, and in worst-case scenarios, actually break the rules because they want to win so badly. There have been cases where prosecutors hated defense attorneys so much that they ignored evidence of innocence and even worse, withheld it. Of all the attorneys that practiced in Ventura County, Vandenbalk was the best example. Scapio knew he had to keep his focus on the defendant.

After the court's venue ruling, Holdman and Scapio met in the office library to prepare for the preliminary hearing and motions. The office library was small, not much bigger than the standard window office at the Ventura DA's office. It wasn't like the law library downstairs, which was enormous. The DA's office library had just California cases and the California Code books. To get anything out of state, you needed to use the gigantic law library downstairs near the cafeteria. With the rapidly developing online libraries of legal research, by 2016, law libraries were becoming an anachronism of a bygone era, much like the phone booth. The office's law library had been significantly downsized.

The window office had become an institution in the Ventura County DA's office under Bill Reddis. They were the most coveted. All homicide attorneys got window offices, as did a select few non-homicide attorneys who had distinguished careers and had probably tried homicide cases at some point. Supervisors also got window offices. To get a window office was a big deal; it either meant that you were working homicide cases, which was itself a big deal, or you were a supervisor—also a big deal, and it paid more than being a homicide attorney—or it was given to you as a lifetime achievement award. The new prosecutors were encouraged by their supervisors to seek out window-office people for advice in trial strategy or legal issues. Part of the price of having a window office was that you were expected to provide that guidance if asked. If you did not have time at the moment, you made sure you provided time later to help out the "baby prosecutors."

Scapio didn't mind that at all. He loved helping and giving advice, plus he would never deny that yes, he had an ego. The window offices were for elite trial lawyers. Yes, he could be eccentric at times and did like to hear himself talk, but he was a great trial lawyer who was looking forward to his career case. He met Holdman in the library because Scapio's office was currently such a mess that he often preferred to work in the library. People even joked that it was Scapio's second office or his "home away from home."

Since the burden of proof in a preliminary hearing is very low, the prosecution only needs to show that probable cause exists that a crime occurred and the defendant more likely than not committed that crime. Scapio and Holdman knew that they had DNA evidence and that would be enough for the holding order to then set the case for trial. They decided that the key motions to admit evidence would wait until the trial brief. A trial brief is a document filed by each side outlining the facts of the case, witnesses expected to testify, and any pretrial issues that the side writing the brief wants the judge to rule on. Holdman knew that he would be arguing for the judge at trial to allow evidence of McCarty's prior threats against Braden as well as his prior abuse of her and a previous girlfriend.

Normally, evidence of other crimes is inadmissible to show that the accused has a propensity to commit similar crimes. The good thing for the prosecution was that California has Evidence Code section 1109, which is an exception to the prohibition of prior-crimes evidence; it specially allows prior acts of domestic violence to prove that the defendant has a penchant for committing acts of domestic violence.

Scapio had checked McCarty's background and found that in 2008, a woman named Karen Loring had filed a restraining order against McCarty. He had no prior convictions besides a misdemeanor domestic battery against the deceased victim, but for trial they hoped to add Karen Loring to their witness list because she alleged in her application for a restraining order that McCarty had choked her and threatened to throw her off the balcony of their apartment.

The threats were going to be a more difficult issue, since it was Jessica Braden, the victim, who told people about the threats. Because she was dead, the testimony would be considered prohibited hearsay evidence, and they wanted to find an exception that would allow the jury to hear about the threats.

As Scapio and Holdman brainstormed, they agreed that the best way to get the victim's statement in—that she had told her friends and family members that she had been threatened—was through Evidence Code section 1370, enacted after OJ Simpson got away with two murders. That section allows statements of a victim relating violence or the threat of violence against the victim by the person now accused. This seemed like a solid way to get the evidence in.

Scapio and Holdman came up with some backup arguments to get the victim's statements in, but as long as 1370 was still good law when they went to trial, they should be able to get the threats in.

* * *

Vandenbalk filed a discovery motion alleging prosecutorial misconduct for failing to provide discovery of expected-witness criminal convictions. This motion was made solely to piss off Scapio. Misconduct is a serious accusation. If an allegation of misconduct is found true, it mandates a report from the judge to the state bar. A prosecutor who commits misconduct can suffer penalties as minimal as a censure or as serious as disbarment.

Scapio knew the motion was frivolous, and Holdman filed a response brief saying that rap sheets showing crimes of moral turpitude are only required to be disclosed before trial, not at the preliminary hearing. Holdman also argued that the defense never requested these from the prosecution and never filed a discovery motion. Vandenbalk knew Scapio was known to be a little quick-tempered and hot-blooded, and he figured if he could file a lot of those motions, he could maybe throw Scapio off his game.

Vandenbalk figured he needed something. He went over the DNA reports extensively and could not find a way to credibly spin reasonable doubt. He knew that he had an excellent expert who had a great reputation for winning cases, and he had worked with him before and won both trials. Here, however, he was faced with very strong evidence and a prosecutor who also had a great reputation. Vandenbalk knew Scapio was good but considered himself to be even better.

A hearing on the motion for misconduct was set for a week before the preliminary hearing. By that time, the issue was moot because Scapio and Holdman had decided to run the rap sheets of all the civilian witnesses and had provided them to Vandenbalk.

Vandenbalk also heard that Scapio did not like Lanny Michaels, so he hired him as his sole investigator. Scapio was going to have to really focus on that quarterback–defensive-lineman strategy, because Vandenbalk was going to do everything imaginable to throw Scapio off his game.

The motion was sent to Judge Curtis. Scapio told Vandenbalk that since he had the rap sheets, he can withdraw his motion. Vandenbalk said that he was not withdrawing it because he had a few things he wanted to say on the record. None of the witnesses had any crimes that were admissible for impeachment purposes. One of the victim's friends that she had confided in had a driving-under-the-influence conviction from four years earlier. Case law on that was very clear: driving under the influence, though dangerous, is not a crime of dishonesty and is inadmissible to attack the witness's credibility.

The unusual thing about this motion was that Holdman was going to argue the motion, but he only spoke three words, and two of them were unnecessary but consistent with longtime court practices of proper etiquette.

Judge Curtis told Vandenbalk that he was to go first, since it was his motion for sanctions. Vandenbalk had only gotten two sentences in when the judge interrupted him and said that he had read Mr. Holdman's response brief and declaration and "apparently you have the information that you requested by this motion." Vandenbalk confirmed that, and the judge asked why they were still there.

Vandenbalk replied that it was to send a message to the government that they must be vigilant in protecting a defendant's right to exculpatory evidence. Judge Curtis responded that he was not in the message-sending business. Phones do that through text messages. There was a time long ago when people used Western Union. They once used carrier pigeons. The judge asked Vandenbalk if he thought "I look like a carrier pigeon." Scapio was trying not to laugh and hoping he would not get caught. Nobody ever wants to get the Joe Pesci line from *Goodfellas*: "I'm funny how? I mean, funny like a clown? I amuse you?" Scapio knows the entire scene, having seen *Goodfellas* six times.

After a few more hostile questions from the judge, Vandenbalk said that was all he had. Judge Curtis turned to Holdman and asked, "Is there anything you feel the need to say, Mr. Holdman?" who spoke his three words: "No, your honor."

Every good lawyer knows when you are winning, shut up. Judge Curtis then said the defense motion was denied as having absolutely no merit, preliminary hearing remains as set. As they left the courtroom, Scapio was giddy, congratulating Holdman on his "great argument," adding that was "the best oral argument I have ever heard. Maybe only three words, but the best thing was the inflection. The fact that you said them all together rather than separate them showed confidence, no hesitation. Just brilliant." He then said that he was hoping Curtis wasn't gonna see him laugh, 'cause he didn't want to get "Joe Pescied," after which Scapio recited the entire "you think I'm funny" speech. Scapio added that Curtis kinda did it to Vandenbalk with the "Do I look like a carrier pigeon?" line.

SIX

When Scapio got back to his office, he had ten voice mail messages. He went through all ten and saved the ones he needed and deleted the two phone solicitations. One of the messages was from Carlos Acevedo's attorney, Lydia Crespino.

Scapio had pulled the jail calls that Carlos Acevedo had made and uncovered over one hundred calls from jail after his arrest for the shooting death of Nelson Castillo. Some of the calls were of no evidentiary value. Many involved his calling family members and friends, asking them to go to the jail and put money on his books. Inmates' money can be used for commissary, which can include food such as candy bars, trail mix, Doritos, and potato chips, as well as hygiene items, radios, MP3 players, or pencils for those inmates who are either doing their own work for their case or writing letters. But some of the calls were highly incriminating. Many were to other gang members or gang associates. He was recorded asking fellow gang members for information on the murder investigation or for them to give messages to certain people, some of whom the police department weren't aware of before.

When Carlos "Sniper" Acevedo talked with other members of the Northside Chiques, he only referred to them by their nicknames. Acevedo was inquiring as to who had search warrants served on them. He was also inquiring as to whether anyone was rumored to be ratting to the police; in several calls he asked if anyone was "eating cheese." When someone mentioned the person the prosecution had turned, Acevedo's reaction was, "Fuck, homie, if the fool eats cheese, that's fucked up, you know what I mean?" He added, "You gotta talk to that one blond hyna he was living with, that hyna is Huero's [a common nickname for a light-skinned Hispanic] prima [female cousin]. You gotta tell that hyna to tell Turtle [the nickname for the prosecution witness arrested in the same car with the gun, and yes, he did look a little like a turtle] to not fuckin' be a rat and to tell the prosecutor and the detective that he didn't see nothing, you know what I mean?" After speaking with gang detectives familiar with the Northside Chiques street gang, Scapio learned that Turtle's girlfriend was twenty-year-old Destiny Reyes.

In yet another call, he said he heard Turtle might be ratting, and the unknown gangster that he was talking to said it might be Mousy, who was the third person in the car; then the unknown gangster referred to Mousy as a "cheese-eating motherfucker."

Sniper replied, "That's fucked up, homes. If anyone rats, I could be doing a long fuckin' time."

The unknown gangster replied, "Don't even sweat it, homie. You'll be home with your little one before Christmas. All they got on you is a fuckin' parole hold, homie. The cuete [gun] could have been anyone's. Me and your homies are getting the word out that snitches get stiches," to which Sniper replied, "and end up in ditches," and they both laughed. They each professed their love for each other as gang members do, and the unknown gang member ended with, "I fuckin' got your back, homes. Neither of those motherfuckers is gonna eat cheese."

The most useful of the jail calls was one that Acevedo made to his girlfriend, Laura Morales. It turned out that Laura Morales, aka Lolo, had been in an on-again, off-again relationship with Acevedo, aka Sniper. In one of the calls, Sniper was professing his love to her and got graphic, saying, "We fucked the last night before I got picked up, babe, and I didn't even want to take a fuckin' shower 'cause I wanted the smell of you to stay with me 'cause I love you so much, babe." She told him she doesn't know whether to believe him because he had cheated on her before. He told her, "That shit didn't mean nothing, I love only you, you're the only hyna for me. Now that I'm fucking locked up again I know when I get out it's just gonna be me and you, babe."

She said she wanted to believe him, and he said, "Come on, babe, you know I'm not lyin'. You are all I want. So how long will you wait for me?" She said she didn't know, she couldn't keep doing this with him going in and out of jail, and that their daughter needed a father. He then asked, "Will you wait a year?" and she said OK. He said, "What if it's ten years?" and she hesitated before she said OK. Then he went into a diatribe, which Scapio found funny but Laura Morales didn't.

Sniper asked if she ever saw *Braveheart*. She said she didn't know. "There is this one part," he said, "where Braveheart yells 'Freedom' a bunch of times really loud. Well, if it was me I would be yelling 'Honesty!' You are lying to me, you aren't waiting ten years, babe, no fuckin' way are you doing that."

"I know. I'm not sure I'm waiting one year, and I don't give a shit about some stupid movie you saw."

"I know, babe. I love you so much. I want to be with you so bad." Then after she said she loved him, he said, "I need a favor. I hear Turtle might rat. I need you to get ahold of his hyna and tell her she is gonna get her ass beat if she doesn't tell Turtle to hand the cheese back to the cops and not take a bite out of it. Tell that stupid hyna to tell Turtle that her ass is gonna get beat bad if Turtle rats."

He continued, "I fuckin' love you so much, Lolo. I can't stop thinking about you. I know I fucked up really bad this time. I could be going away for a long time." Then he caught himself, finally remembering that the calls are recorded, and said, "I mean I didn't fuckin' kill that guy or nothing. Nah, I wouldn't fuck up that bad, you know what I mean? Yeah, I didn't do that shit that they are saying, but they might find my prints on the gun 'cause we went target shooting earlier that day, so I mean I could be fucked." There was an automated warning that the time for the call was almost up, so he concluded, "OK, talk to that hyna and tell her what's up. I love you, Lolo."

Scapio sent the jail calls to defense counsel in discovery. Acevedo had stopped saying anything of substance after a Northside shotcaller with the moniker "Spider" told him, "Don't say nothing over the fuckin' phone! They record all the fuckin' calls. You start even askin' shit and favors or whatever, man, they fuckin' bury you with your own fuckin' words, homie."

When Crespino heard the call with Spider, she thought, "My idiot client should have talked to you first." By the time Spider talked to him, Sniper had already made calls burying himself. Crespino had told him not to talk about the crime because there are informants in the jail and because what you say on the phone is recorded, but she didn't specifically say not to screw himself over the phone by asking homies for favors. Crespino hadn't done many gang cases, but this one was quite the eye opener.

Crespino informed Scapio that she had listened to the jail calls and she really was concerned that her client had screwed himself. She said she'd had four talks with him, and her client realizes how bad the jail calls are. He was distraught that he put his family in this situation, but the confrontation was started by the victim. He said he knew it wasn't a defense to a shooting. Crespino said after the final long talk with her client, with the evidence of the DNA on the gun and Turtle's testimony plus the one other witness from the party—a guy who was not in a gang, who had picked Sniper in a photo lineup—her client was "willing to plead for fifteen-to-life second-degree murder if you drop the gun enhancement." Scapio said that he couldn't make any promises and that DA Bill Reddis made the final call on homicide pleas, but he would advise the family of the victim and get their input before speaking with Reddis.

Scapio liked the idea of taking that plea. Despite the jail calls and the DNA as well as Turtle's testimony, there was little doubt that the victim was the initial aggressor. The victim did not recognize the defendant or any of his friends, according to two witnesses who said that he walked up to them and said, "What's up?" and "Where you from?" Turtle was wearing a Nebraska Cornhuskers baseball cap with the big *N* on the front. Mousy had on a CSUN (Cal State University Northridge) hoodie. Northside gangsters liked to wear Northridge because they liked to call the school "Northridge State" or NS—in other words, Northside. The defendant, Acevedo, was wearing a throwback Minnesota North Stars cap. This cap was common among Northside gang members who had status in the gang. The North Stars were a hockey team in the NHL from 1967–1993.

(Northridge gear was eliminated a few months later when the daughter of the shotcaller known as Veterano, or OG for Original or Old Gangster, enrolled as a freshman at CSUN. Veterano ordered all the Northside gangsters to stop wearing Northridge because "My daughter does not want anything to do with gang shit. I know it's our way of life, but I love Cecilia and we have to respect that our way is not her way." From then on, no Northside gang members wore Northridge, but Nebraska and North Carolina gear was common.)

The victim then said, "Northside, get the fuck out, this is Southside, bitch." At this point, Acevedo pulled his gun and shot and killed Castillo. This was not self-defense, as one can only use deadly force if a reasonable person confronted with the same circumstance would reasonably believe that deadly force was necessary to prevent death or great bodily injury. However, if someone has an honest but unreasonable belief in self-defense, the crime is manslaughter instead of murder.

Second-degree murder with a gun is fifteen to life plus twenty-five years. Second-degree murder without the gun allegation is fifteen years to life, meaning the inmate must serve fifteen years before being eligible for parole. Voluntary manslaughter, on the other hand, is a fixed-term sentence. That means that the defendant would be guaranteed his freedom. Voluntary manslaughter carries a sentence of either three years, six years, or eleven years in state prison, so the maximum would be twenty-one years with the ten-year gun enhancement, but they would be eligible for parole sooner than that.

Crespino had previously mentioned that she would be able to sell her client on twenty-one years for manslaughter. Scapio said that would not happen, as he believed that the defendant brought a gun to a fist fight and was even given the opportunity to leave without a fight. Now that the defense was willing to take second-degree murder, the situation had changed a lot.

This offer made Scapio very happy, because he knew this was not an easy case. The victim was a gang member who started the confrontation. Gang experts would testify that the words "where are you from" are often a prelude to murder. The defendant asked for a lawyer rather than give a story, so he was free to say that he thought the victim was reaching for a weapon. It would contradict his jail-call denial, but that would not be a big deal because he was obviously being cagey on the jail conversations. The victim did not have a gun or any other weapon on him, but if the defendant said he thought the victim was reaching for something, it might get at least some jurors to buy into manslaughter. Although Scapio could present the history of the defendant's Northside Chiques gang—Chiques comes from the city of origin of Latino gangs in the US, Chicago—including past violent acts committed by the gang, the defense could do the same with the Southside gang.

Scapio knew this was a fair deal and he was going to recommend it to Reddis. He also knew Reddis well enough to know he would agree. Scapio would not see Reddis doing the duck on this one. Reddis had always said you should try to settle gang-on-gang homicides, and he would be very happy with a plea to second-degree murder. Scapio was also happy for a second reason. He would be able to spend all of his time getting ready on the McCarty case. The thing he needed to do was sell the plea to the victim's family, so he called Sandra Goldberg, the victim advocate, and asked her to set up a meeting with the family of the victim before April 19, the day of the McCarty preliminary hearing.

The meeting was set for Friday, April 15, at 2:00 p.m. in the executive conference room. Scapio set it there for two reasons. First was that the conference room was bigger and could seat about fifteen people comfortably around the long table in that room. Scapio was told by Goldberg that six family members would be attending the meeting. If six people were in Scapio's office, even though it was a window office, four of them plus Sandra Goldberg would have to stand the entire time. The second reason was that Scapio's office, per usual, was a mess. There were papers all over his desk and files on the floor. There were also boxes that contained additional case material that would not fit in either the files or the trial notebooks he made. These included CDs and DVDs of police interviews of witnesses and scene photographs. Scapio had two boxes of cold case files that he was assigned to work with the Cold Case Unit to see if the cases could be solved.

A little after two in the afternoon on April 15, Scapio got the call from the front desk that the Castillo family had begun to arrive. Scapio had already told Oxnard police detective Jaime Escobedo, who worked the case, that the defense was offering to plead to second-degree murder. Escobedo told Scapio to go for it, because gang cases were not a guarantee. Escobedo also had some insight into the shooter, Carlos Acevedo, from having worked gangs for five years, and he said that even though Acevedo did not have much of a record, he was firmly entrenched in the gang culture and would likely have disciplinary problems and become involved in prison-gang activity with the Mexican Mafia. Escobedo predicted that a fifteen-years-to-life sentence would likely result in a sentence well beyond fifteen years. Escobedo added that if, on the other hand, Carlos could turn his life around and stay out of prison-gang life, then he deserved another shot.

Scapio believed that a part of the reason why Escobedo supported the plea was the victim was not completely innocent here. This was not the same as a robber shooting the clerk at the liquor store. Evidence did support the fact that the victim, Nelson Castillo, was the initial aggressor and was himself a gang member. Scapio knew he had to make this point very diplomatically. Once the defendant pulled the gun out first, the victim was not a threat to him, even if the victim had asked where Sniper's group was from. This was the point Scapio emphasized to Crespino in turning down the previous manslaughter offer.

The victim's parents and sister arrived first. Scapio had not met Aurelio Castillo yet. A forty-eight-year-old truck driver, he looked like an older and heavier version of his son. Scapio already knew the victim's sister, Gabriella, and her mother, Norma. Arriving five minutes later were two cousins and the victim's uncle, Aurelio's brother.

Scapio began the meeting, after shaking hands with everyone, by telling them that he had turned down the defense offer to plead to voluntary manslaughter with the gun use. This was strategic, because he wanted the family to know that he was not just willing to take any plea to get the case over with. It was important in gaining the trust and support of the victim's family for them to know that he declined to accept a plea for anything less than murder. After he explained that, he said the defense had made another offer, which he believed should be accepted but that he also welcomed their thoughts.

He explained the fifteen-to-life sentence and that the best-case scenario without taking the plea was fifteen plus twenty-five to life. But if the defendant never got out of his gang loyalties and they continued in prison, he'd be staying in for a lot longer than the plea-bargain fifteen years, and if that is the case, dismissing the gun enhancement would not change anything.

Sandra Goldberg added that at sentencing, each family member could give victim-impact statements, and if anything was written out, it would go to the prison as part of his record that will be viewed by a parole board. She also mentioned that in fifteen years when he gets a parole hearing, the prison would notify them of the hearing and they could be present to express opposition and could also submit written statements at that time.

Scapio knew that he had to tread lightly on the last topic, and he began by saying that Nelson had been making progress in getting away from gangs but it was a tough process, that the gang members were guys he grew up with, "so we often see two steps forward and one step backward." He explained that at trial, the defense would be allowed to focus on that one step backward. Nelson did not deserve to get shot, Scapio explained, but his initiating a confrontation using gang terms might make a jury hesitant to convict of murder.

After a pause, Norma said that if Scapio thought it was best, then she would trust him. Aurelio said the same. Scapio listened closely as Aurelio teared up and explained how his son had been a great kid but got caught up in a lifestyle that he had been easing out of, and Aurelio agreed with Scapio on the one step backward.

The other family members nodded in agreement. Some family members asked some questions about the process. When the meeting was over, Scapio and Sandra hugged everyone, and that was it. Scapio stopped by Waverly's office and told her about the offer and his recommendation. She said that she agreed, especially if the detective was on board. She also repeated that final approval had to come from the DA.

After speaking with Waverly, Scapio decided to stop by Reddis's office to see if he was in and would approve the deal. As the elected district attorney, Reddis was only in the office about half the time and was often traveling. In fact, Reddis wasn't in, but Scapio made an appointment to see him on Monday the eighteenth, which was the day before the preliminary hearing for McCarty was scheduled. Scapio did not believe that a meeting with Reddis would hurt their preparation of the McCarty preliminary hearing.

At 10:00 a.m. on Monday morning, he got a call from Reddis's secretary that "the district attorney will see you now." Scapio entered the office and Reddis motioned him to a seat in front of Reddis's desk. Scapio looked up at the Rose and Bird posters and laughed, and Reddis said, "Yup, still got 'em."

Reddis first asked how the McCarty prep was going and Scapio told him it was going well, and despite a large volume of evidence and Vandenbalk playing the rush-the-prosecution strategy, they were ready to put on a good case. Reddis then asked why Scapio had wanted to see him the day before the preliminary hearing, and Scapio realized that he had not mentioned the reason why he wanted the meeting, and Reddis had assumed that it was about the McCarty case.

That's when Scapio told him that the defense had made an offer of second-degree murder without the firearm-use allegation in Acevedo. Scapio outlined the facts of the case and told him about his conversation with the family of the victim as well as the Oxnard police detective's support and Waverly's. Scapio figured that Reddis would approve, since he never once got the infamous duck during the entire speech he gave Reddis. Scapio was correct; Reddis said he thought it was a great result, especially since there were substantial issues in the case and you never knew what a jury would do with a case where the initial aggressor was a gang-member victim.

Nobody would know how good a deal that would turn out to be until four years later, when the California legislature, having focused on reducing sentences and freeing inmates as part of a new criminal justice reform movement, would allow inmates aged twenty-six or under to be parole-eligible in murder cases like Acevedo's after twenty years even with a twenty-five-year gun enhancement. It was part of a youthful offender parole law designed to give younger inmates convicted of murder a chance at earlier release.

The law was also retroactive to all cases before the law was passed. That meant that in 2016, Acevedo would have only been eligible for parole after forty years, but after 2020, he would have been eligible for parole in twenty years even without the plea deal if convicted of second-degree murder and the gun-use enhancement.

Scapio thanked Reddis and they shook hands. As Scapio started to leave, he stopped, turned to Reddis, then said, "Oh, never mind, it's nothing." Scapio was going to tell him that he knew Reddis was going to agree to the deal because he didn't do the duck, and he was going to explain the duck. But then he thought that too many people benefited by knowing about the duck, and if Reddis was told, he would stop doing it. No, Scapio thought, this is gonna be revealed at Reddis's retirement, whenever that will be.

Scapio called Lydia Crespino and let her know that he got approval for the fifteen-years-to-life sentence with the gun enhancement dropped. She said she was glad it could resolve, and it was gonna be up to her client to make the deal worth it, because he would have to change in prison.

SEVEN

When they got to the calendar court for the preliminary hearing, Scapio and Holdman waited for Vandenbalk. Vandenbalk arrived late; he walked up to Scapio and shook his hand but ignored Holdman. Vandenbalk asked if they were ready, and Scapio confirmed that they were.

Then Vandenbalk began his next phase of gamesmanship. He told Scapio he had really good news for him. He had spoken extensively with his client and was able to convince him to plead guilty to voluntary manslaughter with use of a knife for a twelve-year sentence, out in around nine with credits already earned. He said, "I know you'll need to run it by your boss, and I'll give you time to do that. I said my client was not going to waive time, but I got him to do that. You should take this deal; it's a win-win, and you save your career." Scapio asked if he could have as much time as he needed to think about it. Vandenbalk was surprised and said absolutely, they would waive time for sixty days if Scapio needed that much time. Scapio then said he thought about it, and the answer was no; they were going forward with the prelim.

Checking his irritation, Vandenbalk asked Scapio who he would be calling as witnesses. Scapio said that he would call the two detectives who found the evidence, crime-scene investigator Sean Murphy, the DNA analyst, the cell-phone expert, and the roommate, who would confirm the relationship and breakup.

Vandenbalk had given serious consideration to what is called waiving preliminary hearing. That would be agreeing or stipulating that there was probable cause, and setting the case for trial within sixty days. The reason he considered doing this was he knew the press was covering the preliminary hearing, and he also knew pretrial publicity could impact the trial. Jurors form opinions, even if they do not admit it, and those opinions become hard to change. That is why he liked to try his cases by press conferences, and the gag order hurt his strategy. The evidence against his client was strong, and the more publicity a preliminary hearing got, the more it could potentially damage the defense.

Then Vandenbalk had looked at the flip side. His first change-of-venue motion wasn't serious; it was just to direct the prosecution's focus away from building their case. The next one would be serious, and they needed a preliminary hearing to make that venue-change case. Vandenbalk really did not want to try the case in Ventura County. He figured LA or Santa Barbara would be a much better jury pool for the defense.

Vandenbalk was also going to use the preliminary hearing to gauge how much he should rush this case to trial. It was a DNA case, and if the prosecution seemed organized and prepared for a thorough presentation, rushing to trial might not be good. He might need Lanny to dig up dirt on the victim. Lanny lived to dig up dirt. His style as an investigator was to try and trash everyone associated with the prosecution. If you wanted to find evidence of innocence, Lanny was probably not your investigator of choice. If you wanted to muddy the waters and find something to make a jury dislike a victim or witness or even the prosecutor, Lanny might be your guy. At sixty-three years old, he'd been diagnosed with diabetes and high blood pressure and he'd had a heart attack, but he thrived on trashing others, and if there was dirt to be found, he would probably find it. Rushing this case to trial might not give Lanny enough time.

Scapio and Holdman completed the preliminary hearing in a little over half the day. Vandenbalk asked very few questions. What Vandenbalk did learn through the testimony of the two detectives, the cell-phone tower expert, DNA analyst Maria Aguilar, crime-scene investigator Sean Murphy, and roommate Michelle Harrington was that the prosecution was ready if the trial started the next day. The original time estimate for the preliminary hearing had been two days. They beat that estimate by a day and a half. One thing was clear to Vandenbalk: he was going to have to slow this thing down a lot. He would give Fat Lanny time to work some magic, and he would try to find some way with his high-priced expert witness to make it work. He had asked very few questions on cross-examination because he was saving anything good he had for trial.

Another reason he wanted to slow down the process was he knew the articles would come out, both in the paper and online. Public opinion would be influenced based on reports of the evidence, and it would not be favorable for the client. If he failed in his change-of-venue motion, which was likely because those motions don't succeed very often, he was going to need time for the bad publicity to die down. Scapio didn't know it yet, but he would soon learn that this case was no longer on the fast track.

* * *

Vandenbalk met with Frank Andrews, who told him that his initial study of the file was supportive of McCarty's innocence. Andrews said he was quite confident that the victim's blood on defendant's clothing had to be unrelated to the murder, because based upon the length, depth, force, and number of the stab wounds, there should have been much more blood on McCarty's clothing.

Andrews said one of two explanations was possible. One was that the blood came from a separate incident, since there was no way to determine how long the blood had been on the clothes. Vandenbalk pointed out that the prosecution was going to argue that it had to be recent because the clothes were recently placed in the trash. Had that not been the case, the clothes would have been in some previous trash pickup and they would not have been found. Andrews explained that the blood could have been from earlier, but that didn't matter. "If the jury agrees with me or thinks that my testimony at least creates reasonable doubt, then you don't explain an alternative theory as to how the blood got there, nor do you need to."

He said that Vandenbalk and the investigator could pursue one of two theories: either the blood came from some other incident where the victim bled and got her blood on his shirt or shoes, or they could pursue the OJ-type defense, that the police planted the blood on the clothes. He reminded Vandenbalk that he was prepared to testify to a reasonable degree of scientific certainty that, based upon the number of and force of the stab wounds, the blood could not have come from the murder because there should have been a lot more of it.

Vandenbalk thought to himself that the guy was impressive, and maybe he could win the case. They would have many more sessions, but Andrews told him he would produce a PowerPoint show that would captivate the jurors. His testimony would last a full day or close to it. Andrews told Vandenbalk that he'd had great success where he testified almost to the end of the day so there would be no cross, and the witness's entire dog-and-pony-show would make a huge impression on the jurors going home for the night. Andrews bragged that after he had testified for a full day, most prosecutors floundered, looking flustered and confused, even with a full night of preparation, and basically "couldn't lay a glove on me." Vandenbalk was excited, and he knew he would be even more excited if he could get the case moved to Los Angeles, or even better yet, Santa Barbara.

The preliminary hearing resulted in defendant McCarty being held to answer on the charge of murder with use of a knife as well as the special allegation for premeditation and deliberation, which had been added when the cell-phone records came in, and the arraignment on information—the next step—was set in superior court.

* * *

In the Ventura County DA's Homicide Unit, the cases are often round-tabled after a preliminary hearing or a grand jury indictment. A round table is a meeting among all the homicide attorneys, the supervisor of the Homicide Unit, and the chief deputy assigned to oversee the Homicide Unit. The assigned prosecutor writes a memorandum that is distributed throughout, so everyone attending the meeting is familiar with the case and any issues that the case might present. The case is thoroughly discussed and a decision is made whether to go forward with the case, file additional charges or allegations, or keep the case as is. Ideas for further investigation are also discussed.

The meetings can be very productive, with some of the most experienced and talented prosecutors brainstorming one case. The round tables are also used in death-eligible cases where, because of a charged special circumstance, a defendant is eligible for a death sentence. There are a number of special circumstances that can make a person eligible for a death sentence, including multiple murder; murder in the course of a rape, robbery, or residential burglary; murder by torture; murder for financial gain; and murder of a police officer, judge, prosecutor, or witness, among many others.

The difference with those meetings, besides the issue of whether to seek death, is the presence of the district attorney. When the Affordable Care Act was passed, there was a provision that called for the coverage of end-of-life counseling for the terminally ill. Opponents of the law called them "death panels" and said that this was the government's attempt to kill Grandma because she had lived long enough. Reddis, not known for political correctness despite being a politician, said that "they need to stop calling those things 'death panels,' because we have the real death panels. Our meetings where everyone votes on whether we should seek death and I decide, those are the real death panels." Prior to such a meeting, every member of the Homicide Unit gets an email with the heading "Death Penalty Meeting Scheduled," noting a day, date, and time, and the name of the accused. A copy of the memorandum is attached to the email.

The round table on the McCarty case lasted only a half hour. There was no special circumstance filed to create death eligibility. Based upon the DNA, there just was not much to talk about.

* * *

The arraignment was set for May 2, 2016. The information or charging document was filed, and a trial date was set for forty-five court days later, which was July 7, with a last day of trial set for July 28. The pretrial readiness conference, when both sides must either agree on a plea deal or advise the court if they would be ready to start the trial when set, was scheduled for Monday, June 27. If a side informed the court they would not be ready, the judge would decide whether or not to grant the request to continue.

At the May 2 arraignment, Scapio asked Vandenbalk for a witness list. Vandenbalk said he did not have one yet. Scapio told him that he at least wanted to get the defense's list of expert witnesses. Vandenbalk said that he would get that to him when he decided who to use, but he had not made that decision. Scapio said that was "bullshit" and told him that when he sent the expert's information, it had to include when Vandenbalk retained the expert and when he was first consulted. Scapio told him, "If that fact predates today, when you are telling me you don't know who you're calling, you will be in deep shit for withholding discovery."

Vandenbalk replied that he had retained an expert but had not made the final decision as to whether he would use the witness. When he decided that the witness would testify, he would then provide everything. Scapio figured that the witness was already on board and that Vandenbalk was playing games so

Scapio would have less time to prepare for the witness's testimony. Scapio mentioned that Vandenbalk knew all of the DA's witnesses, and if Vandenbalk didn't provide his witnesses by the date set for pretrial readiness, Scapio would himself be asking for sanctions for failure to provide discovery. Vandenbalk got the message and told Scapio he would have his expert's name to him before the pretrial date and more than likely within two weeks.

Vandenbalk added, "I have to meet with him one more time, but I will likely call Frank Andrews."

* * *

Carlos Acevedo pleaded guilty to the second-degree murder of Nelson Castillo. Family members of the victim gave emotional victim-impact statements. During the impact statements, Acevedo sat next to his attorney and had his head bent down. There were tears from many family members in the courtroom. Even though Castillo had been a gang member, his family gave truly heartfelt tributes showing Castillo as a loving brother, son, boyfriend, and young father who had made mistakes. At the conclusion of the impact statements from the families, Carlos Acevedo spoke, apologizing for his action, and cried. Scapio might have been persuaded because Acevedo sounded more sincere than most, but he had listened to the jail calls and did not believe Acevedo was sincerely remorseful, and he expected Acevedo to be a hard-core gangster in prison.

Scapio hugged the family members, and the victim's sister, Gabriella, asked what Scapio thought of Acevedo's statement. Scapio said that Acevedo sounded good, but he had heard the jail calls and was convinced that Acevedo talked a good game but was entrenched in gang culture. The victim advocate, Sandra Goldberg, again explained to the family members the parole process and how the family members would be notified.

* * *

Well before the pretrial hearing, Holdman and Scapio had interviewed Karen Loring, the woman who had filed the restraining order against McCarty. Present for the interview was DA investigator Philip Conway. The prosecutors get a DA investigator after the preliminary hearing. Conway had joined the district attorney's investigative bureau in 2011 after serving fifteen years as a Port Hueneme police officer and five years as an investigator for the navy. With silver slicked-back hair, he looked like a US senator. Despite his politician look, however, he had a reputation for honesty and dedication. He was an outstanding investigator, and Scapio and Holdman were happy to have him.

Loring recalled that McCarty was charming at first but became increasingly controlling. The incident where she had gotten the restraining order was the worst of the abuse and the only time when it became physical. She was willing to testify, and Holdman was very confident her testimony would be allowed.

On June 27, the pretrial hearing was held in Courtroom 12 at 1:30 p.m. When the case was called, Scapio referred to the discovery motion that Holdman had filed requesting the list of witnesses that defense intended to call. The prosecution had included the list of people that they would call at trial in the trial brief. Scapio represented that Vandenbalk had said that he would have his witness list. The judge turned to Vandenbalk and asked him about that, and Vandenbalk said that they did not know all the witnesses that would be called, but his forensic expert would be Frank Andrews.

Scapio had researched Andrews, pulling a couple of articles Andrews had written in scientific journals. He read both articles, but they were way beyond Scapio's understanding and contained algebraic calculations about mass and velocity. He kept reading because sometimes you find that needle in a haystack that you can use, but not in this case. Scapio was lost and was not particularly adept at mathematics. He carefully read the two articles start to finish and found nothing but the fact that he'd wasted a day and his brain hurt.

Scapio found a couple of articles about the arson case Andrews was involved with, where a convicted person in Idaho was exonerated. Scapio knew that Vandenbalk was going to really play this one up.

He then went to the expert witness file and found a couple of cases where Andrews did testify. One was a driving-under-the-influence causing serious injury. The case was People v Halverson, and Andrews had been hired by the defense. The prosecution contended that the accident resulting in Halverson's passenger's injury was the driver's fault and was therefore evidence of alcohol-impaired driving. Andrews testified that, based upon his review of the scene photos and the highway patrol expert's report the prosecution relied upon, the accident was the fault of the other driver in that case.

The prosecutor on cross-examination asked the witness if he was being paid to support the conclusion the defense attorney wanted. Andrews got indignant and said, "I am a scientist. I am consulted for my expertise. If my conclusions are consistent with the defense case, I expect that my testimony would be requested, and I would be compensated for my time and testimony. If my conclusion, after reviewing the evidence, does not support the defense theory, I would not be called as a witness; I would be paid for my time in reviewing the case and that's it. Either way is fine. I am a scientist and I do not work for any attorney; I do not care what the attorney wants or needs. I am not beholden to the attorney. My obligation is to science. My integrity as a scientist is too important."

The prosecutor doing the cross-examination was new to the Felony Unit and was stunned by the answer and knew the jury ate it up. The prosecution cross-examination lasted another hour but was never very effective. The blood-alcohol level was .07, but the blood was taken four hours after the accident due to medical treatment and hospital admission of the defendant. Assuming full absorption of alcohol at the time of the accident, based upon burnout rates, the blood alcohol should have been about .115 at the time of the accident. The legal limit was .08. The case was difficult because there were no field sobriety tests done due to the accused's injuries, and the passenger had no memory of the accident or how much the accused had to drink. In the end, the jury was deadlocked five for conviction, seven for acquittal, and the DA's office opted not to refile the case.

The second case involved a shooting. Andrews testified that even though the victim was unarmed and was shot from a distance, the shooter could have seen the victim turn toward him with what he thought was a gun. Andrews testified that the cell phone the victim had in his hand could have been mistaken for a gun, based upon the time of day, reflection of the sun, and distance the shooter was from the victim. The defendant was convicted of assault with a firearm causing serious injury. The defense problem in that case was that two witnesses saw the victim arguing with the shooter with what clearly was a cell phone in his hand. The witnesses were the same distance away as the defendant was. This was a drug deal gone badly. Scapio couldn't have known as he reviewed that case, but Andrews didn't like losing and vowed that would be the last time he would accept a case where his theory had to contradict actual eyewitness testimony.

Scapio gleaned from his review that the prevailing theme of Andrews's testimony was always that, though he had no training in any of the subjects he testified about, everything was subject to the laws of physics, so being an expert on that, he could testify to anything. Scapio found cases in other jurisdictions where he'd testified on blood spatter, another on blunt-force injuries. Still another was an accident reconstruction case. There was even a case involving shoeprints, in which he testified that even though the defendant's shoeprints were near the crime scene, the distance and direction of the prints were not consistent with burglary but rather with an innocent home buyer or a merely curious passerby. This defense was absurd, but one juror held out and the prosecution decided to reach a plea deal for felony grand theft.

Holdman had suggested filing a motion to exclude Andrews's testimony based upon his lack of training in blood spatter or DNA, which could be the only two topics he could possibly be used for. Scapio rejected that idea because he didn't want to risk the case being tossed on appeal. He also said that he loved cross-examining experts, and that if you could damage the expert's testimony, you would hurt the entire defense case. If the jury can't believe the expert the defense paid a lot of money for, what about the defense theories can you trust?

Andrews himself saw this case as a great opportunity. It was high profile, so if he could help Vandenbalk secure a not-guilty verdict, he would reach potentially legendary status and would make a fortune the rest of his life. There was little downside; there were no eyewitnesses to contradict his conclusions, so there was no chance his testimony would be made to look foolish. It was clearly a strong prosecution case and the guy obviously killed his ex-girlfriend, so nobody in the legal profession expected he would win the case, and if he did not prevail, there would be no harm to his status. A victory, however, would cement his legacy as the greatest expert witness in the modern era. When it came to egos in the courtroom, the only one in his league might be the attorney who hired him on the case.

* * *

Scapio and Holdman prepared for trial religiously as the trial date approached. At the pretrial hearing on June 27, a little over a week before trial, Vandenbalk handed Holdman a second motion for change of venue. This motion contained a declaration from a social science expert alleging that she had taken a lengthy survey of a cross-section of eligible voters and many knew about the case, and many others had expressed opinions about the defendant, some of which were unfavorable. Scapio read it and believed that the most it required would be more time for jury selection and the use of written questionnaires to screen out those with a bias toward either side.

Scapio told the judge that he'd just received the change-of-venue motion and that he was going to need time to respond, and the trial would need to be continued. The judge turned to Vandenbalk and asked his position. Vandenbalk said that it was the defense's intention to waive as much time as Scapio and Holdman needed. Scapio asked for a moment to confer with Holdman. After a minute's discussion, Scapio said that, given the defense motion included a survey and a sociologist's recommendation, they would need three months. Scapio turned to Vandenbalk, who was suddenly being more accommodating than he ever had been, and asked if Monday, September 14, for the change-of-venue hearing, and Monday, September 21, for the pretrial hearing with a sixty-day time waiver, worked for him, and Vandenbalk said that was fine. The time waiver gave them sixty court days from September 21 to start the trial. Scapio requested that much time in case the change-of-venue motion was granted. They would need time to fit the trial in and arrange for transportation or possible hotel accommodations for the trial. The trial was given a four-week estimate including jury selection.

Holdman had handled change-of-venue motions before and knew this was going to significantly delay the trial. They would have to do their own counter-study to show that a fair and impartial jury could be selected in Ventura County. This would take time. Time would now be their ally, because the more time passed, the less likely any taint that existed now would linger, as delays would keep the case out of the news cycle.

When Scapio returned to his office he called Philip Conway, the assigned DA investigator, and told him about the change-of-venue motion. He told Conway to work with Holdman on how to conduct a survey to submit to the judge, and that Holdman had responded to venue motions for the DA's office on previous cases.

Scapio did not want a Santa Barbara or LA jury over a Ventura jury, but he did acknowledge that liberal Santa Barbara might be good on a domestic-violence homicide since Santa Barbara liberals tended to be more offended by domestic abuse. The flip side, of course, was that a Santa Barbara jury might be more receptive to a police-misconduct defense.

Scapio was not particularly political, but he did vote. He had just never registered for a party; he'd been independent his entire voting life. Candidate, not party, had been his motto. But despite that, he had a good sense of what type of case the prosecution did better on with liberals as jurors, like domestic violence, sexual assault, and any crime with a gun. They may not be as good for prosecutors on street crimes with defendants of color, or cases entirely dependent on police testimony. Conservatives were favored in robberies, burglaries, and murders. Of course, that was a stereotype, and good prosecutors know when instinct tells them to break the stereotype. Scapio once left a young woman who was a member of Amnesty International on the jury of an assault-with-a-deadly-weapon charge, and the jury convicted; she was one of the strongest guilty votes.

* * *

Scapio checked his messages on his voice mail and had one from his mother, Diane. Diane Scapio was seventy-two years old and had been married to his father, Michael, for forty-nine years. They lived in East Hampton, New York. Scapio was concerned because she rarely called his office.

He called her back and she tearfully told him that his last living grandparent, Salvatore, had passed away. Salvatore "Sal" Scapio was ninety-three and had been in a Florida nursing home when he passed in his sleep.

Ray had known he had been ill. He'd been very close to his grandfather on his father's side as a kid. Sal used to sneak him candy that his mom didn't want him to eat; candy corn was the big taboo. Diane would scold Sal and say, "He's gonna grow up to be a handsome man, but not if he eats that crap. His teeth will fall out!" Sal would smile and say in his old-country accent—he was born in Sicily—"Ah, come on. Don't be like that. Kids love this, he's a kid. When you get to be my age, that's when you worry about shit falling out." Diane was always scolding Sal for foul language too. But Sal was Sal, and Ray, who frequently swore, had always thought Sal might have been the influence there.

Ray hadn't seen Sal for years. They had talked on the phone a few times, but now Sal was gone and Ray was feeling sad. At the same time, he was relieved the call was not about his mom or dad's health. His parents were getting older, and he knew that day would come when they would be gone. But he hoped that Sal's long life was a good sign for his parents' longevity, and his own as well.

Ray and his mom discussed possible funeral arrangements. Sal was in Long Island, so Ray was unsure whether he would be attending. Diane told Ray that she was able to reach his brother. Michael, or Mike Junior, was Ray's only sibling and was four years older, living in Anaheim, California, with his wife Tracy and their two children. Mike was a financial advisor. Ray called him and they talked for a while, swapping stories about Sal.

Mike said he wasn't going to be able to make the trip to Long Island for the service due to several business commitments he couldn't cancel. Ray did go to the service to pay his respects to Sal and to spend a few days with his mom and dad.

* * *

In addition to preparing for the eventual McCarty trial, Scapio tried two other homicide cases before the change-of-venue motion would be heard. The first one was in late June of 2016. That case involved a particularly senseless murder in Simi Valley, a largely white middle-class city in the East County, home to quite a few law enforcement officers, many from LAPD who wanted to live within a reasonable driving distance from LA without having to live in LA County.

Simi Valley is probably known most for the Rodney King trial, but the jurors were actually drawn from a cross-section of Ventura County. The Simi Valley courthouse was never used for jury trials except for the King trial, and that was because the change-of-venue motion from LA County, where the incident occurred, had been granted. The Simi Valley courthouse was more compatible than the courthouse located in the city of Ventura because all the participants lived much closer to Simi Valley than Ventura. Since the accused officers were able to make bail, the Simi Valley court was viable, as there was no need to transfer inmates to court across town.

In the case Scapio tried, a thirty-two-year-old man named Jake Miller had been released from prison for robbery two weeks prior to the incident. Miller attended a party put on by his neighbor Joe Pollinger, thirty-four. Pollinger could not find his cell phone after having had a few too many drinks. Pollinger knew Miller had been in prison for robbery and accused Miller of taking his phone. Miller denied it and went home angry. Pollinger then found his phone. Miller got a knife from his home and returned. Pollinger's girlfriend answered the door and told Miller that Pollinger found his phone. Pollinger went to the door to apologize to Miller for accusing him, and Miller plunged the knife into Pollinger's chest, killing him.

Scapio charged murder, alleging the murder was willful, deliberate, and premeditated. The defense was that it was heat-of-passion voluntary manslaughter. The jury rejected the defense of voluntary manslaughter, finding that the victim's false accusation at a party that the defendant stole his phone did not rise to the level that would inflame the passions of the ordinary reasonable person. But the jurors found second-degree rather than first-degree murder because, although they found the crime was deliberate and premeditated, they did not believe that Miller had the intent to kill, because he did not continue to stab the victim. The jurors found that Miller harbored the state of mind of reckless disregard for life but not intent to kill, and that made the crime second-degree murder. Scapio was not upset with the result because Miller would still receive a life sentence. With the previous robbery conviction he would ultimately be sentenced to 32 years to life and would be unlikely to ever get out.

Scapio's second trial was a drunk driver charged with murder. A man with two prior convictions for driving under the influence had been warned in both those cases that if he became intoxicated and caused an accident that killed someone, he could and likely would be charged with murder. The accused's blood-alcohol level was .29, which was more than three times the legal limit. The defendant was speeding and driving erratically when he ran into a young man riding a bicycle. The young man died at the scene with blunt-force trauma injuries from the accident. Jurors deliberated only two hours before finding the man guilty of second-degree murder. He received a sentence of fifteen years to life.

* * *

With those cases out of the way, Scapio checked on Holdman's progress on the change-of-venue motion. Holdman told him that Conway had completed the survey work with the help of a firm that Reddis approved payment for. By early August 2016, Holdman's opposition to the motion to change venue was complete. Holdman emailed a copy to Scapio, who just skimmed it and told Holdman that he was the expert on that stuff and to go ahead and file it without changes.

Scapio was hoping to get the trial started in October so he could make his December trip to Las Vegas to bet on the bowl games and also get back for family Christmas at his brother's home, when his parents would visit from New York.

Scapio definitely wanted to stay in Ventura, but he also knew that a Santa Barbara jury would not look favorably upon domestic abuse, especially where there was prior abuse. He also figured that Santa Barbara jurors tended to be well educated, so they would not have trouble with the DNA evidence. As for LA, he was not too concerned. They would likely keep it in a courthouse close to Ventura, so that would make it Van Nuys, San Fernando, or Chatsworth, all of which have jury panels close to what you would get in Ventura. Scapio was originally more rabid about staying in Ventura, but after studying the other possible venues, he was less concerned. Of course, the worst-case scenario would be a transfer to downtown LA, where a jury would be more inclined to believe a police frame-up conspiracy. This case did not have a racial angle to it, however, and Scapio was confident they could get a conviction even there.

Once Holdman filed his response brief, Vandenbalk requested additional time to respond. Vandenbalk had realized his hostile, aggressive approach had not rattled Scapio but had motivated him. He knew that from the clear preparation that the prosecution had displayed back at the April preliminary hearing with little preparation time. Gone now were the nasty biting comments along with the bragging about the victory he claimed to expect. Vandenbalk told Scapio that he really needed more time to address Holdman's response. He said Holdman's response was good, and if he just went forward now, he might get second-guessed by an appellate lawyer claiming incompetent representation.

Scapio thought about pointing out that Vandenbalk had been so sure about acquittal, and now he was worried about being second-guessed by an appellate lawyer. Of course, an appeal never happens with an acquittal. But Scapio decided to refrain. If Vandenbalk was gonna play nice, he would too. Scapio reported that he had a vacation in December, and Vandenbalk assured Scapio that wasn't going to be a problem. They agreed to set the venue hearing and trial for Monday, January 9, with a sixty-day time waiver.

Scapio called Vandenbalk a few times and asked him for a witness list and a report from Frank Andrews. Vandenbalk said that he would call Braden's ex-boyfriend before she began dating McCarty. Cody Welch was Braden's ex. Welch was twenty-eight when they broke up and she was twenty-one. Welch was a teacher and assistant football coach at Newbury Park High School when they dated. He had since become the head coach at another high school in the San Fernando Valley. He was single and living in Simi Valley at the time of the murder. In the early stage of the investigation, he was interviewed and was sad about his ex-girlfriend's death but denied any knowledge of what happened. He voluntarily submitted to a DNA sample.

He did admit that when they were dating, he had lost his temper a few times and yelled at her and did kick her car one time but said he never physically hurt her and would never hurt a woman. Welch was targeted by Vandenbalk as an alternate suspect because of the car vandalism. As their relationship came to an end, he kicked her car door hard, causing $500 in damages. Braden had filed a police report, and charges were dismissed after a civil compromise was reached where he paid the damages. He had not admitted to the police that he had done it but did not deny it either; he simply asked for a lawyer. Jessica called him right after it happened, and he did admit to it to her. He almost lost his job as a football coach once word got out, but he was allowed to keep his job if he got counseling, which he did. Had he actually been convicted of misdemeanor vandalism, he likely would have lost his job.

The public defender representing him was Rebecca Mason who was an effective advocate for her clients. She knew that the case was entirely dependent on Braden's credibility, so she thought she might be able to get the DA's office to agree to the civil compromise. She submitted character letters from friends and family who knew Cody Welch. She also informed the prosecutor that Welch would likely lose his career as a football coach with a conviction. The Ventura County district attorney does not normally agree to civil compromises in domestic cases but made an exception in this one. The public defender had represented him well. Welch was excluded from all the DNA samples collected in the investigation of Jessica Braden's murder.

Only a week before the scheduled trial date and venue hearing, Scapio received Frank Andrews's report, and it consisted of just one page. Andrews concluded that based upon the principles of the science of physics, the blood on the recovered shoes and shirt could not have come from the charged incident unless a substantially greater amount of blood had been wiped clean. Defendant's blood found on the brassiere could have been there from any much-earlier event and did not have to be related to the incident at all. The same was true with blood drops linked to the accused.

Scapio asked his investigator, Philip Conway, to call Andrews to see if he would be willing to meet with him and Conway before trial to discuss his report. When he was finally able to reach Andrews, Conway was told that Andrews would need to discuss that with Vandenbalk. Andrews agreed to get back to Conway with an answer but he did not call back, so Conway called Andrews again and Andrews told him that "after discussing the matter with Mr. Vandenbalk, I will not be meeting you to discuss this case before trial."

Scapio had his witnesses lined up to start January 9 but knew that January date was unrealistic. The courts were backlogged, and no case that had a sixty-day grace period was going to be sent to trial by the master-calendar court anywhere close to that January trial date. Scapio would only admit it to his closest friends, but he requested that sixty-day waiver due to the fact that he was going to Las Vegas in the middle of March for the NCAA college basketball tournament. March Madness is, after all, the greatest four days of sports wagering anywhere, and Scapio did not want to miss it. Despite his losses during the last basketball tournament, he was confident that this year would be better. He was shooting for early April as a trial target; that way, he could make his Las Vegas trip and still get back with plenty of time to continue trial preparation.

On January 9, both sides announced that they were ready for trial and for the change-of-venue motion. The master-calendar judge assigned the change-of-venue motion to Judge Darren Malek, a former prosecutor who was elected to fill a vacancy with the retirement of another judge. Malek had the reputation of being favorable to the prosecution on evidentiary issues but more neutral on sentencing. Scapio disagreed with the reputation and considered Malek just good on the law and fair. If the prosecution should get evidence in, such as the previous domestic-violence case, then it would be error to not allow it. Unfortunately, if the evidence was wrongfully excluded, unless the local appellate court would change the ruling right away, the prosecution had no remedy. Scapio considered Malek one of the best judges in Ventura but not one who favored either side.

Vandenbalk had considered what is known as "papering" the judge, which is disqualifying the judge for that case. It's called papering because to do that, you have to fill out a paper alleging that you don't believe that the judge can be fair to your side. Vandenbalk decided not to do that, as he doubted any judge was going to grant the motion, and he didn't want to burn his bridges with the judge because he may have to defend cases in his court in the future.

Malek heard the change-of-venue motion and denied it, sending the case back to the master-calendar courtroom.

The new Vandenbalk had decided he needed to get on Scapio's good side because he had a trip to the Bahamas with his wife planned for May and did not want to have to cancel. When Scapio suggested early April for the trial date, Vandenbalk knew they could end up starting on a day that would wipe out his vacation. They settled on a June 9 trial date with a last day in late August. This would likely mean that the biggest trial of Scapio's career would begin around the middle of August.

Vandenbalk had decided that when he saw how prepared Scapio and even Holdman was for the preliminary hearing, rushing things would not have a beneficial outcome. He needed to make sure that if there was a conviction, no appellate lawyer could say that McCarty did not get good representation. Time gave Vandenbalk an alternate suspect. They were gonna go with the previous ex-boyfriend theory. In the DA's office, this was called the "SODDI defense"—Some Other Dude Did It.

* * *

Tuesday, May 23, was a big day for Sam Vandenbalk. He had returned from the Bahamas trip the previous Saturday and had lined up a practice presentation for Frank Andrews. Andrews was going to have cross-examination sessions with Vandenbalk and two associates who had only been in court for the first appearance but would also be present for the trial.

Craig Atherton was a graduate of Pepperdine School of Law. Young-looking, blond, and an avid surfer, Atherton was looking to gain the confidence of his boss, so he practiced hard for this mock cross-examination. Atherton had worked for the Law

Office of Sam Vandenbalk for three years and was hoping to get his own caseload. Elizabeth (Beth) Delaney was a Cal Western law school graduate and had been captain of the UC Irvine undergraduate women's volleyball team. She was in her fourth year with Vandenbalk and had handled one case on her own, which resulted in a plea to a lesser charge. Both Atherton and Delaney wanted more independence and their own cases, but it was tough to leave because Vandenbalk paid well.

Vandenbalk's office was in the downtown area on Poli Street and near Ventura High School. Vandenbalk set up their PowerPoint presentation, and direct went very smoothly. He was very happy as Andrews explained, in painstaking detail, how blood-spatter interpretation relied entirely on the laws of physics and aerodynamics and that he was well credentialed in both. He explained that it did not matter that he had never been to a crime scene, because science and mathematics are intertwined, and viewing crime-scene photos, diagrams, and most importantly, distances, should allow him to extrapolate conclusions based upon known science provided in the documentation.

Andrews went through each photograph in detail, flipping to the autopsy report and photos to explain how there should have been more blood on the shirt and shoes if the blood came from the murder.

Without counting a couple of breaks, the practice direct examination lasted about two hours and twenty minutes. Adding one twenty-minute break would bring the total time to two hours, forty minutes. That would take them to about 4:30 p.m., given that the afternoon session in a courtroom generally starts at 1:30. Vandenbalk knew that objections add time, but there are very few objections during experts' direct. Any objections are resolved during the motions in limine—motions before trial that limit the scope of the evidence and testimony.

Scapio had filed Holdman's trial brief, and it didn't seek to limit the scope of Andrews's testimony. Vandenbalk was familiar with Andrews's work enough to know that virtually every prosecutor had filed a motion to exclude Andrews's testimony because he had never been to a crime scene and had never taken a course on blood-spatter interpretation.

Prosecutors always failed to keep him off the stand, but they always successfully limited his testimony to saying that he "would expect to see," but he was almost never allowed to reach an ultimate conclusion like "this blood could not have come from this murder." Here, Andrews's report said flat-out in its conclusion, "Based upon the limited amount of blood on both the shirt and the shoes, it is my opinion that the blood on the shirt and the blood on the shoes are from some unknown event unrelated to the murder and that the blood belonging to the victim on the shirt and shoes did not come from the occasion of her homicide."

Courts should limit this, Vandenbalk thought; he knew that on only one prior occasion had the above opinion slipped in. Courts do not allow expert witnesses to do what is called invading the province of the jury. That means giving the ultimate opinion. Here he would be able to say that he would expect more blood if this was related to the murder, but neither Scapio nor Holdman had moved to limit this. Vandenbalk thought either Scapio was not as good as he was cracked up to be, or he had something up his sleeve. Vandenbalk just could not fathom how Scapio benefited by having the jury hear that the defense expert believes that Scapio's most critical evidence is not related to the killing.

Vandenbalk noted that Scapio had blood-spatter expert Sean Murphy on his list. Vandenbalk had cross-examined Murphy before and was aware of how good he was. His strategy was going to be to not do much on cross-examination at all, because Murphy was not rendering an opinion on whether there should have been more blood or about the same amount. What Vandenbalk focused on was that neither witness's reports discussed where nor how the blood got there. Neither Murphy nor the state's DNA expert gave the opinion that the blood was from the murder. To add that now would impair their credibility, since it was not in either's report. They would look so desperate to help the prosecutor that they would add a game-changing additional fact in the middle of trial that was never in their reports. Vandenbalk would love for them to do that. Murphy was going to testify to the same conclusions that he gave Cuevas and Rollins at the scene, including the fact that the killer would likely have gotten blood on his clothes, but he was not giving an opinion as to how much blood there would be.

Once the practice direct examination was completed, the cross-examinations began. Delaney went first and asked Andrews the basics, such as how much he was paid and how often he testified for the defense and how often for the prosecution. Andrews handled it smoothly, noting that his testimony was almost exclusively defense because almost all prosecution agencies had their own labs and their own department experts. Delaney then asked, "You declined to meet with me and my investigator, isn't that right?"

Andrews said, "That's correct."

"Isn't it true that Mr. Vandenbalk would not let you speak with me?"

Andrews chuckled, turned to the imaginary jurors, and said, "Let's just put it this way; he wasn't offering to pay me and neither were you, and I do charge for my time."

Delaney added, "So you are not willing to speak to the other side unless you get paid, isn't that right?"

Andrews replied, "I'm talking to you now and he is paying me"—pointing to Vandenbalk—"so take all the time you need. I'm a scientist, but I don't work for free. I wouldn't talk to him, either, if he didn't pay me."

Delaney was a little flustered by the response but came back with the fact that Andrews had never been to the crime scene or any crime scene. Andrews replied that the latter was not true, and Delaney's eyes lit up. She said, "Didn't you testify in 2012 that you had never been to a crime scene?" Andrews answered with a casual yes. Delaney therefore asked, "So you have been to a crime scene since 2012?"

Andrews answered, "Yes, my car was stolen last year, so I consider that a crime scene, but other than that, no."

Vandenbalk interrupted and said, "No, Frank, don't do that. You're coming off too smug there. If the prosecutor asks if you have ever been to a crime scene, you can say, 'Well, my car got stolen last year, and I consider that a crime scene, but never to analyze evidence.'" Vandenbalk emphasized that Delaney would have scored points with the jury and Andrews would have looked like he was playing games.

Vandenbalk also said that Andrews needed to tone down the "I don't talk unless I get paid" attitude; they would need to make it sound less flippant. He suggested that Andrews just say,

"I do have to charge for my time, and nobody offered me financial compensation for such a meeting."

Delaney then cross-examined on the idea that the amount of blood there should be was just speculation. Andrews disagreed, saying, "The laws of physics don't vary, so you need to understand the laws of physics, which are much the same as mathematics." He added that two plus two is always going to be four and you don't have to keep adding it every time. "Blood spatter is the same way. If you know the angle and depth of the wound, you can calculate force used, and knowing the properties of blood, you can calculate the approximate degree and amount of spatter within a certain range. If you are close, you can't be sure, but here I can tell you with great confidence that the laws of physics dictate that there absolutely should be much more blood than we have here, if this was from the murder.

"Now, your theory about the bloodstains being evidence could only be right if there was lots more blood. That means, what? The killer did a fantastic job of cleaning up about half of it and then just decided, 'OK, good enough, I'm getting tired'? I just don't think that is reasonable." Vandenbalk was absolutely giddy with that answer.

Delaney then moved to the issue that Andrews couldn't prove his theory by example, "because we can't stab someone a bunch of times and then compare spatter patterns."

Andrews said, "Of course not, but the great thing about science is you do not need to. If you understand the laws of physics, you apply them; you don't have to kill anyone. Now, there are a few researchers who slaughter pigs whose skin constitutes a thickness close to humans in the animal kingdom." Andrews turned to the imaginary jury and said, "I myself would never do that; I am an animal lover. But with the laws of physics being discernable and applicable, I don't have to do that which I would never do."

Delaney decided to cut her losses and said, "No further questions."

Vandenbalk was thrilled. He had read a transcript where Andrews had used that example, but Andrews had perfected it here.

Next up was Atherton. He asked some of the same questions and went into the fact that many experts are of the opinion that there are too many variables to determine how much blood there should be. Andrews acknowledged that, but added that "they are not physicists. They do not apply the laws of physics. Those experts can tell you what a particular spatter pattern looks like based on their extensive training on that. They can distinguish between different types of spatter patterns and say whether it is blunt force, sharp force, or gunshot wounds. But they can only tell you what you do see; what they can't tell you is what you should see. You need physics to tell you that."

Atherton had done some research to impress his boss, and he cross-examined on a police-shooting case where Andrews had testified that because the police shot the victim twice in the back, the shooting was not justified. This was a federal civil suit out of LA County. Andrews acknowledged that he did testify to that. Then Atherton asked if he was familiar with a study done at the University of Minnesota at Mankato that concluded that justified shootings often do occur to the back because a suspect turns around with a gun, sees the officer with a gun, and then turns around; the officer shoots, but the shot hits the back because of officer reaction time.

At this point, Vandenbalk said, "I would object here, and would have done so before you got your last question out, as this is way too far afield." Vandenbalk added, "Most judges would exclude this, but you never know, so I want to see where this goes."

Andrews said he was not familiar with the study but knows that the University of Minnesota at Mankato has a law enforcement training center, and their research is likely to skew toward justifying shootings. He added that the author of the study is known to frequently justify police shootings, and in Andrews's opinion, he is biased. Andrews said that he was unfamiliar with the variables and controls the study applied, so he really couldn't comment on it. He said that he stood by his testimony in that matter, as did the jury in their finding.

Atherton then got to the one area that Delaney had planned to cross-examine Andrews on but, becoming distracted, skipped it. She was kicking herself mentally when she sat down. Atherton asked whether Andrews disputed the DNA results that the victim's blood was on the shirt and shoes recovered from the trash can. Andrews replied that he did not have any reason to dispute it.

Atherton then asked, "Assuming it's the victim's blood, do you have an alternate theory of how it got there?" Andrews said that he had never spoken with any witnesses; he had only examined the physical evidence. Atherton asked if Andrews was aware of any other incident where the defendant got the victim's blood on him. Andrews said that he had not been given a family history and he did not have that information. What he could say was that the blood could not have come from the murder, but he did not have sufficient information to know where it did come from. Atherton continued but broke little ground after that.

This was the one area of concern that Vandenbalk had, and he had really wanted to see how Andrews might handle it. It was a dangerous area for a prosecutor to explore, however, and Scapio would never ask that question. Scapio would only argue that there was no evidence that explained how the blood got there other than the murder. If the defense has a story, the expert can give the story the defendant gave him without the defendant being subject to cross-examination. If you ask the expert and they say, "Yes, I believe the blood got there because . . ." you have committed prosecutorial malpractice. Atherton did not have the experience, and he would have made a potentially big mistake, had he actually been the prosecutor and the defendant had an explanation.

McCarty denied the crime but had no explanation of how his blood got on the shirt and shoes. Vandenbalk suddenly thought of that and said, "Maybe we can subtly suggest to McCarty that he think of an alternate way the blood could have gotten on his shirt. That way, Frank, if the prosecutor does ask that question, you can crush him with a believable answer that they cannot cross-examine."

Lanny had come up empty on corruption, aka dirt, on Cuevas and Rollins. The only thing he had was Cuevas got written up for accepting about ten free meals from a local Mexican restaurant as a rookie, and he said that the restaurant comped police. Five other officers received write-ups for the same thing. It was a long time ago, and it was a violation of department policy that Cuevas said he was not even aware of. There was no evidence that the restaurant received any perks in exchange. On Rollins there was nothing. A police-planting defense was unlikely to be successful. Therefore, the jury was going to have to accept Andrews without an alternate explanation for the blood. He thought Andrews handled the questions as well as could be.

Vandenbalk was beaming with excitement at the conclusion of the mock cross-examinations. He asked Andrews how his lawyers did compared to most of his opponents. Andrews said they were better than most prosecutors. Few prosecutors have a science background, and he added that no prosecutor has ever really laid a glove on him. He explained, "I don't win every case, but that is because some cases are almost impossible." Vandenbalk asked him what he thought of this one. Andrews said, "It's tough but not impossible. I think we can win it."

On his way home, Vandenbalk was fantasizing about the verdict as he played out in his mind the jury foreperson handing the bailiff a note, who then gives it to the judicial assistant, who stands up and the judge says, "The court's judicial assistant will read the verdict." The judge asks the defendant to rise. He does, and the judicial assistant, also called the clerk, reads, "Superior Court of California, County of Ventura, case number 2016023575: People of the State of California, plaintiff, versus Allen Jeffrey McCarty, defendant. We, the jury in the above-titled action, find the defendant, Allen Jeffrey McCarty, not guilty of the crime of murder in violation of Penal Code section 187."

It was music to Vandenbalk's ears as he imagined embracing his client and becoming an absolute legend in not just Ventura but the entire country, and Ray Scapio would be the next Marcia Clark. Vandenbalk believed it could happen. The case rested on one witness. Frank Andrews was one heck of a compelling witness. Vandenbalk really believed he could win.

EIGHT

It was Halloween night 2017, and Daisy Guzman always loved Halloween. As a kid, she loved dressing up and going trick-or-treating. As an adult, she just loved dressing up and partying with friends. She made plans with her best friend Veronica (Nikki) Gonzalez.

Veronica and Daisy had been inseparable since high school. They were the part of the group of popular girls but were not elitist about it. Some referred to the two as the "pretty Mexican girls"; the majority of girls in their social clique were white. Veronica was taller than Daisy at five foot six and had lighter-colored hair. In high school, Veronica dyed it blond for a while but later went back to her natural color, medium brown, though she would often tint her hair with purple or red coloring. Veronica's skin tone was slightly lighter than Daisy's and her hair was a lot lighter, but Veronica and Daisy still looked close enough to be sisters.

In 2017, Veronica was working at the pharmacy at CVS in Oxnard. She'd recently ended a relationship with a boyfriend she caught cheating on her, so she and Daisy were both newly single and excited about hanging out on Halloween.

Veronica and Daisy came from different socioeconomic backgrounds. Veronica's father owned a car dealership in Oxnard and was a multimillionaire, but he wanted his kids to go to public school. Daisy had been middle-class when she lived in East Ventura, but her family was lower-middle-class after her father fell on tough times and the family moved to the Avenue. It was never an issue with Nikki and Daisy. Nikki came from family money but she always had to work and never thought more of herself because she had that family wealth.

Daisy drove to Veronica's apartment in Oxnard near the beach. Daisy was dressed as an Aztec princess with long dangling earrings and a very open sleeveless dress showing lots of skin. Daisy would be turning heads all night long, as would her best friend. When Veronica opened the door to greet Daisy, she was dressed as Wonder Woman. That is, if Wonder Woman ever had her hair tinted purple.

Daisy hugged her, then rolled her eyes and said, "Isn't that like the fourth time in the last six years you've been Wonder Woman?"

Veronica replied, "I like Wonder Woman."

Daisy shook her head and said, "Whatever," then added, "You do make a great Wonder Woman, though. I tried it one year, remember? I'm too short."

Aztec princess and Wonder Woman went to a party at their mutual high school friend Jennifer Weinberg's house in Ventura. There were some really amusing costumes at the party. One guy went as the closeted anti-gay rights politician who got caught toe tapping for sex in a men's room stall. The costume came complete with a makeshift cardboard bathroom stall. Daisy only figured out what it was when she read the sign on the cardboard and saw the guy tapping his toes. Daisy showed it to Nikki and the two busted up laughing.

Another guy had a Notre Dame football jersey with the name Quasimodo on the back and what looked like it could be a lot of toilet paper plus a Nerf football attached to his back and covered by the jersey, making him the hunchback of Notre Dame. Daisy and Veronica didn't get the joke, since neither had seen the movies or read the novel to know who Quasimodo was. Both girls just thought the costume was mean because it seemed to make fun of the disabled.

Daisy and Veronica both figured out the girl standing in the middle of a bottom-cut-out painted-white trash can with lots of crumpled up newspapers and empty soda cups attached to the sides. Daisy and Veronica went up to the girl, stared for about ten seconds and simultaneously broke out laughing, pointing to the girl and saying, "white trash." Daisy told the young woman that her costume was awesome and that she should win the costume contest, and Nikki agreed. The young blond woman, who was probably in her early twenties, thanked them and said she loved their costumes too.

They stayed there until midnight, then went to downtown Ventura and hung out at a couple of bars, giving their numbers to a couple of guys they met that seemed nice. They then went to Pirates Grub and Grog on Oxnard Boulevard in Oxnard. At 4:00 a.m., Veronica drove them back to her house. Daisy had been drinking, so she stayed at Veronica's until about 7:00 a.m. and then drove back home sober, as she had to be at work at ten that morning.

When Daisy went to start her car for work, it wouldn't start. She pounded the steering wheel in frustration and threw her arms up in the air and cursed a couple of times. She was about to get her phone out of her purse and call Victoria's Secret and the Auto Club when she heard a rapping on her passenger window and looked up. She saw a man she recognized.

He said it looked like she was having car trouble and that he knew a little about cars, and he asked for permission to take a look. Daisy popped open the hood. The man fiddled with a couple of things and then said, "OK, try and start her now." Daisy tried but the engine would not turn over at all, so she just put her arms in the air and made a sad face. The man said he could give her a lift if she needed to get somewhere.

Daisy smiled and said, "OK, I work at Pacific View Mall, at Victoria's Secret."

"OK, get into my van and I'll give you a ride, save you the cost of an Uber."

Daisy got out of her car and the man got into a gray van. Daisy climbed into the front seat of the van, smiled, and reached out her hand and said, "I'm Daisy, by the way."

He shook her hand and said, "Jack, Jack Macklin—people just call me Mack."

NINE

November 4, 2017, was a beautiful Saturday night. Halloween was being celebrated late because it fell on the previous Tuesday, so Nordhoff High School football players Jabari Clemons, Matt Lyle, and Alvan Williams attended a party in Ojai near the school.

Several of the football players and their friends were going to be there. Williams was dressed as a masked wrestler. A star athlete in high school, Williams pulled off the wrestler look nicely. At five foot ten and two hundred pounds of solid muscle, Williams was the tailback for the team, and he put up some great numbers.

Williams and Clemons were two of the few African American students at Nordhoff. The small school with under 800 students had 40 percent minority enrollment, but the vast majority were Hispanic.

Clemons played both offense and defense. He was a cornerback on defense and wide receiver on offense, and he ran a 4.41 forty, which made him the fastest player on the team. His was excellent, not elite speed, but it was the best on a high school team at a small school. He was dressed as *Friday the 13th* killer Jason with the hockey mask and fake machete.

When Clemons, who was driving, stopped at Lyle's house to pick him up, Lyle opened the door and saw Jabari standing there in his *Friday the 13th* mask. Lyle said, "Great costume. Are you Black Friday?" Clemons took off the mask and just started laughing. Lyle was a blond-haired white kid from Minnesota who played tight end on the football team and power forward for the basketball team. Lyle was known for his quick wit and humor.

In 2017, it was certainly politically incorrect to kid people about their race, but with these three, almost nothing was off limits. On one day in particular, when several other students saw and heard the exchange and could not stop laughing about it, Clemons had yelled at Lyle, "Hey, how's your privileged white ass doing?" and Lyle replied, "You're just jealous 'cause you're black and you suck at basketball. How the fuck did that even happen? Didn't your dad ever tell your mom they should trade you for a kid that could hoop?"

Clemons responded with, "Damn, you're even slow for a white dude. Last game there's twenty seconds left and Sullivan [the team's QB] said, 'OK, Lyle, you go deep,' and I said, 'Man, there's only twenty seconds left in the game—it's gonna be over before he gets deep.'"

Williams usually didn't get in on the banter, but he would burst out laughing with each comment. Lyle and Clemons were like two standup comics and Williams was the audience that could not get enough of the act. But Williams was a physical football player and he liked to carry it over, for fun, in the hallway. If you were Alvan Williams's friend—and everyone that knew him was—and he was coming toward you in the hallway with that big infectious smile on his face, he was going to lean his shoulder into you and bump you to the side. Even if you saw it coming and moved away, he was still going to bump you and then laugh with glee. This behavior earned Williams the nickname "the Bull." Estrogen was the only way out, because he didn't do it to girls, although he did fake it a couple of times. If you were a guy and you were his friend, he was shoulder bumping you, as sure as the sun rises. It did match his running style, as he often bumped and ran through would-be tacklers rather than try to elude them.

The party broke up around 11:00 p.m., and the three left in Clemons's Dodge pickup truck. Their costumes were now in the back seat; they'd brought a change of clothes. Clemons hadn't been drinking because he was driving, and neither Williams nor Lyle was heavily intoxicated. Clemons, as a lot of young people did, often drove too fast, though not so much in traffic. On this night, Clemons was racing up Matilija Canyon Road to turn onto Highway 33. Just as he heard Williams shout, "Look out!" a dark figure stepped out of nowhere into the roadway. Clemons saw the man turn his head, and the next thing he saw was a body hurtling toward his right passenger windshield. The windshield cracked—the sound was loud—and the man went flying into the grass on the side of the road.

Clemons pulled over and all three of the young men were looking for the body when they saw a man in dark clothing lying unconscious on the side of the road. They thought for certain he was dead, and Clemons was moaning, "I didn't see him, he came out of nowhere, oh my God, I killed him."

Lyle said, "We gotta call 911." Williams was asking where the man came from. Lyle said that he stepped out from the side of the road; he had caught a glimpse of him as they were approaching the turn, but he didn't think the man would actually step out into the roadway.

Just as Lyle got his phone out, the man made a low moaning noise and then sat up. He was wearing a black hoodie with blue lining and dark-gray pants that were like sweatpants but a little different. They were baggier with very wide pockets. He shook his head back and forth as if to clear it. He looked to be a man in his early thirties with short brown hair that was messy, like he really didn't care. His eyes were dark brown and set wide apart, and his ears were quite small. He was not ugly, but he was a bit odd looking. He was either white or possibly light-skinned Hispanic as best they could tell, but even that was just a guess.

Clemons asked what he was doing stepping into the road. The man simply said he was lost. He was craning his neck and shaking his shoulders wildly as if trying to shake something off. Then he checked his pockets and looked relieved, stopping the odd neck and shoulder movements, and just said, "I'm OK."

He stood only about five foot seven but appeared well-conditioned, with little body fat. Williams asked his name and the man said he was Zack Morgan. Clemons said, "Well, Zack Morgan, there is a hospital nearby, and we have to get you there." Morgan said he did not want to go to a hospital and said he would be fine. He started to stand up but couldn't put any weight on his right ankle; he started to fall back down as Williams and Lyle grabbed him and held him up.

Williams and Lyle both noticed that the man seemed heavier than he looked, but being young strong athletes, they didn't have that much trouble moving him. Morgan repeated that he did not want to go to a hospital, but he put up no resistance. When they got to the car, they placed Morgan in the back seat with Lyle and put the costumes on the floor.

Clemons gave Williams the key to the truck and said he couldn't drive right now because he was shaken up. Williams said that was understandable. Clemons asked Williams if he knew how to get to Ojai Hospital, and Williams assured him that he did.

Clemons was apologizing to Morgan, who said it was not Clemons's fault and that he, Morgan, should not have been where he was. Clemons said his dad was gonna kill him. Williams arrived at the hospital and parked the truck at the ER entrance.

The three young men carried Morgan out of the car. Morgan was able to put some weight on the ankle but still needed help to walk. They made it to the hospital waiting room, and hospital staff asked Morgan to fill out a form. Morgan said he didn't have his wallet with him, and he had no ID on him. Realizing that he had no insurance information, the ER desk clerk asked him who his insurance carrier was, and Morgan said he had insurance, but it might have expired.

Clemons explained to the admitting nurse what happened and was informed that the sheriff's department would be called to take a report and to photograph the vehicle. Morgan said that it was not needed and it was his fault.

After the deputy arrived, the young men gave a statement of what occurred, and then the deputy questioned Morgan, who said that his head hurt like hell and the accident was his fault, and he had nothing else to say. The deputy, a middle-aged

Filipino man named Gabriel Saqui, asked Morgan what he remembered about the accident. Morgan said that he was going across the highway when he saw the car at the last second. He tried to avoid it, and the next thing he remembered was waking up with his head pounding and three young men trying to help him. Deputy Saqui asked him what he did to get out of the way, and Morgan said he thought that he jumped.

At this point, Saqui began asking Morgan where he had been and where he was going, and Morgan answered that he didn't have to answer questions. He said he didn't mean any disrespect, but he was not feeling like answering questions. Deputy Saqui asked Morgan where he lived and Morgan said he stayed with different friends sometimes but was basically homeless and didn't have a phone. Saqui did get Morgan's height and weight for the report at five foot seven and 155 pounds, and Morgan gave his date of birth as September 4, 1983. Saqui sensed something was off about Morgan and asked again where Morgan was going at eleven at night, and Morgan told him that he already told him he was not getting into that.

When Saqui left, Morgan thought about leaving, but his ankle hurt and he figured he wouldn't get very far. He felt around his skin to see if he had any cuts or was bleeding, but there was nothing.

After waiting another forty-five minutes, Morgan was taken to a room that opened and closed with a curtain. A young nurse took his blood pressure and looked surprised, saying, "It's only 110 over 65; those are really low numbers for someone in an accident who is probably spending the night in ER." Morgan just nodded but didn't say anything. The nurse told Morgan that the doctor would be there soon.

About a half hour later, Dr. John Wong appeared. Wong appeared to be about thirty-five, with a very calm and pleasant demeanor. Immediately Morgan perked up and shook the doctor's hand as the doctor introduced himself. Morgan asked him about where he got his medical education, and Wong told him and assured Morgan he was qualified. Morgan politely said he was not questioning that at all but was just interested in the process.

Dr. Wong did a concussion exam. Morgan was able to pass some of the protocols, but it was obvious he was not fully recovered. He also said that his head felt cloudy. The doctor moved the ankle back and forth and asked Morgan if it hurt with each movement. Morgan said that it was hurting a little with a few of the movements but not nearly as badly as it was before.

Dr. Wong conducted a thorough examination and determined that Morgan likely had a concussion, a mildly sprained ankle, and a shoulder bruise. He said that due to the likely concussion, Morgan was going to stay overnight. He explained that Morgan would not get much sleep, because the nurses would do neuro checks in the room every couple of hours. Morgan said that he expected that would be the case. Morgan would be hooked up to a monitor so they could make sure they could reach him quickly if there were any issues, but staying at the hospital was the best and safest thing in concussion cases.

The doctor said that it was very unlikely Morgan would experience any complications but if he did, he was in good hands, and that he should relax and try to get some sleep and he would check on him in the morning. Morgan said he understood, and began asking some questions about the monitor, which Wong found odd. The admitting documents listed Morgan as jobless and homeless, yet he seemed highly intelligent and had an obvious interest in the technology of the monitor. Wong also noticed that Morgan was unusually well spoken.

Deputy Saqui had worked patrol for the last six years and had taken many accident reports. He inspected and photographed Clemons's—well, it was registered to Clemons's father—Dodge Dakota pickup truck. The damage was all to the front right passenger windshield. The windshield was cracked like a spiderweb, but no glass went inside the vehicle. Saqui just had a weird feeling about this whole thing.

Morgan had to be hiding something. The physical evidence matched the witnesses' stories, but it just did not seem right to him. Saqui had the same thoughts about Morgan as Dr. Wong. Something was not quite right about this guy, but his reasons for thinking that were very different from Dr. Wong's.

On Sunday, November 5, Dr. Wong was waiting to give the family members of a young woman some awful news. He stopped by Zack's room and told him that his vitals looked great and he was free to go. He told Morgan that there would be some paperwork for him to sign at the front desk. Morgan thanked him and shook his hand and said that he would be waiting in the lobby for a ride and would take off when they arrived, but he wasn't sure how long that would be. Dr. Wong said that would be fine, they were not going to be too busy on a Sunday. But he also mentioned that there was a family coming in, and he wished he could give them the same good news he had given Morgan.

TEN

Frank Andrews anticipated that he might get cross-examined on some of his prior testimony, so he reviewed some of the transcripts he'd saved. He'd heard Scapio was good, and that meant Scapio was probably researching past testimony. Andrews knew he'd best look at everything to make sure he didn't contradict himself. He wanted to focus on past cases involving blood spatter and use of force. He figured he didn't need to review his accident-reconstruction testimony as that is a totally unrelated field, and he wouldn't expect to be cross-examined on speed–skid ratios and other complexities of that field. He understood that Scapio didn't have a science background and was unlikely to battle him on his turf.

Andrews was thinking he couldn't guarantee the jury would acquit or even be hung. He was concerned, as Vandenbalk was, that he didn't have a counter explanation for the blood on the shirt and shoes or for what appeared to be two fresh drops of blood belonging to McCarty inside Braden's home. McCarty's problem was that he hadn't been with Jessica Braden for over three weeks before her murder, so he couldn't come up with an explanation for having her blood spatter on a shirt and on shoes that he kept for over three weeks without washing and then coincidentally decided to throw out right when she got murdered.

Vandenbalk agreed with Andrews that letting the lawyer argue it's not defense's burden to offer an explanation would be much better than Andrews offering an explanation that got laughed out of the courtroom. Andrews couldn't predict the outcome, but he was confident that he was going to be easily able to handle what Scapio might throw his way.

* * *

Scapio was feeling pretty good about their preparation. After doing enough work on Andrews, he focused on cross-examination of the defendant, McCarty. He did not believe McCarty would take the stand, but he had to prepare, just in case. The biggest mistake that a prosecutor can make is assuming the defendant won't testify because they have prior convictions that will come in. If the defendant shuns the lawyer's advice and takes the stand and admits their past acts and says they took responsibility for those but did not do this one, the prosecutor is caught flat footed. In this case, McCarty was unlikely to testify due to the lack of a plausible explanation for the blood evidence. So Scapio prepared for something he figured would never happen.

He knew he was going to press McCarty on the shirt, shoes, and brassiere. Why would he have wiped his own blood on one of her bras? Obviously, he would ask him to explain how he got a significant amount of her blood on his shirt and shoes. Of course, when this alleged other incident occurred would be covered, as well as why he chose to throw them away that day. Scapio would also cover shutting off the phone.

Holdman had filed an excellent trial brief, and included within it was a motion to admit, and be allowed to cross-examine defendant on, his refusal to volunteer a DNA sample when asked. If allowed in, Scapio would cross-examine on that. He would cover the past domestic-violence complaints and McCarty's controlling behavior.

The initial police contact with McCarty had been audiotaped but not videotaped. Scapio and Holdman decided not to use it in their case because he made no admissions and did deny the killing. If the defense was going to get into evidence a denial beyond the mere plea of not guilty, it was going to have to come from the defendant. If he testified, then the audio, where he does not sound shocked and does not ask many questions, would have value.

Scapio worked on setting it up. "When the detectives came to you, you didn't know Jessica was dead, did you? Were you curious as to how she died? You didn't ask, did you? You say you didn't know who did it, right? But you didn't even ask if the police had made an arrest, did you? You didn't ask if they had a suspect, did you?"

On June 9, the official trial date, Scapio arrived in court wearing a navy-blue suit from Men's Wearhouse, a red silk tie, and a white dress shirt. That color combination was said to be the prosecutor's uniform. Scapio liked to start his trial very conventionally and conservatively dressed, but as the trial would go on, he would go bolder in the selection of attire. On the off chance they would get a courtroom assignment, Scapio wanted to be ready. Holdman always dressed conservatively, except for the bow ties. He always wore a bow tie.

Scapio and Holdman waited for Vandenbalk in Courtroom 14. All the jury trials and preliminary hearings are sent out from Courtroom 14. If both sides are ready and a courtroom is open, and if you are priority in terms of speedy trial, you get sent to a courtroom for your case unless one side or the other had filed paper against that judge. Scapio and Holdman had arrived at 8:30 a.m. and chatted up some of the young felony attorneys from the DA's office who had preliminary hearings.

Judge Nancy Maloney was the presiding judge there. She was appointed by Governor Brown in 2013 during his second stint as California's governor. She had been a civil and family law attorney from Simi Valley before that. Currently divorced and a devout dog lover, she lived with her three dogs in Santa Paula. She was considered very fair but was also very soft spoken and quite difficult to hear. Scapio never considered his hearing bad, but every time she set a new court date, he always found himself asking her to repeat it or saying, "Was that the fourteenth or the fifteenth?"

Vandenbalk arrived late, wearing a green sport coat with a gray tie and dark-gray pants that really didn't match the jacket. He was not dressed like he was expecting to start a jury trial. Scapio was of the same view; he told Goldberg, the victim advocate, to let the family know that they would likely not get a courtroom.

Judge Maloney called through the last-day cases. Those are the cases that have to get a courtroom or the charges are dismissed. If a judge is papered and there are no open courtrooms, the last day is extended one day, but each side gets only one judge disqualification. Two of the last-day cases got sent to trial, one was dismissed by motion of the district attorney, and the last one was a mutually agreed continuance.

After those cases were called, the next cases were called in the order that the defense attorneys lined up. Scapio had to wait another ten minutes due to Vandenbalk's late arrival. When it was their turn, the six or seven reporters in the courtroom leaned in to listen. Vandenbalk approached the lectern and said, "I request to call the Allen McCarty matter. Sam Vandenbalk for the defense; the defense is ready for trial."

Scapio then said, "Ray Scapio along with Woody Holdman for the people. The people are also ready for trial."

Judge Maloney said she had no courtrooms available that day and asked what the trial time estimate was. Scapio said it would be three to four weeks. Vandenbalk did not disagree. Judge Maloney said, in a louder voice than usual, probably as a courtesy to the media, that there was a sixty-day time waiver from that day, and that she would set the case for trial on August 21, adding, "You will still be about ten days away, but I know this is a murder case, so it is high priority, and I do anticipate I can find a courtroom for you on that date or soon after."

Scapio said, "Thank you, your honor," and he and Holdman began to walk away—when Vandenbalk asked if they could be assigned for all purposes to a judge that day to start on the twenty-first.

Judge Maloney looked exasperated with Vandenbalk's request and said, "Mr. Vandenbalk, I can't do that. I can't clog up one courtroom for that long. We have a really busy calendar, as you can see. I cannot set a specific courtroom aside and say they can't get any cases that would last five days as of four days from the twenty-first. I can't run the courthouse that way.

I understand this is a big case, but to the people who are in custody, they probably could care less about your case. The prosecutors and public defenders have other cases. Come back on the twenty-first and I will try to get you a courtroom, OK?" Vandenbalk and Scapio both said, "Thank you, your honor," and walked away.

Holdman said, "I guess she didn't like Vandenbalk's idea." Scapio said that if Vandenbalk had suggested approaching the bench and bringing that up, he would have advised him not to piss off Maloney, but Vandenbalk instead just came out with it. Scapio said he was surprised but not shocked, because Vandenbalk thinks there should be a separate set of rules for him.

* * *

Scapio now had some time before the McCarty trial, so in July he made a Las Vegas trip to hang out at the Mandalay Bay resort. He lounged by the pool and bet on baseball games for a full week and a day. He needed the baseball action because he had gone cold turkey on his bookie service since getting the McCarty case. He made a decent amount of money on the trip and even added some at the poker table a couple of nights.

The first week of August, Scapio actually pulled a practical joke on a young hotshot prosecutor who was being groomed for homicides. Kyle Irby never saw that one coming.

On Monday, August 21, Scapio and Holdman arrived in Courtroom 14 a little before 9:00 a.m. while the 8:30 preliminary hearings calendar was still being called.

Vandenbalk arrived with an entourage for the first time since the initial arraignment. Craig Atherton and Beth Delaney were there along with the defendant and his new girlfriend, a tall, attractive blond woman in her late twenties.

Vandenbalk introduced Scapio and Holdman to Atherton and Delaney and they shook hands. Vandenbalk leaned into Holdman and asked if he had his apology letter written yet. Holdman responded, "I think your client is supposed to write one for sentencing. That's where he tears up and hopes someone lets him out before he's ninety." Vandenbalk said, "We shall see," then asked if Scapio was ready. Scapio said he was and could not wait to get started. The Braden family was in the courtroom in the front row.

Judge Maloney called through the last-day cases, and none of them were sent to a trial court. Two pleaded guilty, one was dismissed, and two more were continued with time waivers. Vandenbalk was near the front of the line, and after a couple of cases were put over, Vandenbalk stepped to the lectern and called the McCarty case and announced that he was ready. He also introduced his two associates. Scapio said that he and Holdman were also ready. Judge Maloney assigned the case to Judge Darkoza in Courtroom 46.

Judge John Darkoza was fifty-eight years old and a former felony supervisor in the DA's office. He was well liked by the defense attorneys despite his being a former prosecutor. He was appointed by Governor Brown six years prior. Darkoza was from the Bay Area and went to Santa Clara undergrad and Boalt Hall law school. Boalt is, of course, UC Berkeley's law school. Berkeley is often referred to as Cal, and Darkoza was a huge Cal fan in sports. In fact, he jokingly told attorneys in his chambers when a case was sent to his courtroom that he was easygoing, that he understood that witness scheduling issues occur. If there was a problem, he would try to take the heat about keeping the jury waiting when he talked about the delays with the jury. He gave them an overview of the courtroom rules, which were standard, and then added that if he heard any comment from either attorney disparaging Cal football or basketball, "You will be held in contempt." He didn't mention Giants baseball, 49ers football, or Warriors basketball, but he had old ticket stubs from games he attended framed on the wall in his chambers.

The first time Scapio had a jury trial in Darkoza's courtroom was in 2015 when Scapio responded by asking whether it was OK to bash Santa Clara basketball.

Darkoza responded, "You went to Northridge; you can't be bashing anyone."

"You say that now, but in five years we will dominate the Big West."

"We played you once in your own house and beat you down by thirty points."

Scapio said Northridge had an academic scandal that year, so "we probably pulled a bunch of frat boys from the stands to field a team."

Darkoza said, "I was at that game; frat boys would have played better."

Scapio said, "Fortunately, I wasn't."

Scapio liked Darkoza and thought he would be just fine for this case. He didn't know him that well when he had been in the DA's office but thought he seemed like a nice guy and had heard good things about him as a supervisor.

Darkoza was married and had two adult sons. One was a criminal defense attorney in the Santa Barbara County Public Defender's Office. The other was a truck driver. Darkoza's wife was a teacher in the Camarillo School District. The Darkozas were very active in local charities and in the community.

Vandenbalk also was happy with the draw, although he only knew Darkoza by reputation. Vandenbalk was still aware that neither Scapio nor Holdman had voiced an objection intended to prevent Andrews from testifying to the ultimate opinion, that the blood on the shirt and the shoes could not have come from the murder.

Vandenbalk was ecstatic to have the strongest possible opinion from Andrews. He had been expecting to get a watered-down opinion like those he had gotten from previous experts he'd used. For example, a report that said, "Given the depth and number of stab and slash wounds in the case, I would expect more blood on the shirt and shoes than is present in this case," would be helpful, but it would leave open the possibility that you *could* have that much blood. Such a diluted opinion would be extremely unlikely to result in a jury finding reasonable doubt.

From Andrews, he got not only the opinion that if the blood was from the murder you would expect more blood, but that in his opinion the blood could not have come from this murder. This was critical, because with this testimony, Andrews was all Vandenbalk needed to sell to the jury. He did not have to sell his client, who would not testify. Only Andrews, whose testimony might just do it.

Vandenbalk had two things he was really hoping would happen in that first in-chambers meeting with Judge Darkoza. He felt that this first session might be as significant to the outcome of the case as anything that might happen in the trial.

Vandenbalk had scouted Scapio by asking other defense lawyers what some of his tendencies were. One defense attorney said that he had been known to file trial briefs and then bring up additional issues that he didn't brief, which he said were "simple and obvious."

Another point was that on juror questionnaires, Scapio had a question about whether the jurors had ever followed any high-profile cases and if so, which ones. That would be a way to allow him to talk about the OJ Simpson trial. Scapio liked to ask jurors who were old enough to have followed the case of the former football star's double murder trial in the mid-nineties, what their opinion of the case was. Anyone who agreed with the not-guilty verdict or expressed doubt about Simpson's guilt was kicked off the jury. Scapio likely saw it as an easy way to weed out jurors who distrusted law enforcement or who were skeptical of circumstantial evidence.

Vandenbalk knew Scapio was going to do that, because a week after he spoke to the attorney who told him about the OJ inquiry jury-selection strategy, Vandenbalk was emailed a copy of Scapio's proposed jury questionnaire, and sure enough, it included a question about which high-profile trials they may have followed.

As to the first issue, regarding Andrews's expert testimony, Vandenbalk was sure Scapio was going to ask Judge Darkoza to limit the scope. Scapio would be right on the law, but Vandenbalk's strategy was to argue that Holdman and Scapio had a chance to raise this in their trial brief but failed to do so. This was a key component of their defense, and limiting the scope of defense at the trial-court stage would be late notice. He would claim that he set a lot of his trial strategy around this testimony. He believed he would have a decent chance to prevail on that point.

They met in Judge Darkoza's chambers. The judge was a big man and former devoted weight lifter. About ten years earlier, he had to curtail weight lifting due to a major shoulder injury. At six foot three and around 220 pounds, down from his peak weightlifting days at over 250, he still looked intimidating, with a large round head, pale skin tone, 1960s sideburns, and thinning gray hair. He was a pleasant judge to try cases with, as long as you didn't try to showboat or violate an order he made.

Judge Darkoza said that he was excited to have this trial and he knew that he had two outstanding trial lawyers. The first thing the judge wanted to talk about was the ground rules. He did his thing about Cal sports, acknowledging Scapio when he said, "Ray, I know you have already heard this, but just so Sam understands . . ." Vandenbalk laughed and said he hoped his degree from Stanford Law would not be a problem. Darkoza said he never tired of the Stanford band touchdown play.

(In 1982's football game between Cal and Stanford, Stanford thought they had the game won, but on the final play, Cal received the kickoff with four seconds left, trailing after a field goal had given Stanford the lead behind quarterback John Elway. The Stanford band came onto the field, figuring the game was over. The Cal Bears received the kickoff and the band made it difficult for the players to maneuver, so after several laterals, Kevin Moen ran through the band and scored the winning touchdown.)

Darkoza added, "I still remember the name Kevin Moen, and whenever I get upset with my wife or kids or one of the lawyers in my courtroom, I YouTube the Stanford band play and I am at peace."

After that initial banter, they discussed scheduling and the media coverage. Darkoza emphasized that he intended to repeatedly warn the jurors not to read any stories, listen to the radio, or view any TV coverage about this case. He was going to tell them if it came on their TV, shut it off or change the channel, same with the radio. He added that the jurors were going to grow weary of him saying it, but they would get the message.

Everyone agreed that the media could be present for the trial. Vandenbalk was opposed to actual televising of the trial as Court TV had requested. Scapio took no position on it and did not want to get involved in the free-press arguments. Judge Darkoza indicated that he would allow press in the courtroom but would be unlikely to allow audio- or videotaping of the trial.

After ironing out scheduling matters, they discussed the questionnaire that Scapio was requesting to give the jurors. Vandenbalk objected to the question about high-publicity cases that the jurors may have followed and said that he heard Scapio did this to talk about the OJ case, and that should not be permissible. Scapio piped in, claiming this was the first time Vandenbalk had even mentioned an issue with the questionnaire.

What Scapio said was music to Vandenbalk's ears. Scapio complained about late notice and said that Vandenbalk had had the questionnaire for well over a month and never filed opposition. Judge Darkoza said that regardless of the notice issue, he thought it seemed like a fair question, but his ruling was not etched in stone. He pointed out that attorneys needed to know what evidence was coming in and what was not before opening statements, but the concept of what follow-up questions could be used from the questionnaire was fluid. He said that he would not allow a question on the questionnaire that would read "Do you think OJ did it, yes or no?" He explained that the questionnaire was something the jurors believed came from the court, and the OJ verdict was such a travesty that to put it in the questionnaire would make it look like the court was siding with the prosecutor, but this was different. Here the prosecution was proposing to ask his question as a follow-up. "That might be OK, but we will cross that bridge when he asks the question."

The judge advised Vandenbalk he could put his objection on the record where it could be reviewed by the court of appeal, should there be a conviction. (Chambers conferences rarely have court reporters unless it's during trial on something that can't be handled in open court.)

Vandenbalk knew that if Scapio brought up limiting Andrews's testimony, he was going to absolutely slam him with the late-notice argument Scapio just made. Vandenbalk was doing all he could to hide his excitement. He submitted a couple of questions he wanted added to the questionnaire and showed them to Scapio and the judge. Scapio said that he would have liked to have had them sooner so he wouldn't have to rush his secretary. He also added that the questions covering the concept of reasonable doubt were covered in question 16. Judge Darkoza looked at Scapio and told him that the additional questions went a little further than question 16, and he would have the entire afternoon to have the secretary add the questions to the questionnaire, so he was granting Vandenbalk's request.

Scapio then brought up his trial brief. The judge said that the prior domestic violence was coming in. The law was very clear on that. He said he wanted both sides to look at the limiting instructions that were to be given to the jury that would tell them evidence of prior domestic violence could only be used to show that defendant might have a tendency to commit domestic violence, but it was not sufficient to prove it beyond a reasonable doubt or to prove the crime charged beyond a reasonable doubt. If the jurors believed to a preponderance of the evidence that the alleged prior domestic violence occurred, they could weigh it how they chose, but it did not substitute for proof beyond a reasonable doubt. Vandenbalk said that he might request a stronger second instruction.

Judge Darkoza also said that evidence of the threats would be allowed under Evidence Code section 1370, but that Vandenbalk could put his objection on the record and make his argument during trial.

The last issue they discussed in chambers was Holdman's argument that McCarty's refusal to provide a DNA sample and demanding a warrant should be admitted. Scapio and Holdman had tentatively decided not to use it in their case, but they also wanted to keep their options open. It could open the door to McCarty's denial, but his failure to ask basic questions would also come in. Scapio and Holdman wanted to see how the trial played out before making the final decision. Judge Darkoza asked Scapio if he was prepared to do an opening statement without it. Scapio said that he was. Judge Darkoza gave a tentative ruling that the prosecution would not be allowed to use it during their case because requesting a warrant was a little different from a flat-out refusal. He did say that if the defendant should choose to testify, they could revisit the issue and he would hear additional argument.

Judge Darkoza asked both sides for a witness list, and Scapio handed the judge and Vandenbalk one and told the judge that there was also one attached to the questionnaire.

Vandenbalk was asked if there were any witnesses on his side, and he said, "You can add Frank Andrews to the list." Scapio made a note to add that name to the names on the back of the questionnaire. One of the questions was whether the prospective jurors knew any of the witnesses, and the witnesses were listed on the back of the page.

Judge Darkoza asked if there was anything else either side wanted to bring up. Scapio said oh yeah—and immediately Vandenbalk thought Scapio was gonna talk about Andrews's testimony. But he didn't. Scapio just said that he had pulled the jury instructions and he gave the judge and Vandenbalk a copy. Judge Darkoza said, "Thanks, but I always have my secretary pull these from my research. But I'll use these as a guide to make sure I didn't miss anything." With that, Judge Darkoza said they would go out and make their record.

They would take the afternoon off and start fresh in the morning with hardshipping jurors, referring to excusing jurors who had a valid reason for not serving on a trial that would last that long. A good reason would be financial hardship because the potential juror would lose pay, childcare or eldercare issues, physical disability, scheduled vacation, medical procedure, or missing class for students.

Scapio left happy that he would likely get to ask about the OJ trial, since he felt that would weed out potential jurors. Vandenbalk could hardly contain his glee. He said to himself, "Ray Scapio has to be the most overrated attorney ever. A first-year misdemeanor attorney might have known to exclude that." Vandenbalk thought Ray Scapio just lost the biggest case of his career and would probably be doing misdemeanor trials after this. Vandenbalk could not wait to get started.

* * *

The next day, the first panel of seventy jurors was called into the courtroom. Scapio would scan to see individual reactions when they heard the charges. As the jurors walked into the courtroom, he looked to see if jurors recognized McCarty. If anyone did, they did not let on. The bailiff did the "All rise" announcement after all the jurors had entered, announcing the name of the case and "the Honorable John Darkoza, presiding." Judge Darkoza entered and motioned for all to be seated, then introduced the parties to the case, who stood and introduced themselves. The clerk then called roll, announcing the jurors' names in alphabetical order.

Scapio paid close attention to this part and tried to match names to faces as each juror said that they were there. Scapio always looked for anything out of the ordinary. He once excused the eleventh juror on roll call because the first ten had said the word "here" when their name was called, and the eleventh juror said "present." Scapio's reason was that with everyone else using the less formal "here," the person who would deliberately stand out by announcing "present," the more formal term, might be the same person proud to be the sole holdout in an 11–1 hung jury. Scapio did not understand Vandenbalk's cockiness; Scapio believed that if they got twelve jurors to agree, it was going to be guilty.

Roll was called and only a couple of jurors stood out. He wanted to avoid women that might fall in love with McCarty, which was a danger in this type of case. One of the jurors in the trial of Richard Ramirez, the Night Stalker, fell in love with Ramirez and frequently visited him after his conviction. It was unlikely to be a problem with married women with children or those who were well educated, but there was no guarantee. This may be the reason that McCarty's new girlfriend would be completely absent from the trial. A potential obsessed fan might be turned off by the presence of a girlfriend.

Scapio would say it's hard to describe it, but he was looking for a weird vibe, a gut feeling. Scapio subscribed to the "when in doubt, they are out" theory of jury selection. The last thing you want to do is leave a juror on that you had doubts about. If you have a strong case, the best-case scenario is the jury convicts, but you had unnecessary agony worrying about having kept a juror on that maybe should have been excluded. Worst-case scenario is they hang your jury and then you are kicking yourself, trying the case again, and losing lots of sleep.

Jury selection is part science and part gut instinct. To avoid a hung jury, you want people who will get along, and you don't want people whose personalities may clash with others. The prosecution does not benefit from an ally who alienates the jurors who disagree. The angry nasty ally just makes the opposing jurors dig in their heels more.

That said, how you interact with jurors during the questioning process, known as voir dire, is critical. Many people, including Scapio, remember the other high-profile case that got almost as much coverage as OJ, and that was Scott Peterson. There was a young woman on the jury the media referred to as "Strawberry Shortcake" because of her dyed-red hair and tattoos. The pundits repeatedly criticized the prosecution for leaving this juror on. One famous pundit even speculated that this juror would hang the trial. Strawberry Shortcake turned out to be one of the prosecution's staunchest advocates for both guilt and death.

Another juror in that trial was dismissed early in the trial for reasons that were not made clear. The juror, a twenty-eight-year-old airport screener, gave interviews critical of the prosecution and very supportive of an acquittal, even though the prosecution had not rested its case yet. Scapio remembered seeing the interview and remembered thinking, "Good thing they got that idiot out of there, hope nobody else is that stupid." There was one juror who seemed friendly with the man even though jurors are forbidden to talk about the case until deliberations. Some of the media pundits began speculating that the juror who was friendly with the dismissed juror would be an acquittal vote but they also turned out completely wrong about him. This juror was another of the strongest prosecution jurors in the case. It just shows the inexact science of reading people.

* * *

The initial phase was screening the jurors for hardships. The attorneys gave a three-week estimate, but the judge added another week and agreed they would seat three alternates in case they lost any jurors. Of the seventy jurors called into the courtroom, more than half declared a hardship. The most common reason given for the hardship was not getting paid for jury duty by their employers. The second most common cause of hardships was that people had scheduled vacations. This was the summer, and that is when jury duty most often conflicts with scheduled vacations.

Once those twenty-eight jurors who could serve were given questionnaires to fill out, they were sent to the Jury Assembly Room on the first floor near the elevators, and the closest exit to the courthouse cafeteria, to fill out the questionnaires and leave them at the reception window at the Jury Assembly Room. Scapio would later go to the Jury Assembly and collect the questionnaires and have copies made for the judge and the defense attorney as well as Holdman and Conway.

After a half-hour break, another seventy panelists were sent in. The Braden family stayed outside throughout this process because there was no room for family members in the courtroom; every seat, including those in the jury box, would have to be filled by prospective jurors.

The second batch of panelists included two jurors who tried to claim hardship based on their lack of trust for the system. They were denied a hardship excuse on that basis. The judge told them to fill out questionnaires and those concerns could be discussed later.

This second batch had fewer people who were unable to serve. One young juror claiming hardship obviously did not want to serve but he seemed to get his excuses wrong. His first excuse related to his company not being able to lose him for that long. Judge Darkoza told him that hardship to your employer is not one of the recognized grounds. Darkoza asked him whether he would get paid while on jury duty and he said he thought so for a while but wasn't sure for how long. Judge Darkoza said that he would like the young man to check with his employer at a break and find out if that would be a hardship.

The young man then said he had a vacation but when asked when it was, he gave a date that was over a week past when they thought they were going to be finished. When the judge informed him of that, the young man was exasperated and said, "I think I'll just go with whatever the cops say. If they think he did it then I will go with that." Judge Darkoza explained that what he was saying, even if true, could be explored later but was not the basis for hardship.

Once the list of jurors who could not serve was complete for the second panel of seventy, Judge Darkoza had the attorneys approach the bench and the judge read off the names of those that qualified for a hardship. The first group was obvious but this time Vandenbalk suggested the young man who said he would believe the cops. Vandenbalk's point was that the young man was obviously lying, and he was never going to stay on the jury. Judge Darkoza said that he did not think there was a legal hardship, but if both sides agreed, then he would add the juror to the ones to be excused. Judge Darkoza asked Scapio if he was willing to agree to add the juror to the excused list. Scapio turned to Holdman and nodded. Scapio turned to the judge and said that was fine, he could be included on the list. Judge Darkoza then said that the parties were stipulating to the removal of the juror. For that panel, thirty-one jurors filled out questionnaires.

They now had fifty-nine jurors filling out questionnaires. Both sides get twenty peremptory challenges, a challenge to a juror where no reason need be given. The side exercising the challenge simply says that they request to thank and excuse the juror.

The exception to the rule is a challenge made for an impermissible reason, such as race or gender. If the other side contests a challenge, the side asking that the juror be excused must show a race-neutral reason for the dismissal of the juror. This is known as a Batson/Wheeler motion by the defense. US v Batson was the case where the Supreme Court ruled that challenges may not be used to exclude people by race or gender. People v Wheeler was the California case holding the same.

Each side gets an unlimited amount of challenges for cause but must show that the challenged juror shows actual prejudice against their side. Defense attorneys tend to be able to use more of these. Sometimes it's the nature of the crime. Challenges for cause are frequent in driving-under-the-influence cases, since jurors may have lost a loved one to an intoxicated driver. Cases involving the use of a firearm can generate strong emotions from jurors. Strangely enough, murder cases actually generate fewer challenges of this type than other crimes such as drunk driving. Even people who know someone who was murdered understand that the prosecution has to prove who did it. Driving-under-the-influence cases often involve the gray area of how much is too much. The family member who lost a loved one to an intoxicated driver is not often open to that gray area. "If you drank and drove, then you are guilty" is the view frequently expressed. That comment will generate a successful challenge for cause. Prosecutors' for-cause challenges in most cases usually involve jurors who distrust law enforcement.

The last group of jurors filled out thirty questionnaires, bringing the total to eighty-nine.

The next morning, Wednesday the twenty-third, enough questionnaires were completed to begin the process of selecting a jury. Both sides would have all Wednesday afternoon and all day Thursday plus the evenings to go through all the questionnaires. Judge Darkoza said that both sides needed to confer and stipulate off all the jurors whose questionnaire responses meant they obviously were going to be excused. Darkoza emphasized that it would be very difficult to get eighty-nine people into the courtroom.

Scapio and Holdman had a system that they brought Conway in on. They would each read all the questionnaires. Each one would rate each separate juror on a one-to-ten scale. Ten would be a superb juror who would vote to convict and would not alienate others but would instead be persuasive to others. Tens are easy to spot based upon their answers to the questions, and it would be unlikely that they would get many of those.

Jurors scored eight or nine would be rated as solid and likely guilty votes and wouldn't alienate others. Sevens would be likely guilty votes but most likely followers. Sixes and fives would be neutral, and they would kick these if they had a group of five or six behind them in order who have higher rankings. Threes and fours would be ones to use peremptory challenges on as being likely pro-defense. Any jurors below three they would try to excuse for cause for being actually biased against the prosecution if they could show that.

Those numbers can change after questioning the jurors. Scapio once had a juror he rated a nine after reading his questionnaire, but after hearing him, the juror dropped to a one. It could work the other way too; there had been jurors rated with low scores but whose rating went way up after speaking with them.

Scapio also had the ability to run jurors on the office computer to see if they'd had past jury service and whether the jury convicted or not. At the conclusion of a jury trial, prosecutors write jury trial reports that include the facts of the case, name of the case, name and occupation and residence of each juror, and verdict rendered or hung jury. There are comments sometimes about the individual jurors. There is a section called significant excused jurors, which includes the reason the juror was excused. That can help weed out a potentially bad juror.

For the next day and a half, Scapio and Holdman read the questionnaires, and the biggest ratings disagreement was on a juror named Diana Carbone. She was a very attractive single schoolteacher who was thirty-three years old. She once dated a police officer, and her father had been a detective for the LAPD before retiring. On the flip side, about her views of the criminal justice system she wrote that the system was slanted against minorities and that sometimes people were sentenced to ridiculously long sentences for minor crimes.

On questions about domestic violence, she said she could be fair in evaluating the evidence in deciding whether it happened or not, but she believed that there was no excuse for domestic violence. She was also a member of the Sierra Club and Greenpeace.

Scapio gave her a nine, Holdman gave her a one and Conway gave her a four. Scapio liked her for her law enforcement family background and her strong position against domestic violence. He wasn't bothered by her view that minorities might not get a fair shake, because McCarty was a rich white guy. He didn't think her liberal environmental views were a problem. Plus, Scapio had dated a couple of jurors after trials since his divorce. Neither worked out long-term, but he did notice when roll was called that Carbone was single and very attractive. He also figured as a paisan, "Carbone" being Italian, she was more likely to fall for him than for the defendant. He chose not to mention that as a reason he liked her.

Holdman, on the other hand, labeled her a liberal do-gooder bleeding heart and he didn't want her at all. When she ended up getting called up to the jury box the second day, Holdman leaned in to Scapio and whispered, "I see where the nine came from now. On the scale you're using, I give her a ten."

Conway gave her a four because he liked the law enforcement background of her father and noted no bad feelings toward her ex that was an officer. He liked her stance on domestic violence, but he did not like that she was a teacher and didn't like her expressed liberal views.

Scapio's review of the jury trial reports had revealed that six prospective jurors had been on juries before. One was in Los Angeles County; three were on juries that found defendants guilty and the comments about the jurors were just "good juror" or "would keep again in a future case." One was on a hung jury in a 10–2 where the majority was for conviction. This juror was identified as being in the majority and not a holdout. Since that jury trial report, as well as all of the reports, was not discoverable to the defense because they were considered work product, Scapio had knowledge that Vandenbalk would not have, and he did not want to inquire further to tip Vandenbalk off, once that juror got in the box. Sometimes when you really believe a juror is going to be great, once they get in the box you limit your inquiry so as not to tip off the other side, and Scapio made note not to do that on jurors he rated tens. There was no report on the last juror who served in Ventura on a criminal case. That wasn't surprising, since some deputy DAs neglect to write reports, and some older reports had been lost when they transitioned computer systems.

Scapio, Holdman, and Conway identified ten jury questionnaires where they were willing to agree they could excuse immediately without having to go through the questioning process.

From the questionnaires they filled out, it was obvious that they could not give the defense a fair trial. They also identified eight that they thought were so anti-law enforcement or just plain bizarre that Vandenbalk should agree to excuse them.

Scapio called Vandenbalk and he shared with Vandenbalk the ones for which he would request a stipulation of removal. Vandenbalk agreed to four of the eight and gave Scapio a list of fourteen he wanted off. Of the fourteen, seven were on Scapio's list to excuse. Another was a juror that all three of the prosecution team were shaky on that Scapio rated a five, Holdman a six, and Conway a four. This was a juror Scapio figured he might have to spend some time questioning, because she gave long written answers, most of which seemed to go against the defense, though some seemed like she could be a holdout. Scapio was more than happy to agree to excusing this juror.

When they returned to the courtroom on Friday, August 25, several more jurors who filled out questionnaires said they had hardships they did not realize. Three said they found out that their employer only pays for ten days and they thought it was unlimited. Two said that they had childcare issues. One had severe back pain since Tuesday and did not think he could sit through it. All six were excused, leaving seventy-one questionnaires. Most of the jurors averaged seven or higher between the members of the prosecution team. The four Vandenbalk would not agree to remove were rated two or lower. There were a couple of jurors that averaged three or four. Several in the five to six range.

Judge Darkoza read the charges to the jurors again and instructed them on proof beyond a reasonable doubt, the presumption of innocence, what evidence was, and what things were not evidence, such as questions by attorneys and rulings by the judge. These were pretty standard things that occur in the courtroom before jury selection begins in a trial. Judge Darkoza instructed them again to not follow the case in the news. Then the clerk called the names of twelve jurors to fill the seats, and the trial of People v Allen McCarty for the murder of Jessica Braden was underway.

The names called were already known to both prosecution and defense, as the order was selected randomly and that list was given to the attorneys before they even began reviewing the questionnaires. Of the first twelve, nine had a collective average rating of eight or higher. Scapio's lowest rating was a seven and he had three tens in the group. One was a collective six and the others were threes. The two threes expressed distrust of police and the system.

Vandenbalk was first to question the potential jurors. He made a show of having memorized their names, and he skipped around so that nobody would know who was next. His technique was smooth and effective. He asked them more details about their jobs to convey that he was interested in them. Scapio liked going second because those types of questions were already out of the way, so he wouldn't look uncaring if he asked fewer questions about their jobs and families and got more to the point.

Vandenbalk questioned jurors about presumption of innocence and about the defense not having to prove anything. He also covered the defendant not having to testify and that they were not allowed to speculate about why. That if the prosecution failed to meet its burden, the defendant had no obligation to do anything. He covered keeping an open mind throughout the entire case. He said that things might look one way after they heard one side but then they would hear more evidence and might see it differently. He covered their ability to keep an open mind the entire way. He talked about expert testimony and asked jurors what things they would evaluate in deciding to believe expert testimony.

After about an hour, Vandenbalk was done, and he declined to excuse anyone for cause. He did try to get one of the jurors Scapio rated a ten to say he would always believe the police no matter what, but the juror did not take the bait, so Vandenbalk would have to use one of his twenty challenges.

Scapio noticed something very significant. It was not anything Vandenbalk said; it was what he didn't say. Scapio believed that in at least his last twenty jury trials, the defense attorneys always emphasized the fact that the defendant is entitled to the individual opinion of each juror. They would typically say that even if the other eleven jurors disagreed, it was each juror's individual obligation to hold to their opinion and not cave in to pressure just because others disagree. The good ones point out that this is true whether you are the lone holdout for conviction or for acquittal. That way they don't sound like they know their case is terrible and they are begging for a lone holdout, though they really are. Some may not go as far as to give the 11–1 example, but defense attorneys always talked about sticking to beliefs and not caving under pressure.

Except Vandenbalk, in this case. He never did it once. Scapio realized Vandenbalk was really banking on an acquittal and would be satisfied with nothing short of that. Since he had basically committed to the defendant not testifying, he was banking on Andrews giving him reasonable doubt. Scapio said to himself, "This is gonna be fun."

* * *

Scapio conducted the voir dire for the prosecution. He brought the grid with him and went in order of seating rather than at random like Vandenbalk. He wanted to make sure that he didn't skip anyone. He started out with a comment that he routinely used. It worked in getting at least a few smiles and building a rapport with the jurors. He basically told them that jury selection was not a science, and if a juror was excused, it could be for as trivial a reason as what part of the county they lived in or what some family member did for a living. The side that excused the juror could be completely wrong, so nobody should feel rejected if they got excused, and nobody should rack their brains trying to figure out why. He then added, "On the other hand, if you are really happy about it, try and hold your celebration until you get outside the double doors." That comment always got a laugh, and it made the jurors like Scapio because he was expressing concern that they might feel hurt if rejected from the jury.

He then asked the first juror, a 57-year-old married woman from Thousand Oaks who worked in banking, what she thought the purpose of a trial was. She answered, with some uncertainty, that it was to find out if the person on trial was the right person. Scapio then paraphrased it and said, "So would you agree that the purpose of a trial is to reach the truth?" The juror said that she agreed. Scapio followed that up with, "In the perfect scenario, if the defendant is guilty, he should be held responsible and found guilty, and if not, he should be found not guilty; would you agree with that?" She answered yes. Scapio then asked the rest of the jurors if everyone agreed with that, and if anyone disagreed, to raise their hand and they could talk about it. Nobody raised their hand.

That line of questioning served several functions for Scapio. First, it boosted his credibility because he was seen by jurors as a pursuer of truth, not an advocate for a result. Defense attorneys frequently countered by correcting Scapio with the jurors by saying that it was not correct to say that the purpose was to reach the truth, but rather to see if the prosecution could meet the high burden of proof beyond a reasonable doubt.

Technically both were correct, in that truth was the ultimate goal, but defense attorneys had to be careful how they responded. The ones who got back up and said, "Mr. Scapio is wrong, the purpose is to see if they meet their burden of proof," came off like they were playing games. The best defense attorneys said that the prosecutor was right that the goal was to reach the truth, but there was a burden of proof to prevent the innocent from being convicted just because some thought it was more likely that they did it. That burden was proof beyond a reasonable doubt.

That response was good, but Scapio had heard many young deputy district attorneys who got a not-guilty verdict relate that they had spoken to the jurors afterward, and the jurors had told the prosecutor that they "knew the accused did it, but they just had that reasonable doubt." Scapio believed that getting the jury into the mindset of finding the truth prevented that from happening.

After going over the purpose of a trial, Scapio covered circumstantial evidence. He explained that circumstantial evidence was indirect evidence, but it included evidence like fingerprints and DNA. A juror could conclude that because a person's DNA was there, that person was there, as opposed to an eyewitness who actually saw the person there. A fingerprint was circumstantial evidence that the person touched the object. He gave another example of that by saying it could be where you had one really big cookie in your house and you told your friend not to eat it because it was specially made for another person. You took a quick bathroom break, you came back, the cookie was gone, and the friend had cookie crumbs all over their face, and they shrugged their shoulders and said, "Sorry." That was circumstantial evidence.

Next he gave the more elaborate example of the bank robber who handed the teller a note that said, "This is a robbery, give me all the money in the drawer, don't push any alarms, don't do anything stupid, do as I say and nobody gets hurt." The guy was wearing a fake beard and mustache. Police got video of cars leaving the area. Defendant's car was one of them. That video was circumstantial evidence, but not enough to convict. Maybe they showed photos to the teller and defendant was one of the people and she said it looked like him because of the eyes. That is direct evidence because she was an actual eyewitness, but again, not enough to convict. But then they executed a search warrant at the guy's house and they found a hundred practice notes that were variations of the "give me all your money" note, which was found outside the bank and had no DNA or prints because the robber wore gloves. They also found stacks of money consistent with the large amount the robber got.

Then Scapio asked the jurors, "What do you think now?"

Scapio explained that some circumstantial evidence like the written notes was a lot better than the direct evidence from the teller's identification. If any juror, given that hypothetical, no matter their previous score, had said anything like, "I would want the practice notes tested for prints; maybe someone else lives at the house and used his car to do the robbery," that person would have been gone. Of course, the prosecution would have tried to get DNA off the notes, but they had powerful proof before they even got to that point. If any juror had theorized that the police might have planted the evidence, they would have been gone. If anyone had said, "Why didn't they find the beard and the mustache?" they would have been gone. The robber could have ditched that at any time.

Some of the jurors answered in their questionnaires that they did follow the OJ case, others Scott Peterson, and others followed Casey Anthony. Scapio asked if any of those cases affected their view of the criminal justice system, hoping they would reveal their opinions about the case. When one juror gave a vague answer—"It showed that money talked"—Scapio eventually asked them if they agreed with the verdict in the OJ Simpson case in Los Angeles. This led to the trial's first objection.

Darkoza thought for a moment and said, "Overruled." Vandenbalk asked to approach the bench.

He said, "It does not go to cause and is too close to the facts in this case."

Scapio said, "It shows how they evaluate circumstantial evidence, and this case is far different in that there is no dispute about the DNA results. But the defense is arguing that their expert's report shows that the blood had to have come from a different incident because he says there should have been much more blood if it was from this."

Darkoza then said, "Ray, normally I would allow this question, but this case is too close. You have defendant's and victim's blood on different items of clothing, and you have a cut hand in both cases. The only difference is McCarty plays tennis and OJ played football. I know I indicated in chambers I would allow it, but I am reconsidering and am going to say no OJ questions."

Scapio asked if he could question them about Casey Anthony and Scott Peterson. Darkoza turned to Vandenbalk, and Vandenbalk said that "if you allow him to ask about the other cases but don't let him ask about OJ, you are telling the jury that my client is as guilty as OJ. Some of them are going to be smart enough to figure that the judge thinks my client is like OJ, and that is never good. Plus, I did not object to his stupid practice-note robbery example." Darkoza said that he would have overruled him on that one but was sustaining the objections.

A few jurors had indicated that they knew of McCarty before the murder in this case, and Scapio questioned them about that. He tried to get jurors who he rated very low to admit they would not be fair, to save a peremptory challenge he might need later. He was unsuccessful there. After Scapio declined to excuse for cause, the peremptory challenges began.

To speed things up, Judge Darkoza had the lawyers approach the bench. That way they would be able to make multiple challenges in a row. Scapio really preferred challenges to be in open court because he liked to have jurors see defense attorneys excusing obviously smart people.

Scapio and Holdman wanted smart jurors since this was a DNA case. Defense attorneys prefer people who are more prone toward skepticism. That would mean people who might be more susceptible to reasonable doubt when a common-sense evaluation of the evidence shows reasonable doubt does not exist. Vandenbalk would love the juror who thought they were the smartest person in the room but was not. It turned out Vandenbalk had more confidence in his case than was typical, and the jurors each side was looking for were not that different. Scapio asked for a moment to confer with Holdman and Conway, and Vandenbalk did the same with his two associates.

When the attorneys approached again, Darkoza asked Scapio if he had a challenge. Scapio exercised his first against a juror he rated low because of distrust of law enforcement. Vandenbalk excused one that Scapio rated a ten, but he knew that was coming because Vandenbalk had tried to get that juror out for cause. Scapio then excused the other juror that he rated low. Vandenbalk excused a juror who was very troubled by domestic violence. Scapio declined to use any further challenges. Vandenbalk excused one more that Scapio had rated a ten.

At that point, Judge Darkoza said that since it was 4:25 and they normally broke at 4:30, they would call up the next five jurors in the morning. He reminded the jurors of the admonition not to read anything about the trial, not to watch any coverage on television and not to listen to radio coverage, and he reminded them not to research any of the parties or witnesses on social media. He then said he would see everyone back at 9:00 a.m.

The next trial day was Monday the twenty-eighth. Five new jurors were seated, and they were questioned. Scapio asked many of the same questions. One of the prospective jurors in listing high-profile cases mentioned a local murder case from just before Scapio had joined the Homicide Unit, and the juror expressed relief that the defendant was convicted. Although he was restricted from asking his OJ question—he had to credit Vandenbalk with good lawyering there—Scapio raised this juror's score from a six to an eight. After conferring with Holdman and Conway, they agreed this juror was a keeper.

Of the other four, three were rated from eight to ten by the prosecution team, with Scapio being the highest grader, giving two tens and a nine. The fourth juror was a one across the board. The juror wrote long rambling diatribes that caused the juror to frequently write on the back of the questionnaire. Vandenbalk had declined to stipulate this juror off, reasoning that this was going to be a high-profile and high-pressure trial, and it would be good to be able to laugh. Vandenbalk added that he was 99 percent sure that Scapio would succeed in getting a challenge for cause and added that he would not oppose that.

The juror was a forty-eight-year-old self-employed blogger who was living on Silver Strand Beach in Oxnard. It was not completely clear, but it seemed that he was living off a trust fund. He answered a question about his attitude toward law enforcement by saying most of them were fair but some were stealth representatives of the new world order and the deep state. He explained that local law enforcement had representatives of the deep state, as did the FBI, and his blog was designed to expose the dangers of globalism. He rambled that Donald Trump recognized the problem but some had infiltrated the inner circles led by Trump's own daughter and her husband, Jared Kushner.

When his name was called, Judge Darkoza called the attorneys up and asked how this juror was not on the stipulation list. Scapio pointed to Vandenbalk and said he tried. Vandenbalk explained his reasoning and that he would not be fighting a for-cause challenge. Judge Darkoza was clearly irritated and said that Vandenbalk was wasting the court's time but that technically the juror had not written anything that would guarantee a for-cause challenge would be upheld on appeal.

Vandenbalk started the questioning of the juror and asked him about how he recognized someone in law enforcement who is part of the deep state. The juror answered that you had to follow the money. Vandenbalk then asked the juror what to do if you cannot get their bank account information. The looks on the other jurors' faces were priceless at this point. Vandenbalk asked if he thought Scapio might be part of this deep-state conspiracy. The juror acknowledged he might be, but without following the money, you couldn't be sure. Vandenbalk thanked the juror and then turned to the judge and said that defense was challenging the juror for cause.

Scapio realized what Vandenbalk was doing. Vandenbalk was making the jurors think that he was the one being fair and was just looking for jurors who were not unstable, even if unstable would benefit his client. When Judge Darkoza asked Scapio if he agreed to stipulate the juror off the case, Scapio pointed out that of course he would, and he wanted to when he read the juror's questionnaire, but someone else had insisted on questioning this juror. Vandenbalk objected and said that Scapio's comments were totally improper. Judge Darkoza then said, "OK, gentlemen, I don't need to hear this from either of you. The stipulation to excuse this juror is granted. Sir, thank for you your time, you are excused."

The next juror called up was none other than Diana Carbone, the teacher that Scapio rated a nine. Vandenbalk did a very limited voir dire of this juror. Scapio asked which school she was a teacher for (that way if she got excused, he would know how to contact her). He asked a question about how she resolved disputes between students and if she had to evaluate who was telling the truth and who wasn't. She gave an answer that Scapio liked.

He mentioned that she said that she had previously dated a police officer, and he asked what department he worked for. She said that it was the Simi Valley Police Department. He asked her if there was anything about that experience that made her say that she would never date cops again. She said that there was not, and that the breakup was mutual.

He asked her what she thought the purpose of a trial was, and she said, "As everyone was saying before; to get to the truth." He asked if she could keep that in mind throughout the process. He did not ask about domestic violence and her answer that there was no excuse for it, because he did not want to highlight that she would be a good juror. Scapio turned to Holdman when he got back to counsel table and said that he thought she would be good. Holdman agreed.

Scapio conferred with Holdman and Conway as to whether they had any challenges, and then he said, "The people accept the jury as presently constituted."

Vandenbalk then said, "The defense would like to thank and excuse juror number eleven, Miss Carbone."

Scapio's shoulders slumped ever so slightly. Holdman whispered, "There goes your future ex-girlfriend." Scapio laughed and another juror's name was called.

A few more jurors were called up. Vandenbalk got one juror excused for cause because she did not think she could be fair if the case involved domestic violence. Scapio excused a psychologist, an occupation he tended to think leaned defense unless he heard something that overrode that. Both sides accepted the jury.

Three alternates were selected, to make sure they would be able to continue with the trial if any jurors could not stay on due to illness or other unforeseen circumstances. A jury trial must have twelve people unless both sides agree to less. If it goes under twelve and three are lost and there are only two alternates, it's a mistrial, and the trial would have to start all over again. The witnesses who already testified would have to do so again.

The jury consisted of seven women and five men. Ten of the twelve jurors had at least some college education. Three were Ventura city residents. Two were from Oxnard. Three lived in Camarillo, one lived in Thousand Oaks. Of the other three, one lived in Simi Valley, one lived in Santa Paula, and one in Fillmore. Seven jurors were Caucasian, four were Hispanic, and one juror was Asian. The alternates were two men and one woman, two Oxnard residents and one Camarillo resident. The lowest rating Scapio gave any of the jurors was a seven. Ventura County is a majority white and Hispanic county, so it wasn't surprising that there were no black jurors and only one Asian juror.

The trial would begin with opening statements and evidence the next day, August 29.

ELEVEN

Scapio had his opening statement on a PowerPoint slide presentation. His tech wizard was fifty-four-year-old Penny Jones. Penny was a white "hippie chick" who knew computers inside out. In her youth, she worked in the film industry in the technology department. After her divorce at thirty-seven—she had been married seven years—she moved to Ventura County to be near her parents, who lived in the Ventura Keys, a beautiful area near the ocean. After the death of her father, she moved to Ojai because she felt it fit her. Scapio was not confident with computers and was paranoid of a glitch, so he always had Penny clean up his PowerPoint presentations and set them up for the courtroom.

She was the master at multitasking. She could turn a sloppy slide production with no pizzazz into a masterpiece, including zooming-in evidence and fading-in new slides in an attention-grabbing way, while regaling anyone who would listen with stories about concerts she attended, rockers she partied with as a young "hot hippie chick," and backstage passes she got before the after-parties. She could and would tell you what actors and rock stars were "cool" and which ones were "jerks." Her hair was still as long as ever but now gray with streaks of pink, and she still wore the Native American-style jewelry of her youth.

Scapio delivered a powerful opening statement in front of a packed courtroom that included the victim's family members and about a dozen young prosecutors, encouraged to watch as much of the trial as they could. Several TV and print reporters were also in attendance. Scapio laid out the motive and abusive behavior of the defendant. He detailed the physical evidence of the murder and showed photos of the shirt, the shoes, and the blood-smeared brassiere. He then showed the DNA results and explained the compelling nature of the numbers that were the result of the analysis, leaving no reasonable doubt that the victim's blood spattered onto the defendant's shirt and shoes as she was being stabbed to death. He explained how defendant inadvertently smeared his own blood onto one of her bras as he pulled items out of drawers, desperately trying to make it look like a robbery. The defendant had the victim's blood on his hands as well, as demonstrated by the fact that the blood on the brassiere was a mixture of both the defendant's blood and the victim's. He explained the cell-phone evidence and how it proved premeditation and deliberation.

Scapio then put up slides of the blood drops in the house, showing the two drops that belonged to McCarty up close and then giving the odds of it being anyone else's blood as astronomical. Scapio concluded with a basic slide explaining the law of murder and premeditation and deliberation, then asked the jury to hold this man accountable:

"Unwilling to accept rejection from a woman he thought he had control of, he chose murder as the ultimate act of control. But he got sloppy. He failed to discard all the evidence, and detectives found the shirt she spurted blood on and the shoes that her blood spattered upon as she was being slaughtered for daring to break up with this murderer. He wiped his own smeared blood as he desperately tried to escape responsibility for his crime; he thought that his wealth and power would allow him to do just that. At the conclusion of the evidence, I will ask you to hold him accountable for the crime of murder with deliberation and premeditation and use of a knife."

Vandenbalk gave his opening statement next, and it consisted of two themes. His first slide was labeled "Rush to Judgment." This was a theme he had covered in jury selection. In his opening, he talked about what evidence was not found, like the pants the defendant was wearing, and the murder weapon used. He had that under a bullet point labeled "missing evidence." He also had a bullet point labeled "other suspects ignored." His opening was closer to argument than a true opening statement, and Scapio thought about objecting but decided he wouldn't gain anything by doing that, and he let it go. He also recognized that the last part of his own opening might have crossed that line too.

Vandenbalk next talked about Andrews and called him a true American hero for his work exonerating an innocent man convicted of arson and murder. Vandenbalk said that Andrews was a world-renowned physicist and he would testify that the blood on the shirt and shoes could not have come from the murder.

Judge Darkoza was puzzled that Scapio had not objected to Andrews making this conclusive assertion. He was thinking that if Scapio had made the proper pretrial objection, he would have narrowed Andrews's testimony to saying that in Andrews's opinion, the amount of blood was "less than one would expect" from the murder and therefore was "likely" from some other event.

Vandenbalk, after asking the jurors to keep an open mind to all the evidence, told them that he was confident that they would find reasonable doubt and acquit Allen McCarty.

* * *

The prosecution's case went smoothly. They opened with the defendant's prior domestic violence against victim Jessica Braden. They covered his conviction for domestic abuse and called her friend Michelle Harrington to testify about Jessica telling her that the defendant said he would kill her if she did not get back together with him.

The first officers on scene were next. Then Sean "Lucky Charms" Murphy did his thing. He used a diagram and photo boards to thoroughly explain the crime scene, including the garage and the interior of the home. He explained the difference between blood smear and blood spatter so that McCarty's blood on the brassiere was consistent with a person who had a bloody hand wiping that blood off onto the object rather than it spattering off as a result of force impact. Scapio also asked Murphy if there was any way to determine how much blood one could expect to be on an attacker's clothes. Murphy said, in his thick Irish accent, that there were so many variables, and he went on to explain all the different variables, such as exactly where the victim and suspect were standing, the size and sharpness of the weapon, the thickness of the clothing the victim was wearing, the exact distance and body positioning.

Vandenbalk cross-examined that Murphy couldn't know how long individual blood drops had been there and that he couldn't be sure that the blood drops were from the same incident. Murphy responded by pointing out that the blood drops did not seem to differ significantly, and it would make sense that they were from the same incident. Murphy added that he "would not expect a house full of bleeders that drop blood all over at different times, but I guess anything is possible." Several of the jurors laughed.

Murphy also testified that it was obvious from the amount of blood spatters on the shirt and the shoes that the spatters had to have come from an event involving significant trauma, and that McCarty had to have been in close proximity to the victim when that very significant event resulting in substantial bleeding occurred.

Vandenbalk asked Murphy where he got his degree in physics from. Murphy said he didn't have one. Vandenbalk asked if he ever took a class in physics and Murphy said he had taken one in college in Dublin. Vandenbalk asked if he had written any scholarly papers. Murphy responded, "I wrote an article on the Irish World Cup Soccer team in college and I considered it pretty scholarly, but other than that, no, I haven't taken to writing yet, but I might. Unfortunately, I've been in the field so much I haven't had actual time to do that yet." A lot of the jurors were smiling. Vandenbalk would have argued Murphy's credentials further, but he realized that now was the time to back off. It was clear the jurors liked Murphy, and Vandenbalk was going to have to rely on Andrews to really drive home the point that by using physics, you could actually determine what Murphy said that you couldn't.

Wednesday, August 30, began with Holdman calling Rollins and Cuevas. Scapio was impressed. He had picked Holdman for his legal research skills and not for his trial skills, but both of his direct examinations were well organized, and he got all the evidence in that he needed to. Scapio and Holdman had changed their strategy and decided to present McCarty's first contact with the detectives. Holdman covered the cut to McCarty's hand and his snide-sounding "cutting celery" explanation as well as his failure to ask any questions about how the victim was killed or if there were any suspects or leads. Per the judge's order, he refrained from discussing McCarty's lack of cooperation upon the initial request for DNA, then got to the actual collection of the DNA later.

After some argument at the bench, Vandenbalk was able to get in the fact that McCarty denied committing the murder when asked. Scapio was hoping to keep that out, but he realized that by getting in the fact that McCarty did not ask questions, the defense might be entitled to get in his denial. Scapio and Holdman initially had decided to leave that out, but then decided unless they put it in, it would never come in, because McCarty was not going to testify.

Holdman also called the medical examiner, Michael Quisenberry, who had been the Ventura County ME for five years after coming from Oregon. Small and thin with a pale complexion and short light-brown hair, Quisenberry was a thorough witness but tended to be tentative in his conclusions. That was not an issue in this cause of death, however, as he concluded that Ms. Braden had been stabbed a total of fourteen times with an object consistent with a kitchen knife. Her throat suffered a deep slice wound, which was what killed her, but Quisenberry testified that she would have died from loss of blood from the stab wounds eventually; the cut throat only sped up the process.

There was a kitchen knife missing from a set of knives in the victim's kitchen, which had been testified to.

Quisenberry determined that the cause of death was sharp-force trauma to the throat, resulting in significant loss of blood. He was only able to put time of death as estimated at up to twenty-four hours prior to the autopsy, which was performed that evening at 5:00 p.m. A neighbor did hear screams at around 9:30 p.m., and Quisenberry testified that 9:30 p.m. on April 23 could have been the time of death.

The neighbor who heard the screams testified next and said she wished she had called 911 but thought nothing of it at the time, because there was never any crime in the neighborhood. She was quite distraught about having not called, and Vandenbalk asked her no questions.

The DNA testimony was impressive and compelling. Maria Aguilar made a superb witness. Bright and attractive with long brown hair, tawny-beige skin, and a warm smile, she had an easy, friendly manner. At thirty-five years of age, she was not too young to be credible as a scientist or old enough to be bored by the courtroom experience. Some lab people don't like testifying and would rather spend all day in the lab. Not Aguilar. She enjoyed the teaching part of her testimony.

Scapio had her lay out the numbers—the odds of the sample's DNA matching the defendant's DNA—for the blood drops and for the blood on the shirt and shoes as well as the mixture on the brassiere. She also established the exclusion of the victim's previous boyfriend, Cody Welch, as a source of DNA for any of the samples. She testified that there were over fifty visible spatters on the shirt and more that you could only see with a microscope. She also mentioned that there were three visible spatters on each shoe. This corroborated that McCarty had to have been nearby when a traumatic event happened to the victim. The testimony only lasted a little under two hours and was very effective.

Vandenbalk did not cross-examine much there, other than to establish that DNA could tell you who bled at a location, but it couldn't tell you when they bled. He also got the analyst to agree that DNA couldn't tell you what particular event the DNA came from.

On Thursday, August 31, Scapio called Cody Welch, who testified that he had dated the victim. He admitted vandalizing her car and paying for the damages. He denied killing her, and he established that he was willing to give a DNA sample.

Anticipating the very remote possibility that McCarty would testify, Scapio asked, "When the detectives asked you for a DNA sample, did you provide it willingly or did you demand they get a warrant?" Vandenbalk's objection was overruled. The witness answered that he gave his DNA willingly.

Scapio asked why he didn't ask for a warrant, and Welch said, "I didn't do it. It had been a long time since I had been to Jessica's, and I didn't want them to have to make the police waste time when they could spend it on finding out who killed my ex-girlfriend." Vandenbalk objected again, but it was overruled.

Vandenbalk was not planning on calling the defendant as a witness, so the jury would not hear that McCarty did ask for a warrant. Nevertheless, he didn't like that Scapio was slicing holes in his rush-to-judgment theory.

Scapio asked about the vandalism, and Welch said he was stupid and lost his temper over the breakup of the relationship, but that he would never physically hurt a woman. He said he paid for the damages and apologized, and he became a better person as a result of his mistake.

Vandenbalk cross-examined about how he was so angry when he kicked in her car. He asked what made Welch so angry. He was asked if he went looking for the car with the intention of damaging it. Vandenbalk tried to play it out like it was some premeditated act of viciousness and cruelty. Scapio could tell the jurors were not buying Cody Welch as an alternate suspect.

Welch was a good-looking, athletically built man who came off as genuinely nice. He was now married, with a baby on the way. Cody Welch was gonna be a tough sell as an alternate suspect, and Vandenbalk knew it.

Karen Loring testified to the prior incident by and the restraining order against the defendant. She explained the nature of his behavior during the relationship. She related his controlling behavior. The testimony was interrupted by multiple objections but ended up going well. She related the choking incident where he threatened to throw her off the balcony. Vandenbalk's cross was only about the fact that she did not lose consciousness, the choking only lasted a few seconds, he never threw her off the balcony, and he never used a weapon on her or battered her on any other occasion. Not great, but it was all he could really do.

The last prosecution witness was Rhonda Antonopoulos, the sheriff's department cell-tower expert. She had been heading the Crime Analysis Task Force for five years. Very knowledgeable, she came off like a librarian. She was in her mid-forties, had grayish hair, olive skin, and thick glasses, and was just five feet tall but projected confidence and stature once she began her testimony. She presented a slide show clearly demonstrating defendant's pattern of phone activity. The fact that McCarty's phone was shut off during the crucial hours surrounding the murder, but was otherwise always active, was compelling.

Vandenbalk tried to make it sound like he could have just not received any calls, but the witness made it clear that there was some activity and the phone was always receiving information, so you could tell when it was off. Vandenbalk did point out a couple of other periods where there may have been no activity, consistent with the phone being off. Those, however, were for much shorter times than this two-hour gap. Scapio pointed that out with the witness on redirect.

The prosecution's case lasted only a week, so with jury selection taking just under that with the questionnaires, the case was well ahead of schedule.

* * *

On Friday, September 1, it was the defense's turn to begin. Vandenbalk recalled a couple of the officers to ask some questions regarding the time of the first call that Braden didn't answer. If she was already dead, this would have been before the neighbor heard the scream. This was an anomaly, but Scapio would explain she may have shut off her phone to avoid him, since the phone records Scapio offered showed McCarty had frequently called her and texted her in the days leading up to the murder.

Her friends and family were concerned because of the threats, so it's not a shock that she might have shut her phone off or simply not answered it before he actually did kill her. If true, that was more evidence of his guilt. Scapio had made this point in closing. The defense intended to create confusion around time of death and to lay the foundation for the argument that the blood could be related to the murder or to some previous incident.

Once that examination was completed, Vandenbalk asked for a short break to set up the slide show that he and Andrews had put together.

After the twenty-minute break, the defense began. Andrews introduced himself with a long narrative about his credentials. Vandenbalk covered the standard prosecutors' questions about fees. He also covered the fact that Andrews was almost exclusively a defense witness in criminal cases but that was because prosecutors have their own crime lab and crime-scene experts, and when his conclusions agreed with the prosecution's conclusions, he ended up not testifying. He turned to the jurors and added that it happened quite a lot.

Vandenbalk asked if his work was ever instrumental in exonerating a man who was wrongly convicted. Andrews said that he had been and went into a lengthy, painstaking description of the arson homicide case. Jurors seemed to be impressed and on the edge of their seats. He explained in great detail his physics background and his scholarly works. He explained the peer-review process and how his scholarly articles had been published in many of the most prestigious scientific journals.

He was asked about the subject matter of prior expert testimony he had given and explained that he had testified on accident reconstruction, blood-spatter interpretation, use of force by police, boating accidents and safety equipment, and crime-scene interpretation involving disturbances in the ground documented by shoeprint movement, as well as ballistics and bullet trajectory.

Vandenbalk asked how he could testify in all those areas without formal training in the subjects. Andrews explained that the laws of physics are immutable, meaning they don't change, and a basic knowledge of physics was key to understanding how objects move. He went back to the arson case and talked about how that state's expert had been to arson schools and fire scenes and had investigated hundreds of fires, and he was a convincing good-ole-boy expert witness who was dead wrong, because he did not understand the laws of physics. That took them to the lunch break.

As Scapio, Holdman, and Conway exited the courtroom, victim advocate Sandra Goldberg approached Scapio and said the Bradens wanted to meet with him.

Scapio said they could use one of the DA's office conference rooms. Upon returning to the office, Scapio secured the executive conference room. He entered with Conway and Holdman, and Diane and Phillip Braden followed with Sandra Goldberg. Scapio could see the worried look on Diane's face, so he asked what she was concerned about. She said that up until now she had been very confident in a conviction but was now feeling scared. She felt this witness was bamboozling the jury and she was worried. Phillip added that he shared his wife's concerns and he hoped Ray had something that undermined the expert's testimony.

Scapio said he was very confident in the evidence they had, and that he did believe he had some good questions that would change how jurors viewed the expert. He added the jurors might be impressed with the witness's knowledge and effort, but that did not mean the jurors had any doubt about who killed their daughter. That made the Bradens feel better. Scapio told them to always look confident. "Even if you think things might be a bit tough, jurors pick up on little things."

They started back up at 1:30 p.m. and the slide show continued. Andrews was a professional witness. He was smooth and knew when to look at the jurors and how to explain complex science in a way that didn't necessarily make it that much clearer but made him sound smart. He went through each of the exhibits he viewed as well as critical crime-scene photos to lay out what was to be the climax of his testimony. Scapio began watching the clock; he also was starting to get anxious to jump in on cross-examination. The way it was going, he might not get the chance, and it was Friday. The testimony would stick with the jurors all weekend.

Scapio could feel his blood pressure rise as he knew he had questions he wanted to fire at Andrews; he had prepared a long time for this moment. Andrews then began to move deftly through Vandenbalk's well-crafted direct examination toward its conclusion. He was asked about the blood on the brassiere, and he said that the blood could have already been there when pulled out. The vast majority of the blood on items pulled out belonged to the victim. Andrews added that since no fingerprints of the defendant or anyone else were found, the killer was likely wearing gloves, so it would likely have been from another incident.

He repeated that you couldn't tell how long the blood had been there, but the fact that all the other items pulled out that had blood on them had only the victim's blood and this one had a mixture meant it must have been from a separate incident. He covered the two blood drops by repeating that they could have been from any time.

He then went to the shirt found by Rollins and Cuevas in the trash can at defendant's home. "Based upon the laws of physics," he said, "the number of stab wounds, and the depth of the slice wound, if the killer was wearing that shirt at the time of the murder and while committing the murder, I would have expected to see much more blood on that shirt. There was some blood and it was clearly visible, but it could not have been from the murder, as there was just not enough blood."

Judge Darkoza was waiting for Scapio's objection. He had already decided that he would overrule it as untimely. The objection never came. Darkoza still wondered what Scapio was doing and figured maybe next week he would find out if this was part of a great plan or a potentially monumental oversight.

Vandenbalk showed the exhibit with the shoe photos up on PowerPoint, as he had with the shirt. He asked Andrews if he had an opinion as to whether the blood spatter on the shoes could have come from the murder or have been worn by the person committing the murder. Andrews responded, "In my opinion, had these shoes been worn during the murder, there would have been much more blood on them than there is here. This is based upon laws of physics, and so it is my opinion that the blood on the shoes is unrelated to the murder and must necessarily have come from an unrelated event."

Vandenbalk then proudly stated, "No further questions."

Fat Lanny Michaels, the defense investigator, could not stop himself and, in a packed courtroom, walked from behind the defense table and over to Holdman and whispered, "Time to start writing that apology letter." Judge Darkoza looked at Michaels with a scowl and Michaels said, "I'm sorry, your honor."

Judge Darkoza looked at the jury and looked at Scapio and said, "Well, it's four fifteen. I am sure your cross-examination will be much longer than fifteen to twenty minutes, so I think we'll break for the evening."

Ray Scapio, the recreational sports bettor, as he liked to call himself, looked at trials through the lens of sporting events. The trial was like a football game, but cross-examination of an expert was like a boxing match. You can jab and move and pile up points, or you can go for a quick knockout. The packed courtroom, including eleven young deputy DAs eager to hear Scapio's cross-examination but figuring they would have to wait till Monday if they could even come back then, were shocked when Scapio looked at Judge Darkoza and said, "Your honor, fifteen or twenty minutes should be enough time. I'm ready now."

Vandenbalk thought, "Scapio thinks he's going to just spend a few minutes, so as not to convey that the witness's testimony hurt the prosecution." He thought that was a mistake.

Andrews thought, "This is interesting. I think I'll stall this guy and make him look really bad when he has to finish on Monday. No prosecutor has ever laid a glove on me in hours, and this clown thinks he is gonna nail me in fifteen minutes? Good luck with that."

Over the last sixty-five years, more people have claimed to have seen Bobby Thomson's "shot heard 'round the world" to put the old New York Giants in the 1951 World Series than could have been in the ballpark that day. The same could be said of Franco Harris's 1972 "immaculate reception" to win the Steelers' playoff game. Ventura County trials never get the same national fame as a major sporting event, but for years to come,

Ray Scapio's fifteen-minute takedown of Frank Andrews would achieve that kind of legendary status, so here is the transcript:

Q. Good afternoon, Dr. Andrews.

A. Good afternoon, sir.

Q. Let's talk about the arson murder case. Isn't it true that three arson investigators had already decided the initial investigation was flawed, and they brought you in as someone from a different background? You were fourth to come in, right?

A. I don't see how the order matters. We worked as a team and achieved the goal of justice. If you asked the man freed from prison, he would tell you we were all of equal significance, because it was critical to have someone from a different discipline contribute corroborative information.

Q. I promised twenty minutes. My question called for a simple yes answer, but you went on to give a dissertation about teamwork, which my question did not call for. If you keep doing that and I go over, it's gonna be your fault.

[Objection was sustained, but Judge Darkoza admonished the witness to answer the question.]

Q. Three arson investigators already reviewed the case and thought the initial investigation was wrong, and they brought you in after, right?

A. Yes.

Q. About five years ago, you testified as an accident-reconstruction expert in People v Halverson, didn't you?

A. I do remember that case.

Q. You were asked by the prosecutor if you were paid to reach conclusions that help the defense.

A. Most prosecutors ask me that. I'm surprised you haven't yet.

Q. You got indignant and talked about how you are a scientist, right?

A. Yes, because I am.

Q. In fact, your exact words were, "I am a scientist. I am consulted for my expertise. If my conclusions are consistent with the defense case, I expect my testimony would be requested, and I would be compensated for my time and testimony. If my conclusion, after reviewing the evidence, does not support the defense theory, I would not be called as a witness; I would be paid for my time in reviewing the case and that's it. Either way is fine. I am a scientist and [Scapio read this part loudly] I DO NOT WORK FOR ANY ATTORNEY; I DO NOT CARE WHAT THE ATTORNEY WANTS OR NEEDS. I AM NOT BEHOLDEN TO THE ATTORNEY. MY OBLIGATION IS TO SCIENCE. MY INTEGRITY AS A SCIENTIST IS TOO IMPORTANT." That's what you said in Halverson, isn't it?

A. Yes.

Q. My investigator, Mr. Conway, called you and asked if you would be willing to meet with us, isn't that true?

A. Yes.

Q. Didn't you tell him that you had to run it by Mr. Vandenbalk?

A. Yes.

Q. A week later, Mr. Conway called you and asked if you were willing to meet with us, and it was at that time you said, "Mr. Vandenbalk is not allowing me to do that," right?

A. That is what I said, but you were not offering to pay me.

Q. So when you said you don't work for any attorney, you are a scientist, what you are telling us today is you don't work for any attorney that doesn't pay you?

A. I don't work for free.

Q. You didn't even ask Mr. Conway if we would pay you for your time, did you?

A. No.

Q. And you did not discuss that issue with Mr. Vandenbalk either, did you?

A. No.

Q. Is Vandenbalk paying you a lot more money than Halverson's lawyer?

[Objection was overruled.]

A. My rates are standard but may have gone up over the last five years.

[At this point, three jurors who had been taking notes closed up their notebooks.]

Q. Doctor, let's talk about the scientific method, OK? The scientific method is critical in making and validating a theory or hypothesis, isn't it?

A. The scientific method is the foundation for all advancements in science.

Q. The scientific method means I have a hypothesis or a theory, I conduct an experiment, and I document my methodology in a scientific journal. Other scientists review my work and conduct their own tests or experiments to see if I got it right. It's called the peer-review process, isn't that right?

A. Correct.

Q. You are not a blood-spatter expert, are you?

A. As I have already explained, my expertise is in physics, and that allows me to reach conclusions that are based upon the immutable laws of physics, and that applies to many fields, including blood-spatter interpretations.

[Scapio objected that the answer was not responsive. The objection was sustained. Scapio re-asked the question slowly and the witness acknowledged that he was not a blood-spatter expert.]

Q. You have never been to a crime scene to examine blood spatter, have you?

A. No.

Q. You have never been to a training class on blood-spatter interpretation, have you?

A. Again, it is not necessary.

Q. You have never had an article published about the laws of physics and how they relate to crime-scene evidence, have you?

A. No.

Q. You do agree, though, that the blood on the brassiere was smeared or transferred blood and not spattered blood, right?

A. Yes.

Q. You also agree that the blood on the shoes and shirt was spattered blood, not smeared or transferred blood, right?

A. Yes.

Q. OK, let's talk about your conclusion. Victim's blood is on defendant's discarded shirt and shoes in the form of spatter; in other words, some traumatic event. Most people would say that is not good for the defendant, but you have a different conclusion. You say, based upon the laws of physics, that blood had to have come from some other time when the victim suffered a traumatic injury and the defendant was standing right near her that caused her to bleed on him, but it couldn't be from the murder because there wasn't enough blood. That is your theory, right?

A. Essentially, yes.

Q. But you can't verify that through an experiment that can be peer-reviewed, can you?

A. I don't have to; the laws of physics don't change.

Q. OK, so let's say I get bored with my job and decide to play in the NFL. I write to all the teams and say that all those other guys like Brady are bums, and I can throw a football and hit a dime someone is holding 240 yards away. Do you think teams are gonna just take my word for it if I say it's based on the laws of physics?

A. I don't follow football because of all the concussions.

Q. You follow it enough to know that there are concussions, so you do know that throwing a football 240 yards and hitting a dime is pretty good?

A. It would be impossible.

Q. So if you were an NFL team, you wouldn't sign me just because I said, "Of course I can do it, it's physics"?

A. It's ridiculous.

Q. You can't verify how much blood should be on an object of clothing. For example, you can't go looking for young women about the same height and weight as Jessica Braden was and go up to them and say, "Hi, my name is Frank Andrews and I am a physicist. I am working for an attorney representing a man accused of murder, and I will pay you one thousand dollars to volunteer for an experiment. I have another volunteer who is the same size as the accused. He is going to use an ordinary kitchen knife and will plunge it into you fourteen times and then he will slash your throat, and we want to see how much of your blood gets on his shirt and shoes. Here is my card, it will be at my office address, it's right here, how does 3:00 p.m. sound?" You think she is showing up at your office?

[At this point, multiple jurors are laughing.]

A. No, but it isn't necessary.

Q. You are not going to find a guy about the defendant's size to be the stabber—and if you do, let's hope he is already serving life.

[Objection sustained on that one.]

Q. You do agree that that is not something we can apply the peer-review scientific method on.

A. Not that specific example.

Q. Although you have this theory that the blood had to have been from some other traumatic event recent enough that the bloody clothes were still in the trash, you are unaware of any recent hospitalizations of Jessica Braden from some other event, are you?

A. No.

Q. And you are not aware of any 911 calls that Jessica Braden made that could explain the blood spatter?
A. I am not.
Q. And you are unaware of any statements to friends or family relating some traumatic event that might explain the blood on the shirt and shoes, are you?
A. I have not spoken with any family members or any of her friends.
Q. You and I have never met before today, right?
A. True.
Q. Now, I hope this does not happen, and I can tell you if it does, it won't have been me that did it. I have to do this hypothetical and I apologize in advance, but let's say when you come home tonight, there is someone waiting inside your home—not me, but someone else—and that person has a knife like what was used in this murder. That person stabs you fourteen times with the same amount of force as in this murder and then the assailant slashes your throat [strenuous objection is overruled; Vandenbalk asks to approach and the judge says no] just like in this case.
How much of your blood should be on my shirt?
A. Well, that depends. Maybe you were waiting in the car for my assailant, and when the assailant ran to the car, some of the blood from the knife spattered onto your shirt.
Q. No, I already said I'm not mad at you; it wasn't me, I wasn't in the car. How much of your blood should be on my shirt?

A. Maybe you visited me at the hospital and you hugged me and got some on you then [juror laughter].

Q. No, I did not go to the hospital, I didn't even know you got stabbed. I was home in front of my TV; the Angels were playing the Yankees. I had no idea you got stabbed. How much of your blood should be on my shirt [more laughter]?

A. None.

Q. How much of your blood should be on my shoes?

A. None.

Q. No further questions.

It was now 4:45. Scapio's cross went ten minutes and some seconds. Judge Darkoza said, "We are adjourned for the day." He gave the jurors the standing admonition not to talk about the case or follow the news.

Whenever jurors enter a courtroom, the attorneys stand, and when they leave, the attorneys also stand. It's a traditional show of respect. Vandenbalk had always stood up as the jurors would come and go. This time, as Scapio, Conway, and Holdman rose, Vandenbalk sat in stunned silence. Atherton had to tell him to stand. When the jurors filed out—the jury is always seated closest to the prosecution—several passed Scapio and smiled.

After the jurors left, Judge Darkoza asked Vandenbalk if he wanted to put anything on the record. Vandenbalk, still stunned, said no. Judge Darkoza said that he had just loudly objected to the hypothetical of his witness getting murdered. Vandenbalk said, pretty much as all one sentence, "Oh right—that was ridiculous! He was trying to humiliate my witness with a horrifying story and it was over the top and I move to strike all that testimony and ask that the jury be admonished to disregard it on Monday and be told that he should not have been allowed to do that!"

Judge Darkoza said that it was a little graphic, but it was a fair line of questioning, given the witness's testimony. The judge then gratuitously added that "the hypothetical was a bit uncomfortable, but what was worse was watching your witness get murdered on the stand in under fifteen minutes." After wishing everyone a good weekend, Judge Darkoza said that he would see everyone Monday.

Scapio, Holdman, and Conway went out of the courtroom, and Mrs. Braden had the first smile on her face that Scapio had seen. She said, "I'm not worried anymore."

Holdman was gushing and saying, "I couldn't believe when you said you could be done in fifteen minutes and then you completely destroyed the guy." Holdman then saw Lanny talking to Atherton and Delaney, and he walked up to Lanny and said, "You know, I'm not thinking I'm gonna be writing that apology letter."

Lanny responded with two words: "Fuck off."

The baby prosecutors that had stayed to watch could not wait to tell their supervisors what they had just witnessed. It was a great day for the people in People v Allen McCarty, and it took just over ten minutes.

As Judge Darkoza drove home, he realized that one of the mysteries was just solved. He had wondered why Scapio never sought to limit Andrews's testimony, instead allowing Andrews to give the opinion that the blood on the shirt and shoes were not related to the murder. Scapio knew that he could utterly destroy that theory, so he did not want to limit his cross in any way. He also knew that the defense had put all their eggs in one basket, and if he destroyed the eggs, the basket would go with it. Darkoza had to hand it to Scapio; that was the best cross-examination he had ever heard, and it only took about ten minutes.

* * *

After the cross-examination, Vandenbalk met with McCarty, who said he wanted to testify. Vandenbalk asked him what his explanation for the blood on the shirt and shoes was going to be. McCarty said the cops planted the blood. Vandenbalk told him that it would never fly. Vandenbalk said that the cross-examination of Andrews went poorly for the defense and probably eliminated any hope of an acquittal. But the prosecution still needed all twelve, and if one or two stayed with them, maybe a hung jury was possible, and they could do better next trial.

Vandenbalk told him that if he was convicted, he would be eligible for parole in around fifteen years if it's second degree, and he would still be young enough to have a full life. Parole boards looked at remorse as one of the things to consider. Perjury at trial could be a deal breaker to any claim of remorse and could kill any chance of parole. He also said, "You saw what that prosecutor did to a professional witness. What do you think he's going to do to you? Besides, we already decided you weren't going to testify. If you do now, it's a concession that we are getting destroyed. It tells the jury we are now desperate." McCarty agreed that testifying was a bad idea.

Vandenbalk met with Andrews on Saturday. Vandenbalk asked Andrews if there was a way to salvage this. Andrews said the quote was out of context when he said he didn't work for the attorney, and that what he had meant to say was that he would not agree to the interview because he was not being paid for his time to be interviewed by the prosecutor and his team. Vandenbalk pointed out that Andrews admitted that he had not asked if he would be compensated for doing the interview. Andrews suggested a few other things they could get done, but it was obviously bleak.

Vandenbalk asked Andrews about his claim that no prosecutor had ever laid a glove on him. Andrews said that it was true until Friday night. Andrews said that the fifteen-minute thing caught him by surprise, and he got stung with the quote from the old Halverson case. He added that he took the McCarty case knowing it had problems, so Vandenbalk shouldn't be shocked when a skilled prosecutor pounded those weaknesses in cross.

Scapio had custody of Amy that weekend and took her to the Pacific View Mall and dinner at Red Robin on Saturday. On Sunday he went to work and showed Amy around the office before finalizing his PowerPoint closing by adding some slides covering Andrews's testimony. He was surprised it took so little time. Scapio was feeling so good about how the trial went that he called Holdman and asked him if he would like to do the rebuttal argument. Holdman declined and said, "This is yours, you should have the very last word. I was honored to have three witnesses and to do the legal research."

* * *

On Monday, September 4, Andrews was back on the stand as Vandenbalk tried to salvage something. Andrews explained his answer the way he wanted to on the Halverson case. Scapio's re-cross-examination was repetitious, and he soon realized that the jurors seemed tuned out, so he said, "No further questions," much to the relief of Andrews. The defense rested their case.

The prosecution did present evidence in rebuttal from friends and family members of the victim that she had never related any recent traumatic injury before the murder, and she had never been hospitalized for any major blood loss incident that they were aware of. Vandenbalk offered no cross-examination.

The jury was excused until 1:30 p.m. while the lawyers and the judge finalized the instructions for the rest of the morning.

At 1:30 p.m., the courtroom was packed for closing arguments. Judge Darkoza read the instructions to the jurors, and that took a little under an hour. After a twenty-minute break, during which tech assistant Penny Jones set up the PowerPoint and made sure it was running smoothly, Scapio was ready.

Scapio's closing began with discussing circumstantial evidence, pointing out that witnesses can lie, but circumstantial evidence never does. He put up a slide of a rope and said that circumstantial evidence is like a rope that is held together by thousands and thousands of tiny strands. You can't cut the rope by cutting one strand. He then pointed to the strands in this case. He went through the defendant's history of domestic violence. He went through the threats to the victim and her fear of him. He went through each slide photo of DNA evidence including the brassiere, followed by a chart showing the results, then the two blood drops at the scene belonging to the defendant, and the astronomical numbers indicating the killer bled at the scene and the defendant bled at the scene. He went to the shirt and the shoes and those results.

He then talked about how Frank Andrews tried to pull the wool over the jury's eyes. He blasted Andrews as a conman who got self-righteous about his role as a scientist, then acted in complete contradiction by asking the lawyer for permission to speak with the other side. He contrasted the honest testimony of Sean Murphy (he slipped and called him Lucky Charms once and had to explain to the jury that Lucky Charms was his nickname because of the Irish accent and the breakfast cereal; that got a laugh from a couple of jurors) and of Maria Aguilar, the people's DNA expert, with the junk science of Andrews.

He went through the cell-phone evidence in detail and then discussed the law of murder and willful deliberate premeditation.

Scapio was never ashamed of borrowing a strategy or argument from another prosecutor. The rope argument came from the late great fellow-Italian American and Manson prosecutor Vincent Bugliosi. Scapio concluded his argument by paralleling Bugliosi's argument from so long ago when he told the jury how Sharon Tate cried out for justice from her grave.

"Jessica Braden could not be with us today, but from her grave, she cries out for justice. She told us who killed her, not from the witness stand, but with her blood as it spattered all over her killer as he was murdering her. She told us as she fought and resisted, causing him to be cut and leave drops of his own blood. She told us with her own words spoken to her friends and family about the past violence and her fear that he would kill her, as she echoed the words of Karen Loring who filed a restraining order for the same reason. Jessica probably even shut her phone off or did not answer any calls because she wanted him to just go away. Karen Loring was lucky, but Jessica Braden, a beautiful person inside and out, was not so lucky.

"Where Jessica has been silenced, the evidence has not been silent. The defendant silenced the victim out of rage, control, and arrogance. He then silenced his phone by shutting it off. Frank Andrews tried to silence the evidence in this courtroom. He failed. It is time to give Jessica justice, and that can only be done when you find this killer"—pointing to McCarty—"guilty of first-degree murder with the use of a knife. Thank you for your time and attention."

Vandenbalk argued for less than an hour. He talked about something he never talked about in jury selection. He urged each juror to stick to their guns or their opinion unless they were convinced they were wrong, but to not change to go along. He read the instruction from his screen that said the defendant was entitled to the individual opinion of each juror. He only became animated when he accused Scapio of a vicious personal attack on a hero scientist who helped free an innocent man. He tried to defend Andrews's conclusion about the blood spatter but could see it was falling flat. He proposed that the victim may have had a date with an unknown man who she rejected, so he killed her. He conceded that his client may have been abusive in the past, explaining the blood. He insisted this new unknown man was the real killer. He also suggested that maybe Cody Welch was. He talked about reasonable doubt and rush to judgment. His argument relied on the thoroughly discounted testimony of Andrews. He asked the jury to find reasonable doubt.

Scapio's rebuttal was short but ended on the pile of coincidences. He argued that for the defendant to be innocent, he would have to be the unluckiest guy on the planet. On the night he finally decided to throw away the clothes he was wearing when he beat and likely stabbed his former girlfriend so badly she bled all over him, some unknown guy murdered that former girlfriend for an unknown reason and left no evidence of his presence. The unlucky man left the only evidence because on that unknown previous occasion, he cut himself and bled at her house, leaving two drops, and some other non-bleeding killer happened to pull out a bunch of clothes to make it look like a robbery and one item actually had the unlucky man's blood on it. The unlucky man also happened to shut off his phone for the longest time ever on the night this other guy who wasn't bleeding killed the unlucky man's ex-girlfriend. And the bad luck piled up more for the unlucky man as he happened to get hungry and cut himself while slicing celery, making the police think the two drops of blood must have linked him to the murder, when they were really related to a previous unknown assault and stabbing that she never reported, never sought a restraining order for, and never told her friends or family about, or went to the hospital for.

"Use your common sense. He's not unlucky. He's just guilty." With that, Scapio concluded. He decided to pass on the entire Santa Claus–tooth fairy argument, because he figured he made his point well enough.

The jury returned on Tuesday, September 5, for deliberations. By 3:00 p.m., the jury announced they had a verdict. Before a packed courtroom at 4:00 p.m., the verdict of guilty was read by the court's judicial assistant. They also found that he used a knife and that the murder was willful, deliberate, and premeditated.

Braden's family cried tears of relief, but it didn't make the loss go away. McCarty's family, whose attendance was spotty during the trial, sat motionless as the verdict was read. McCarty, who was so cocky during the investigation, sat stoically as the verdict was read and he was pronounced guilty. The judge thanked the jurors and told them they were free to talk about the case but only if they wanted to, and they were discharged. Conway left the courtroom to get contact information from the jurors so they could talk about what they thought was important. Scapio and Holdman hugged the family members. Scapio went back to his office but soon went home, relieved and excited. Judge Darkoza ordered McCarty remanded into custody without bail. McCarty was handcuffed without resistance.

On Wednesday, September 6, Scapio got a call to see DA Reddis in his office. When Scapio arrived, Reddis shook his hand vigorously, saying, "I heard you had one hell of a cross-examination of the expert." Scapio said he'd prepared for it, and Reddis said he knew he picked the right prosecutor for the job. He asked Scapio if he had Amy that weekend, and Ray told him that his ex did; he'd just had her, and they had a great time at the mall, and she even got to see his office with the paper clips in formation.

Reddis said, "Good, because I reserved the Mandalay Beach Resort bar for Friday night to celebrate the conviction." Reddis added, "No driving for you, because as your boss, I'm ordering you to drink like it's St. Patrick's Day and your name is Patrick O'Flaherty. We'll make sure you have a designated driver."

Scapio said that sounded good, and he might just call the hotel and stay overnight. Scapio liked the hotel, which was in Oxnard, and had stayed there a couple of times. Reddis said that if he wanted to take a couple of weeks off, it was well earned. Scapio told him that he already had his December Vegas trip scheduled and he didn't want to use too much vacation time, but he was hoping to get no new cases until after his on-call week at the end of October.

On-call week was when senior prosecutors were obligated to stay in-county after hours, because if there was a murder, they would respond to it and assist in the initial stages of the investigation. They got two days off without having to use vacation time in exchange for being on call for an entire week. The call could come at any time after 5:00 p.m., and it could require them to respond to the police station, a crime scene, or a hospital, depending on the circumstances.

Scapio said he was just hoping to catch up on his other cases, as he had been living this one for a while now. Reddis agreed to make sure he got nothing new until November, and he would make sure Waverly knew that.

The rest of the week, Scapio was on cloud nine. He was approached by one of the new deputy DAs, Jeff Pweeg, who looked like he hadn't turned twenty-one yet. Scapio recognized him from when he taught cross-examination to the new prosecutors. Pweeg said, "Hey Ray. I have just one question for you."

Scapio was a little guarded and said, "What's that?"

"How much of your blood should be on my shirt?"

Scapio laughed and said, "All of it! Or, I don't know, maybe I was waiting in the car for your killer so we could hug it out, or maybe it squirted all over me when the real killer waved his knife around."

"No, remember, I don't know you, I never saw you before today. I'm not waiting in the fucking car; I'm at home eating pizza."

Scapio laughed and said, "You do a better me than me! If I ever get famous, I have an impersonator."

Pweeg then introduced himself and said, "That was so great. I've never seen anything like it." Scapio invited Pweeg to go to the Mandalay to celebrate. Pweeg said he would be there.

Ray thought about calling Diana Carbone, the excused juror that he found attractive, but since she never got on the jury, he felt awkward about it. He figured if she was interested, she would have read about the case result in the paper and would have called and congratulated him. In fact, Diana Carbone did find Scapio attractive, she was single, and she did think about congratulating him when she read about the case in the paper, but then she thought that might seem a little awkward and desperate, so she decided against it.

He did speak with some of the jurors, and they did not have trouble with the case at all. Although three jurors put down their notebooks after the destruction on cross began, the jurors thought the defense was ridiculous.

Friday night at the Mandalay was a great time. Woody Holdman was there and about thirty other prosecutors showed up. He even took congratulations from Flynn. He was not happy that Flynn didn't want him on the case, but he felt like it would be breaking a confidence to say anything. The young deputy DAs he'd taught cross-examination to were all there, and they asked him about how he prepared for that. He spoke with Reddis and his wife, who bought one of the six mixed drinks he consumed that night. It was just a fantastic time.

He retired to his room at the hotel about 1:00 a.m. and woke up a little hung over but still excited about the trial and the party the night before. He thought how much he loved his work. Though he felt like he was being a little egotistical, feeling so great about all the accolades, he did always manage to praise the other members of the prosecution team. He bought Penny Jones four boxes of See's candy and called her the "unsung hero."

He didn't know it then, but it would not be too long before his on-call week would send him on the strangest and most horrifying case he would ever see.

TWELVE

Macklin noticed the purple daisy tattoo and complimented her on it. That would be the last nice thing Macklin would say to Daisy. He drove from the Avenue to Main Street and headed toward the mall. He knew that when he got near the mall, if there was too much traffic for him to get over quickly and onto the 101 freeway, he was just going to have to drop her at the mall and wait for another time. Mack was feeling lucky as he moved to the right lane, which would get him onto the freeway rather than to the Pacific View Mall where Daisy worked.

Daisy told Mack to get in the left lane, but he ignored her and sped up toward the 101. Daisy asked what he was doing and said she had to get to work. Macklin sped up more and was now entering the 101 heading north. Daisy became very frightened and asked where he was going. He told Daisy to shut her mouth. Daisy knew the car was going too fast to jump out. She begged to be dropped off and promised she would not say anything. She was saying to herself, "Oh God, Daisy, why didn't you just have Mom drive you?"

Daisy got her phone out of her purse but Mack hit it out of her hand. The phone hit the dashboard and bounced. She started looking for it, but Macklin struck her with a backhand blow in the mouth, cutting Daisy's lip. Macklin was speeding, but Daisy saw no police cars. Macklin drove about eight miles and turned rapidly off Highway 33 toward Ojai. Daisy realized she was probably going to die. She began crying, and Mack yelled, "Quit crying, you stupid little bitch." Daisy continued crying and begging to be released. She began thinking of her parents, her friends, and her little brother, and was terrified she would never see them again.

Mack turned off Cañada Larga Road and made a fast right turn. Daisy saw the road was isolated, and now she was certain she was going to die. She was crying uncontrollably. She tried to open the door, but it was locked from inside. Mack grabbed a fistful of Daisy's long black hair and pulled it toward him, then flung her to the passenger window. Daisy's head smashed against the window. Her head was pounding, but she was conscious enough to know that she knew who he was, and there was no way he was going to let her live.

She tried to grab the steering wheel and drive it off the road, but Macklin pushed her away. She tried again and he backhanded her in the head. Daisy was able to scratch Macklin's arm with the fingers on her left hand and she tried to punch him with her right hand, but he smacked her again on the side of the head. Daisy thought maybe if she fought hard enough, she could cause him to crash the car and she might have a chance. She lowered her body and kicked Macklin as he was driving, and she did land several kicks as Macklin called her a fucking little cunt and said she would be dead soon. He took his right hand off the wheel while maintaining control of the wheel with his left hand. He again grabbed Daisy's hair and almost ran off the road but straightened out. He then thrust his big arm and slammed her head into the door. She gasped and felt herself close to passing out.

The road was becoming isolated now; Macklin had driven at least five miles into the middle of nowhere. Soon Daisy would lose track of time and distance. She knew death was certain unless by some miracle a police car would be in the area. She tried to suppress her crying but she couldn't. She would never get to say goodbye to anyone who ever cared about her. She was never going to have children or have a career. Though she wasn't particularly religious, Daisy had been to church, and she began to pray. Mack heard her and smacked her in the face again, while shouting, "God can't hear you, you stupid little cunt." Daisy was so terrified, she hoped it would just end. Mack was laughing at her fear. He was thinking to himself that he had never had this much fun in his life.

He pulled over a long way up Cañada Larga Road, where there was nobody around. Daisy decided if she was going to die, she was going to try to hurt him as much as she possibly could. He stopped the van on the side of the road, overlooking a very steep ravine. Daisy jumped out and ran. Macklin was surprised at how fast Daisy was, but he had a much longer stride. He caught her after about forty yards. She kicked him hard in the thigh, but she was off balance and missed what she was aiming for. She tried to scratch him with her long polished purple nails, but Mack grabbed her wrists.

He dragged Daisy toward the edge of the road, pinning her arms to her side in a bear hug. Daisy was grunting and screaming at the top of her lungs, but there was nobody around to hear her. Mack threw Daisy down onto the ground and pinned her arms so she couldn't scratch him and leave more evidence. She was unable to lift her arms to fight back; Mack was so much larger and stronger than she was. In her last act of defiance, she spit right into Mack's face. Mack slammed Daisy's head three times on the ground while calling her a fucking bitch. The third head slam knocked Daisy out cold.

Jack Macklin returned to his van and slid it open. He was mumbling that she was lucky because he was no longer in the mood for "romance," so he was just going to kill her. He grabbed a plastic container filled with sulfuric acid, which he had purchased just for this occasion. He walked back to Daisy, unscrewed the cap, and poured the liquid all over Daisy's face and chest.

Daisy woke up to the most horrific pain she could ever imagine. She screamed, and Macklin kicked her, and she tumbled down the embankment. Macklin got back in his van and sped away.

As Daisy was tumbling down the embankment, she grabbed a large weed or bush. Despite the harrowing pain, she clawed and climbed her way up the ravine about ten feet. Had she not grabbed the branch or weed or whatever it was—at this point Daisy couldn't see—she would have fallen well over one hundred feet to certain death.

She got to her feet and ran onto the road, but the pain was excruciating. All she could think about was identifying the man who did this to her before she died. In unbearable pain and miles from the road, Daisy felt her face burning away. The only thing that kept her from begging to die was getting justice.

Macklin pulled over about two miles up the road when he heard Daisy's phone ring. He got out of the van. Shut the phone off. Threw it on the ground and stomped on it, smashing it. Then he threw it down the ravine. Returning to the van, he retrieved Daisy's purse and threw it way down the ravine where he figured it would not be found for a long time. He drove about a mile and stopped again and tossed the container of sulfuric acid. He felt fortunate that it didn't go all the way down and got wedged in some bushes. He saw that it wasn't visible from the roadway and might never be found. Even if it were, he thought that the weather would probably wash away all the DNA.

When he got home, he was going to wash the van himself, then take it to an auto detailer and car wash. His initial washing should clean it up enough to prevent an auto cleaner from noticing anything suspicious. Then a professional cleaning should do the trick. He couldn't do anything right away about the crack in the right front passenger window where he slammed Daisy's head, but he figured he would just say some vandal must have cracked the window trying to get in to steal something.

He believed that the police wouldn't be able to tie him to Daisy's murder. They might suspect him, but they would never prove it. Even if they were smart enough to check if her abductor tried to help her with the stalled car, he actually didn't touch the interior under the hood; he only pretended to. And before he touched the part to lift the hood, he had put his hand inside his untucked shirt, so unless his DNA was on his shirt and it transferred, he would not be linked. He also figured that he always had the option of telling them that he noticed her car would not start and he tried to help her get it started, but he never gave her a ride.

He hoped a thorough cleaning would wipe her DNA from inside the car. He had planned on abducting Daisy, raping her, and killing her, and the fact that his anger overcame his desire to rape her might have been a good thing, because none of his semen would be inside her. He figured any other DNA would decompose by the time they found her body.

THIRTEEN

Kent and Millie Hooper had been married for fifty-two years. Kent, seventy-four, was a retired farmer, and Millie, seventy-two, a retired legal secretary. They lived in Ojai and liked to sometimes take long drives with the windows down. Kent suggested they take one the morning of November 1. Millie suggested they head toward 33 and take the exit for Cañada Larga and drive up the isolated roadway and check out the sights. They got in Kent's new pickup truck.

As they drove up Cañada Larga Road and got to where the road seemed deserted, they saw a dark-colored van speeding toward them and then past them. Both Kent and Millie thought that was odd. They wondered why someone would be up there in broad daylight, racing down this remote road. They decided to keep on driving.

About seven minutes later, they saw a figure in the middle of the road. They could see it was a young woman with long black hair and a green tank top. As they got closer, they heard her scream in agony and saw she was clutching her face. Kent stopped the truck and ran to her. He picked her up and put her in the back seat and took off his overshirt and gave it to her to hold against her face, which seemed to be burning off. She just kept screaming, but they couldn't understand much of what she said. They were sure of one thing; she had repeatedly yelled the name Jack or Mack.

Kent knew the Ojai Hospital was the closest and easiest to get to. He drove that new pickup truck as fast as he had ever driven it. Daisy was screaming as she entered the hospital, and she was immediately sedated and taken to the ER. She was intubated and put into a medically induced coma due to the severity of her burns.

That afternoon, the hospital notified the Ojai Sheriff's Department of what had occurred. Detective Chris Whatley, forty-six, was called to investigate. He was told that the victim was transferred from the ER into a room but that she was still comatose and bandaged up. He was also told that she was never able to give her name and she had no phone, purse, or identification.

Whatley was one of the sheriff's department's finest and had been considered a strong possibility to be the next sheriff of Ventura County. A white man and former athlete with a youthful appearance, Whatley had grown up in Ventura but had attended college at Montana State, where he was a power forward on the basketball team. Though he was still athletically built, his light-brown hair was turning more salt-and-pepper.

Whatley had been a well-respected sheriff's homicide detective for ten years. Before that, he had worked patrol, custody, and property crimes for thirteen years. Whatley had a twenty-two-year-old daughter from a previous marriage and a four-year-old with his current wife.

When he peeked into the victim's hospital room, he saw a bandaged-up young woman but could still tell that she might be about the same age as his eldest daughter. He wanted to get justice for this young woman, but he first had to find out who she was. Based upon the grim medical prognosis, this was likely to become a homicide investigation.

The first thing Whatley did was check missing-person reports. If this young woman was someone with a family and a home and job, it should be easy to at least build a strong case for who she was that could be corroborated by DNA. If she was a street girl, it was going to be very difficult unless they could get fingerprints, but even that would take time since her hands were currently bandaged because she had touched her face.

She was wearing blue jeans and a green tank top that was from Nordstrom Rack. Her shoes were high end. She had spent some money at a nail salon, based on her long polished purple nails. He did get a look at her skin tone; although heavily bandaged, her arms were visible and her coloring seemed most consistent with her being a young Latina. She also had long black hair. The combination of these factors made Whatley think that this victim was likely a young middle-class Hispanic woman who should be easy to identify, even if confirmation might take a while.

* * *

Around 1:00 a.m., Whatley spoke to John Wong, who was the young woman's assigned doctor. He confirmed his previous grim prognosis. He told Whatley that the young woman was unlikely to survive her injuries. He added that when they identified her, it would be likely that they would ask the family to take her off life support. He added that if by a miracle she survived, she would be facing a lifetime of surgeries and would always be easily recognizable as a burn victim. Whatley decided it would be a good idea to call the on-call attorney at the DA's office since this was likely going to be a homicide.

Ray Scapio was the on-call homicide prosecutor for the week that ran from the end of October through the beginning of November. His ex-wife had their daughter that week due to his being on call to respond.

Scapio rolled out of bed, awakened from a just-achieved deep sleep. He had stayed up until midnight watching TV on the couch in his one-bedroom condo in Ventura. He got the call from the service that works the on-call process and was given a number to call. He called that number, and it was Chris Whatley's cell.

Scapio knew Whatley from a couple of cases they had worked together. Whatley also attended a homicide conference in Monterey that Scapio had attended. One night they hung out in the bar at the hotel, discussing their respective divorces. Scapio and Whatley, as well as several other deputy sheriffs and detectives attending the conference, went to dinner a couple of times on the Monterey Pier. Scapio was the only prosecutor in attendance from Ventura because one investigator and one other prosecutor had to back out due to a trial, so Scapio had hung out with the sheriff's crew. Scapio liked and respected Whatley and the feeling was mutual.

Whatley told him about the girl in the hospital, and all Scapio could say was, "Oh my God." He felt guilty that he had been still basking in the glory of his victory in the McCarty trial when he heard about this horrible case. His heart went out to this poor girl, whoever she was.

Scapio changed into jeans and a green button-down shirt and drove to the Ojai Hospital, where he met with Whatley and Dr. Wong. They led him to a room on the first floor. Dr. Wong pulled back the curtain on a young woman who was bandaged up everywhere but her forearms and the outside part of her fingers, which had no burn damage. Her palms were bandaged and there were some Band-Aids on the inside of her fingers. Scapio noticed that some of her nails were broken and that there was visible dirt. He figured that she might have crawled out from somewhere she had been left for dead. He also noticed the long black hair. Her forearms were slender but not skinny. Her skin was a golden-brown shade, probably not black or white; Scapio thought this young woman was likely Hispanic. He also thought she was probably a beautiful girl before this happened. He knew that beauty would be gone.

He teared up looking at her and said, "I hope the sick fuck that did this to her burns in hell, and I would love to be the prosecutor that sends him there." He told Whatley that he was going to clear it with Reddis to be assigned the case. Ray thought about what he would want to do if someone did that to his daughter or someone else he loved. He thought about whether it might not just be best for her if she died but then realized she was going to likely have to live in order for this sick person to be caught. Scapio commented on her nails and said they should call a crime-scene investigator to collect fingernail clippings or scrape under the nails, because maybe she scratched her attacker. Whatley said he would call in the morning, but they would be closed now.

On Thursday morning, Whatley reviewed the missing-person reports that he had requested. The newest case out of Ventura looked promising. Twenty-four-year-old Daisy Guzman was supposed to be at work in the Pacific View Mall in Ventura yesterday morning, but she never showed up. Her parents could not reach her on her phone, and she had not called anyone. Daisy had gone to several Halloween parties with her friend Veronica Gonzalez the day before that. Ms. Gonzalez had said that Daisy left her house at 7:00 a.m. on the first of November. They knew Daisy got home because her parents reported that she left to go to work that morning. But her car was still on the street near their house. She was wearing jeans and a green tank top and had long black hair. Whatley contacted the assigned Ventura police detective to get an update.

Detective Davon Washington was the first African American to head the Homicide Division for the Ventura Police Department. Whatley knew him from homicide round tables when different agencies met to discuss pretty much everything law enforcement homicide-related. Washington would later earn the nickname "J Edgar" because of his uncanny resemblance to the actor Jamie Hector, who played Detective Jerry Edgar, or J. Edgar as they called him, on the Amazon Prime series *Bosch*. That show started in 2014, but Whatley's nickname didn't take hold until 2019 when one of the newer detectives started watching the show and noticed the resemblance, with the notable exception of the unexplained scar on the character's cheek.

Whatley told Washington about the case he had at the Ojai Hospital, and Washington said that he was aware of it and was about to contact him. He said he was hoping it wouldn't be her, but given what he had already learned about Daisy Guzman, he did not think she just left without contacting family or friends. She also would not miss work without calling.

Washington mentioned that they had an interview set up in an hour with her ex-boyfriend who was a low-level Ventura Avenue Gangster named Steve Alvarez. Alvarez worked at an auto body shop in Ventura. He had a criminal record, but it was minimal. The most serious charges were a drunk driving and a tagging—vandalism by spray paint—when he was seventeen.

There was one call for service when Daisy was briefly living with him in Ventura. A neighbor called and complained about shouting from their home. When the police arrived, neither requested that anyone be arrested. They both claimed that the argument never got physical. Reading the report, it didn't seem like the type of incident where a victim was physically abused but denied it out of fear. According to the patrol officer's report, Daisy called Steve an asshole in front of the officers. Whatley decided it would be a good idea to go to Ventura and interview Alvarez with Washington.

When Whatley arrived at the Ventura police station, Washington came out and greeted him warmly with a hug and a handshake. Washington commented that Whatley was looking good, except his once-light-brown hair had gotten a lot grayer. Whatley joked that it was the job and told Washington, "What are you, twenty-six? When you've been working these cases as long as me, you'll get salt-and-pepper real fast. Then you'll need a good hairstylist to keep the pepper in there."

Washington said, "I'm thirty-five, but I'm beginning to know what you mean." Then he went on, "This is gonna be the most horrific case in Ventura that I have ever seen." He added that he kept hoping that the next call from the Guzmans would be that Daisy was home safe and it was all a big misunderstanding. But if it wasn't her, it was someone else, and that was a tragedy too.

They met Alvarez at a body shop on the Avenue. Esteban (Steve) Alvarez was a good-looking young man, too pretty to be the gang member he was known to be, but he did have multiple tattoos that covered both arms. He was a couple of years younger than Daisy at twenty-two. He came out and greeted them, they shook hands, and the two investigators introduced themselves.

Alvarez immediately asked what this was about. Washington asked Alvarez when the last time was that he saw Daisy Guzman. Alvarez immediately became distraught and asked if Daisy was OK and if anything had happened to her. Washington told him that they did not know, but she had been reported missing. Alvarez said, "Oh my God, how long?" Washington told him they couldn't go into a lot of details, but they just needed to talk to all the people that were close to Daisy.

Alvarez seemed genuinely distraught and volunteered that they were a couple for about a year but had broken up a couple of months before. When asked the last time he talked to Daisy, he said it was a few weeks ago, and he had just called to say hi and ask how she was doing. When asked the last time he had seen her, he said it was a week after they broke up; she had left a couple of things at his place and she came to pick them up.

Whatley asked why they broke up and Alvarez said it was more his fault, because he was hanging around with the Avenue gangsters too much and Daisy did not like that. He added that they had probably already looked him up and that he was documented Ventura Avenue, meaning law enforcement recognized him as a documented member of the Ventura Avenue Gangsters.

He said that Daisy and her friend Veronica were really classy and they didn't like the cholos and cholas or the entire gang culture, but he grew up with those guys and two of them worked at the shop, so it was really hard for him to break away.

Washington asked him about the time the police were called, and he said it was about that. He had promised Daisy he was gonna break away from the gang but she had checked his phone and he had a lot of texts where he and others were flashing signs—gang signs with their hands—and he had posed in a photo with a couple of the cholas where he was holding a gun. He was still on probation and Daisy got furious and started screaming at him. He had yelled back, telling her that he already had a mom and he did not need another one. The argument got so loud that the police were called.

Washington asked if he had any information about Daisy's whereabouts. Alvarez denied any knowledge and said that even though they weren't together, she was the best girlfriend he ever had and she only wanted what was best for him, and he asked them to call him if they found out anything. He added, "I guess I'm not over her, 'cause I'm worried sick right now." Washington asked Alvarez if he was willing to give a DNA sample and he said, "Sure, anything you guys need." Washington pulled out a packet and then took a Q-tip and asked Alvarez to open his mouth, which he did, and Washington swabbed his cheek and put the Q-tip in the packet.

Washington asked if Daisy had any enemies. Alvarez said that as far as he knew, everyone liked her, and he had no idea who would want to do anything bad to her. They each gave Alvarez a business card and asked him to call if he heard anything.

Washington and Whatley agreed that it was unlikely Alvarez was involved in her disappearance. Washington mentioned that if Luis "Psycho" Gutierrez wasn't serving time for kidnapping and rape, he would be a good suspect. Gutierrez was a very active Avenue gangster who grabbed a female jogger and forced her into his van and drove her into the hills and raped her. He ended up getting convicted and was serving life for kidnapping and rape. Whatley said that it might be someone like that though, a gang member who saw Daisy and decided to stalk her and take her. Washington agreed that was possible, and he mentioned that he looked at her DMV photo and she was an absolute knockout, so this could be about her looks. Whatley said that they couldn't rule out a female perpetrator or perpetrators in a jealousy thing. Washington said that this wasn't the type of crime females usually commit but agreed that it couldn't be ruled out.

Washington suggested they go to Oxnard and interview Veronica (Nikki) Gonzalez, Daisy's best friend. Washington had a cell number for her, and she answered on the first ring, hoping it was Daisy. Washington identified himself and asked if she was at work and she said that she was. She asked if they found Daisy and if she was OK. Washington said they had not but were working on it. He asked if they could come by and speak with her and she agreed.

Washington recognized her from her DMV photo right away. Veronica Gonzalez was twenty-four years old, born on March 12, 1993, so just a month older than Daisy. When they met Veronica, two things were obvious. Veronica, like Daisy, was physically beautiful. Long brown hair, curvy hourglass figure perfectly proportioned. Veronica had streaks of purple in her hair. That was a thing that she was known for; she always had long brown hair but with different colors streaked into it. Sometimes blond, red, and now purple. She had the face of an angel but a very sad one. The other obvious thing was that she had been crying.

She went over the previous Halloween night and was asked if there was anyone who acted strangely. She said it was Halloween so everyone was a little weird, but nobody stood out as creepy. Whatley asked if Daisy had any enemies, and Veronica said no, that everyone loved Daisy, she was the sweetest girl in the world. Washington asked how long she had known Daisy, and she said since high school, and they became friends fast.

Whatley asked if she ever had any enemies back in high school, and Veronica said that there was one girl in high school named Becky who didn't like Daisy and used to call her Ditzy Daisy, so Daisy started calling her Bitchy Becky. She said it was over some guy that Becky liked who ended up liking Daisy instead. Whatley asked if the issue between Daisy and Becky ever got physical, and Veronica said that as far as she knew it never did, and Daisy was not the type to start a fight. She mentioned that Daisy had once confided in her that she was afraid that Becky would beat her up, but she didn't want to show that she was scared. Veronica added that if Becky had assaulted Daisy, Veronica would have known about it because Daisy would have told her. She said Daisy had never even gone out with the guy and was distraught that Becky hated her so much. Veronica said that Daisy was her friend, but she tried to stay out of the drama and added with a laugh that Becky was bigger than her too, and she did not want to get in a fight with her.

She said that it was a long time ago and everyone had moved on from high school, so she seriously doubted Becky would do anything to hurt Daisy, and she didn't even know where Becky was. Veronica said that the two girls just talked shit to and about each other, but neither one ever talked about violence or made any threats. Then she remembered that Daisy saw Becky afterwards, "like years later," and Becky was really nice and felt terrible. Veronica had forgotten the whole story about where they saw each other but thought it was where Daisy was working. She remembered it was kind of a cute story.

Washington asked some questions about the ex-boyfriend and Veronica mentioned that Daisy loved him, but he just did not want to break away from the gang, and that was a source of conflict for them. Veronica asked if they thought she herself had anything to worry about because she lived alone in Oxnard Shores and was afraid that if someone had some grudge against Daisy maybe they would come after her too. Detective Washington said that they had no reason to believe that but told her to always be cautious and keep her doors locked and to not accept rides from people she didn't know.

Veronica said she knew something terrible had happened because she and Daisy would text or talk every day, and now she called and texted and got nothing. She said that even if Daisy was mad, she would never ghost someone—intentionally not respond, like a ghost that you can't see or hear.

Detective Whatley asked if there were any men that had wanted to date Daisy that she rebuffed. Veronica said that Daisy had a boyfriend up until a couple of months ago, so most guys respected that. Veronica added that men definitely liked Daisy, but that Daisy never mentioned a stalker, or a guy who would not take no. Veronica mentioned a previous boyfriend from a few years back named Trent Rogers, but he had moved to Colorado. They gave Veronica their cards and asked her to call if she remembered or could find Becky's last name. They also asked her to call if she thought of anything else.

Veronica called back because she'd remembered Becky's last name. Washington found a number for her in the cell-phone database. He called the number and identified himself as a detective with the Ventura Police Department. He asked her to come in the next morning, and she asked what it was about, and he said a missing person. She asked who and she was told that they would talk about it the next day.

At 9:00 a.m. on Friday, Rebecca Holland, formerly known as Becky Patterson, came in. They figured with the name change she had gotten married and that would make her an unlikely suspect to carry a high school grudge over a boy.

Washington and Whatley met her in the lobby. Both detectives immediately noticed the rock on Becky's finger, confirming the marriage. Rebecca Holland asked who was missing and was told it was Daisy Guzman. Holland, a tall, pretty blond woman around five foot nine with blue eyes and a fit athletic figure, said, "Oh my God, do you have any leads? That's horrible."

Whatley asked Rebecca, without answering her question, what her relationship was with Daisy. Rebecca said that in high school they didn't get along, but she said that it was her fault. She related that a guy she had made out with told her he didn't want to see her anymore because he was attracted to Daisy. She said because of that, "I was a bitch to Daisy and called her 'Ditzy Daisy' and 'Mexican Barbie' and she called me names back. Then after high school, one of the guy's friends told me that his buddy never even went out with Daisy, but that she was his dream girl. I realized then that I had been mean to Daisy for nothing.

"Then one night about three years ago, my husband and I, well, he was my fiancé then, went to Yolanda's in Oxnard and who turns out to be our server but Daisy Guzman. As soon as she came to our table, I apologized for having been mean to her and I said how stupid it was. She seemed a little skeptical but smiled and was nice the whole time. It was a fifty-dollar bill and I tipped her forty dollars on top of the fifty, so she got ninety. Daisy came running out and said that she thought I overpaid. I told Daisy that I intended to tip her that much because she deserved it for how much of a bitch to her I was in high school." She also said that Daisy hugged her and even cried and said that meant a lot to her.

She asked when Daisy went missing and sounded sincerely worried. They talked a little more and she mentioned that she is a stay-at-home mom with three kids. After some small talk, they gave her their cards, and she said she was going to pray for Daisy. She added that she should have figured out that since everyone else loved Daisy, she was probably wrong about her. Besides, she added, "Who cares if she dated that guy, I didn't own him. God, I was such a bitch in high school."

Whatley and Washington agreed Rebecca Holland was a very unlikely suspect. Washington observed that her story was corroborated by Veronica, who remembered they had made up but had not recalled all the details.

It was getting late on Friday, but Chris Whatley and Davon Washington decided to confer on what they thought happened, assuming the girl in the hospital in Ojai was Daisy Guzman.

Washington posed the question of where they thought Daisy had been abducted. Since her car was still on the street, she was either abducted before she got to her car or she was already in her car. They reasoned that if she'd been abducted in her driveway or outside her car, she would have been likely to scream, and someone would have heard it.

Washington suggested the possibility of an accomplice. One guy grabbed her from behind and put his hand over her mouth and the other guy opened the door of the vehicle, and the guy holding her mouth forced her inside without her being able to scream. Whatley said it would be hard to sneak up on her because she'd be aware of a stranger who was that close to her house. Whatley added that it could be one assailant if he took her at gunpoint and threatened to shoot her if she offered any resistance.

Washington suggested perhaps she was already in her car when abducted. Whatley said that would make sense if the car wouldn't start and the kidnapper offered her a ride. Washington said that would likely mean she knew her abductor and trusted him enough to get into his or her car. Whatley added that they needed to tow the car and have a mechanic check it out. They didn't have Daisy's keys because they were missing, as was her purse, but a mechanic should be able to determine if the vehicle had a dead battery or other starter issue. Washington said if the abduction happened that way, Daisy would not have screamed or fought back until she realized that he wasn't taking her to work but got on the freeway.

Washington said, "Here's another reason that this unidentified woman is Daisy Guzman: If someone is driving to the mall and detours to the 101, the first isolated road they get to where they can drive and a commit a horrible crime with little chance of being seen is Cañada Larga Road off Highway 33. This woman was found by the couple on Cañada Larga Road."

Whatley said that if her car did break down, it was likely a neighbor who gave the ride and did this horrible thing to her. They agreed to check out all the neighbors, especially the men, since it was looking much more likely that Daisy's abductor was a man. Washington theorized that since Daisy was fully clothed, she probably fought her attacker and he decided that committing rape would be a problem, so he just tried to kill her.

They discussed Friday's agenda. They would get the car towed to the mechanic service that the Ventura Police Department uses and verify that her car would not start. They needed to make sure that the mechanic service made this the number-one priority. Washington mentioned that he had not gotten a DNA sample from the Guzmans for Daisy. They could get some hair from a hairbrush. They also wanted to get a full statement from the Hoopers, the couple that drove Daisy to the hospital. Additionally, they wanted to find out who her neighbors were by checking county records and then running rap sheets.

* * *

Jose and Marta Guzman could not sleep for even one second. Their daughter was missing and they didn't know what to do. They wanted to know where she was, but they feared the worst. Jose said that he dreaded receiving the phone call from the police because he was afraid that it would be that they found Daisy's body. Marta shared that fear.

To try and calm her, Jose told Marta about the girl that was kidnapped out of her home and returned safely, several years ago. He didn't remember the name but hoped maybe it would be what would happen with Daisy. Secretly, he doubted it. He feared he had lost his loving daughter. Their young son Juan was constantly crying and saying that he wanted Daisy to come home.

When the detectives arrived, Marta asked about going on TV and begging whoever took Daisy to return her safely. Jose said that since they do not have that much money, this wasn't about ransom, and there had been no demand for that anyway.

Marta saw Daisy leave for work in the morning; Jose had already left. Marta never heard Daisy scream, but her car was still on the street near the house. Marta wondered if maybe Daisy's car stalled and she got a ride from someone. Marta dismissed that at first, thinking Daisy would just call her and ask her to give her a ride. Then Marta thought if it was somebody she knew, she might have let him give her a ride. Marta thought about the neighbors and her mind focused on Macklin, but she didn't even know his name.

Detective Washington asked Jose if Daisy had a spare car key. Jose said they thought she did. They searched Daisy's room and found a few loose keys; one looked like her car key. They went out and tried it and it fit the door to Daisy's Honda Civic. After trying the ignition, they knew they wouldn't need to send the car to a mechanic right away; the car would not even turn over. Detective Whatley called for a tow truck and a forensics team from the lab.

Jose broke down when he saw Daisy's car wouldn't start. He cried that as a father, the one responsibility he had in life was to protect his daughter. He sobbed uncontrollably, saying, "Daisy,

I'm sorry, I failed you. Please forgive me. Oh God, please help Daisy, please don't take my little girl."

Marta told the detectives that they had a big "scuzzy"-looking neighbor that moved in not long ago that gave her the creeps, and Daisy was way too trusting. Washington asked what his name was, but Marta didn't know it. He wasn't very friendly to her or Jose and didn't seem approachable. She pointed out where she thought he lived.

When the forensics team arrived, the detectives suggested areas to swab for DNA, including the windows outside in case he tapped on one, the hood of the car and the lever under the hood that opens it, and the battery and wires.

Detective Washington asked the court officer that brings all the Ventura PD in-custody filings to go to the county records department and get ownership information on all the houses within two blocks from where they now believed Daisy was abducted. He told her when she got that information to run rap sheets on all the owners. This would turn out not to be helpful, because Jack Macklin wasn't the property owner of the home he was living in. They would, however, make some progress once they canvassed the neighborhood and spoke to people that were home.

Davon Washington checked the registered sex offender database under Marcy's Law requiring persons convicted of sex offenses to register within five days of their release and again before their next birthday. Washington had suggested it Thursday night and Whatley thought it was a good idea. Washington figured that whoever did this probably didn't register if he had to. They hoped that if they could identify a suspect who turned out to have failed to register, they could arrest him for that, and that could give them time to build a case while keeping their suspect in custody.

After running the database for sex offenders in Ventura, Washington was shocked that he may have hit gold. Two looked promising. The first was a forty-eight-year-old African American named Lawrence Hill. He lived in Ventura about a mile from Daisy's residence. His convictions were from when he was a Los Angeles resident. He was convicted of two counts of child molestation and served six years in prison. He was also convicted of stalking and attempted rape and served ten years. The negative on this pervert was that Daisy was already probably too old for him. His oldest victim had been seventeen.

Washington liked the next one a lot more. John "Jack" Macklin was convicted of forcible rape, and a kidnap-for-rape charge was dropped. Macklin was thirty-eight and was recently paroled. He lived just two doors down from Daisy Guzman. Washington phoned Whatley and gave him the news.

Whatley told Washington that he got a call from Daisy's friend Veronica who said that this was probably nothing, but she called because they said to call if she thought of anything. Veronica told them that Daisy had mentioned a heavily tattooed neighbor that was kind of good-looking in a real bad-boy sort of way that said hi to her a few times and seemed to be checking her out. Veronica asked Daisy if she would go out with the guy, and Daisy said her parents would kill her if she did. Veronica said that if that neighbor was offering Daisy a ride somewhere, she might get in. She said she never asked the man's name and Daisy never said what it was.

After pulling up photos of Macklin, they were scheduled to speak with Kent and Millie Hooper. Washington drove to the

Ojai sheriff's substation and from there they drove to the home of Kent and Millie Hooper. It was a small house on a little street behind Highway 33. Kent and Millie related what they saw and heard. Millie said the girl was screaming in pain and some of it was "Help" and "Oh God." Some of it she could not understand, but she is sure she heard the name Jack or Mack or both several times. Kent confirmed he was sure he heard "Jack," but the rest he was not sure. He added that his hearing was not great.

Whatley asked if they had washed their truck. Kent said that they had. There was a lot of blood and skin and he wanted to get it out as soon as possible. Washington was told about Kent taking his shirt off and Washington asked if he still had the shirt. Hooper said he threw it out. Washington asked if the garbage had been collected yet; Hooper said that it came on Thursday. Whatley asked him to describe the shirt. He was thinking about checking where the trash went to see if they could recover it. They would later look into that, but they were too late. Washington wished they had impounded the truck, because the lab could have confirmed what substance was used on the poor girl, but sulfuric acid seemed like the most likely candidate.

The two detectives asked the Hoopers where they first saw the girl. Before answering, Kent asked if she was dead. Whatley said that she wasn't yet, but they didn't know if she would survive. Kent and Millie expressed deep sadness over what they had seen. Whatley said if she did survive, "you two are the reason." Millie responded that she wasn't sure that would be a good thing because the woman had been in so much pain.

The detectives requested that Millie and Kent go with them up the road and try to estimate where they saw the girl and where they saw the van speeding by. Whatley thought they should check vehicles registered to Jack Macklin to see if he had a gray or black van.

Millie and Kent gave an approximation of where the van sped toward them and then where they saw the girl. The detectives walked along the road and looked down the very steep ravine but didn't see a purse or a container of corrosive liquid. Whatley brought up bringing out a team over the weekend to search the ravine for evidence. He commented that the abductor must have thrown her down the ravine and she had to have stopped the fall and crawled back up. Washington said, "Daisy, assuming it's Daisy, has a ton of heart and courage in that small frame." They took some photos of the area before driving back.

They had driven about ten miles out on Cañada Larga Road before coming to the approximate area where they saw the girl and the van. Washington was curious as to what had brought the Hoopers out there, and Millie said it was a drive they just liked to take sometimes. It was peaceful and truly out in the middle of nowhere. After spending a couple of hours with the older couple, both detectives were impressed with what nice people they were. Kent asked if the detectives could call if they got any word on the girl and Millie agreed. She said they both could not stop thinking about her.

On the ride back, Washington, for the first time, mentioned jurisdiction and conceded the long-standing rule that the assault and probable murder happened in sheriff's jurisdiction in Ojai so it's going to be a sheriff's case. Whatley said that the two of them had been working the case since the beginning and had worked great together.

He said, "We've made a lot of progress so far and tomorrow we're going to interview our prime suspect. Our substation is down a detective, so I'm putting in a request for joint jurisdiction, allowing us to see this to the end." Washington liked that and laughed that they would "have to put up with each other a while longer."

Whatley called in to records and requested vehicle ownership of a John or Jack Macklin DOB 1/19/1979. After a minute wait, Whatley announced that Jack Macklin had recently bought a 2008 gray Dodge van.

* * *

By Friday, family members of the Guzmans had learned that Daisy was missing. Marta's brother Jorge had called her Thursday evening and asked about Daisy, and Marta couldn't lie, so she told him Daisy was missing. Jorge told his wife, and soon the entire extended family was worried too. Everyone knew that Daisy would not just take off and leave.

On Saturday morning, Washington waited for Whatley because they were going to do a second neighborhood canvass. Whatley was a little late arriving, mentioning that his youngest daughter got sick and his wife had been at the grocery store. He would have called but he was dealing with his daughter. He thought he could get out earlier but his wife took too long to shop, even though it was just the grocery store. Whatley told her when she got back that she was expected to be late if it was Nordstrom's, but how long did it take to find lettuce and burgers? He said the wife did not appreciate his comedy routine. Washington replied, "I don't have to worry about that drama—I'm still single."

They headed out to Ventura Avenue where Daisy lived. They noticed the gray van in Macklin's driveway, so they knew he was home. They also noticed that it appeared to have been recently cleaned but there was a small crack in the passenger-side window. They were not really planning on speaking with Macklin first, but he stepped out of the house, likely because he saw the two plainclothes detectives.

Macklin said, "Something I can do for you?" They approached Macklin and introduced themselves and offered handshakes, but Macklin snubbed them. Washington asked him about the crack in the window and Macklin said that someone probably tried to break into it or they vandalized it. He added, "Bad neighborhood." Whatley asked if he reported it. Macklin laughed and said, "You really think I'm gonna report some bullshit like that? Fuck. I'll get around to fixing it at some point."

Macklin then mentioned that he was sure two undercovers did not come to talk about a cracked window, and he asked what was up. Washington said they were investigating a missing-person report. Macklin asked who was missing and Washington said, "Daisy Guzman." Macklin said he didn't know her. Whatley said she lived two doors down. Then Macklin said that he didn't know her name but that's probably the "cute little wetback girl with big tits." Whatley, ignoring the racial slur, asked when the last time he saw her was. Macklin said maybe a week ago, he wasn't sure. Washington asked where he was on November first, which was Wednesday, in the morning. Macklin stared at Washington for about ten seconds with a look of disdain, then finally said that he was right there at home. Washington asked if anyone could verify that. Macklin said nobody came over, then added, "If you find that missing girl, she'll tell you I wasn't with her."

Whatley asked if they could take a look in his house just to make sure he wasn't involved. Macklin answered Whatley with a smirk and said, "If you and your nigger want to come inside, you are gonna need a warrant." Washington had been called the N-word a couple of times before and wasn't going to let Macklin bait him. He also couldn't say he was surprised. Whatley said they would be going but that "you never know, maybe we'll be back." Macklin smiled and said, "Look forward to it."

Whatley said, as they walked across the street to speak with other neighbors, "If it walks like a duck and quacks like a duck, it's a duck."

Washington replied, "This one quacked like he just killed a girl and is challenging us to prove it."

The two detectives canvassed the rest of the neighborhood. Nobody had seen or heard anything Wednesday morning. Unlike Macklin, the rest of the neighbors were all genuinely concerned about Daisy. Even the Marquez family, who'd had run-ins with law enforcement in the past, were very cooperative. Elvia Marquez was at work, but her husband and son were home.

Bobby Marquez had a long history with the Ventura Avenue Gangsters and had been to prison twice. He was a big guy with a big belly to match. He had lots of ink on both arms and his neck. He looked like the guy you would get right out of central casting for a Latino gang member veterano and shotcaller. His son Bobby Jr. was following in his father's footsteps. Elvia was trying to steer Junior away from that lifestyle, but his father wasn't much help there. Bobby Jr. volunteered that he was friends with Daisy's ex-boyfriend Steve and added with a laugh that he was sure they knew how he knew him.

Washington asked Bobby Sr. if he thought Daisy's ex could have anything to do with her disappearance, and he said there was no way. Steve Alvarez told him Daisy was missing after Alvarez talked to the cops. He said Alvarez was shook up over it. Bobby Jr. confirmed that and said that Alvarez cried when he talked to him. He added that Alvarez fell hard for Daisy. Bobby Sr. said that he usually didn't talk to cops and that he was on the opposite side of cops but on something like this, "we are on the same side." He said he hoped Daisy was OK, because she is a really nice kid.

Washington asked if they could take a look around inside, and Bobby Sr. said, "I will probably never say this to cops again, but mi casa es su casa. Come on in, you guys want anything to drink?" Washington said they were on duty and couldn't drink, but Bobby Sr. said, "No, we got Pepsi and water." Washington said he would take water and Whatley said that a Pepsi sounded good. They knew they weren't going to find anything but were more interested to see if the Marquezes were as sincere as they sounded.

Washington popped his head into Junior's room. Junior was eighteen and looked like a skinny version of his dad. He had a tee shirt on the bed that said "Ventura Ave 805 for life." Of course, 805 is Ventura's area code. The room had about ten other items of gang paraphernalia, plus spray paint. As Washington and Whatley were leaving, Washington said to Bobby Jr., "Junior, next time you guys let cops in, at least try to hide the gang shit. I'm not gonna bust your chops for it, but you're probably on probation, so next time your PO comes by, I'd probably hide that shit." Junior laughed and thanked him. The detectives gave the Marquez family their cards and asked them to call if they heard anything.

On the doorstep, Whatley asked them if they knew their neighbor Jack Macklin and described him as the big tatted-up white guy. Senior said that he knew who he was, seemed to keep to himself but also seemed like an unfriendly asshole and predicted that they might have a problem someday. Senior laughed and said, "But you know me, I like to stay out of trouble, my kid here takes after me." Then Marquez got serious and asked if they thought Macklin did something to Daisy. Whatley said that they were looking at a lot of possibilities and the case was still under investigation.

The detectives went back to the station, and Whatley said that it was going to be weeks before they got DNA back on anything. Washington said they should call Dr. Wong and ask if he could speak to Daisy's family on Sunday. Whatley agreed, so Washington called and was eventually able to reach Dr. Wong and found out that Daisy was still comatose, and her condition was unchanged. Washington told him that they believed the girl's name was Daisy Guzman and they would like him to speak with the family tomorrow. Dr. Wong acknowledged that this was going to be tough.

Washington waited until 8:00 a.m. the next morning, as he did not want them worrying an entire night before finding anything out. Marta answered her cell phone and he told her that Daisy was at Ojai Hospital and she had been abducted. Marta cried and asked if Daisy was going to be OK. Detective Washington told them that he would like them to get the information from the doctor because they would have many questions and he would be able to answer them better. She kept trying to find out more but that was all Detective Washington would tell her.

She cried while telling her husband, and they agreed to go to the hospital immediately, as soon as they arranged for a sitter for their younger son. Marta figured they would choose what to tell him later, when they had more information. The couple were very nervous as they hurried to Ojai, relieved that apparently Daisy was still alive, but fearing that horrible things might have happened to her, and that they could still lose her.

Detective Washington had also told Marta that it was very important that they keep Daisy's presence at the hospital a secret except for immediate family and Daisy's closest friends, and that "under no circumstances should you tell any neighbors that Daisy has even been found. For everyone but her immediate family and Daisy's closest friends, this is still a missing-person case. And for those few people you do tell, make sure they know not to go blabbing about it."

When the Guzmans got to the lobby, there was only one other person waiting there, a man who seemed to be reading a magazine. He appeared to be in his early thirties, short but muscular. He had floppy light-brown hair and a confused look on his face.

Dr. Wong approached the couple and asked if they were Mr. and Mrs. Guzman. He then introduced himself and told them that he wished he could give them better news. He told them that Daisy had been abducted and her kidnapper had poured an acid-type substance on her face and left her for dead, but Daisy had climbed out of a ravine and was given a ride here. She had suffered extensive facial damage. He told them that she was in a medically induced coma and they were not sure she would make it, but if she did, she was looking at a lifetime of surgeries. Marta and Jose cried. Jose asked if she would ever be back to how she looked, and Dr. Wong said that under current medical science, that was not feasible, and she would always look like a burn victim. Jose asked, "Who could have done this, do they know?" Dr. Wong said that they would have to speak with the police on that one.

Jose asked if she would be able to speak and see. Dr. Wong said she could not see when she was brought in, but that didn't mean she would be permanently blind. He did say that very little got into her throat or lungs, so speaking should not be a problem, should she survive. Dr. Wong was asked her chances of survival, and he said that it could go either way. They asked if they could see Daisy and he said there were some more things they had to do, and that she was bandaged up and they would not remove bandages unless she came out of her coma. Dr. Wong apologized for having to relay such horrible news. He told them that they would be notified of any updates.

After Dr. Wong left, the young man said he'd heard what the doctor said, and he was very sorry to hear what happened. They cried and did not really want to carry on a conversation but politely thanked him. He then asked if they had a recent photograph of Daisy, because he wanted to pray for her. Jose looked a little annoyed, but Marta, not wanting to be rude, pulled out the photo of Daisy that she had in her wallet. The photo was taken shortly before Daisy turned twenty-two. She was posing next to a tree while wearing a black halter top. It was a pretty good close-up photo. The young man looked at it and kept looking at it. He was not saying any prayers as far as they could tell, but he looked intensely at the photograph for a couple of minutes before handing it back to Mrs. Guzman and thanking her. As the devastated couple walked out of the lobby, the man was still sitting there, and it appeared that he had picked the magazine back up and was reading again.

Marta and Jose contacted their family and told them the sad news. They told eleven-year-old Juan that his sister had been hurt and was at a hospital, saying she was hurt badly but they hoped she would come back to them. They told him that if she did come back, she might not look the same as before. Then they told Juan not to talk about it in school or on the street. "Always say that you don't know where Daisy is."

Juan asked what happened to her, and they said a bad man took her and hurt her. Juan cried and asked when Daisy would be home, and they said they did not know but hoped it would be soon. Juan asked why the bad man hurt Daisy, and Jose told him that there are just some bad people who like to hurt others. Juan asked if the bad man was going to hurt him, and they said he was going to be OK and they would protect him. Juan said when he grew up, he wanted to kill the bad man. But his parents told him that revenge comes from the courts and the law.

Their other son, Joshua, called back, and when told, he cried into the phone and exclaimed, "Oh my God, my baby sister." He asked them to call him, and when he could visit, he would get time off from his job. He had been somewhat estranged from the family over some differences with his father, but nobody cared about that now.

Jose was getting a bad feeling about the man in the lobby that Marta had shown the photo to. He began wondering why the man was there just sitting in the lobby. Why had he wanted to see a picture of Daisy? Why was he staring at it so closely for so long? Jose wondered if maybe this was the man who had hurt Daisy. He said that he was going to call Detective Washington. Marta said that she doubted he was the man; he seemed nice. But she admitted that the entire encounter was odd.

Jose did call Detective Washington, who seemed interested at first and asked for a description. When Jose gave the description, Detective Washington said that they were looking at a possible suspect who did not look like that. He also said that it was very unlikely that the man who hurt Daisy knew that she was in the hospital. Detective Washington did say that he would get to the hospital and see if he could find out who the man was but again emphasized that very few people knew that Daisy was in the hospital. He also reiterated not to tell any of the neighbors where Daisy was.

On Monday, November 6, the Ventura Police Department and the Ventura County Sheriff's Department put together a team to search the ravine, looking to find Daisy's cell phone, purse, and possibly a container with the substance thrown in Daisy's face.

It took a while to rappel the search team down the steep ravine. They didn't know how far down the items might be. They brought a metal detector to help find the cell phone. The search was going to cover the area from where the Hoopers said they first saw the speeding van to a little past the area that they said they saw Daisy in the road.

The first four hours of the search turned up nothing, then they broke for boxed sandwich lunches. The choices were turkey, roast beef, or veggies. Washington opted for turkey and Whatley went for the roast beef. Soda and water were also available. They knew this search could take a while. The terrain was terrible, and the ravine was very deep. It seemed like the length of a football field. Whatley was shocked that he had not been familiar with this isolated location, but he knew if someone were to do a crime like this, here would be the place.

It was approaching 5:00 p.m. when one of the searchers yelled that he had something. It turned out to be Daisy's purse. It had her wallet with her driver's license. Now they knew with certainty that the beautiful Daisy Guzman was lying comatose in Ojai Hospital and that she would never again remotely resemble that driver's license photo. They searched a little farther in that area and the metal detector went off again. The smashed cell phone was located close to the bottom where they thought they might find it, since the phone could be thrown farther down than the purse or container. It was getting dark and they had not found the container yet. If he tossed it there, they could hopefully find it the next day, but if he was dumb enough to keep it, they might find it when they executed a search warrant.

* * *

On Tuesday, November 7, at a little after 10:00 a.m., Daisy woke up. Dr. Wong received word that Daisy was out of the coma. He stopped the protocol infusion and extubated her. At first, she didn't remember where she was or how she got there and thought she had to get to work. Then it hit her, and she remembered everything. She began crying. She knew her life as she had known it was over.

Daisy's return was sooner than expected. A nurse took her pulse, which was racing, and her blood pressure was now high at 153/94. Dr. Wong asked her some questions and she was able to answer them. She asked if she was going to be OK. He explained that her vitals were good, and she was likely to survive. He asked if she remembered what happened to her and she cried and said that she did. He didn't have to ask who; she said the name Jack and she thought his last name was Mackey. She described him and said that he was her neighbor.

Daisy's eyes were covered in bandages, so Dr. Wong did not know if she had vision. The doctor asked what kind of pain she was in and if she had any itching sensation. She said that her face itched some, and that her chest had a little bit of itching and her lip hurt. She also said her head hurt a lot.

Daisy asked, "Can you fix my face?" Dr. Wong said that it was likely to be a long process. He told her she would have some bandages—only a few—removed on Friday and they would have a better idea of the healing process. He told her that she may want to have friends and family there for support. Daisy gave him a list of names and a nurse jotted them down along with their phone numbers.

Daisy asked if she would be able to see herself, and if she would want to. The doctor said that they would know more when they removed some of the bandages. Daisy said she wasn't sure if she wanted anyone to see her face, and Dr. Wong assured her that they were just going to remove enough bandages to get an idea of the damage. He added that the surgeries would likely be performed at the USC burn center, once they had an idea of the extent of the damage.

Later that day, Marta and Jose visited Daisy. She tried to be strong for her parents but couldn't. Jose broke down as well and apologized to Daisy for not protecting her. Daisy tried to comfort Jose by saying it was her fault for getting into the man's van. She told her father that she knew he loved her, and she loved him, and it wasn't his fault. The three cried together for a good ten more minutes, proclaiming their love for each other. Marta and Jose told Daisy they would be back tomorrow, and headed home.

Daisy had thought that after she got revenge for what happened to her by identifying her abductor and testifying, she would take pills and end her life. She was torn because she didn't want to hurt her family any more. She was tormented and confused but did not know how she could live the way she thought she would have to. Eventually, she decided that her family would understand if she took her own life.

The sheriff's department and the police department pitched in to put Marta and Jose and young Juan in a hotel near the beach in Ventura. They didn't want any of the Guzmans on the Avenue near Macklin. The plan was to keep them there until they were ready to arrest him.

The team had just begun the second day of searching the ravine when Detective Whatley got a call from the hospital and was told that Daisy had emerged from her coma. He asked if she was talking and Dr. Wong informed him that she was, and she said the man who did this to her was Jack Mackey, and she said he was her neighbor. Whatley asked when they could see her and talk with her. The doctor said that he would like her to rest all day with no visitors except her parents, but they could get an initial statement from her on Wednesday.

When he got off the phone with Dr. Wong, Whatley yelled out, "Davon!" and Davon Washington walked from the truck over to where Whatley had gone to take the call. Whatley told him everything that Dr. Wong had told him. Then he called Ray Scapio and told him the news and asked if he could get to the hospital tomorrow, and Scapio said, "Absolutely." Whatley also told Scapio that they confirmed it was her earlier because her purse and phone had been located during the search.

Around 3:30 p.m., and quite a long distance from where the purse and the cell phone had been located, they found an empty plastic container wedged between two bushes, so it had been hard to see. The lab would have to test it for DNA and any liquid residue, but at least they thought they might have found the last object they were looking for.

* * *

Macklin thought about driving the route back toward 33 and Cañada Larga to retrieve the items and permanently get rid of them and to make sure Daisy's body had not been found yet. He then told himself to calm down. He reminded himself that the police said it was a missing person, not a dead person, so that means they hadn't found her yet. He thought that it was now Wednesday and they might follow him, plus he didn't want to attract attention. He assured himself that he picked the perfect spot and it was going to take months, if ever, to find her.

* * *

Daisy could not stop crying. She knew that someday her looks would fade, but now she could not bear to think that people would turn their faces away because she looked like a monster. Daisy asked, "Why me?" She could not understand why this happened to her. Why couldn't someone have saved her?

She still felt that she didn't want to live after she got justice for her attacker. She could feel her hands and knew people always complimented her on them. Even with a couple of broken nails she thought they probably looked great, but she thought it wouldn't matter because all anything anyone would see would be her disfigured face.

She thought about how much fun she'd had with Nikki in her Aztec princess costume. She knew she would never have that experience again. She tried to joke to herself that Halloween might be the only time she would fit in, but the joke only made her cry more. She was not sure if she wanted to be able to see again. Since she was about twelve, everyone told her she was beautiful, and people could not take their eyes off her, and she wondered if she could ever handle nobody wanting to lay eyes on her.

Veronica Gonzalez was working the checkout stand at the Oxnard CVS when she saw a call had come in from Daisy's mom. She wanted to take it so badly, but she had customers in line, and whatever the news was, she was going to have to take a break and call. She asked for a break and said she might have information on her missing friend. As soon as she got her break, she called Marta back. Marta told her that Daisy was alive and at the Ojai Hospital. Marta explained what had happened to Daisy. Veronica cried and promised that she would be there for Daisy when they would remove some bandages.

When she got off the phone, she was distraught and her boss asked her what happened. She told her what Marta Guzman had said, including the fact that they had to keep the information absolutely secret. Her supervisor told Veronica to take the rest of the day off. Veronica also asked for Friday off because she was going to want to be at the hospital for Daisy. Her supervisor said, "Of course. I hope your friend is OK."

Marta called Jennifer Weinberg, the young woman who hosted the Halloween party. Marta had never met Jennifer, but she was one of the friends Daisy had listed. Marta told her what happened to Daisy, and Jennifer broke down on the phone and promised her she would be there for Daisy at the hospital, and promised to keep it secret.

Jennifer had initially gone to high school in Simi Valley, where she was living. She had been a pudgy girl with very frizzy hair and pimples. She was also one of the few Jewish girls in her high school. Sadly, Jennifer was a victim of constant bullying. She was tormented by the so-called popular girls in the school. She was so depressed, she had contemplated suicide. She believed only her mom and dad would ever love her or even like her.

Fortunately, she was able to transfer to Buena High School in Ventura when her father, partly to get his daughter a new start, changed jobs and the family moved to Ventura. When she started at Buena, she made her first high school friend, a Vietnamese American girl named Kelly Ng. Jennifer asked Kelly who the popular girls were and she was told that Daisy Guzman, the really pretty Mexican American girl, and her friend Veronica Gonzalez were probably the two that were the popular girls along with about ten other girls that hung out with them.

Jennifer confided in Kelly that she did not want to meet Daisy because she had been bullied by the popular girls throughout her first year at her old high school. Kelly said that Daisy wasn't like that, and that she was really sweet. She said the only thing you have to worry about with Daisy is that if you end up sitting next to her in class, she could get you in trouble because she will talk to you all the time. Daisy was sweet, but kind of a chatterbox. She said Daisy doesn't bully anyone, so Jennifer wouldn't have to worry about that.

It turned out that Jennifer was in Daisy's history class. Jennifer didn't sit next to her but she very quickly saw what Kelly was talking about, because Daisy was talking a lot to the girl next to her—so much so that the teacher finally stopped and said, "Miss Guzman, is there anything you want to share with the class?" Daisy replied, "No, sorry, I'll shut up." The teacher responded, "Not sure if that's possible but I would appreciate if you would at least give it a try." The entire class, including Daisy, laughed.

After class, Daisy went up to her and said, "Hi, I'm Daisy, I heard you're new here," and stuck her hand out. Jennifer was hesitant at first because of how the popular girls at the Simi Valley high school had treated her. She paused a moment but did put her hand out and introduced herself. Daisy sensed the hesitation and said that it was nice to meet her, and took off.

The next day, Jennifer saw Daisy in the hall, called her name, and apologized to her for being hesitant. She explained that she knew Daisy was one of the popular girls, and she told Daisy what happened at her last school. Daisy said that was terrible and "that wouldn't happen here." She never really got in Daisy's group of popular girls, but Daisy invited her to some parties, and she attended a couple of them. Daisy was always nice to her and she did consider Daisy a friend.

By her senior year, Jennifer had lost weight and gained confidence. She proudly told her parents that the most popular girl at the school was a beautiful Mexican American girl named Daisy and Daisy was her friend. She talked about Daisy a lot, but her parents had only met Kelly and a couple of her other friends, not Daisy. Her parents had discussed whether she had made up

Daisy as a defense in her mind because of what had happened in Simi Valley.

Jennifer's parents came to her graduation, and after the ceremony, Jennifer saw Daisy and thanked her for being nice to her and told her that she made her not hate popular people. Daisy told her she was popular herself and had friends, and that being nice to people is just good. Jennifer asked if she could introduce Daisy to her parents. Her proud parents saw Jennifer walking toward them with this beautiful Hispanic girl with long black hair, and they knew this had to be Daisy.

Sure enough, she said, "This is my friend Daisy Guzman." Daisy shook hands with the parents and they both said that Jennifer spoke really highly of her. They asked Daisy what she was going to do after graduation, and she said that she was thinking about going into journalism but had to go to Ventura College first. Then she joked that "I didn't study as hard as Jennifer." Daisy looked at Jennifer and said, "UCLA, huh? Congratulations!" Jennifer thanked her and told Daisy that her being so nice made a huge difference in her life. Daisy said, "Now you're going to make me cry!" They hugged, and Daisy congratulated her again on graduating high school and getting into UCLA.

After that meeting, Jennifer's parents kept a secret from her that they would take to their graves. They would never reveal that they had doubted there was a real Daisy Guzman.

Jennifer would go on to graduate from UCLA with a degree in business management. She would meet her first boyfriend and they would date throughout her four years of college. She also had a secret she didn't reveal until much later. Had Daisy Guzman and her friends bullied her, she believed she would have committed suicide.

It wasn't until after college a little over a year ago when Jennifer, now a sleek 127 pounds, with styled long curly hair and a confident pretty face, walked into Victoria's Secret and recognized Daisy Guzman putting bras on the sales racks. She called Daisy's name and Daisy didn't recognize her; then Jennifer said her name. Daisy's face lit up and she hugged her and said, "Oh my God, you look gorgeous." Then Daisy was embarrassed and tried to backtrack, saying, "Not that you weren't before, I mean, you know what I mean, you look great." Jennifer said it was OK and she knew exactly what Daisy meant.

They talked for a while and caught up, exchanged phone numbers, and promised to get lunch. Jennifer and Daisy had met up regularly from then on, Veronica often joining them. Jennifer had come from being bullied by the beautiful, popular girls to now being good friends with the two most popular girls from her days at Buena High School. Jennifer thought to herself that some things didn't change. Daisy was as sweet, beautiful, and popular as ever, but she was still a chatterbox, but in a really good way.

Jennifer had hosted the party on Halloween where Daisy and Nikki had spent much of that night. Daisy had been there for her when she was in despair; now Jennifer was going to be there for Daisy.

Marta wanted to call Daisy's ex-boyfriend Steve because he was on the list Daisy had provided, but Detective Whatley had told her not to, because Alvarez had too many connections to the neighborhood, and telling him could result in the word getting out.

Daisy's childhood friend, Misty Herrera, who was living in Arizona and still kept in contact with Daisy, was invited to attend and agreed to drive out. Misty cried when she heard the news. They would visit each other every couple of years, sometimes in Phoenix where Misty was living with her boyfriend, and sometimes Misty would come to Ventura.

Misty remembered when they picked players for sports in middle school, Daisy would get picked higher than her athletic ability justified. Everyone liked to have her on their team. Daisy wasn't a terrible athlete; she was OK and was a fast runner, but she was small and her coordination was basically very average. Yet she had been consistently picked just after Misty, who was a great athlete. Misty had become a soccer player at Arizona State and even tried out for the Olympics but was not selected.

Marta had a thought, as she clung to any hope that things might not be so bad. She called Dr. Wong and asked him if the fact that Daisy had a darker skin tone might help. She said Daisy was closer to her father's skin shade and that of Marta's sister, and that maybe the scars would be less visible, and they might heal faster. Dr. Wong said that he didn't want to give her false hope and that skin tone didn't really affect things, but they would know a little more what the road ahead would be when they removed a few of the bandages.

On Wednesday, Scapio and the detectives went to the hospital, but Daisy didn't want to take any visitors other than her parents. The three decided to not press the issue and would come back on Friday.

FOURTEEN

It was Friday, November 10, 2017, the day Daisy would have some bandages removed. Dr. Wong was the first to see her, and Daisy begged him not to take the bandages off. She said she couldn't look and didn't want to see that her old face was gone forever. Dr. Wong tried to be as reassuring as possible without giving her false hope. He told her that "the sooner we can remove some bandages, the sooner your rehabilitation and surgeries can begin." Daisy cried as Dr. Wong said she had another visitor. He told her that the police wanted to speak with her before they got started with bandage removal.

Detectives Washington and Whatley introduced themselves. They took a statement from her about what Jack Macklin had done to her. She struggled through tears to get the words out. They said they would be there for her, every step of the way. They didn't tell her about photos that she might be shown, because they didn't know if she would have vision.

At that point, Ray Scapio introduced himself to Daisy and explained his role as the prosecutor in the case. He mentioned how sorry he was that she had to go through this. He explained that he was going to do everything he could to get justice for her, and he could put the guy away for life so he would never hurt anyone else again. Scapio would be in the room, along with the detectives, when some of the bandages came off.

He left her with the comment that science kept advancing, that maybe they couldn't fix what happened right away, but not to give up hope. He told her he needed her, to get justice for her. She interpreted it as him telling her not to kill herself before the case was over.

"Don't worry," she said, "I'm not going to kill myself and let this psycho get away with what he did to me." Scapio felt bad and said that he wasn't saying she would do that. He told her that everyone out there loved her and thought she was one of the best people they would ever know. She thanked him through a voice that was cracking from crying.

* * *

The time had come to remove some bandages and find out if Daisy could see. Dr. Wong entered through the curtain. Daisy's hospital room was small. The friends and family were there, but not everyone could fit into the room. Everyone identified themselves for Daisy and they all said they loved her and were there for her. She cried the whole time. She was really overcome with emotion when she heard from her friend Misty and her older brother, Joshua. At that moment, Daisy changed her mind about suicide. All these people were there for her and she did not want to disappoint them by giving up.

Dr. Wong told Daisy that he would start by removing the bandages that covered her eyes, to see if she had vision. He told her to close her eyes really tightly, because he was going to use a needle and scissors to cut the bandages. He pulled the bandages up and punctured them with a needle. He slowly began cutting around the bandages. He noticed that some of the bandages were wrinkled and discolored and some weren't, and he was concerned that Daisy might have been fiddling with them.

Scapio had seen the driver's license photo of Daisy and figured this was going to be the hardest thing he was ever going to have to see in his career. Dr. Wong slowly and carefully cut circles and removed them, exposing Daisy's big brown eyes. Dr. Wong turned toward Daisy's parents and said, "There is a lot of redness, but that could just be from crying. I don't see any ocular damage." He asked Daisy if she could see anything, and she said that it was really blurry, but she could see him.

Daisy blinked, then said she could see him a little better but it was still blurry. The doctor told her she had been bandaged up for a while, so that was why her eyes hadn't adjusted but they would, and she should have full vision. She then said hi to Nikki as well as Nikki's parents and brother and sister and to Jennifer, then said hi to her mom and dad and everyone else, and said she was really scared.

Dr. Wong asked Daisy if she felt any pain or itching. Daisy said that her head hurt and the back of her head was really sensitive from when he slammed her head into the ground. She said she touched back there a few times. She also said her lip was really sore. Dr. Wong asked if her face itched and Daisy said no, that the itching had gone away. Dr. Wong looked puzzled.

But he went on, saying, "I'm going to remove some bandages from your face. These bandages will stick a little bit to any hairs on the back of your neck and might have attached to head hairs as well, so it might hurt a little."

Sure enough, he began to remove a bandage that caught a strand of Daisy's hair, and Daisy exclaimed, "Ah!" The doctor said sorry, and that it might happen a few more times. He removed another bandage. Daisy's vision was starting to come back a little better. She could see her mother and father hugging and could hear them sobbing, and she figured this was going to be bad. She could not yet be sure about the expressions on the faces of her cousins, aunts, uncles, and friends as she squinted to try to see well.

In a rather odd tone, Dr. Wong said, "OK, I'm going to go ahead and remove all the bandages." Daisy was confused, because she thought that only a few were going to be removed. A few more times Daisy made pain noises when her hair got caught. She could hear crying as Dr. Wong worked faster.

Daisy saw the bandages were almost all off, but nobody was offering her a mirror. She thought that was a bad sign. The first person to speak was Nikki, who said, "Daisy, you're still beautiful." Daisy figured that Nikki was being nice, but Daisy knew her days of being beautiful were long behind her. Then she heard an angry rant, a rant she at first did not understand. The rant began naming people that she did not know. It wasn't until the end of the rant that Daisy asked for a mirror.

The rant was from the prosecutor, Ray Scapio, who had shouted, "What the fuck is this? Goddamit Davon, come on Chris, did Kyle Irby put you up to this? Irby's an asshole. You can come out, Irby, you got me. Come on man, was it Reddis, did he set this up? Come on, this is nuts, I'm not falling for this. It's bullshit. You guys get me up at 1:00 a.m., tell me some girl got kidnapped and got acid thrown in her face and her face is coming off, and you pull the bandages off and I'm looking at Miss Oxnard 2013 with a split lip."

Daisy said, "Mom, can I have a mirror?" Nikki pulled one out first and Daisy grabbed it and stared into it. She sat in silence, tears flowing.

Jennifer spoke next and said through tears of joy, "I hope someone is filming this, because this is the longest Daisy Guzman has ever been silent."

Daisy's vision was a little blurry, but it was good enough. She saw herself in the mirror, and other than the cut on her lip, she looked the same as when she and Nikki spent Halloween night partying. Daisy said, "Please tell me I'm not dreaming." Everyone said it was real. She turned to Dr. Wong and said, "Thank you so much! You are the greatest doctor ever!" Mr. and Mrs. Guzman agreed. Dr. Wong said he wished he could take credit for it, but he had no medical explanation for what happened.

Daisy began talking a mile a minute. She said to Nikki, "Next year, Halloween again, all of us, Jennifer you gotta do the party again. Nikki, you can't be Wonder Woman again, four times or whatever is too many, I mean you're the best Wonder Woman even with purple streaks or red, but we will have sexy costumes 'cause it's Halloween."

Jennifer laughed and said, "Our girl is back." Daisy laughed too and apologized and said she was so happy, she still couldn't believe it. Dr. Wong let her entire family and her friends cry. Even the detectives and Scapio teared up.

Scapio whispered to Washington, "Did this really just happen? I mean, this isn't a joke?" Washington said it was not.

Dr. Wong waited until it had quieted down a little, but there still was not a dry eye in the house, including his own. He tried to be as professional as he could and told Daisy that she had been in a coma for a while. She asked what day it was, and the doctor told her it was Friday, November 10, and that she had been in a coma for a week. He took her blood pressure, and it was 122/78. He said all her vitals were excellent, but she had taken a pretty bad beating. They wanted to monitor her overnight and then go through concussion protocol the following morning before they would release her.

Daisy said that the man who did that to her was still out there. Veronica spoke up. "Daisy, you can stay with me as long as you want. I have a spare bedroom. And your parents and brothers can visit you there, since they aren't staying at home." Veronica said she would be back tomorrow to pick her up from the hospital. Daisy said that would be great.

Scapio told Daisy he was really happy for her, and he no longer believed it was a joke and was sorry for how he reacted. Daisy asked who that Kyle guy was. Scapio said it was a long story, one he'd tell her at some point.

Gradually, Daisy's friends and family left, feeling absolute joy but not having any idea how the miracle happened. Scapio asked to talk with Chris and Davon. Davon knew right away what Scapio wanted to talk about. Detective Washington asked straight out, "We still have a case, right?" Whatley said to wait a second, he would be right back.

He went back to Daisy's room and asked her if her vision was good enough to look at some photos the next day. Daisy said it was, and that she could see as well as before. She said that her vision wasn't perfect, and she had glasses, but she didn't usually wear them. Still, she knew the guy and she could pick him out easily. Whatley said he would come by the hospital with the photos the next day at 9:00 a.m., so he told her to wait for him and not leave with her friend until he could do that. He added that he believed what happened to her was real, and he was happy she got a miracle.

Whatley returned to Scapio and Washington. Scapio was saying that they had to get all the DNA, including off the container, the back seat of the Hoopers' car, Daisy's phone, her purse, and her car, as well as fingernail clippings. They also needed to get statements from everyone who saw her burned—all the doctors and nurses—and they had to re-interview the Hoopers. He emphasized that they had to get every detail of what they saw of Daisy's face.

Even then, Scapio said he believed her, but there was no medical explanation for her recovery, and he was unsure whether the office would file. He said he would try to persuade, but it would be hard. The three agreed to keep in regular contact, and they discussed what to do in terms of priorities. Scapio said it was wonderful, whatever did happen, but it complicated it. He said, "I know that girl wasn't acting, but can we prove it?"

Whatley said he would come back in the morning and show her a photo lineup. He told Davon he was welcome to come by. Davon said he probably would and wanted to check some video at the hospital. Whatley said he and Washington would do whatever Scapio would need to make a case. Scapio said again that he believed Daisy and he would do everything he could to convince his office to go forward, "even if we can't explain this miracle." They then parted and agreed to stay in touch.

Wong stopped Whatley before he left and asked him if he knew why he pulled the bandages off so quickly after removing the ones blocking her vision. Whatley said he did not, but he did notice the doctor wasn't gentle at that point, because he ripped the girl's hair a few times. Dr. Wong said his first hint that something inexplicably wonderful might have happened was when she said she had no itching. He said that burn victims itch. Daisy's skin should not have healed yet, so she should have been itching. In fact, the itching was usually unbearable, but Daisy was talking about a sore lip.

Once he could see her eyes, he said, he knew something miraculous was going on, and at that point he wondered if there was going to be any scarring at all. He said that the acid got in her eyes; he emphasized that he was there when she came in. He concluded, "I was not looking forward to this day. I thought I would be revealing a blind and horrifically scarred young woman. Once I saw her eyes, I couldn't wait to remove the bandages. I was like an artist removing a drape to unveil a beautiful work of art I didn't paint. I don't know how this happened. I am very happy for that nice young woman that it did."

Washington asked to look at video footage before he left. He found out that they did have a camera that covered the hallway to the rooms but there were no cameras in the rooms. He vowed to watch all day if he had to, because he believed that the answer to his question might just be on video.

* * *

Mrs. Guzman and Mr. Guzman were speaking in Spanish. She suggested stopping by the market before going back to their hotel so they could get a bottle of wine to celebrate. But she then told Jose that there was something missing about Daisy; something just didn't seem the same. She was excited about Daisy's miracle recovery, but she admitted something did not fit. Jose said that she seemed just fine to him and that today was the best day of his life, "other than when I met you. Maybe this is even better, because Daisy is our little girl."

The Guzmans arrived at the market and Marta grabbed some groceries and a bottle of Chardonnay. They went to the check-out line and Marta got out her wallet and was looking for her credit card when she saw it. It was staring right at her, and she told Jose they had to go back to the hospital and see Daisy. Jose asked why and what was going on. Marta said, "I think I know why Daisy has no burn scars." Jose asked why, and Marta said that she would visit Daisy and confirm what she saw before she said any more.

They got to the hospital and said they needed to see Daisy again. As they approached her curtain, they could hear her singing in Spanish. They walked in, and Daisy smiled and said, "Mom, you're back so soon, and Dad! That's OK, I want to tell you again how much I love you."

Marta said, "I love you, too." Jose said, "We love you," and he added that he was so happy she was OK and that he could now forgive himself. Daisy corrected him and said it was her fault, but especially it was the fault of the man who did this to her, and she said she would not have blamed her dad in a million years.

Marta then asked Daisy to sit up so she could see her bare left shoulder. Daisy did, and Marta looked closely. Daisy looked as well and said, "My tattoo is gone! It's OK, you never liked it any-way." Marta said she loved Daisy and they would see her soon.

Once they were back in the car, Marta told Jose that she now was positive why Daisy wasn't burned. She knew what was different about Daisy once she saw Daisy's picture in her wallet:

the tattoo was gone. "That the man in the lobby, that asked to see a photo of Daisy, had to have fixed her face."

Jose asked how she figured that. Marta said, "Daisy herself said that the tattoo was gone. You could see Daisy's shoulder; the tattoo wasn't there. It wasn't in the photo either. It was taken before Daisy got it." Marta reminded Jose how long the man stared at the photo. "It looked like he was processing it," she told him. Then she said that had to be how he fixed Daisy—just like the photo, but he didn't know she had a tattoo. Jose pondered it and said whoever the man was, Jose was glad Marta had that photo. She agreed.

* * *

Washington watched hours of footage of the hallway leading to Daisy's room. He would fast-forward until he saw a person; he'd watch their movements, then return to fast-forwarding. He got to Sunday, the day when the Guzmans met Dr. Wong in the lobby. He watched and fast-forwarded until the late morning, and then he saw it. He slowed it down. Then he still-framed it, played it forward again, then went back and freeze-framed the image. Washington took out his iPhone and took several still photos. He then fast-forwarded for two hours and got another still photo. He stared at the photo and said six words: "Who the fuck is that guy?"

Washington had been watching video the entire day, so he decided he'd stay in a motel in Ojai for the night; he wanted to get to the hospital early. Before leaving the hospital, he went to the front desk of the lobby and showed the still photo to one of the receptionists, a thin, gray-haired white woman in her fifties, and asked if she recognized the man in the photo. The woman said that she did not. He then showed the photo to the other receptionist, a heavy-set Hispanic woman in her twenties. She looked at the photo and said she thought he had been there about a week ago but wasn't sure. Washington asked if there was any way to get a name. The receptionist said the only way would be if one of the doctors or nurses knew who he was.

Washington checked video of Daisy's arrival at the hospital but her face was not visible in any camera angles to corroborate the burn damage.

On Saturday, November 11, Dr. Wong gave Daisy the concussion protocol, and she passed. Washington and Whatley arrived at the hospital a short time after, and Daisy was still in her room. They entered and told Daisy they were going to show her a photo lineup, and that the person that hurt her might or might not be in the lineup. They told her not to feel obligated to pick someone out just because they were in a photo. Daisy looked at the lineup and instantly picked number four, which was John "Jack" Macklin.

Detective Whatley gave Daisy her wallet, which still held her driver's license and forty-seven dollars in cash. Daisy was beaming when she said, "You found my purse? Where was it?" Washington told her that Macklin had thrown it down the ravine, and that it was with the lab for DNA testing, since he'd touched it. Daisy asked about her phone. Whatley said it had been smashed and thrown down the ravine. Daisy made a sad face and said she had all her contacts in that phone.

Then she smiled and said she couldn't complain; what happened yesterday was a miracle and she still sometimes thought she dreamed it. She said she woke up that morning and looked in the mirror and saw she still wasn't burned up. She asked if anyone knew why her face was normal. They both said they didn't know yet. Daisy mentioned her mom coming back and looking at her left shoulder and commenting on the missing tattoo like that meant something. Washington said they would speak with her mom. Daisy didn't ask her next question, because she thought maybe she should ask Mr. Scapio instead.

Veronica arrived at the hospital and the two friends hugged for a long time. Daisy said the police gave her wallet back to her, and she asked Veronica if they could stop by a store so she could buy some clothes—just jeans and a couple of tops and some flip-flops, since all of her clothes were back at her family's house. Veronica asked if the police had arrested the man who did this to her, and Daisy said that they hadn't. She told Veronica that they had more work to do, and she thought that her face healing made it harder to prove what had happened to her.

Veronica said that she didn't want to be paranoid, but the guy could show up anywhere, and if he saw Daisy, they would both be in danger. She said that she knew Daisy's size and style and she could buy some clothes for her while Daisy stayed in. Veronica said she had food she could cook, and they could sometimes get takeout; the place across the street delivered and had really good salads and hamburgers.

Daisy was tearing up and told Veronica that she was the best friend anyone could ever have. Daisy said she was so overwhelmed that she couldn't stop smiling. She then raised her right arm and said, "When we get to your house, I'm gonna shower and shave my armpits."

"Oh, gross! That's more than the little stubble you sometimes have. OK, I admit I sometimes do, too."

"OK, you know what? These dark stubbles have been growing on me since before I got to the hospital. I'm gonna let them stay for a couple of more days before I tell them they have to go. We've been through a lot together."

"Daisy, you're my best friend for life, you're beautiful, you're smart, you're sweet, but you are fucking insane. You know that, right?"

Daisy said two days ago she thought she would have to live without a face; "now we're talking about my armpits." She said she just couldn't believe how happy she was. She added that she was going to have to get a phone at some point and she wanted to call Victoria's Secret to see if she still had a job. Veronica told Daisy she couldn't go back to work until they arrested that guy. Daisy agreed. "He knows I work there."

Whatley went to the front desk as Washington was at the water fountain. Whatley asked if Dr. Wong was in. The receptionist said he was, but he was starting a surgery. Whatley asked how long the doctor would be in surgery, and she said two hours approximately. When Washington finished his drink, he walked over. Whatley told him he wanted to show Wong the photo, but Wong was going to be in surgery for the next two hours.

They talked to whatever hospital staff they could find and showed the photo of the man that Washington took with his phone. Only one of the fifteen or so doctors and nurses thought they recognized him. She said he looked like a patient that came in late at night around a week ago or more, but she didn't treat him. She remembered him because he was distinct looking, but she didn't know his name.

Whatley called the Hoopers, and Millie answered. Whatley asked if they could come by because they had a couple more questions. Millie asked how the girl was. Whatley told her that "we are keeping it really quiet for now," but they would let her know as soon as they could.

They went by the Hoopers' home and got the best descriptions they could of Daisy at the time they found her. They said her hands covered her face a lot, but it did seem pretty horrible. They both confirmed there was blood and liquid in the back of the truck, but they had cleaned it because nobody had told them not to.

Whatley and Washington headed back to the hospital and found Dr. Wong. After shaking hands, Washington asked Dr. Wong if he recognized "this guy" and showed him the photo on his phone. Wong said he did. He was a patient that had been brought in by three young men over a week ago. He said that "he was in the lobby when I told the Guzmans about what had happened to their daughter."

Washington asked what he was treated for, and Wong told him that he had a sprained ankle, bruised shoulder, and a concussion, and that it was a vehicle-pedestrian accident. Dr. Wong asked if he was the man who hurt Daisy. Washington said, "We don't think so." He then turned toward Whatley and said, "We're good to tell him, right?" Whatley didn't answer Washington directly but told Wong that the man might have been the reason Daisy's face healed. Wong looked confused and asked how that was possible. Washington asked him if the patient gave a name. Wong remembered his name was Zack. He said the name was a common last name. He then said he would pull the records and look it up. He walked over to patient medical records and pulled files from the records for Saturday night, November 4.

After shuffling through papers, he finally said, "There it is, Zack Morgan." Washington asked to see everything they had on Morgan. They went through all the patient information, but nothing was helpful. Morgan had claimed to be homeless and had no phone. His Social Security number was so scribbled, they couldn't read it. He gave a date of birth and they could run that through records, but they seriously doubted that the information was true. Zack Morgan, or whoever he was, had all the indicia of someone who did not want to be found.

Dr. Wong asked why they thought that man had healed Daisy's face and how it was even possible. Before Washington could answer, though, Dr. Wong said he remembered something about the man. He said that it was weird; he was very well spoken for a homeless guy with no phone. Wong related that he was very friendly when he met him and asked a lot of questions about where and how Wong got his medical license. The man wasn't questioning his credentials, instead saying he was curious about the process. He also seemed to have knowledge of the equipment in the room and discussed that.

Washington then explained what he had seen on the video. He said that at a little before noon, this man could be seen walking down the hallway where patients' rooms are. He checked the names on the outside of the walls before moving on. He approached Daisy's room and checked the name tag, and then he slowly opened the curtain to her room and entered. About two hours later, he emerged with a big smile on his face. He looked up at the camera and stared at it for about twenty seconds. He then shrugged his shoulders and did an odd celebration dance for the camera before walking away out of view.

Dr. Wong stood in silence and then mumbled, as if in shock, "Who the hell is Zack Morgan?"

Whatley said, "That's the same question we've been asking."

Washington checked to see if there had been a police report of the accident and found the sheriff's report from Deputy Gabriel Saqui. He called Deputy Saqui and asked if he remembered the Zack Morgan pedestrian-vehicle accident. Saqui said not only did he remember it, but he would never forget it as long as he lived. Washington told him he would like to meet with him and talk about it. Saqui asked him if Zack Morgan had done something. Washington said, "We think he might have."

Saqui said, "I'm not surprised; that guy gave me the creeps."

Washington said he couldn't go into detail, but what he did might not have been bad. Saqui told him that he really had him curious. Washington arranged a time to meet Saqui, then told Whatley it had been set for the Ojai substation at 4:00 p.m.

Deputy Gabriel Saqui was born and raised in the Philippines but had been in the US for almost thirty years. He was a twenty-two-year veteran of the sheriff's department. His assignment was traffic investigations and he often worked closely with the highway patrol.

Saqui told the two detectives that he interviewed the three young men in the car and Morgan. He said they all told the same basic story, with minor variations. The basic story was that Morgan stepped out onto the highway as the driver, Jabari Clemons, was racing around the curve. At ten feet or less they noticed each other, and Morgan was hit, cracking the windshield. Based on witness statements and skid marks, Saqui believed the truck was going about sixty miles per hour upon impact.

He said he thought the story was bullshit and that all those guys were hiding what really happened. But after examining the truck and Morgan's injuries, he thought that maybe it did happen that way, but Morgan had to be some kind of freakish athlete. Whatley asked what he meant. Saqui said that what Morgan supposedly was able to do happened in action movies all the time but not in real life.

He pointed out that "if someone steps in front of a car that's going fast around a curve and they're too close to move out of the way, they are going to be dead. The car will strike them in the front, and they will fall and likely be run over. Even if they're not run over, they'll suffer extensive lower-body damage, and the landing will be so far from impact it would kill them if they were not already dead. Now imagine a pickup truck that is higher in front than a standard automobile."

He explained that he treated Morgan for injuries, but the injuries were limited to a concussion, a sprained ankle, and a bruise on his left shoulder. Saqui further explained that he had no injuries to his lower extremities other than the ankle sprain. What that means is that Morgan had to have seen the truck and instinctively leapt from a standing position, clearing the entire front fender of the truck while contorting his body in such a way as to protect his head and launching his left shoulder into the windshield, then falling relatively unharmed to the side of the road.

Saqui concluded, "Do you have any idea what kind of insane athleticism that would take? I don't think LeBron James could do that. Neither could Bruce Lee when he was the king of martial arts. This guy Zack Morgan did, and I can't explain that."

Washington asked him his thoughts about Morgan as he interviewed him. Saqui said that he was definitely hiding something. He said Morgan was cooperative until he started asking routine personal questions; then he got very defensive. "He was saying that those questions didn't matter, and it was none of my business. He became very uncooperative. I figured the guy was shady, but I really didn't have probable cause to go further, and I didn't want to agitate the guy any more.

"Can you guys tell me what you think he did?"

Whatley replied, "No, but we aren't saying what he did was bad."

* * *

Washington and Whatley took Sunday off. Daisy still didn't have a phone, but she used Nikki's phone and called Victoria's Secret in the mall and spoke to her boss. Her boss was thrilled and surprised to hear from Daisy. Daisy told her that she had been gone because she had been abducted. The case was still open, but she was hoping the shop would take her back. She said she couldn't come back right away because she was still dealing with some things that needed to be resolved before she could go back to work.

Her boss had always liked Daisy and thought she was a good employee, but Daisy hadn't called or come in for days. The police did call to see if Daisy had called or shown up for work, so she was afraid that something bad might have happened. Unfortunately, they had to hire a replacement, and she told Daisy that they couldn't fire the new girl.

She then asked Daisy what happened and if she was OK. Daisy said she was. Her boss asked Daisy who did it and what he did to her. Daisy told her boss people will not believe what happened to her, but it was horrible, and that if there was any way she could have, she would have called.

Daisy told her that she couldn't talk about the details yet and then asked if they could have a spot for her without firing the other girl; she didn't want them to fire anyone. Her now-former boss told Daisy that as soon as something opened up, she would hire Daisy back if she was still looking for work, but they didn't have an opening now. Daisy thanked her and handed the phone back to Nikki and shook her head. Nikki told her it was OK and she could stay as long as she needed to. She said that once they arrest the guy, she could get Daisy a job at CVS; they were usually hiring, and they would hire her in a second.

Veronica was awakened at 2:00 a.m. by Daisy screaming from the spare bedroom. "Please go back and drive me to work, I promise I won't tell!" Veronica rushed to Daisy's room and Daisy had woken up. "Oh my God, I'm so sorry Nikki, I had a nightmare."

Nikki told her it was OK; she was happy Daisy was "still with us" and was still the same Daisy she always had been. She assured Daisy that "we will get through this," and she gave her a hug.

* * *

On Monday, November 13, Scapio was assigned to cover the morning calendar in Courtroom 12. The morning calendar covered felony arraignments for charged defendants, requests to modify terms of probation, and requests to delay remand dates for people sentenced to jail asking for more time before going into custody, as well as sentencings and probation violations.

The calendar ended at about 11:00 a.m. and he returned to his office. He checked his voice mail and heard the voice of a young woman. "Hi, Mr. Scapio, it's Daisy Guzman, the girl from the hospital. I have some questions about my case. I was hoping you could still put him away. I don't have a phone right now because of what happened to me, but I'm working on getting one. I can give you my friend's phone number. Her name is Veronica, the number is 805-555-0199. Thanks; if you call her, she can give me the phone. I'm staying with her right now. OK, well, I appreciate everything you're doing, and I'll wait to hear from you. Bye." Scapio thought that her voice was as lovely as she was. He wanted to call back, but he was uncertain what to tell her.

He knew she was scared and wanted so badly to promise her that they could go forward with the case, but he needed to persuade Bill Reddis that it really happened exactly how Daisy said, despite no rational medical explanation as to why her face showed no evidence of it. His plan was to talk to Reddis in the afternoon and call Daisy back. He hoped he could promise her that he would take her case. Unfortunately, Reddis was in Sacramento at a meeting with the California District Attorneys Association and wouldn't be back until Wednesday.

He did call back that afternoon and spoke to Daisy. She asked if they could still prosecute her case, and she said that other people saw her and could testify to what happened. Scapio said he agreed with her and wanted to go ahead but had to wait for some DNA tests to come back, and he mentioned that his boss was out of town.

She said that she was scared for herself and anyone else he might do this to. She knew that something wonderful happened that caused her face to be restored and she didn't have an explanation, but she was scared that next time he would finish her off. Scapio could hear Daisy fighting back tears. He assured her that he was on her side, but ultimately the decision was his boss's, though he would have input.

Daisy said that she googled him and saw he was the one who put away the tennis player who killed his girlfriend. "I'm glad you're my prosecutor," she said. Scapio told her he would keep her informed. After getting off the phone, he thought that if Daisy was trying to charm him, she definitely succeeded. Scapio wasn't usually one to beg, but he would get on his hands and knees and beg Reddis to take a shot here.

FIFTEEN

Washington came to work at 10:00 a.m. on Monday. As head of homicide, he had his own office; some of the detectives just had cubicles. He headed into his office after saying good morning to his secretary, Roxanne—who he had jokingly told many times to not turn on the red light, as if she hadn't heard that comment referencing the song by the band the Police a billion times—and she stopped him and told him there was a young man in his office waiting for him. "He said he was a witness in the Daisy Guzman case." Washington asked what his name was. Roxanne said she wrote it down and that "it was here somewhere."

Washington walked into his office and took a look at the man seated in a chair in front of his desk. Washington stood in shocked silence. The man was dressed a little oddly in plaid shorts and a pullover shirt, but it was obvious looking at him that he was muscular. There was no doubt about the face.

The man extended his hand and said, "Hi, I'm Zack Morgan, but by the look on your face, I think you already knew that. You've seen the security video, haven't you? I am guessing Daisy's bandages are off by now, right?" Washington just nodded his head. Morgan asked, "Did I do a good job?" Washington said that he would have to describe it as an amazing job. Morgan continued, "I thought I did. As you saw, I did a little dance, I was so pleased with my work. You know I thought about smashing the camera, and I should have done that. It would have been the smartest thing, but I have a bit of an ego. I'm not too bad, but I did want credit, I admit that.

"You know what the hardest thing was? The damn bandages. I pulled them off to fix her face and they wrinkled and got caught in her long hair, so I tried to just put them back on after I was done, but that wasn't working too well. I put the ones back on that didn't wrinkle too badly. The rest I had to stuff in my pocket to toss later. I had enough of what I needed to make some new bandages, but if you looked closely you could clearly see the difference. I was afraid someone was going to notice that and take the bandages off too soon and ruin what I did, because what I did needed a little time to set. That was critical to her recovery.

"You know, fixing her face wasn't hard. I was just nervous that a doctor or nurse might come in. I wouldn't hurt anyone, but I would have had to make them take a nap, because I was determined to do this. Her mother had a really good photo, so I had a pretty easy job there. That part only took me a half hour. The rest of the time was spent on the whole bandage situation."

Washington asked an obvious question. "Who are you?"

"I can't really tell you that yet. I can tell you that I was not supposed to be at the hospital. I screwed up. I was expected to leave as soon as I was better, but I was waiting in the lobby and I heard the doctor tell the girl's parents what happened to that poor girl. Like I said, I have a bit of an ego, I admit, but I really am a good guy. As a good guy, how do I walk away from that, when I know I can help?

"But you have a problem, don't you?" Washington had a million thoughts spinning in his head, but he just asked Morgan what he meant by a problem. Morgan said, "Someone did something absolutely horrible to this girl. You want to put that person away, maybe even execute them if you could; now you can't. Is she gonna come into a trial and say, 'Hi, my name's Daisy and this person sitting there poured stuff on my face and burned my face off and look at me now, where is the next local beauty contest? I think I can win it.' You see what I mean? You can't make a case. That's a problem."

Washington said that the local prosecutor was going to talk to his boss about going forward anyway, and the girl wanted to. Morgan said, "I can't stick around for trial and do a demonstration for the judge or whatever, and you can't explain why she looks the same. So yeah, you have a problem, and I caused it."

Washington asked if he had a solution. Morgan said, "I do. That's why I'm here." Washington asked if he could call his partner Chris, who he had been working with, to come down. Morgan said that would be fine, and he added, "You also must call Daisy Guzman and get her down here." Washington asked why, and Morgan said, "It's not for her to thank me, although I don't mind that, but she has to be part of my solution. I don't want to get the wrong person. She knows who did it."

Washington called Whatley and said, "I walked into my office this morning, and guess who was waiting for me?" Whatley declined to guess and just asked who it was. Washington said, "Zack Morgan," and Whatley said he'd be right over.

Whatley's heart was racing as he drove over to the Ventura Police Department.

Nikki answered her phone and Washington asked for Daisy. Nikki said that she was at work and that Daisy was staying at her apartment by herself until things calmed down. Washington said that he thought they were about to calm down, and asked if she could bring Daisy to the station when she got a break. She said she had a break in an hour, and she could go then. Nikki added, "We need to get Daisy a new phone."

Washington said that he could have an officer pick Daisy up, but he didn't want to scare her. He asked if there was a landline, and Nikki replied that Daisy wouldn't answer a landline because she was scared it could be him. Nikki said she believed the guy thought Daisy was dead, but Daisy was scared and had been having nightmares.

Morgan interrupted Washington and said Daisy was going to need a car. Washington told Morgan that they would figure something out when she got there.

Whatley arrived and he recognized Morgan right away. He remembered the amazing feat of athleticism Morgan had to have performed to survive that car accident. He noticed that Morgan was very strong looking, but not like a body builder, because it just looked natural, like he had always been that way.

Whatley introduced himself and they shook hands. Whatley asked how he did it. Morgan played dumb and smiled while asking Whatley what he was talking about. Then he said, "Oh, you mean fixed Daisy's face." Morgan said there were things he was not yet at liberty to explain, but that after he did what needed to be done, they could all have a nice conversation.

Whatley asked what he was talking about. "What is it that needs to be done?"

Morgan looked at Whatley and Washington and said the best thing would be that "you don't know. That way when it happens, nobody can criticize your judgment. You didn't know, and that works best for everyone."

Whatley tried to ask questions, but Morgan just kept telling him that he couldn't answer. He did tell Whatley something similar to what he told Washington earlier. He mentioned that he was not supposed to be at the hospital and added that he definitely wasn't supposed to be at the Ventura police station. There was some awkward silence as they now waited for Daisy.

Morgan reached under his chair and said he had almost forgotten, but he made some muffins for everyone. He handed one to Washington, who bit into it and said, "Wow, that is really good." Whatley took one too and agreed. Morgan said that he had one for Daisy when she got there.

Morgan asked who had hurt Daisy. Washington looked at Whatley and Whatley nodded. Washington told him that they believed it was a man who lived a couple of doors down from Daisy and who had been in trouble for hurting another girl. Morgan thought for a moment and then decided not to speak. Washington was pretty sure Morgan was going to say that the man would not hurt anyone else ever again.

Washington asked why Daisy needed to be there. Morgan said Daisy needed to be free, and that was the only way. He also said Daisy was the only one who could make sure that "I don't make a mistake." He said Daisy would know who hurt her, and "when I see the look on his face when he sees her, I'll know."

Washington got a call that there was a young woman named Daisy Guzman there to see him. Washington told them to escort her in. When she arrived at his office, Washington told Daisy that there was someone she had to meet, and he introduced Zack Morgan. Daisy had her hair tied in a ponytail. She was wearing jeans and a light-blue blouse and black flip-flops. She was wearing virtually no makeup, but it didn't matter; Daisy Guzman was still stunningly beautiful. Her lip had even mostly healed.

Morgan looked at her and said, "You know if you had done your hair that way it would have made it a lot easier." Daisy looked confused, and Morgan said, as he looked at Daisy, "I was telling these guys I was good, and I do try to be humble, but an artist has to admire his work." Daisy stood staring in disbelief until Whatley spoke and told Daisy they were convinced that Zack Morgan fixed her face. Daisy put her hand out and said, "Well, I'm Daisy and it's so nice to meet you." Morgan stood up and Daisy pulled her hand away and hugged him and cried. She held on for over a minute, and then she said she had so many questions.

Morgan told her he would answer her questions but they had to do something first. He said, "Even before that, though . . . here, try one of my muffins." He handed the muffin to Daisy, who was not going to turn down a gift from a benefactor, although she was sort of on a low-carbs diet. Daisy bit into the muffin and her face lit up. She said, "Oh my God, that is so good! What flavor is that?" Morgan said that it was regular flavor. Daisy laughed and said, "Well, OK, that was the best regular flavor ever."

Daisy asked what she had to do. Morgan told her that it was going to be something very hard, but it was the only way. He said they had to go to the horrible man's house, and she would have to stand outside, and when he opened the door, she would say if that was him. Morgan said he would protect her and that she would be in no danger. Daisy said she couldn't. Morgan asked if she'd been having night terrors.

"You mean nightmares?"

Morgan nodded and said, "Daisy, I fixed your face; you know you can trust me. I will never let him hurt you." Daisy put her hands in his and nodded. He asked Daisy the man's name.

Daisy said his first name was Jack. "His last name was Mackey, or something like that." Washington said that it was Macklin. He added that Daisy was very courageous, and though she could identify Macklin, Washington didn't want her put in any danger. Morgan said that what he had planned was the best way to deal with the situation. Morgan told Daisy they needed to rent her a car if she didn't have one there at the station. She asked why, and Morgan told her that she had to drive. They could park away from his house and walk over there.

Morgan turned to Washington and Whatley and asked if they had talked to the guy yet. Washington nodded and said that the guy was an asshole and used a racial slur on him and on Daisy. Daisy asked, "What racial slur did he use on me?" Washington said that he called her the "wetback girl with big tits." Daisy said he got it half right. "I'm not a wetback. I was born in Ventura." Daisy asked what he called Washington and he told her. Daisy said, "He's one of those. Figures."

Washington asked to speak with Morgan and Whatley away from Daisy. Morgan said OK, and they stepped outside.

Washington said that Daisy picked Macklin out of a photo lineup. He said he could give Morgan the picture and that he could do what he needed to do without involving that girl who has already been through hell and back. Morgan said that it can't go that way. He said the man could have a relative staying over that looks like him. He said he could not make a mistake. When the man saw Daisy, Morgan would know by the look in his eyes that he had the right person, just like Morgan knew as soon as he saw Washington look at him that Washington had seen the security video.

Washington turned to Whatley, who said, "Are you 100 percent sure that Daisy is in no danger?"

Morgan said, "Yes, she'll be fine and this is the best thing. Remember, I never told you guys what I was going to do. I never told Daisy either. What you think you know, nobody else can be sure of. Always remember I never told you what I was going to do. It probably will never even come up." They walked back into Washington's office.

Daisy was told that one of the newer officers was going to drive her to Enterprise Rental in Ventura. She came back with a white Honda Accord, and she and Morgan left together. Washington said he was going to head over in an undercover and park nearby, just to make sure it didn't turn to shit. Whatley said, "It's going to turn shit for Jack Macklin. I would hate to be him right now."

* * *

Jack Macklin was pacing inside his home. He was thinking the next one would be a hooker; much less risk. He was considering going back to Cañada Larga Road and getting rid of that purse and that container. Mack was concerned that the cops had checked out Daisy's car. They had to know she was taken from here. He also knew that if the cops tried to figure out where the first isolated road was, they would come to Cañada Larga. If they searched long enough, they would find Daisy's body and all the other evidence. But he thought again and figured that was a very long stretch of road.

"They need me to fuck up," he thought. "They probably have the road staked out. I go up there, I will lead them right to shit they might never even find. Just fucking stay calm. They do not know where the girl's body is. Even if they find it, they may never be able to identify her. Well, dental records, I guess. Even if they think Cañada Larga Road, it could take weeks. I don't even know if they can get a dog down there. That ravine is like a cave."

His thoughts were interrupted by the doorbell. He growled through the closed door, "Who is it? What do you want?"

The man said, "I have a check for you and you need to sign for it." Macklin opened the door and saw a powerful-looking short guy in funny plaid shorts.

The man had a goofy smile on his face. Then he stepped to his right and back and said, "Daisy. Is this the guy?"

Daisy said, "Yes, he tried to kill me."

Mack looked to the right and about five feet behind the man at the door. He thought, "This can't be real, this can't be her . . ."

He started to speak, but the young man said, "You look like you've seen a ghost."

Mack thought, "He's a short punk, I can—"

Mack felt a sharp powerful blow to his chest, then he felt the bones in his nose smash. Blood spurting everywhere, he fell to his knees.

Daisy had heard Zack say, "You look like you've seen a ghost." The only fight Daisy had ever been in, in her entire life, was when she tried to escape from Mack. She had taken the aerobic kickboxing class at her gym a couple of times, but she preferred the spin class and yoga; Daisy really liked yoga. She did watch boxing whenever she would get together with her cousins, who were big fans and bought the big fights on pay-per-view.

So Daisy knew what a good punch looked like, but she had never seen anything like this. The first punch was the fastest jab she had ever seen, straight to Mack's chest. The next punch was a crushing right hand. She heard the bone crunch and she saw blood spurt from the scumbag's nose. She then saw Morgan kneel slightly and thought he was throwing another right but instead something came out of his sleeve. She thought it might have been a dart or even a bullet.

Jack—or Mack, or whatever his name was—fell to his knees and clutched his chest. Morgan then kneeled so he was eye to eye with the profusely bleeding giant.

Daisy heard Morgan speak. He said, "I'm gonna need you to stand up for me. Come on, I know you can do it." Mack started to fall, but immediately Morgan grabbed him and easily slammed him against the wall of the house and held him up. Morgan continued, "I want you to know what the rest of your life is going to be like. But don't worry, I'm only going to need two minutes, 'cause that's all you got.

"The first thing is that your temperature is going to rise."

Daisy heard her attacker cry, "I'm sorry, please don't hurt me. I'm sorry."

Daisy walked up to him, got right in his face, and shouted, "Quit crying, you stupid little bitch."

Zack Morgan turned to Daisy, put his arms in the air, and said, "Daisy, come on, please."

Daisy said, "Sorry, I had to do that."

Morgan continued as the big man fell to the ground. "By the way, I think you know my friend Daisy. Doesn't she look gorgeous? I did that. You, on the other hand, won't be looking so good. Your temperature is rising 'cause of that little dart I hit you with. I actually missed the spot I was aiming for, which means it's gonna take a little longer. That means more pain."

Macklin looked at Daisy and mouthed, "I'm sorry," and in a dying voice, said, "Please help."

Morgan continued, "Oh, she isn't going to help you. Did you show her mercy? No, you did not. But here is the worst part. Even if she took pity on you and started saying, 'Oh, he's had enough, please stop'—do you hear her saying that? 'Cause I don't—even if she did, and I started feeling bad too, which I don't, the bad thing is I have all this technology, and you know what I don't have? A fucking rewind button. How crazy is that? I put that dart in you and you are burning up. I just can't stop it. It's like that email. You hit send, and then you think, 'Oh man, I should not have said that.' You can't undo it. You know why. No rewind button. So, you might as well, as my good friend Daisy so aptly put it, quit crying"—he turned to Daisy and said, "What was that phrase again?" and Daisy said, "Stupid little bitch," which Morgan then repeated.

"You got about a minute left in your miserable life. Here's the thing. I can see how much pain you are in. I could tell you to think of something that makes you happy, like how you tortured this poor beautiful person. Maybe you got some religious beliefs, maybe you think if you repent you will get into that good place or you will get another life. Now if you end it trying to jerk off over tossing shit in this poor girl's face, and that religion thing is true, damn you are fucked. So that pain you're feeling right now, that might last forever.

"You now can't speak at all. I know you gotta try to get your mind out of the pain. My best suggestion, I have been told I have a calming voice. That is a good thing for my profession. So, you can listen to the sound of my voice. Unfortunately, I got more bad news for you. I've run out of shit to say."

At this point, Macklin began to literally evaporate. His blood drained, creating a large pool on the doorstep, but Jack Macklin was otherwise gone. Not even bones. Zack Morgan stepped back and did an odd little victory dance. Daisy looked at Morgan said, "Why not?" and busted out her best dance moves.

Daisy and Zack walked back to Daisy's car. Daisy hugged him and said, "I almost feel bad for saying this, but thank you. That was awesome. I think I'll be able to sleep now."

Zack got in the passenger seat, and Daisy climbed into the driver's seat and put on her seat belt. She asked Zack to put on his and laughed, reminding him that she'd gotten a couple of speeding tickets. She said, "Since you saved my life, I've decided to pursue my dream of being an investigative reporter. I have some questions for you, and I hope you'll be willing to answer. Then after, you can tell me if I asked good questions and if I missed anything." Zack said it was time she knew, and he was willing to help.

He commented that he'd got some of Macklin's blood on his clothes, and some went on hers when she hugged him. He said she should go back to her house so she can get a new top. They had to detour to Nikki's, since Daisy didn't have the keys to her parents' house on her. She changed into a sleeveless light-blue top and threw the light-blue blouse in the washer.

They got back into the rental car, and the investigation began. Daisy asked how he fixed her face. He said he was a doctor. Daisy said Dr. Wong couldn't do it, so how could he? Morgan said he had technology that Dr. Wong did not have. Daisy expressed doubt that Zack Morgan was his real name, and he confirmed her suspicions, but suggested it would be easiest for her to keep calling him by that name.

Daisy then said that she didn't think he was from around there. He confirmed that he was from quite a distance away. Daisy asked him straight out: "Are you from outer space?"

Morgan said, "We don't refer to it that way, but yes, technically you are right." Daisy asked where that was, and Morgan replied, "Your scientists actually know it, and have given it a name; you call it Kepler-452b. It's in the Cygnus constellation, and it's fourteen hundred light-years from here." He added that his planet was much older than Earth, and that was why they had advanced space travel that allowed him to get there in less time than what anyone would expect. Morgan said that he guessed that his planet was probably named after the astronomer who discovered it but he never researched the origin of the name.

Daisy asked why he was on Earth. Morgan explained that his planet had had difficulty growing crops due to soil contamination, which threatened their existence. He was a medical doctor on his planet and was part of a team, consisting of himself as the doctor and three geologists, whose directive was to collect and analyze soil samples for compatibility with their planet. "An area of Earth that we liked was the Ojai Valley. Our geologists thought that might work to allow us to bring back samples and clone the soil and replace our contaminated soil."

Daisy asked why Ojai, and Zack explained that he wasn't a geologist so he couldn't answer that, but of their three crew members who were geologists, the female member of the crew was very high on the soil in and around the entire Ojai area. He had never asked why because he figured he wouldn't understand it, but she was very excited and optimistic on that area. Daisy said, "She sounds smart; I'd like to meet her."

Daisy asked what his real name was, and he answered, "You really should just go with 'Zack Morgan,' because we use a different system for names—a numeric system. It would be like if your name were 4,853,658⅔. Not knowing our numeric system, my name would make no sense to you and would be unpronounceable."

Daisy wanted to know why he had been at the hospital, and he explained that he had been wandering when he got hit by a car at night. He said he'd become bored and the others were sleeping, and he wanted to explore but was unfamiliar with the roads. He was wearing dark clothes and he got hit.

Next, Daisy asked how he fixed her face. Morgan said, "If someone on an exploratory mission gets cut, the wound could be exposed to bacteria that are harmless to you but potentially fatal to us. As soon as possible, that open wound must be closed. As our vessel's doctor, I carry this mimetic compound, or skin salve. It's essentially a mimetic binding in that it mimics the surrounding skin and closes the open wound. In your case, as long as I had a picture of you, I would know exactly how much and where to apply the compound to the open wounds and damaged or burned skin. The compound mimics your actual skin, and in a short time, you are good as new. The compound comes in a concealable tube; I'll show it to you when we get back to the police station. I just needed a recent photo of you, and fortunately, your mom had one."

Somewhat alarmed, Daisy asked, "If the compound mimics my skin, is it not really my skin?"

"No, it is, it's exactly the same on the outside. It's a much more advanced version of how your planet treats burn victims. You replace parts of skin on the face with transplants of skin from other parts of the body, but our compound actually recreates the skin in place. If your nose was replaced with skin from your hip, everyone could tell that you had a serious accident and you had skin there that might have some functionality, but it's obviously not your natural nose. With your nose, I just recreated the parts that had been burned away, so your nose is exactly the same.

"The part that became a little problematic was the bandages they put on you. I had to remove them. Because of your face and hair, that was really hard. The bandages wrinkled and folded. Putting them back on was even harder. The second knob on the tube creates bandages, but they are not the same as the ones they had on you. I rebandaged you with the ones originally on you that I could salvage, and the rest I made with the compound tube. I was concerned someone might notice a difference, but I couldn't imagine they would do anything about it."

Daisy said, "My mom figured out that you had to be the person who fixed my face." Zack asked how she knew. Daisy said she had talked to her mom on her friend's phone and her mom explained it to her. "My tattoo. When the asshole you killed attacked me, I had a tattoo of a purple daisy, for my name, on my left shoulder. My mom didn't like it but I got it right after the photo was taken, so it wasn't in the photo you were shown. The tattoo is gone; that's how she knew."

Morgan said, "Your mom is a really smart lady, that was excellent logic. But she's wrong. I'm not a tattoo artist, and the compound can recreate skin and the tone that is natural but it doesn't recreate body art. Obviously, some of what he poured on you burned your shoulder, and I remember working on your chest and shoulder and just a little on the palms of your hands. If your tattoo burned off, even if it were in the photo, it would still have been gone. By the way, we have body art, but I don't have any myself."

Daisy asked why he decided to help her. He explained that when he heard what the doctor explained to her parents, he had to help. He said that on Earth, there is an oath doctors take—he said he didn't remember the word because he took a crash course in English before they left for Earth but forgot some words—but "that oath is the same one we have. I had two conflicting instructions. I was told not to interact with the people on the planet any more than is needed and to be very careful about revealing myself. But I also have the oath to help others as a doctor, and I chose to help you because I could not live with myself, knowing I could have and didn't."

Daisy started crying and thanking him again. She asked if he was going to get in trouble. He said, "Oh, without a doubt. Not for fixing your face; I have a defense for that. My oath as a doctor is a pretty good defense. On the other hand, what I just did? I'm gonna be in deep shit for that."

Daisy said, "He would have come after me and my friend Nikki and other women. You saved lives! You should get a medal. You're a superhero."

Zack said, "I don't think they are gonna see it that way. But I'm going to explain exactly why I did it."

Daisy said, "Just don't say anything. They won't know." He explained that everything they do is monitored; they agree to that before they go on a mission.

As Daisy continued driving, he added, "They were already pissed at me for going bowling." Daisy laughed and asked him to explain that. Zack said they'd had a lot of spare time on Earth, and they had satellites that could pick up TV. "I like to watch sports, but many of your sports are very similar to what we have. There are subtle rule differences, dimensions are different, and the ball, like in baseball, is very different. But still, very similar.

"Bowling, on the other hand—we don't have anything like it. I really wanted to try. It looked easy, but it was really hard. I couldn't get it to go straight when there was one pin left in a corner. And at first, I couldn't get anything to go straight. I didn't want to roll too hard or I might have given myself away with how fast I could roll it. I was trying to blend in because I knew I was gonna be in trouble, but if nobody noticed anything unusual, I could say that it was no problem."

Daisy asked if he did a dance when he made a shot, like he did when he killed that guy. Morgan answered, "I probably did, why?"

"OK, Zack, or 8,000,556⅔, or whatever your real name is. I love you; you gave me my life back and I would do anything for you, I will never forget you. But I have to be honest; with that dance, you stood out. I'm surprised nobody got on a megaphone and said"—Daisy covered her mouth with her hand—"'We have a space alien special on lane 6, space alien special.'"

Zack laughed and complimented Daisy on her sense of humor. "That bad, huh?" Daisy smiled and nodded.

Daisy asked, "How were you able to kick that guy's ass so easily? He was huge, and I know I'm not very big, but he made it seem like I weighed ten pounds."

"Because of gravity. On Kepler-452b, our gravitational pull is twice as strong as yours. Picture if you ran up a hill with a backpack strapped to your back from the time you were two years old. Assuming you developed no health problems, you would be that much stronger as you got older because you would have worked those muscles so hard. That is how we are, because it takes more work to move with stronger gravity; things like squats and sprints are twice as hard. That builds up far greater muscle. You go to gyms and work out, but every instant we are on our planet, the gravitational pull necessarily exerts us more."

He asked Daisy to guess his weight. She guessed 165. He said, "Around 235."

"No way. You're obviously strong, but you're still a little guy."

"Not when you consider bone and muscle density. My bones weigh more; they're the same basic size, but they're dense from the strength development due to our gravity." He said if anyone on Earth had asked him to step on a scale, he would have refused and told them that he had a rare condition where he feared scales. He couldn't step on a scale because that might have led to all sorts of medical investigations.

Daisy laughed and said that she's afraid of scales after she eats her mom's Mexican food. He laughed and continued that when he's on Earth, because the gravity is lighter, he is faster. It would be like throwing punches with fifteen-pound weights attached to your hands for weeks and then shedding the weights. Also, they had extensive martial arts training on his planet, so that, combined with the fact that he knew he was much stronger and faster than the guy, meant Zack didn't figure there would be a problem. Plus, Zack really hated him for what he had done to Daisy, so that helped too.

She asked if she would have died if he hadn't fixed her face. He said, "Once all the burns were replaced with new skin, you were in the healing process. I won't go into a long medical explanation, but I don't think you would have died, because the acid didn't get into your lungs, but you could have. The best-case scenario would have been a lifetime of surgeries, and your beautiful face would have been gone. I am so glad I got hit by that car." Daisy agreed.

Finally, Daisy asked where she would be if she had died. Was there life after death? His answer was that on his planet, some people were religious, and some were not. He said he believed in what was called intelligent design and a higher power, but he was not sure. Even with their advanced technology, there were some questions that could only be answered when it was our time, and "Daisy Guzman, it wasn't your time." Daisy was glad to not have an answer; she just knew she had her life back.

She pulled into the parking lot at the Ventura Police Department and asked how she did with her questions. Zack said she did great, and if he were in the news business, he would hire her. Daisy said, "We have to go bowling before you go back. I will make you feel great, because I'm terrible. I always throw gutter balls, but it will be so much fun."

He thought to himself that he had to leave, and he couldn't fall for an Earth girl, but it sure would be nice. Daisy asked if he had a wife or girlfriend back home. He said, "There was someone, but . . ." He then said he had to go back that day; he had no choice.

Daisy cried a little and said, "Just when I get to know you, you leave in your flying saucer."

"Daisy, you are beautiful—"

"Thanks to you."

"No, you were beautiful before, and you are a super-nice human, but why do you Earth people insist on saying we are in flying saucers? They are not saucers. Picture that bowling ball; it's a lot closer to that."

Daisy laughed again. Then, "Should we tell the cops what happened?"

"No, just that the problem is solved, and I'll tell them who I am."

He added, as they sat in her rental car, "You are going to have to figure out who in your life to tell how your face got fixed." Daisy said that people wouldn't believe her. He asked who was there when they took the bandages off. Daisy named them, and Zack said, "They were there for you. When they all thought the beautiful face was gone for good, they were with you. They were with you because they loved you no matter what your face was going to look like. Those people saved you as much as I did. Tell them all. They all love you, and they will believe you."

Daisy cried again; she was so emotional, she could only nod her head. She finally said, "Let's go inside." After they got out of the car, Daisy hugged and thanked him again.

Morgan pulled an object out of his pocket that looked like a thick tube of toothpaste. It had two buttons on the side. He explained that pushing the top button would create the skin salve, and the bottom button would produce bandages. Daisy asked to see it and he handed it to her. Daisy kissed it and thanked it, then handed it back to him.

They went back inside and entered Washington's office. Washington told Morgan that he had a really impressive right jab, but that if he really wanted to learn to dance, he needed to ask Daisy to teach him, because as Washington put it, "That was terrible."

Morgan said he'd already heard it from Daisy and then said that Washington should have stayed at the office. Now he'd seen something he shouldn't have, and he could face problems with his job if anyone knew he saw it.

Washington said that was extremely unlikely because they already knew that there were no security cameras on the street. "It would have been nice if you'd brought a change of clothes, though; you got his blood all over you." Morgan agreed, acknowledging that he hadn't thought of that.

Washington asked Morgan who he was and where he was from. Washington was told exactly what Daisy was told. He said he wasn't surprised, and that he thought it had to be something like that. Morgan nodded and continued to explain to Washington and Whatley all that he had explained to Daisy.

Daisy mentioned that she was getting a phone and wanted to know if there was any way that she and Zack could stay in touch. He told her he didn't think that was possible, but he would never forget his experience here. Daisy asked if he thought his planet would be OK, and he said they were very optimistic that this trip had provided the breakthrough they needed. She asked if other planets besides his and Earth had life. He replied that there were probably quite a few, but his people hadn't been exploring that long. They had found others, but Earth so far had the most intelligent life besides their own. Still, there were many galaxies that likely had planets that could sustain life.

She told Whatley and Washington that she had called Scapio's office and left a message about her case before today. He had called back and said he would try to work the case, but his boss had the final say. She asked what she should say when he called her back again. They both told her to act like nothing had happened today, but the two detectives argued about whether they should tell him.

Morgan said he had advised Daisy to tell the people that were there for her when the bandages were taken off. "It would be good if at least one of you was there to explain how her face was fixed, and maybe show the security video."

Whatley asked how he did fix her face, and he was given the same explanation that Daisy got. Washington told Daisy that for now, it would be best to keep quiet about what happened today when she talks to Scapio.

They sat talking for another five minutes before Roxanne came in and said that there were three people in the lobby for Zack Morgan. Zack turned to Daisy and said, "That's my ride, I guess you could say." Daisy asked if he had to leave, and he confirmed that he did. Daisy asked to say goodbye to him and maybe she could meet his friends. Zack said goodbye to the two detectives. "Nobody is gonna believe a space alien killed that guy; you guys will be fine."

They shook hands, and Daisy and Zack walked to the lobby, where Daisy saw two men and one woman. They were stocky and powerfully built, but Daisy understood why. She walked up to them and introduced herself, and they greeted Daisy warmly.

They were all polite and introduced themselves with generic names. Daisy told the woman that it was great to know that smart and powerful women could succeed where she was from. As they were talking, one of the men pulled a towel out of a bag and squirted something onto it, which he used to remove most of the blood on Zack's shirt.

Daisy turned to Zack and told him that she would never forget what he did for her. She said she wished he didn't have to leave. She put her arms around him and kissed him on the mouth. Morgan was also wishing he didn't have to leave at that moment. The kiss and embrace lasted almost a minute. Morgan finally said he had to go. He told Daisy he had never done anything in his life that he was prouder of than helping her. They grasped hands and said goodbye. He teared up.

He turned around and saw his three companions smiling and basically saying in their own language, "You dirty dog, we can't take you anywhere." Daisy saw their hand gestures and the smiles on their faces and figured it was their version of a thumbs-up.

Daisy rushed up to him and hugged him one more time and asked him if he was gonna be in trouble. He said he'd get yelled at for the bowling. He should be fine for helping her at the hospital, and he'd hope for the best and that they just dock his pay for the other thing. He added that wandering off and getting hit by a car may have consequences. The worst would be that he could do some time for it, but there was lots of mitigation, so he should be OK. Daisy said she would miss him, and if he ever came back, "We have a bowling date!"

Daisy drove back to Nikki's and waited for her to get off work. Daisy hadn't decided whether to tell people what had happened to Jack Macklin. She decided when she saw Nikki, and she told her everything. She also told Nikki she wanted to set up a meeting with everyone that had been there for her at the hospital.

Nikki told Daisy that she should stay and they could be roommates. Since she was using the spare bedroom, she could stay for free until she got a job. Daisy agreed and was excited; she hugged Nikki and thanked her, telling her they would be best friends for life.

The next day, Daisy got a new phone, and they were able to upload most of her contacts and data from the iCloud. Next, she got a new battery for her car and drove to her parents' motel. She was going to tell Marta and Jose everything, because she wanted them to know they could go back home.

Daisy's younger brother, Juan, saw Daisy for the first time and smiled and said, "Mom and Dad said you would look different, but you don't, how come you look the same?" Daisy told him that a really nice man helped her out with that, so she's still the "same old Daisy."

Daisy then spoke in Spanish to her parents, telling them that the man who hurt her was their neighbor Jack. She explained that her car wouldn't start, so she took a ride from him, and she told them what happened next. They embraced, and Daisy said she had more good news. She said Jack was dead. She told her parents what Zack had done for her the day before. If they walked up to his porch, they would see lots of blood. "But that's all that's left of Jack Mackey, or Macklin was his name—anyway, he will never hurt anyone again.

"The best part was I got to call him a stupid little bitch and told him to quit crying before he died." Daisy being Daisy, she added, "When he was in all this pain, Zack—that's not his real name, it's a bunch of numbers—but he was telling the guy that he could tell how much pain he was in but he couldn't undo it, even if I wanted him to, and he said, 'which she doesn't,' he said they don't have rewind. Then he said something about he could take his mind off the pain by listening to Zack's voice because he has a calming voice. Then he said he had more bad news 'cause he ran out of shit to say. Zack is the coolest person ever, that was so great." Daisy did get part of it right.

* * *

Scapio talked to Reddis and detailed the case. He listed all the physical evidence that could corroborate Daisy's injuries. He said he could not explain why she wasn't burned, but he believed her and really wanted to go on it. He talked about where Daisy's purse was found and her smashed phone as well the container. He said that all of that backed up her story.

Reddis said that if her DNA and sulfuric acid were found in the back seat of the Hoopers' truck, he would OK it. If not, then if Scapio thought that the hospital staff that saw her burned were credible, he would approve it, but he wanted Scapio to speak with them personally. Reddis told him that he did a fantastic job on the McCarty case, and the ten- or fifteen-minute cross was the stuff of legends. Reddis concluded with, "You have a tough one, but I have faith in you."

That afternoon, Scapio called Nikki's number and she explained that Daisy just got a new phone. Scapio called Daisy, who did a superb job of acting. Scapio told her that he expected to go forward with her case, but he needed to speak with the hospital staff that treated her. Daisy's voice sounded excited and she thanked him. He told her that he would be in touch, and they would meet and go through his questions with her before the preliminary hearing.

Scapio felt good about helping her, but one thing, he admitted, was odd. She didn't seem scared anymore. She didn't ask when they were going to arrest Macklin.

That same day, Daisy called Detective Washington and said she really needed to thank some people and she begged him to give her a ride to where she needed to go. At first, he didn't think it was a great idea, but Daisy was a persuasive young woman.

Kent and Millie Hooper were relaxing on their porch when a squad car pulled up. They recognized Detective Washington. He was with a pretty and young Latina they did not recognize. Davon approached and asked them how they were doing, and they said that they were doing well. Kent asked if they were finished with his truck, and Davon said they still had a little more work to do. He then introduced them to Daisy, and Kent said that if she was his girlfriend, he was a lucky man. Davon said no, she just came along for the ride.

Millie said, "I keep thinking about that poor girl, I feel so awful for her. Did she die?"

Washington had a big smile on his face and said, "I know this is going to seem impossible, but that girl is right here. This is Daisy, the young woman whose life you saved, and she begged me to bring her here to thank you in person."

The Hoopers were in disbelief, but then Daisy said, "You found me staggering in the middle of the road—if you drive up this street, then make a left on 33, then another on Cañada Larga, how far I'm not sure, because of all the horrible things that happened to me along the way. I was in agony, screaming.

I tried to say the name Jack and Mack, that's how he introduced himself before he abducted me. I was crying for help and I was in so much pain.

"I could tell you how my face was saved, and Detective Washington can verify it. What is most important, though, is that I would be dead if you hadn't stopped for me and taken me to the hospital, but it really is me."

The Hoopers both cried and hugged Daisy and said they were so happy. Kent asked how she had no burn scars. Daisy let Washington explain the whole story. Kent then said, "Millie, remember a couple of days ago there was a report on the local station about a UFO?"

Daisy said, "I bet it was round, not a saucer. They're kind of sensitive about that. Zack is super nice, but he made sure to tell me that he didn't like it when I asked him about his flying saucer."

Millie touched Daisy's face and said, "Is that really you?" Daisy said it was, and that she knows lots of people would have driven by and not stopped, or just taken off when they saw what shape she was in. They hugged Daisy again and said they were so happy.

Kent said, "We are old and retired and we've both had some heart problems, but we're out here every day, and if you ever want to stop by and make a couple of old folks really happy, we would love to have you as our guest."

Daisy said she would love to. She said she had a new cell phone because "that asshole smashed my old one," so she gave them her number and said again that both of them saved her life, and if there was anything she could ever do for them, she would; just call her. She then got their number and entered it into her new phone. She added that she started a new job at CVS in Oxnard, but her hours were weird, so when they call, they could work out a time when she could come by.

Millie asked if the man was in jail. Washington anticipated that question, and he didn't want Daisy to say too much because, well, Daisy could say too much. He told them he could not yet discuss the situation.

They drove back and Daisy thanked him, saying that seeing the Hoopers and letting them know she was OK and being able to show her gratitude meant a lot.

Washington thought that Daisy was a really nice person. She did not have to do that. A lot of people would have just moved on and not even bothered to thank the old couple. Not Daisy; the girl had a heart of gold. Washington had just started dating a woman that he really liked. He thought if that had not happened, he would have asked Daisy out. His mom preferred black girls for her son, though, and his new love interest was a young black girl living in Canoga Park who was about Daisy's age. She was a nurse at Northridge Hospital.

Back at their apartment, Daisy told Nikki that she wasn't ready to start dating again. She admitted that she had fallen for a space alien and needed to get over that, to let go of her feelings for "Zack Morgan," before she could start dating again. Nikki said that she understood and that the alien visitor had saved her life. She said they could hang out and be single together; Nikki was still getting over her last cheating boyfriend.

* * *

It was Wednesday, November 22, when Scapio interviewed Dr. Wong, who told him about Zack Morgan. Scapio was shocked, partly because nobody from law enforcement had told him. He called Washington, and as soon as Washington answered, Scapio said, "Who is Zack Morgan and why didn't you tell me about him?" Washington said they needed to talk but they should do it in person. He said he would call Whatley and they would all talk.

On November 23, Washington's commanding officer, Tom Heath, knocked on Davon's office door and Washington told him to come on in. Heath congratulated him on a job well done on the Daisy Guzman missing-person case. Heath asked what the latest was. Washington told him only that the assigned prosecutor was working on putting together a case, even though Daisy had no burn scars.

Heath said that sounded good and then said the reason that he stopped by was that he had another missing-person case that might be related. He told him that Paul Macklin had called. He said that he was Jack Macklin's cousin, and that he had tried to reach his cousin for a few days and the phone went to voice mail first, and then did not even connect. He said that he went to visit his cousin when he couldn't reach him and found a large pool of dried blood on the porch.

Washington asked if Heath wanted him to investigate it. Heath confirmed that he was assigning the case to him. Washington said he would, but Macklin had lots of enemies and it could be a tough case. "I'll get a forensics team out there and collect samples. Macklin's DNA is in the system, so they should be able to determine if it's his blood." He also said he'd do a neighborhood canvass.

When he did the canvass, only one neighbor said that they heard anything unusual. A lady who lived next door said she heard what she described as an argument between two young women. The one thing she heard for sure was a woman calling another in a shouting voice a "crying little stupid bitch," or something like that. Washington successfully suppressed laughter, because he'd heard that too. He asked if she heard if the other woman responded. The neighbor said she couldn't say for sure. She did hear a female voice shortly after, but she wasn't sure what was said, because it wasn't as loud. The only thing she was sure about was the shout, calling the other woman a "crying little stupid bitch."

Washington asked if she saw any physical altercation. She said she didn't want to look outside or get involved in any way. She said her neighbor gave her the creeps. He asked her what day that happened. She said it was Monday, November 13, because that was the day her daughter came by in the afternoon, and she had mentioned it to her. Washington asked what time she heard the shouting, and she said it was in the morning after 9:30 for sure, could have even been after 11:00.

On Friday the twenty-fourth, Washington updated Heath about what he had learned. Heath focused on the "bitch" comment and said maybe Ms. Guzman wasn't as innocent as people might have thought. Washington said, "I wouldn't call her innocent. She is a genuinely nice person, but she does have certain qualities and she is not above using her natural charms to influence people. But she wouldn't do that to achieve evil goals. Anyway, it couldn't have been her shouting."

Heath asked why not, and Washington told him that "she has a really good alibi for November thirteenth in the morning: she was here. We did follow-up interviews that day, so Daisy was pretty much here the entire morning. Plus, the last place she would go would be to his house, after what happened." Heath said OK. Washington said his recommendation was to close the missing-person case until they got the DNA back. If the blood was his, he was most likely dead. If the DA filed charges on him for what he did to Daisy Guzman, they'd issue a warrant. If he turned up, they'd prosecute him.

Washington pointed out how many possible suspects there could be. "If they find his body, we can reopen. If someone wants to come in and confess to killing him, we take their statement. Bottom line, he was a suspect in his neighbor's murder years ago; he raped a dancer and went to prison. She could have friends. He was Aryan Brotherhood in prison, so this could be a prison-gang thing. Daisy has motive but she would have needed a ton of help, given she's 120 pounds dripping wet. She had gang connections because she dated an Avenue guy, but they aren't even together now. She doesn't have enough money to hire a hit man. I don't see who she could have gotten to do this. Once we confirm that the blood on the porch is his, I think we've done all we can for now."

Heath agreed and said to write up a report closing it pending DNA, but if the blood turns out to be a female's, then Macklin likely killed her and is in hiding. For obvious reasons, that thought had not crossed Washington's mind. Heath said he would bet lunch that the blood turns out to be a woman's and that Macklin and some girlfriend are on the run. Washington did not believe in betting when he already knew the outcome. He simply said, "Next lunch is on me either way, but I do think you're wrong. Macklin had a lot of enemies and this was probably a hit totally unrelated to the kidnapping and torture of Daisy Guzman."

* * *

Daisy phoned all the people who had come to the hospital except Veronica, who was now her roommate, so she already knew. Daisy set up a meeting at her parents' house for all her friends and family who had attended the bandage removal. She included a co-worker and good friend from Victoria's Secret who was not there for the bandage removal because she didn't know Daisy was in the hospital. Daisy hadn't given her name initially but thought about it afterward and wanted to include her.

The meeting was Sunday afternoon, the twenty-sixth. Washington agreed to attend, and he brought the still photos on his phone. The friends and family from out of state couldn't attend, but they agreed to be on a conference call. The only people present at that miraculous day that were not there at the Guzman home were Dr. Wong, Ray Scapio, and Detective Chris Whatley, who was out of town.

There were chips and salsa as well as carrots and celery with ranch dressing on the living room table. There was also a bowl of grapes. Daisy's mother and father began the meeting with the day they were informed about what happened to her. They described the man in the lobby and the conversation they had with him. Marta showed the photo that she showed to the man. Washington spoke next and talked about his investigation after seeing Daisy's face was still gorgeous. He showed the still photo and explained that the man had entered Daisy's room, stayed two hours, and left. He included the "celebration dance." He then talked about seeing the man in his office and told the story of what happened up until Daisy and the man left.

Daisy took over from there and told the rest of the story. When she finished, there were shocked looks throughout the room, but everyone said they believed her. Daisy explained that she would not tell that story to people she met from then on out, but that she had to tell everyone in this room.

Daisy then related what the alien had told her about telling the people in the room. She said she knew people she met in the future would think she was delusional. "But," she said, "Zack was right. You were all there for me on what we all thought would be the second worst day of my life, the worst being the kidnapping. It was when I saw you all there for me that I decided not to kill myself once I got justice. Before I saw all of you, I had decided if things were as bad as I thought, I would take pills. But you were there for me; I will never forget that, and we are friends for life. Mom and Dad, I moved in with Nikki, but you are not rid of me. I will visit a lot, we will have dinner, we will hang out a lot. I love all of you so much."

Everyone cried. Nikki and Jennifer were skeptical that Daisy would not tell others. They believed she had every intention of talking to nobody else about it, but it was Daisy, and she loved to talk.

On Monday the twenty-seventh, Whatley and Washington had a conversation about Scapio, and how much, if anything, to tell him. Washington informed Whatley that Scapio had talked to Dr. Wong, so he knew about the video. Whatley acknowledged that they should have figured that, but there was nothing they could have done about that because you cannot tell a witness to lie to the prosecutor.

On Wednesday morning, Washington called Scapio and asked him what the status of the case against Macklin was. Scapio told him that it was likely to be filed.

Washington said, "Ray, we've been friends for a while. I had drinks with you and your ex-wife before the divorce a few times. You recruited me for a softball team about five years ago. You're friends with Chris too. I am going to ask you a hypothetical, and you have to promise me an honest answer."

"Go ahead, shoot," Ray said. "You know me; I'm an honest guy unless I'm playing poker."

Washington said, "What if you found out Macklin was dead? Would you prosecute his killer or anyone who may have had a part in it?"

Scapio said that it would depend on why. "Assuming we're not talking about self-defense, if it were some guy who thought Macklin smiled at his girlfriend so he walked up to him and shot him, I would. Even though Macklin is as evil as they come, we can't let guys shoot people just because they don't like the way he looked at his girlfriend. If we let him go, the next victim might be a real good guy who would have cured cancer or something. On the other hand, if it was retaliation for what he did to Daisy Guzman, in all honesty, I'd let it go."

Washington asked, "Will you be in your office tomorrow?"

Scapio didn't answer right away. Instead, he said, "It was Zack Morgan, wasn't it?"

Washington said, "We'll see you in your office at 2:00 p.m. tomorrow."

Scapio became the fourth person to ask, "Who the fuck is Zack Morgan?"

* * *

On Thursday morning, Scapio called Eric Goren, his buddy from college, and caught up with him, since they hadn't spoken for a while. At 1:50 p.m., Whatley and Washington arrived, early for their two o'clock. Scapio closed the door to his office and became one of the few people on Earth to be 100 percent convinced that we are not alone in the universe. He heard the entire story and was riveted to each word. At the end, he simply said, "Thank you for telling me."

Whatley asked what his opinion was of what the alien did. Scapio said he completely understood it. "Though part of me wishes he would have talked to me first. I really feel I could have gotten justice for Daisy at trial. I don't think I would have emphasized Zack Morgan. Even if I had him as a witness, I don't know that I would have put him on unless he could levitate a pen or perform some feat of strength for the jury.

"I think I would have put everything on to persuade the jury that what happened to Daisy was real. I would have shown the video and presented the suggestion the man identifying himself as Zack Morgan might have been responsible for fixing her face. It would be up to the jury to decide who he might be and how he did it. Maybe some very religious jurors would believe that God chose to spare Daisy for some unknown reason when others suffering a similar fate were not. Maybe some might believe she had some medical anomaly that allowed her skin to fully heal. Someone else might think he was an alien.

"As long as I could convince a jury that it's not our burden to show how Daisy did not burn up, that it's only our burden to convince them he did try to kill her with battery acid, then he's guilty. I honestly believe I could have, but I could see why he felt he could not bet on me. If I failed Daisy, she or someone else would be in danger. Maybe many people. He didn't want his saving one woman to result in more death and suffering."

He assured the detectives the secret was safe with him. He would file charges on Macklin and get an arrest warrant, knowing that it would be "an arrest warrant that can never be served, because it already was served, in the Twilight Zone." The detectives complimented Scapio on his Rod Serling impersonation.

Whatley went back to his office and made another phone call. On the third ring, Becky Holland answered. Whatley identified himself and said he had good news. He said Daisy was OK. She said, "Thank God," and asked what had happened. He told her that Daisy had been abducted but had managed to escape. She said, "She is gonna be OK, right?" Whatley told her that she had only minor injuries and she was a little shaken up, but she was going to be just fine. Becky asked who took her and what happened to him. Whatley said it was a neighbor and he had since killed himself. She thanked him and said she was glad Daisy was OK and she looked forward to seeing her at the ten-year reunion.

Whatley stopped by Steve Alvarez's body shop and he said that Daisy called him and said that she had been abducted but got away and was okay. Steve mentioned that he brought up getting back with Daisy but she said she needed time to sort things out. He was relieved that she was okay. She did not give him details about what had happened but she wanted him to know that she was doing well and was not a missing person.

It was Friday, December 1. Scapio arrived at his office at 8:30, still overwhelmed by what he had learned. Some of his colleagues asked him if he wanted to get lunch later. He said that any day next week would work, but he had some errands to run at lunch. At 11:45, he headed for the parking lot and got in his car. He went down Victoria toward the 101 and turned onto the frontage road past the freeway, heading for the bowling alley and one of the few pay phones left. He approached the pay phone and put the coins in and punched in the number.

The young woman said, "Sports Today, how can I help you?"

Scapio said, "This is RS32452."

"What can I do for you, RS?"

"What is my current balance?" After getting that info, Scapio said, "I want a three-team NFL parlay: Titans over the Texans, Chiefs over the Jets, and Jaguars over the Colts for $100." He then placed four straight bets for $110 each.

The woman on the other line said, "Good luck, RS." Scapio would lose the parlay because the Chiefs decided not to play defense that day. He split his four straight bets for a net loss of $120, but he was back betting again.

On Saturday, December 2, Kent and Millie Hooper were sitting on the porch, sipping tea. Millie said, "We should call Daisy."

Kent said, "She's probably back to her old life and doesn't have time to hang out with old folks like us. It was nice that she stopped by and thanked us, but I doubt we'll hear from her again. You know how things go."

A half hour later, Millie's cell phone buzzed. She looked at the display and saw one name, "Daisy." She answered, and Daisy told her she was sorry she hadn't called before, but her hours at CVS had been crazy. But she had today and tomorrow off, so if they were around, she could come by and bring them lunch. Millie said, "We would love to have you, and lunch is on us, because Kent can fire up the grill for us." Daisy said she would come by with a bottle of wine. Kent and Millie smiled from ear to ear.

Daisy got back into Ventura College for the spring semester in 2018. She took several journalism classes and excelled. She also took Professor Peterson's popular speech and debate class. She knew she liked to talk, so she figured, why not? She ended up loving that class. One day early in the semester, Professor Peterson wanted to get students used to arguing a position. He asked, "Do you believe in the death penalty?"

Daisy was one of the first to speak and said that some people were so horrible that they did not deserve to live, so she was for it, but only where the evidence was really certain. She fought back tears, saying that there were just some people who did not deserve to be here. People thought Daisy, or someone close to her, had been a victim of a terrible crime because of the emotion in her voice.

Professor Peterson then said, "Do you believe in gun control?" Daisy wasn't the first to speak, but she raised her hand and said that she did, because there were way too many school shootings. The discussion got pretty heated. Daisy had a back-and-forth with a gun-rights guy.

Professor Peterson then asked about universal health care. Daisy did not participate in that discussion. Next, he asked, "Do you believe we are alone? In other words, do you believe in life on other planets?"

Daisy raised her hand and said, "There is no such thing as flying saucers."

It was Tuesday, February 13, 2018. Daisy was off that day and spent the morning with the Hoopers in Ojai. This was the fourth time she had been over there. She had a busy schedule, but she knew that she was important to them and she knew she would not be alive if not for what they did. She also liked them and enjoyed their company.

She had learned that Kent had been a farmer and had also raised pigs. Millie had helped on the farm and had also been a legal secretary. They were from Iowa but moved to Ojai twelve years before, when they retired. They'd had a nice place in the downtown part of Ojai but had to sell their house because they got hit hard by the recession and lost a lot of their retirement savings, so they moved into a cheaper place. Daisy said that she was lucky; if they hadn't moved, she would be dead.

Daisy talked about finishing at community college. She said she was still working at CVS and rooming with her friend Nikki; she was paying one-third the rent since her hours were part-time because of school. She told the Hoopers she was definitely going to pursue journalism. She was sure she could get accepted into Cal State Northridge or Long Beach. She preferred Northridge because it was closer, and she wouldn't have to move. She was also promised an internship at KVTA Radio during the summer. Kent Hooper said he could not wait to see Daisy on the nightly or morning news, and that she would make a great reporter.

Millie said she was worried for Daisy because the man that attacked her was still out there. Daisy decided to tell Kent and Millie that they need not worry. She explained exactly how Jack Macklin became nothing more than a pool of blood on a front porch.

Daisy hugged the Hoopers and they told her that their daughter doesn't speak to them anymore because they said her husband was a lying con artist—he did 180 days for embezzlement from a charity—and they felt like Daisy was their long-lost Latina daughter. Daisy told them she loved them. She said she was going to relax and reflect on how lucky she was. She was going take a ride along Pacific Coast Highway and get lunch at the Malibu Seafood Market, and she promised they would stay in touch. Millie told Daisy that the thing they were most proud of themselves for was having stopped to help her. Daisy hugged them again and said that she would call soon. They knew she would.

Daisy had sold her Honda Civic and bought a used Mustang convertible a few weeks before. She took the 101 and exited Las Posas in Camarillo with the top down on her convertible, and she reflected on her life. She remembered her despair in the hospital. She thought about the nights of crying and believing nobody would ever want to look at her again. She thought about Zack Morgan and wondered what he was doing now. She hoped that soil they found did its job.

She reflected on the day Ray Scapio described her as Miss Oxnard. Scapio did tell her that he would have charged the case, but he was OK with what happened. She reflected about how he was funny and kind of cute when he apologized for the Miss Oxnard comment. He said he knew Oxnard was largely Hispanic, but he was not trying to be racist, and he felt terrible about how it came out.

She told him that nobody else was saying anything that day in her hospital room except Nikki, who she thought was just trying to be nice. She said it took his comment to realize that maybe it would be a good thing to ask for a mirror, because Miss Oxnard was not what she was expecting to look like.

Daisy knew that people had always considered her beautiful. When she thought she had lost that for good, she had thought she'd lost everything. Now that it had been brought back, she realized that she was more than just a pretty face, that she could make a difference. It doesn't hurt to have her looks, but she knew she could and would become so much more. With her hair tied in a ponytail so as not to get in her eyes, she thought about her life as she sang along to her iPod, belting out the lyrics to her favorite song, the Evanescence hit "Bring Me to Life." The words had more meaning than ever before, as she drove the Pacific Coast Highway, ready to take on all the challenges and excitement the world had to offer.

EPILOGUE

As a veteran prosecutor in Ventura County working homicides and serious and violent felonies, I dedicate this, my first novel, to the victims of violent crime and their loved ones. Many of those victims were not as fortunate as the young woman depicted in this courtroom drama-science fiction crossover. Their courage, in spite of horrible adversity and loss, to get justice and protect potential future victims is the inspiration for my story.

Bring Me to Life is also a story about kindness to each other in an era of fear and division. Three young athletes could have driven off into the night, but they were more concerned about the person who may have been injured than any consequences that they might have faced. A man in a waiting room in a hospital, a place where he was not supposed to be, heard a horrible story about an innocent victim. He knew he could help but that it might cause more trouble for himself should he do so. He did not hesitate to help.

Daisy Guzman was the beautiful and popular girl in high school. Would her friends stand by her when nobody believed she would be beautiful anymore? For those that did, they have a friend for life.

If not for the kindness of the two most popular girls at a bullied girl's new school, that bullied girl's life would have had a tragic ending. A little kindness goes a long way.

An elderly couple in their golden years came upon a tragically injured woman in such horrible condition that placing her in their car could endanger them. They did it anyway.

That tragically injured young woman, now healed, could have forgotten about the lonely old couple who saved her life and gone on to just focus on picking up life where it left off. She didn't; she made sure that they would always have a place in her life. For the couple, their golden years would be much happier for it.

Not long ago, the United States Navy released a report of a navy pilot's UFO sighting. The Department of Defense has authenticated three videos of inexplicable alien encounters. The AATIP (Advanced Aerospace Threat Identification Program) confirmed the pilot's video and contemporaneous sightings.

Alien life is often portrayed as desiring to kill us, eat us, and take over our planet, or in the alternative, cure us of all of our flaws and make us denounce the error of our ways as they save us from ourselves.

More likely, it's neither of those. Perhaps a technologically more advanced alien likes much of the things we like. Perhaps they have many of the same strengths and weaknesses that we humans have. Perhaps they have good and bad and many in between, as do we. Our alien visitor in *Bring Me to Life* was more technologically advanced and physically capable, yet he wasn't a whole lot different from many of us. Possessed of compassion, decency, humor, and pride, his qualities guided his choices. When someone like him does arrive, shouldn't he be welcomed with cautious optimism and friendly expectations, rather than fear and hostility? It is likely that we are not alone.

www.ingramcontent.com/pod-product-compliance
Lightning Source LLC
LaVergne TN
LVHW010559100826
845148LV00014B/2779
9780578307480